URSULA LAKE

URSULA LAKE

a novel

CHARLES HARPER WEBB

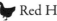 Red Hen Press | *Pasadena, CA*

Book design by Mark E. Cull

Library of Congress Cataloging-in-Publication Data

Names: Webb, Charles Harper, author.
Title: Ursula Lake / Charles Harper Webb.
Description: First edition. | Pasadena, CA : Red Hen Press, [2022]
Identifiers: LCCN 2021034286 (print) | LCCN 2021034287 (ebook) | ISBN
  9781636280219 (trade paperback) | ISBN 9781636280226 (epub)
Subjects: LCGFT: Novels.
Classification: LCC PS3573.E194 U77 2022 (print) | LCC PS3573.E194
  (ebook) | DDC 813/.54—dc23
LC record available at https://lccn.loc.gov/2021034286
LC ebook record available at https://lccn.loc.gov/2021034287

The National Endowment for the Arts, the Los Angeles County Arts Commission, the Ahmanson Foundation, the Dwight Stuart Youth Fund, the Max Factor Family Foundation, the Pasadena Tournament of Roses Foundation, the Pasadena Arts & Culture Commission and the City of Pasadena Cultural Affairs Division, the City of Los Angeles Department of Cultural Affairs, the Audrey & Sydney Irmas Charitable Foundation, the Meta & George Rosenberg Foundation, the Albert and Elaine Borchard Foundation, the Adams Family Foundation, Amazon Literary Partnership, the Sam Francis Foundation, and the Mara W. Breech Foundation partially support Red Hen Press.

First Edition
Published by Red Hen Press
www.redhen.org

ACKNOWLEDGMENTS

Ursula Lake has been a long time in the making. Many people have helped out along the way.

First among these is my wife Karen, who has read so many drafts that she knows the story better than I do. Thanks, Karen, for many great suggestions, for believing in this book from the start, and for never wavering.

Thanks to my longtime friends Ron Koertge and Bill Trowbridge, who, by their examples as well as their astute editing of my prose and poetry over the years, have made me a better writer than I would otherwise be.

Thanks to Shelly Lowenkopf, who saw a young novelist worth nurturing before I saw it myself.

Thanks to Jack Cady, John Rechy, and William Goyen, who taught me the importance of craft, and taking risks, and thinking big.

Thanks to Kate Maruyama, Diana Wagman, and Ivy Pochoda, who helped me to improve this book and my fiction writing in general.

Thanks to Jennifer Pooley for valuable insights.

Thanks to William Loving, Laura Gold, and Lola Ogunyemi, the talented and perceptive members of the writer's group that coalesced out of Ivy Pochoda's class.

Thanks to Kate Gale and Mark Cull who have made Red Hen a national literary force, and who have been in my corner for many years, never more than with this book.

URSULA LAKE

"This is my bed-rock objection to the Eastern systems. They decry all manly virtue as dangerous and wicked, and they look upon Nature as evil."
—Aleister Crowley

"The Promised Land always lies on the other side of a Wilderness."
—Havelock Ellis

"Our dead never forget this beautiful world . . ."
—Chief Seattle

FIRST DAY

Scott Murray was an hour out of Vancouver, British Columbia, heading north on Highway 97, when he saw, ahead and to his right, a deer sprawled in a heap beside the road.

"Aw, man," he said. No animal on earth ever evolved to deal with cars.

A sense that he as human was to blame, made Scott slow down as he passed the deer, and so, saw its head move. Checking his mirror—no cops; no cars at all—he pulled to the road shoulder and stopped. His watch said 1:04, but the air felt like morning, misty and cool as he eased out of his blue Datsun pickup, braced himself for what he'd see, then started down the shoulder toward the deer.

Across the road, pines, spruce, and fir rose like a green fortress wall. A few feet from the gravel shoulder where he walked, a canyon plunged toward a silver creek, wriggling and glittering far below. In the States, there would have been a guardrail. In BC, they would run out of guardrails long before they ran out of risky roads.

Reaching the deer, a good-sized whitetail, Scott saw that yes, it was alive. He also saw there was no hope. The creature's dark, luminous eyes stared straight ahead, its ear-cups twisting as if listening for Death.

The deer's hindquarters were caked in blood. Its back legs were crooked. Snapped. Its spine probably was too. Hit, most likely, by a big-rig that just kept blasting on.

The decent thing would be to end its misery. But how? His only weapon was a hatchet in his truck. Could he, as an act of mercy, hack this deer to death?

He'd read a William Stafford poem where a traveler finds a dead doe on a canyon road, drags it to the shoulder, and feels a fawn moving inside. But the deer in front of Scott was not a doe. Antlers had sprouted: four blunt prongs like velvet-covered coral. As Scott stared at the antlers, he saw that the deer's eyes were fixed on him. Fixed, he would have sworn, in pain and fear. And something else: a gratitude that he was here. A wish not to die alone.

Anthropomorphizing, science would say. Still, Scott touched the creature's flank: just barely moving up and down. He felt lightheaded, probably from seeing so much blood as he stroked the quivering flank. "I'm here," he told the dying animal. "I'm here."

The deer gave something like a sigh as Scott kept stroking, staring into those lucent brown eyes. What did they see, he wondered, when they looked at him?

He pictured himself standing like a deer in thick woods, smelling the pine, the damp, the tang of leaf-decay. The greenery around him swayed in a slight breeze. As if it were breathing.

In his mind, he began to run. Still a man, but with the grace and power of a deer, he bounded up high hills, and down. Following trails that squeezed under gigantic trees and through tangles of briared brush, he ran with what felt like unlimited power and a sense that the deer had called him here for something special. Something grand.

Was this some kind of Keatsian *reverie*? Whatever it was, he kept running, the thrill turning to fear. Something was chasing him, coming up behind. He neared a chasm too wide to jump. And still he ran. Ran and ran, then launched himself into the air.

At that instant, the deer gave another sigh. As if unplugged, the light left its eyes. They didn't close, or turn away from Scott. They simply ceased to see. And with that ceasing, his reverie or vision or whatever it had been, ceased too.

He stopped stroking, and let his hand rest on the deer's rib cage. No movement up or down. Stone-still.

"Good," he told the forest. "No more pain."

The sight of the deer's antler-buds watered his eyes. No telling how big they'd have grown, how many bucks he'd have fought, fawns he'd have sired. The antlers weren't what anyone would call a "rack." Still, some driver might decide to take the head, stuff it, and mount it on a wall.

That was not going to happen. No damned way.

In Stafford's poem, the speaker, knowing he couldn't save the fawn, "thought hard for us all," then pushed the dead doe off a cliff. Scott gripped his deer by its forelegs and, straining every muscle he'd developed at the gym, dragged the creature to the edge of the drop-off. It wasn't sheer, but it was steep. Given a shove, the deer might roll all the way down.

Dropping to his knees, Scott placed his hands on the still-warm belly, choosing spots where the coarse red-brown hair was free from blood. Three hard shoves, and the deer was sliding, then rolling into the canyon. Scott watched it roll faster, then snag on a rock and stop halfway to the creek. Some mountain lion, coyote, or bear might find it there. Vultures and crows would feast for sure. Anything left of the carcass would rot and, bit by bit, finish its journey to the creek.

As for his own journey: two more hours would get him to Winoma. An hour more, and his pilgrimage to Oso Lake would be done.

2

Jerking upright, Scott mashed his brakes as SLOW TO 80 pierced his driving-daze. Eighty kilometers per hour meant about fifty on his speedometer.

He checked his mirror. No cars. No cops.

Twenty miles away, Oso Lake lay thawing in the mid-May sun. Ice-off in Cariboo Country meant big Kamloops trout, starved all winter, gorging on the hordes of insects that erupted from lakes and streams and forests as, like a green-furred colossus coming into heat, the North Woods came into spring.

"Hurrah, hurrah, hurrah for the lowly fish!" Scott brayed in an operatic baritone, just as he and Errol had done five years before.

Instead of making him laugh, the song embarrassed him. And made him sad. About Errol? Or was the sadness left over from the deer?

His speedometer, still at sixty—roughly one hundred kilometers per hour—made him mash the brakes again.

At what point does a speed limit take effect, he wondered: when the driver sees the sign, or passes it? Not that a cop intent on stopping him would care.

A new sign ordered SLOW TO 50. Scott slowed to 30 mph, and rolled officially into Winoma, BC. His legs ached. His tailbone throbbed. But the bulk of his long, solo drive was done.

He checked his watch. 4:45. Rush hour. Meaning, in Winoma, ten cars on the street, and half a dozen loggers rushing into Trixie's Bar.

The town had changed so little, it seemed strange he couldn't turn back time a measly five years. In other ways, it felt like five lifetimes since he'd been here—May of 1987, two months shy of twenty-two, with a new college degree in Honors English, his band poised for rock glory, his best friend Errol beside him, and back in Seattle, Sara: the love of his life.

Now, May 1992, all that he had left was his useless degree.

A sign, HOWDY DO CAFE, reared above the fiendish Howdy Doody face—bright blue eyes, bloody grin, and crimson hair—that had drawn Errol and him inside the faded brown-and-yellow eatery. Errol had rated the food "minus two stars," but the prices had been good for this far north.

Scott signaled just in case a cop was lurking, and turned in.

Two cars with BC plates sat in the parking lot. So did a brand-new, shiny green full-sized Ford truck—Washington plates—complete with hydrocephalic truck-bed camper, and a boat very much like his, mounted, jaunty as a party hat, on top.

Damn. Oso Lake was not on many maps. But once the States found a Canadian hotspot, it cooled off fast.

Scott wanted to park underneath Howdy, as he and Errol had done. But the green giant had hogged that spot, slanting across three spaces to ward other drivers away. Its front end was unmarred. Still, count on it: the owner was the kind of self-absorbed Ugly American who would hit a deer and curse it for damaging his grill.

Okay, my strutting countryman, he thought. *You asked for it.* He was not in the woods yet, but he felt the woods in him. "The wilderness effect," as he and Errol called it, had likely brought on his deer-vision, too.

Squeezing his older, smaller pickup in close to the Ford, he opened his door—whack!—into the unblemished green flank. Then, as if realizing he'd parked too close, he backed away and parked across the lot.

How often, home in Seattle, had he ached to penalize some bloated re-source-hog? Now, having done it, he felt slimy and small.

Seeing no witnesses, he eased from his truck and walked on stiff legs into the burger-eggs-coffee-and-grease miasma of the Howdy Do.

A burly, towheaded cook—albino, or nearly—lounged behind the count-er, whispering to the dark-haired waitress who slouched against it. They, or their doubles, had been here the last time, too.

The sole customer, a hulking, bear-like man, sat faced away from Scott, blond hair curling over the collar of his blue Pendleton shirt. From behind, he looked a lot like . . .

"Errol!"

The name jumped out of Scott's mouth as the door slammed behind him, and the big man whirled to see who dared disturb his meal.

"Scott! Son of a bitch!"

Scott froze. Was Errol still mad at him?

Another instant smashed that fear.

"Christ at a clambake! I was just talking about you," Errol practically roared, bounding up to pump Scott's hand.

At six-foot-five, Errol towered over Scott, and seemed twice as wide. With his blond hair and blue eyes, his square-jawed Nordic face, powerlifter's body, and tendency toward emotional thunderstorms, he could have been typecast as Thor. Not to mention Guy Who Drives an Oversized Camper-and-Truck.

"Pieces of feces," Scott said, rhyming it the way they used to. "What is this? The Twilight Zone?"

"Feels like it," Errol said. But there was nothing otherworldly in the paw that gripped Scott's hand. That clean, firm grip made Scott feel lower than slime. But what could he say—*Great to see you. Oh, I dinged your truck?*

He'd apologize later. For now, he only said, "What brings you here?"

"Chef's reputation. Same as you," Errol said deadpan, then erupted in ap-proval of the joke. He'd majored in Drama at the U, and his expressions fit the stage: big and broad and, when he wanted, comical.

Something that was half sorrow, half relief broke free in Scott, and he was laughing as loudly as Errol. Laughing as he hadn't laughed in years.

"Let me guess," he said when he could catch his breath. "You called Tom's Fly Shop. They told you Ice-off was May 5. Add a week for this far north . . ."

Errol nodded. "You too?"

Scott nodded back. "Right time, right place. It sorta figures you'd be here." He looked away, surprised to be fighting back tears. Had he and Errol really not spoken in four years?

"Remember last time?" Errol said. "Best fishing I ever had. The best time, too."

"With the best friend," Scott said.

This time, Errol looked away. "We were," he pronounced, "the best of friends."

"Errol," Scott said on an upswell of emotion, "I'm sorry about . . . you know. I was a dick."

Errol stared, as if to make sure he'd heard right. Then he nodded. "That makes two of us," he said. "Two giant dicks."

Though they'd never embraced before, Scott thought, for an instant, they might now. Then Errol, whose favorite era was the 1920s, did his best Groucho Marx eyebrow-wiggle, and said, "Mine's bigger, of course."

"Of course," Scott said, and they laughed again. As if they'd never been apart. As if it were agreed they'd fish together now.

With a theatrical bow and sweep of the hand, Errol indicated a chair at his table. "Kind sir, prithee park thy rear."

Scott did. Then Errol did, too.

Scott had an impulse to tell about the deer. But what could he say? *A roadkill deer sent me a vision?* Instead of that, he said, "So tell me—how've you been?"

"Pretty fair." Errol leaned back in his chair, joined his hands behind his head, and looked expansive. "Got a nice house in Spokane, a good job, and . . . well, look who's here."

The door marked LADIES had produced one.

She stood maybe five-seven. Honey-blonde hair curled down her back. Her face, high-fashion beautiful, looked friendly too, softened by full lips and blue-green eyes that simmered with intelligence and warmth. Though Scott tried not to see, her gray sweatshirt and baggy green sweatpants couldn't hide her curves as, walking up to Errol, she slid her hand across his neck in a proprietary way, then kissed his cheek.

"Claire, this is Scott Murray," Errol said, and kissed her hand as she sat down beside him. "Scott, this is Claire. My wife."

"Scott Murray." The clipped precision of her voice was faintly British. She raised her eyebrows—meaning what?—and held out her hand. "*The* Scott Murray?"

"My mother thought so," Scott said, and gave as masculine a shake as he could manage for so feminine a hand. "I'm glad to meet you. Errol always had good taste."

Smooth move, Einstein, Scott told himself. He'd just cast Claire as property, and Errol as the player he was. Or used to be.

"When'd you get married?" he asked Errol, to change the subject.

"June 1988." Errol looked to Claire for confirmation. "Feels like a week. But it's going on four years."

Claire's smile and nod said she was happy to agree.

"Time flies when you're in love," Scott said, and hoped he had implied just enough irony not to seem either a scoffer or a sap.

"I tell you, Scott, marrying Claire . . . it's like I won the Triple Crown." For an instant, Errol's face turned so serious, he seemed in pain. Then his eyes lit up in that manic way he had, as if he'd finished a tap dance and, arms spread wide, was gathering applause. He made fists of his hands, pawed the air, and said, "Now if I could get rid of these hooves . . ."

Bada-boom!—he was his madcap self again.

Claire, Scott observed, had dropped her eyes. Pleased? Embarrassed? Upset that he was here?

He felt the waitress loom over his shoulder.

"Sorry," he said. "Give me a sec." Five years ago, the woman might have been pretty. Something—boredom, disappointment, grueling winters?—had carved frown-grooves in her forehead, weathered her skin, and puffed her cheeks with fat. She might not be much over thirty, but she looked a bitter forty-five.

Wilting under her poised pen and glassy stare, Scott ordered "The Special," whatever it might be.

"So how's Oso?" he asked Errol as the waitress slumped away, moving as if she had pebbles in her shoes.

"We got here yesterday at three." Errol grinned. "Remember how lost *we* got?"

Scott rolled his eyes. "The Pathfinders."

Errol gave a *commedia dell'arte* grimace. "History repeats. By the time we found the lake, the sun was going down. Not much to do but sleep, and fish the morning bite. And I mean *bite*: one eight-incher."

Uh oh, Scott thought. Sometimes a great fishing spot would simply die.

"Claire wanted stuff in town, so we drove back to eat," Errol said. "However . . ." He drew out the word dramatically. "As we were coming in, I saw a pod of trout, just cruising. At least a dozen, all like so!" He held his hands a yard apart. "The smallest would've gone ten pounds."

"All *right*," Scott said. Errol would, of course, be fishing with Claire. But Oso Lake was plenty big enough to share. The campground, though, was small. Would Errol mind if he shared *that*?

More to the point, would Claire?

"I threw everything at 'em," Errol was saying. "Including spoons, spinners, three colors of flatfish, and a stupid Hula Popper."

"Lucky you didn't land a warden."

"Fuck *Fly Fishing Only*. If my teeth were sharper, I'd have grizzly-beared in after 'em."

Scott's nod emphatically agreed.

"Nary a strike, rise or follow," Errol went on. "Then, poof, they disappeared. They were there, and then they weren't. But Christ on a crocodile . . ."

Faster than she should have been, the waitress was shoving a plate in front of Scott. It held a dollop of instant potatoes with jelled gravy, green beans awash in what might have been bile, a roll shaped like a Paleolithic hand ax, and the entree: three greenish sausages.

Here's hoping, Scott thought, and dug in.

A minute later, Claire, stood and walked up to the waitress. They spoke quietly; then Claire walked back to the table, looking annoyed.

"Local calls only," she told Errol.

"Not even if you pay 'em cash?"

She rolled her eyes. "There's no service to the US."

Errol shrugged. "We'll have to get by with no input from your dad," he said with . . . was it satisfaction?

Claire gave a sigh—resigned or exasperated?—and sat back down.

Feeling he'd seen something he shouldn't have, Scott concentrated on his food. They must have changed chefs, because it wasn't bad. He'd nearly wolfed it all when the door flew open and two green-uniformed Royal Canadian Mounted Police stomped inside.

Sit still, Scott told himself. But he was on his feet. "Catch you later," he told Errol, which sounded like a fishing joke he realized as, not waiting for an answer, he dropped eight dollars US on the table, and walked outside as casually as he could. How many years did it take *post-traumatic stress disorder* to go away? He might as well be one of Pavlov's drooling dogs . . .

The sound of footsteps made him whirl. Just Errol, thank God.

"Claire handles finances," the big man said, then added in an undertone, "Cops still freak you?"

Scott nodded in disgust. "If anything, it's worse."

"Hell," Errol said. "These small town heat are fat and lazy. They don't want trouble."

"Those Houston cops were fat and lazy," Scott said. "They *loved* trouble." He shoved the memory away, and slid into his truck. "A cop's a cop."

"Can't argue that," Errol said as Claire marched stiffly out of Howdy Do's. She handed Errol some change and, without a word, made for—where else?—the big green truck.

She's pissed, Scott thought. *Pissed that I'm here.* He'd driven six hundred miles for a chance at Oso's lunker trout. But if three proved a crowd, he'd leave. Maybe look for Ursula Lake. See if the tales of thirty-pound Kamloops were true.

"Follow us," Errol offered. "Save yourself a week."

"You got it!" Scott said. So Errol *did* want to fish with him! That was good. Fishing was more fun with a friend. Safer, too.

His engine started perfectly.

"*Good* truck," he said, as if it were a dog. All he needed was to break down way up here.

Errol's big Ford pulled out first. Relieved to see no damage where his door had banged, Scott lurched after his old friend, through the chugholed parking lot, and into the street. A day or two, and any ding he'd inflicted would blend with dings the woods were sure to give. It might be best to confess after that.

The RCMP station sprang up on his left, one of six units in a faded strip mall that included a drugstore and laundromat. Next, on his right, came Winoma's one gas station, its yellow SUNOCO sign pierced by a red arrow, Mechanic On Duty dangling below.

Another block, and he was passing Trixie's Bar, then stopping at the town's lone stop sign, its cross street lined with shacks and mournful-look-ing Indians. *First Nations*, Canadians called them as a group. What did they call just *one*? His college friend Duane Yellowhorse had loathed *Native American*. "It's like when people say *Spanish* instead of *Mexican*," he'd said. "*Indian* is fine with me."

Considering how they'd been treated, Scott would have called them any-thing they liked. The ones he saw here didn't look militant, like some in the States. Nor did they seem to be spiritual paragons like on TV. They seemed dazed. As if they'd missed a turn, and wound up in the wrong century.

On his left, just past the stop sign, an assault of red, white, and green candy-stripes trumpeted, BIG VALUE GROCERIES! SAVE!!! *That* wasn't here five years ago. A US invader, almost for sure.

A hundred yards more, and Winoma was behind him. Next stop: Oso Lake.

The day was perfect for a drive: air cool, sun hot, with not a cloud to block one ray. The old Honda Civic he'd owned until last year had lost its sun visor, so Scott didn't think, at first, to use his truck's. When he remem-bered, and pulled the white shield down, he felt a pleasure as warm as the sun. If nothing else, his years of playing bars had netted him the truck-and-boat combo he'd coveted.

For now, bar-bands were behind him. The liars in Lyinhart would come tonight to pick him up for their gig at The Hideaway, and he'd be gone.

Seeing Errol's turn signal blink, Scott slowed, then followed him off the highway onto a gravel road that quickly changed to dirt: spurs shooting off spurs shooting off spurs into the unknown. He and Errol had spent a whole day ransacking these woods in search of Oso Lake—eating dust, cursing Canada, trout fishing, and their fates as they rattled over logging roads that would have cowed a mountain goat, and test-fished roadside potholes "as ignorant of trout," Errol had said, "as a lemur of Chinese."

Today, Errol banged down the pitted road with a native's nonchalance. Jolting behind, Scott felt elation swell. Out here, a guy could sit where he liked, spit where he liked, yell as loud and drive as fast as he liked without the Law skulking behind trees, dispensing beatings and jail terms.

There was magic in these woods, like what he'd felt with the deer: something sacred and powerful, left from ancient times. His breakup with Errol—how else to put it?—had been the first domino down in the collapse of his life. Now fate had brought Errol back. If their friendship returned, other things might, too. The confidence he'd lost. The power and drive. The success.

"Hurrah, hurrah, hurrah for the lowly fish!" he sang at the top of his lungs, then followed that with, "Twenty-pounders here I come, / Heading back to get me some"—choking on Errol's dust, but bellowing words as they came: stupid words, dirty words, any words he by-God pleased.

3

The sun was sinking in a sea of evergreens as the trucks banged and rattled to the edge of Oso Lake. Errol parked on the far left, pleased to see Scott take the hint and park as far right as he could: maybe thirty yards away. Many times in the past years, Errol had cursed the tantrum that cost him his best friend. Here was his chance to put things right.

All the same, he'd come here to be with Claire. She had to take priority.

Leaping out of his truck, Errol threw open her door, grabbed her hand,

and pulling her behind, ran to join Scott in the small campground they'd left five years before with shouts of thanks and loud vows to return. Here were the same two battered trash cans, the same rough circle of stones, ash, and half-burnt logs over which they had fried fat trout and proclaimed, "This is the life!" Gray in the lowering sun, and still half-ringed with snow, Oso Lake looked pristine, primeval, and every bit as alluring as before.

"Take a breath of that!" Errol dramatized sucking in the scent of pine, then spread his arms as if embracing every tree. "Makes a man feel ready to win the West all . . . hey, what have we here?"

Walking to the clearing's edge, he plucked up a stick and used it to spear a crumpled pair of pale blue panties. "Some sweet thing gave her all on this very spot," he said as Scott, then Claire hurried to see.

"What's *on* them?" Scott pointed at what Errol realized was a red-brown stain, just as a fat black millipede dropped from the panties to the ground.

Errol dropped the panties and jumped back as the millipede scuttled away. "Oh shit, that's blood!" he said and looked at Scott.

Before Scott could answer, or Errol could squelch an unreasonable rush of fear, Claire said, "Calm down, boys. See any tampon-trees out here?"

Errol felt his face heat up. "Oh yeah. That's right."

Scott poked the damp gray campfire ash with his boot, then stooped to lift a foot-long shaft of charred, half-buried bone. "Whoa! Look at this!"

"Deer," Errol said quickly. One overreaction was enough.

Scott leaned down and pulled another blackened bone. "There's more!"

"They look human," Claire said.

"They're not," Errol declared as Scott passed him the new find. "Looks like they cracked this thing to eat the marrow," he said and, turning the bone over in his hand, forced down the case of creeps that clambered up his spine.

Scott scrutinized the bone he'd kept. "This looks too thick for a deer. Maybe elk. Or moose."

Errol offered the bone to Claire. "Check it out."

She shook her head no. "Get rid of it. Throw it away."

"Fine. No problem," Errol said, glad to heave the bone, spinning like a propeller, into the trees.

Scott did the same with his.

Errol glanced up at the blue sky. The sun had dropped precipitously.

"Come on! We'll miss the night bite," he said, and dashed for his truck. "Claire, grab your gear. Scott, leave your boat. We can use mine."

Working efficiently, just like in the old days, the men unracked Errol's shiny aluminum fifteen-footer and lugged it to the lake. Scott pulled his rod, reel, and fishing vest out of his truck, and rigged up while Errol tossed life preservers, oars, plus assorted gear into the boat, then bolted the motor on, and called, "All aboard."

Watching Claire climb in ahead of Scott and sit in the prow, Errol hoped the snit she'd fallen into wouldn't last. What was he supposed to do: tell Scott, "Great to see you, man. Now go away"?

No, he told himself. She'd understand. Especially if he made it up in other ways.

"Ready?" he called, and without waiting for an answer, gave his starter-cord a herculean yank. The motor roared. Then they were off, chugging over a shallow bay toward open lake.

◆ ◆ ◆

To Scott, settled in the middle seat, the water looked as clear as on their first trip here. *Gin-clear*, fishermen called it. He saw no fish, just bits of ice and, on the bottom, sunken logs, drowned leaves, green weeds, and silt as white as cottage cheese.

"I saw those giants right around here," Errol said. He peered down into the lake, then leaned forward, urging the boat on. "Jeez, night comes fast."

When his friend moved toward a goal, Scott recalled, it was best to stay out of his way.

Reaching in his parka pocket, Errol extracted a black stocking cap, and pulled it over his ears. Scott pulled his cap on, too. His first few outings with Errol, he'd resisted stocking caps as more suitable for gangsters and street poets than fishermen. But the things were warm, easily carried, and in his case, so red no hunter would mistake him for a deer. Not only that, the hats protected heads from flies: those with hooks, and those without.

Claire's cap, gold with black stripes and a black pompom, wasn't woodsy, but looked good on her, Scott had to admit. After all the times he'd fished with Errol, it felt strange to have a woman in their boat. Strange, but okay.

A loon's yodeling lament floated down the lake. The bird itself was lost in fading light. The lake bottom was fading too, the deeper water turning murky: perfect home for dark spirits and mythic monsters.

"Let's fish," Errol said, and throttled down to trolling speed. "Scott— Claire's already rigged up. Can you help her?"

"Glad to. Sure." While Errol steered closer to shore, Scott finished letting out his line, then turned to Claire, who passed him her fly rod.

"We'll try twenty pulls." He demonstrated one *pull*: gripping her fly line at the reel, then extending his arm. Nineteen more, and he handed her the rod.

Her "Thank you, sir," sounded genuine.

"The lake's changed," Errol said. "That deep hole on the far side's gone. Water's up, too."

Scott played out more line. "If we knew what they were eating . . ."

Steering toward the center of the lake, Errol cut a wake in the gray glass. "That eight-incher I caught was empty."

"Maybe it was fasting," Scott said. "Oso's a spiritual place."

Claire laughed: a warm, sexy laugh, Scott couldn't deny.

"Who wants Tang?" Errol asked.

"I do," Scott said.

"*Want* may be a little strong," Claire said. "But okay."

"It's in the cooler," Errol said. "And plastic cups."

While Errol piloted, Scott tucked his rod under his arm, poured the Tang, and passed it out. Tang had been their go-to drink in the old days.

Errol gulped his down. Scott did the same. Claire was still sipping, rod in her left hand, when she said, "Errol, I felt something. Oh!"

Her rod tip dove and her reel screeched. She dropped her Tang, which splashed all over the boat's floor as Errol yelled, "Get your tip up! Quick! Strip *in*! Strip *in*!"

He killed the engine as Scott speed-reeled to keep his line from crossing Claire's.

"Don't give him slack!" Errol said. "Tip up! Let him run!"

Claire's rod flexed and unflexed as the fish changed directions and Claire didn't respond.

"Tip up! No slack!" Errol yelled.

Claire thrust the bucking rod at him. "*You* do it! Here!"

Errol reached across Scott to seize the rod as the fish ran. Fly line sizzled through his hands. "No giant," he said. "But strong."

A swirl, a splash, and there it was: a fat, eighteen-inch silver torpedo thirty feet from the boat. "That'll go two pounds. All *right*," Scott said, net already in hand.

Careful not to splash and spook the fish, he lowered the net into the water. He could see the fly, a purple woolly bugger, sunk into the trout's jaw. "Looks well-hooked," he told Errol, who coaxed the fish in toward the boat, its runs shorter and shorter until, with one smooth motion, Scott lifted net and rainbow, dripping, from the lake.

"Got him!" Scott crowed as, grinning, Errol leaned over Claire to shake Scott's hand.

"Always good to get that first one in. De-scent the skunk," Errol said. Scott watched him struggle to unhook the fish as it flipped in his net. The flipping, coupled with the dimming light and Errol's excitement, made him clumsy.

"Hell with it!" he said. Gripping the fish in his left hand, he used his right to grasp the head behind the gills, then pulled quickly up and back, as if opening a box.

The spine broke with a squishy crack. "Indian-style," Errol called the method, which looked and sounded sickening, but was a quick and humane way to kill a fish.

"We can check its guts in camp," Scott said as the limp trout thumped onto the boat's Tang-splattered floor.

"Right," Errol said, and turned to Claire. "Score one for the girls' team."

"Yippie skippie," she said, and pulled away as Errol reached out to muss her hair. "Spare me the fish-slime mousse."

"You wouldn't guess to look at her," Errol told Scott. "But this rustic fisherwoman was Phi Beta Kappa at UW, just like you."

"What year?" Scott said.

"Before your time, Sonny."

Claire's smile felt magnetic. Literally.

Scott edged back on his seat, away from her. "What was your major?"

"Art," she said. "Drawing and Painting."

"English," he countered. "Poetry."

"Practical people in a practical world," Claire said, and smiled again. She was one of those women, Scott decided, who couldn't help attracting men. Like Browning's "My Last Duchess," she was promiscuous with smiles.

How could that not be a good thing?

Far out on the darkening lake, the loon continued to lament. What had been a slight breeze was turning into a cold wind. Errol was right. Night came down fast up here.

"Might as well head in," Scott said. "Unless you brought a flashlight."

Errol looked around, then whacked his own head. "I left it in the truck." He shrugged. "Oh well, mornings are better anyway."

He restarted the motor, then steered the boat back toward a shore that glowered, blacker than the lake. There were few stars and only a sliver of moon to light their way. But thanks to Errol's sense of direction, they were soon in their bay, aimed toward the outline of their trucks.

For an instant, Scott thought he saw a deer's silhouette between the trucks. Then it was gone. If it had been there at all.

"Don't leave food outside," Errol said. "This is bear country."

"Don't worry," Scott said. "Getting mauled's not on my list of things to do."

Errol killed the engine, letting the boat glide the rest of the way in. "I know you're out there, monster trout," he called across the lake, then climbed out of the boat and, with loud, sloshing steps, dragged it ashore.

4

Through his open camper door, Scott saw Claire give Errol a quick kiss, then, with a roll of toilet paper in her hand, tromp toward the woods, her flashlight's white circle bouncing as she strode. Arranging his six one-gallon bottles of "Spring" water along the right side of his camper, Scott cleared a sleeping space, then made for the woods himself. In the opposite direction Claire had gone.

When he returned, Errol's camper door was open wide. Despite the cold, Claire was sitting topless in her sleeping bag, brushing her hair in the camper's yellow light. Even a hundred feet away, her breasts looked large on her slim frame, and very white.

Scott killed his flashlight, breath catching in his chest even as he turned away. He would *not* goggle-eye Errol's wife!

Tearing off two arm's-lengths of toilet paper from the roll he'd taken to the woods, he folded the paper square by square, and placed it in his left back pocket. No telling when, out on the lake, Nature would call.

He raised his arms above his head, stretched, then leaned farther back. As if someone had turned a rheostat, the sky broke out in stars. So many stars, there seemed no black space between them.

To see even a few stars in Seattle was rare. Too many clouds. Too much smog.

He wished he'd caught a fish. *De-scented the skunk*, as Errol had said. The spirit of this morning's deer had sent no aid. Not that he'd thought it would. Or that the deer *had* a spirit. At any rate, Claire's fish proved the lake was healthy. Find the right fly, and he'd catch his share.

He stole another glance at Claire. If she thought of him at all, she'd assume he was out of eyeshot in his camper. Where he should be.

Opening his camper door, he crawled in and switched on the overhead light. His air mattress had deflated, so he blew it up while bugs strafed the light. The first ones were tiny and white. Next came green ones with transparent wings. Then, whining, mosquitoes moved in.

Denying himself a last glance at Claire, Scott shut and locked his door, stripped off his clothes and, with a wet washcloth and soap, wiped himself down. Cold and tingling, he dried with a ragged towel, mashed what bugs he could against the plastic cover on the light, then flicked it off and crawled into his sleeping bag. Cold would immobilize surviving insects soon.

"Good for Errol," he thought as warmth rose up around him. "Caught himself a beaut."

He'd parked as far away as possible, but he was still too close, he realized when he heard Errol's voice: ". . . sorry I yelled."

The sigh of wind through trees dispersed Claire's words.

"It *will* be," Errol said. "We're miles from the huddled asses. Just us and the wilderness."

Claire spoke again.

"Trees soak up sound," Errol said; then, after a silence, "I promise, he can't hear."

A sleeping bag unzipped. "I should take off," Scott told himself when he heard thrashing, then Errol's grunts and Claire's high cries. For now, he burrowed deeper in his bag, using the smooth fabric to plug his ears.

If only Julie Jorgensen were here. What a great first date this place would be!

Except for Julie, Scott realized—Julie, and now Errol and Claire—no one knew where he was. Like those big trout Errol had seen, he'd disappeared.

◆ ◆ ◆

Claire's voice reeled Scott up from deep sleep. Had she called his name? The wind had died. He could hear everything now.

". . . best friend I ever had," Errol was saying.

Scott winced inside, remembering Errol's dinged truck. Tomorrow he'd confess.

"What's so great about him?" Claire said.

Scott pulled his sleeping bag over his head. It didn't help. He could still hear.

"For one thing," Errol said, "he plays world-class guitar. And sings like . . ." He gave a short laugh. "Like a guy who can really fucking sing. If he's not a star yet, he *will* be."

"Where'd you meet him? In a club?"

"In poetry-writing class," Errol said. "He was the star, for sure. He'd won the Roethke Prize, and had a 4.0. *And* spent half his time nursing his mom."

"His mom was sick?"

"Car wreck. Some drunk driver," Errol said. "Anyway, Cartwright—the professor—he thought Scott walked on ... not so much water as cologne. Ol' Carty smelled like he gargled Aqua Velva."

Strange, Scott thought, to be remembered from before his alpha-to-omega dive. And good to know that Errol thought well of him, despite their fight.

It was hard to think about that fight. He saw himself bounce off his crippled Ford Escort and slam into the ground as Errol scowled down. Then his mind squeezed its eyes shut and turned away.

"One day I brought in a really hot poem," Errol was saying. "Sexy, I mean."

Claire said something Scott couldn't make out.

"All fiction. One hundred percent," Errol said, and boomed a laugh. "Anyway, Carty called it 'a monument to self-indulgence.' But Scott, who didn't even know me at the time—Scott said, 'This poem has gonads. Poetry could use more of those.'"

Scott missed Claire's response, but heard Errol laugh. "Carty looked like he'd deep-throated a persimmon," he said. "He wound up giving Scott a B, and wrecked his 4.0. And Scott thought it was a hoot!"

Errol didn't know about the hole Scott kicked in his bathroom wall when his grades came in.

"An *enfant terrible* after your own heart," Claire said.

"Damn straight." A brief silence; then Errol said, "Speaking of straight ..."

A longer silenced followed. Then, more grunts and cries.

Scott dragged his stocking cap down over his ears, drew his head deeper into his sleeping bag, and tried to erect a soundproof wall of his own thoughts:

A few months after Sara dropped the Brown Helmet on his should-have-seen-it-coming head, his roommate Blake had introduced him to Julie.

"Who would've thought I'd ever date a beauty queen?" Blake had said.

"*Miss Puyallup*'s like being voted Tallest Dwarf," Julie quipped.

Scott liked her instantly: irreverent and beautiful. But she was Blake's.

Years before, in the first flush of high school Existentialism, Scott had listed *Personal Commandments* he'd *chosen* to uphold: "Play fair and square," "Don't take the easy road," "Stand up for what's right"—that sort of thing. Life had hammered those Commandments into mush. "Never mess with thy friend's girl," though, had survived. He'd steered clear of Julie until, three days ago, he'd seen her on The Ave.

Blake was ancient history, so Scott had asked her, "Like to grab some lunch?"

"It's not polite to grab," she said. "But okay."

They kissed in her driveway. One kiss, in broad daylight. But a good one.

"Call me when you get back, Great White Fisherperson," she'd said.

It had been two years since Sara. Two years without a serious girlfriend. Maybe it was time . . .

In the black fog before sleep, Scott halfway thought he heard a gunshot, far away. A hunter? Not at this time of year. Not legally.

Could those campfire-bones have been human, as Claire had said? Had they been cracked for marrow like in caveman days?

Not possible. No way.

He carried Dad's old pocket knife in his jeans. But its rounded, two-inch blade wouldn't offer much defense.

His hatchet would. But it was in the cab of his truck. His fishing knife was, too.

The air outside was freezing. His sleeping bag was warm . . .

The last sound he heard was Errol, groaning, "Christ in a crockpot." Then, "Jesus!"

SECOND DAY

5

Errol's bladder felt tight as a football, but he lay still, mustering nerve to face the cold outside his sleeping bag. Claire lay curled in her own bag, dead to the world. After several tries to zip their bags together, they'd sacrificed cuddling for sleep.

"I love you, Claire," he whispered. Marrying her, he *had* won the Triple Crown. As with all big winners, though, there'd been unintended consequences. Most of these concerned Claire's dad. Half of their fights had to do with him. And they fought a lot. Sometimes he feared their whole marriage was crumbling.

That thought cramped his chest and clutched his throat. He tried never to let negative thoughts have their way. Now they'd caught up. All he could do was ride them out.

His moods were a problem, he knew. His temper got shorter every day. He'd never dreamed how bad a boss Claire's dad would be. But he'd needed a job, and "Pop" Gunn (as, to Claire's annoyance, he called the old man) had offered one. Now he had to hang tough. As he'd learned when he wrestled in high school, the surest way to lose was to give up.

Gently, he touched Claire's tangled hair and peaceful face. "We'll have a great time. I promise," he whispered, leaned to give her a light kiss, then, quietly as he could, wriggled out of his bag, gathered his clothes, and slipped through the camper door, outside.

"Aw, no," he said under his breath. *White* breath. The air felt polar. Thick gray clouds covered the sky. A winter gale slammed off the lake.

"It'll die down," he told himself as he pulled his wool pants over his Fleece long underwear, laced his boots, and strode to the water. He felt like a boy as he peed, melting the ice-film that had hardened close to shore. Freeze-your-prick-off wind or not, life was just better out here.

A loon spewed its crazy laugh, its black-and-whiteness bobbing fifty yards off shore. Half a mile past the bird, the far shore threw up a green bulwark of trees. He pictured a moose stepping through, scanning the scene, then wading out to graze. That would be something to see.

He walked to the campfire and kicked the ashes. Moose or not, those bones hadn't looked human, he assured himself as he clomped to Scott's truck, banged on his camper, and boomed, "Rise and shine, Wolverine!"

Scott had claimed that name on their first trip to Brewster Lake. Errol had been *Grizzly*. His twelve-year-old cousin Joshie had been, despite, and then because of his shrill protests, *Fieldmouse*.

A thrashing started in Scott's camper. "Right with you," came his muffled croak. Something, probably Scott's head, bonged the top of his "camper": the kind of simple shell they'd slept under on their last trip here. A chipmunk could barely stand upright in one of those.

A moment later, Scott raised his door flap, lowered his tailgate, and slid outside. "Colder than a well-digger's refrigerator," he said, pushing hair out of his eyes. "What'd I get, two hours of sleep?"

"You'll live, trooper," Errol said, and hustled off to get his gear.

It felt like fate, Scott's walking into Howdy Do's. Each year, it seemed, friends got harder to find. People's interests narrowed as they aged. Fewer and fewer were compatible. Not that he'd ever had a lot of friends. He was, in his mother's words, "too too"—too big, loud, brash, opinionated. Too extreme.

But Scott was extreme too—interested, like Errol, in everything. Science, art, math, sports, music . . . Scott shared his passionate approach to life. They'd had great times before the fight. How could he have let himself deck his best friend? Scott had his faults, but his virtues outweighed them by far. With his talent, old Wolverine must've done wonders in the last five years.

Errol dreaded to confess what *he* had done. Maybe Scott's influence would get him back on track.

Zipping his fly box into his vest, he remembered Claire's fish, and triple-timed toward the lake. He'd been so tired last night, and so ready to be in bed with Claire, he'd not only failed to gut their fish, he'd left it like a bear-magnet in his boat.

He was twenty feet away when a gray-and-white Canada jay flapped, with fish guts dangling from its beak, out of his boat and up into a nearby pine.

"Son of a bitch!" Errol said, but had to smile. People didn't call them Camp Robbers for nothing. They'd steal food off your tongue, and take the tongue with it.

Throwing what little was left of Claire's fish into the lake, Errol strode over to Scott's truck, called, "Any time now, Wolverine," and slipped back into his own full-sized camper. The thing was loaded with amenities: shower, kitchen, refrigerator, flush toilet. He'd get them all to work, eventually. But even now, this was a good place to stay, he told himself as he climbed to the platform "bedroom" over the truck's cab.

"Babe," he said, "Scott and I are going fishing. Want to come?"

"That would be redundant," she murmured, "after last night." She raised her arms for a hug, but didn't crack her eyes.

Errol scootched up next to her, and took her, sleeping bag and all, into his arms.

"I'm so sleepy," she said as he cradled her. "Do you mind if I stay here?"

"Are you sure?" Errol said. If she was opting out because of Scott, that would be bad.

"I'll fish this afternoon," she said. "Promise."

He felt better, hearing that. Felt relieved and grateful that she understood. With her in the boat, he'd spend more time teaching than fishing. And right now, for the sake of his sanity, he needed to catch fish.

"I'll be back soon. I love you," he said, kissed her cheek, then added, for himself as much as her, "We're going to be okay."

"That's good," she mumbled. "Love you too." And dropped back to sleep.

6

Claire jerked upright to bright daylight, then remembered: no school. "Thank the Lord," she said, and dropped back onto her air mattress, which was nearly flat.

Had Errol given her the leaky one?

She should have gone fishing, she knew. But sleep had felt *so* good. All except one dream. The dream had vanished, but a bad feeling remained.

Those bones they'd found, deer or moose or whatever, had creeped her out. And what if somebody drove up looking for trouble, and found her here alone? Errol's pistol was in the cab. Her father had taught her to shoot—rifles *and* pistols—when she was barely big enough to lift the guns. But could she shoot a person, even in self defense?

It's okay, she told herself. *Who'd come out here?*

Pulling her sleeping bag over her head, she snuggled down. But she kept thinking she heard footsteps. And fretting about school. When she returned, she'd have twice the work to do.

Three years ago, she couldn't wait to help save public education. Now, after six semesters of lesson plans, standardized tests, insolent kids, hostile parents, and administrators concerned mainly with snagging promotions and avoiding lawsuits, she felt as burned out as the thirty-year veterans looked.

Still, she loved Sabrina, with her freckles; Marcus with his big, round, buzz cut head; little John Paul who, at eleven, didn't realize he was gay . . .

"I came here to get *away*," she said aloud as she unzipped her bag, sat up, and dressed. In Hemingway's "The Snows of Kilimanjaro," gangrene started in a man's feet, and climbed, killing him inch by inch. Pine Hills Elementary felt more and more like gangrene.

So why not quit? "With your dad's cash," Errol said, "why deal with kids who aren't your own?"

Errol never missed a chance to jab her about having kids. Neither he nor her father could see why she didn't plunge straight into motherhood, screaming "Yay!"

"If kids are so great, why'd you just have one?" she'd challenged Dad one night.

"Ask your mother," he'd said. But if Robert H. "Bob" Gunn had truly wanted more kids, he'd have had them. Errol's working for him had been a clash of dictators. And Errol had lost. He lacked the killer instinct—"money-lust," he called it—of a top-flight businessman. Still, he refused to let her father call him a quitter. That's probably why she kept teaching: not to give her father that chance.

Something rustled behind her in the woods. She stuck her head out of the camper, saw no danger, and pulled back inside. *Some animal*, she told herself. Animals lived in the woods. What did she expect?

She should have held out for Hawaii.

She gave her sleeping bag a shove that, instead of jamming it into its stuff-bag, pushed it out so that she had to start over. Damn Scott Murray! She'd come here to resuscitate her marriage. To be a team: just her and Errol, like when they were dating. They'd seemed unbeatable, standing at the front desk of the Lake Union Holiday Inn, Errol's hand on her behind while a Born Again convention glared, and Errol told the desk clerk, in an outrageous Southern drawl, "We're Reverend and Mrs. Brain from Tennessee."

Back then, Errol had seemed the kind of powerhouse who could force the world to take him on his terms and (if she were being honest) make it do the same for her. Now she was stuck here, a million miles into the sticks, and he was off fishing with Scott. Outside of bed, she'd be about as welcome as a nosebleed.

Stop, she told herself as, lifting Errol's bright green Coleman stove, she opened the camper door and stepped outside into a cool, gorgeous day. Scott seemed nice enough. At—what? five nine?—he looked like a boy next to Errol. But he was put together well. With his coppery rock-and-roll hair, he was even kind of hot. Why blame her troubles on him?

As long as she'd known Errol, he'd raved about "my friend Scott." She'd never been clear why they parted company. Errol fixed Scott's car, Scott claimed he botched the job . . . something "manly" like that. Manly and dumb.

"It was stupid," Errol had said. "And stupider to let it split us up."

If he and Scott could reconnect, it might be good for her, too. Errol needed the kind of friend Katie and Nyla were for her. A happier Errol might mean a happier marriage.

Setting up the stove as Errol had showed her, Claire pumped the metal fuel tube, turned on the gas, struck a long-stemmed match, then touched it to the burner, which hissed to life on the first try. Their camper had a real stove, but it didn't work. How *Errol* to seize a "deal" on a camper where nothing worked, then reframe the problem as a benefit. "It'll be more like real camping. Roughing it."

Still, she did feel outdoorsy, setting the Coleman's flame to heat water for coffee. Once it was brewed, tasting as good as instant coffee ever did, she turned off the stove and dug a carton of vanilla yogurt out of the ice chest. She'd never liked the slimy goo. But it was good for you. And low calorie.

Errol was right about one thing: this place was stunning. As the sun climbed and the day warmed, the lake sparkled like a blue sapphire in a brooch of forest-green. No telling how far the lake stretched away, or how far away the guys were now.

A cheerful, Christmas tree fragrance filled the air, as different from "pine-scented" air fresheners as strawberries were from strawberry soda. The clumps of snow, already melting in the sun, were pretty, too. She would have brought her paints if she had known she would be spending time alone.

Well, she could still sketch. Good subjects were everywhere. Silver-gray birds flitted bush to bush. Redwinged blackbirds ringed the shore, flashing their shoulder-patches, cheerfully creaking, "Kong-ka-*ree.*"

So why was she on edge?

Two years ago, the "Intro to Parapsychology" teacher at The Learning Company had called her "moderately gifted." Wasn't that the story of her life?

Shutting her eyes, she tried to activate her *moderately* good "psychic sensors." But, all she felt was vague unease which, like her bad dream, likely came from the thin ice she and Errol were skating on.

She downed her coffee, started to tidy up, realized it was pointless, and sat back down. When the woods rustled again, she jumped up, ready to run, then saw a big gray squirrel burst into the clearing and, like an undulating eyebrow, lope to a tree that hung above their truck. Brown bark flying, the squirrel raced up the tree, ran out on a thick limb and, glaring like some half-pint sorcerer, made a sound like a cat throwing up: *Whump! Whump! Whump! Whump!*

Claire understood that the squirrel was cursing her. When she stayed put, it increased its demands that she go away: *Choonk! Choonk! Choonk! Choonk!* it threatened. *Hohnh! hohnh! hohnh!*

"Piss off," she said. Unnerved by its angry black eyes, she picked up her fishing rod and strolled to the edge of the lake. If she cast better, fishing would be more fun for her *and* Errol.

The lake water was like smoked glass on which the woods were painted upside down. She could work all her life, and not paint anything that good.

She thought of her then-professor Peter Langford bending over her at the London Academy, his long, gray hair almost in her face. "Getting better," he'd said in his prim Oxford accent. Then he'd asked her out.

Unhooking her fly from her rod's metal fly-loop, she tugged her leader past the guides. When four feet of green fly line hung down, she waved the rod as Errol had showed her, pulling out line from the reel.

She heard and felt a *THWACK* as the fly hit her parka, then clung to her coat sleeve like some demonic feathered bug.

"Bloody hell!" She pulled the coat off, and studied the fly: barb buried deep in Fiberfill. Pull out the fly, she'd rip her parka. Snip off the fly, Errol might be mad.

Parka in one hand, rod in the other, she made for the truck as fly line wrapped her feet and tried to trip her up. "Christ on a credit card!" she snapped, but had to smile. *Remember that for Errol*, she told herself as, glad the squirrel was gone, she dumped her gear on the truck's hood. Feeling grimy and disgusting, she threw open the camper door and dug out a wash-cloth and a bar of soap. Maybe getting clean would lift her mood.

She could wash up inside the camper. But since neither the sink nor the shower produced water, it seemed a timid choice. Since she was here, she should bathe like an outdoorswoman, she told herself as she closed the camper door. She almost locked it, then remembered that Errol had the key. Which was good. He probably had spares; but if she lost his keys, she'd never live it down. And what if she had to get inside the camper fast?

Screw it, she thought, and stalked toward the woods.

She planned to walk inland a little ways, then follow the shore until she found a private spot. But three steps into the dark, tangled, underbrushy woods felt like three miles. Almost at once, their campsite disappeared. Crows cawed in the distance. High overhead, a huge hawk soared.

Out of the sunlight, strange forces held sway. What if she stumbled on the source of those burned bones? Moose were gigantic. A dead one would be gigantically bad.

A dead *person* would be gigantically worse.

But if the bones were human, Errol would have known. Wouldn't he?

With a laugh to show herself she wasn't scared, she backed out of the woods and rushed to the lake shore. She couldn't see Scott and Errol out on the water, so most likely, they couldn't see her.

Despite the snow clumps on the ground, the air was warming up. She double-checked to be sure the coast was clear, pulled off her sweatshirt, then, reluctant to remove her bra, stood pressing the sweatshirt to her chest.

Strange how deeply *modesty* sank its claws into girls. She hated being ruled by ideas that crushed freedom and, in this case, made no sense. No one was near. She would hear approaching cars from miles away. All the same, she walked farther down the shore to where thick brush set up a screen. Draping her sweatshirt on a low limb, she knelt to dip her washcloth in the lake, and saw a school of minnows hanging together in the shade of a fat bush.

She tossed a pebble. Like one creature, the minnows darted several feet away, then hung in place as if nothing had changed.

She looked around, feeling as if the woods were some shaggy monster crouched to attack. Which was ridiculous. When something rustled in the trees, she told herself, "Another squirrel," and didn't look.

She soaped her washcloth and rubbed her neck briskly.

Instant goosebumps.

She rubbed harder, causing ice water to zip between her breasts into her bra, which turned clammy right away.

"Bollocks," she said, unhooked the bra and pulled it off, then whisked the washcloth back and forth across her skin. Her nipples contracted to the size of wrinkled peas. Still, she liked the shock of cold water in clean, open air.

Pulling off her shoes and socks, she unsnapped her jeans and wiggled out. The ground, studded with rocks, made her wobble, but her thighs were strong and firm. Thirty-three, though, was a long way from seventeen. And five years from Errol's twenty-eight. How many more years would he call her *callipygian*? Especially if she had a child.

There was nothing sexy about freezing your breasts off. Yet she felt aroused. She'd read somewhere that women evolved to be exhibitionists. At the time, she'd thought the notion sexist crap. Now she wondered if it might be true.

Had the woman who'd left her panties at the campsite felt sexy, stepping out of them among the trees?

A quick step plunged her right foot ankle-deep into the lake: so icy-cold, her diaphragm seemed to freeze. She couldn't breathe. But she refused to step back. Refused to retreat.

When she'd relaxed enough to grab a breath, she placed her left foot in the lake next to her right. Almost at once, her skin felt warm. Exhilaration surged up from her feet, making her whole body glow.

Turning her back to the lake, she thrust both hands under her hair, and lifted it above her head the way, at thirteen, she'd practiced *sexy* in the bathroom mirror.

"God of the Forest," she intoned, "take me!"

Her words sounded ridiculous. And very loud.

Her sexy feeling vanished. Pray that the men hadn't heard!

She stepped out of the lake and, all business, resumed washing until something—a heightened stillness—made her turn to face the woods.

When nothing stirred, she went back to washing, humming "Ode to Joy." But Beethoven couldn't quell the sense of being watched. And the smell. Had it always been there? Like locker room sweat dripped on rancid meat.

Trying to seem at ease, she gathered up her clothes and, not bothering with socks, jammed her feet into her shoes.

A twig snapped. She spun around, then, oblivious to rocks stabbing her feet, raced for the truck.

She'd seen a yellow eye. Behind it, something huge and brown.

7

"Claire didn't want to fish?" Scott said as he and Errol trolled across the lake: smooth as a mirror in the lifting mist. The wind had stopped. The sky was clearing fast. But no fish were rising. Neither man had had a hit.

"Claire's up at five thirty every school day. For her, heaven's sleeping in till nine," Errol said. He waved his hand, encompassing the scene. "If a Martian ever asks you, 'Define *beauty*,' show him this."

Bare-breasted Claire leapt unbidden to Scott's mind. "I should give you two some privacy," he said. "I can go fish somewhere else."

"Abandon me to a dead lake? That's cold!"

Scott reeled in to try a different fly. Maybe the lake *had* died.

"You watch," he said, tying on a black #12 woolly worm. "They'll start a feeding frenzy as soon as I'm gone."

Errol shrugged. "Go if *you* want to. Not because of *me*."

"What does Claire think?" Scott shifted his head from side to side, as if to shake water out of his ears. Some sort of sleep-residue had hazed his brain.

"Claire only fishes to keep me company," Errol said. "She's glad you're here." He flashed his most roguish grin. "It gives her respite from my sexual demands."

Scott rolled his eyes, but had to smile. "Errol Wolfe: bonsai priapist."

"More like *banzai*!" Errol said. "How many guys do you know as . . . how shall I put this? . . . as *Rabelaisian* as you? Who love fishing, too?"

"Not many," Scott said. "None."

"Remember our motto? No wimp artists. No wimpy art."

Scott nodded. They'd dreamed of world-class collaborations: Errol directing Scott's shows and rock videos, Scott scoring Errol's films.

"No wimp fishermen!" Errol said. "Oso's changed, but we can still kick its ass."

"Okay," Scott said as they chugged forward. "But if I start to be a crowd, please let me know."

"You got it, Wolverine," Errol said with so much warmth, Scott almost mentioned The Ding. Errol might see it, though, as payback for their fight. *Why risk a blow-up, with things going so well?* Scott was thinking when Errol groaned. "Aw sasquatch shit!"

"What's wrong?"

Scott followed Errol's finger-jab, and saw a boat flash like a mirror in the distance. "Must be another way in," Scott said. "Let's check him out."

◆ ◆ ◆

The boat's owner was anchored in a largish bay, casting expertly: smooth, re-laxed, and easy. Errol killed his motor thirty yards away and glided in, speak-ing softly so as not to spook the fish.

"Any luck?"

"A little." The man, white-haired and at least sixty, finished a fifty-foot cast, bent, and held up a glistening four-pound trout. "I kept this one to eat."

"Whoa! What'd he take?" Errol battled down an urge to cast right then and there.

"My own pattern. Anything small and green should do the trick."

Errol sculled an oar to keep from drifting in too close. The water was gin-clear, the white silt bottom crosshatched, probably by snails.

The old man was anchored on the deep side of a drop-off, casting toward shore. He had a creased face and startling blue eyes.

"Fish here a lot?" Errol asked.

"When my heart lets me."

Errol's question—"What's wrong with your heart?"—jumped out before tact could intervene.

"I've had a couple heart attacks," the old man said.

"That's no good." Errol hoped he seemed sympathetic, not pitying.

"I had one right where you're camped," the man went on. "I drove up with my wife. And a girl's head was lying in the campfire pit."

"Just her head?!" Errol craned forward so fast he wobbled the boat. A puff of wind hit, dropping the temperature several degrees, then scooted off across the lake.

"That's all there was," the old man said. "Red hair spread out like a table-cloth."

Errol shot a glance toward camp and Claire. "They find who did it?"

"Her boyfriend turned up drunk, covered with blood. He claimed a wen-digo ate her."

"Those are like Indian zombies, right?" Errol said. Was this guy messing with *their* heads?

"They never did find the girl's body." The old man raised his eyebrows. "*Or* the wendigo."

"I hope I don't find either one," Scott said.

"If my wife hadn't had my pills, I'd be dead as that boyfriend," the old man said.

"They executed him?" Errol said. "I thought Canadians were . . . gentler."

"He hanged himself," the old man said, and twitched his fly. "Turned out he'd been committed twice before."

That, Errol thought, explained the "wendigo." The boyfriend was a head case.

"When did this happen?" Scott asked.

"Last fall. Just before snow closed the roads."

"You had a heart attack that recently?" Scott said. "And you're fishing?!"

"Doc says fishin'll kill me. *I* say *not* fishin' will." He twitched his fly again. "Seen the ghost trout?"

Errol craned forward again. "What's a ghost trout?"

"A school of giant rainbows cruise this lake."

"I've seen 'em!" Errol barely managed not to shout. "Big as steelhead."

"What's ghostly about 'em?" Scott said.

"They showed up last year," the old man said. "Who knows from where?" He flashed Errol a crafty smile. "Get 'em to hit?"

"Not yet," Errol said.

"Not *ever*," the old man said. "They swim past your flies like they're in some different dimension. Then they disappear."

This old guy might be a head case too, Errol thought. Still, the guy knew how to fish. With a crisp flick of his arm, he plucked his line out of the water, letting it uncurl behind him leisurely. Then, as it hung suspended like a clothesline, he brought his right elbow down, making his rod flex tip to butt. His line reversed, curled forward, then uncurled and laid out perfectly, dropping his fly, gently as a real insect, inches from a sunken log.

He sat motionless for several seconds, then twitched the fly. Something in the water flashed. The old man's rod bent double, and the fight was on.

Rod high, he let the fish run, always facing it, with just enough tension on his line.

When the trout leapt in a silver shower, Errol bellowed, "Christ on a crumpet! That's five pounds!"

The fish dived again—this time, under the boat. Errol feared to see the old man fall, clutching his chest. But no. He guided the line expertly around the prow, not rushing, snagging up, or giving slack.

Errol fought down a crazy urge to grab the old man's rod. He'd come to Oso for this kind of fish!

The trout hugged bottom, letting his weight fight for him.

Slowly, the old man pumped him in, then stooped to grab his net.

The fish chose that instant to run.

"Too soon," the old man said, and tried to brake his screaming reel with his left palm. The fish faltered, slowed, then went all-out, and dived under the sunken log.

The old man's line stayed tight a moment, then went slack.

"Broke off, damn 'im." Breathing hard, the old man plopped onto his seat. "The bugger beat me fair and square."

"Think a green Carey'd work?" Errol's hands were shaking. He felt wild with envy. Desperate to land a trophy fish.

"Lake's full of scuds," the old man said. "You got a green scud, I'd try that. 5X tippet, no thicker. These fish get leader-shy when the water's this clear."

"I've got an *orange* scud," Scott said, examining the feathery rows of flies that crowded his fly box.

Errol didn't have a scud of any kind, so he chose a small, nameless green nymph that, once and only once, had knocked 'em dead at Brewster Lake. He wracked his brain for a way to justify fishing right here. But etiquette was absolute: no horning in.

"Knock 'em dead," he told the old man, then rowed resolutely away. "Don't take any wooden wendigos," he muttered as he rowed.

"Wendigos are East Coast monsters. Algonquin, I think," Scott said. "Ten-foot-tall man-eaters that smell like rotten meat."

"I think I dated one of those," Errol said, and had to grin when Scott cracked up. It felt great to fish with his old friend again. And would feel better when they started catching fish.

Once out of the bay, he stopped rowing, and they tied on 5X tippet. Thin as spider web.

"This stuff's so light, we'll have to sweet-talk a big fish into the net," Errol said, more to himself than to Scott. Restarting his motor, he moved into a slow troll along the shore. With luck, they'd find a drop-off, creek inlet, or other spot where fish hung out.

They were barely ten yards off shore when Scott yelled, "There's one!" and set the hook on what, when Errol got it in the net, proved to be a ten-inch dink. Its girth, though, proved it had been eating well.

"Skunked no more!" Scott proclaimed as, with his knife turned dull-side-down, he whacked the fish twice on the head. *A wimpy way to kill a fish*, Errol thought. But the trout shuddered, flipped once, and went still.

◆ ◆ ◆

"Let's see what's in the guts," Scott said. Steeling his own guts, he shoved his knife into the trout's anal vent, then sliced upwards toward the head. Red gouts of blood, plus runny black gut-goo splashed onto the boat's floor. Stringy intestines draped across Scott's seat as, with a quick tug, he ripped out the viscera.

Errol frowned. "Could you not crap up the boat?"

"Sorry." Scott sheathed his knife, set his fish on the boat's floor, and tossed the guts overboard. Errol had always been touchy about his "stuff."

He wasn't going to like The Ding.

"That underwear we found—it could've been that girl's," Scott said to change the subject.

Errol looked grim. "Snow would've hidden 'em."

Scott felt, suddenly, as if he were being watched. So many places a watcher could hide on shore. Or a sniper. Had he heard a gunshot last night, or had he dreamed it?

Scanning the shore, he would have sworn he saw a deer with budding antlers step out of the woods, then fade back in.

"You think those bones could've been human?" he said.

"Hell, I don't know!" Errol said, and frowned as if he *did*. "Don't mention that girl's head to Claire. She'd fill her pantaloons."

"Not a word," Scott said. "I'm just glad they caught the guy."

"Didn't help the girl," Errol said, then smacked the side of his face. "Die, bug!"

Scott checked his own face for feeding insects. Finding none, he said, "That old guy's got some balls. Heart like a Swiss cheese and *knows* no one can fix it. And fishes anyway."

"What's he gonna do? Give up and wait to die?"

"People do," Scott said. "They decide everything's futile, and just quit."

One great thing about fishing with Errol had always been the conversation. No statement was too outrageous or uncouth—"immature," Sara would have said—to liven up the downtime between fish.

Unfolding a paper cup from his shirt pocket, Scott filled it with Tang from Errol's jug and gulped it down before he spoke: "Dr. Zepeda at the Free Clinic said I felt *helpless* with the Houston cops and Mom, so I avoid that feeling by not *taking risks*." He raised his rod, and felt a drag. "Not a good mindset for an aspiring rock-god," he said, and started reeling in to check for weeds. The slightest bit of "spinach" on a fly would spook the fish.

Errol shook his gas tank to check it. The slosh told Scott it was half-full.

"'Failure-of-nerve,' Claire's father calls it," Errol said. "Any time fear keeps you from taking care of business, that's failure-of-nerve."

Scott kept reeling in. When had he let out so much line? "In that case, my nerve's flunked out and works at McDonald's," he said.

Errol didn't laugh. Something—the gut-mess in the boat? some memory of their fight?—had soured his mood. "Did Dr. Zapata do you any good?" he said.

Scott shrugged. "We did roleplays where I chewed out the cops who clubbed me and the drunk who hit my mom. Mostly, insight was supposed to do the trick."

"You mean to tell me," Errol said, "that thinking about thinking about thinking didn't help?"

"I'll have to think about that," Scott said, and drew in his legs as Errol mimed a kick to his kneecap.

The sun was bright, bouncing light off the now-blue lake as Scott lifted his fly out of the water. Finding no spinach, he unbuttoned his shirt pocket and pulled out the polarized sunglasses he'd bought for this trip. Eighty bucks, but worth it. Not only would they fend off headaches, they'd help him spot fish, even in high glare. Maybe help him spot watchers-from-shore, too.

They saw several good-sized rises. But though they tried dry flies, emergers, nymphs, and streamers, they couldn't coax a hit.

"They're in here," Errol said. "We've just got to find a fly they'll eat."

"I should have checked the guts before I threw 'em overboard," Scott said.

"I shouldn't have bitched about the mess," Errol said.

Scott nodded, less in agreement than thanks that he wasn't being blamed. "We'll open up the next one," he said.

They fished in silence for a while, Scott pondering failure-of-nerve. "Remember in *The Godfather*," he finally said, "when Michael shoots that cop who broke his jaw?"

Errol nodded. "Sure."

"If I could shoot the cops who kicked my ass, and that drunk scrote-lick who ran into Mom, I'd feel a lot better," Scott said, and gave a snort of scorn. "Tell Dr. Zepeda that, and she'd have called the National Guard."

Errol seconded Scott's snort, a frown darkening his blue eyes.

Scott made a roll cast back into the lake, then let out line as the boat chugged ahead. "School was easy for me," he said. "But in the world, I'm like a guy trying to fence with a beach towel."

At this point, Errol should have laughed and offered a confession of his own. When he did not, Scott knocked back another Tang, and kept talking. "I thought if I did well in school, my life would be great by Natural Law," he said. "My bike broke, Daddy'd fix it. My back broke, doctors would. World without pain, amen, amen."

He slapped his face, and this time felt an insect mash. Rolling the body off his cheek, he flipped it overboard, then realized that it might have told him what the fish were eating.

Errol gripped the tiller, glared ahead, and didn't speak.

Scott downed another Tang and floundered on: "I wanted to be Robin Hood when I grew up. But I've never saved a maiden. *Or* seen a severed head." He scanned the shore again. Just trees. "I'm so sick of being *homo inepticus*, I almost joined the Marines."

"The Middle East could solve your problems," Errol said. "Permanently."

"I'd have gotten used to men in uniforms," Scott said. "And if someone gave me shit, I'd know how to throw it back. With interest."

Errol hinted at a smile. "I've done that once or twice."

Scott saw himself sprawled on the ground, Errol snarling down, "You're too damned puny to punch out . . ."

Scott squashed the image, and leapt into joking mode. "Look at the *size* of you!" he said. "Us non-pituitary types are scared, if we let down our guard enough to live, something'll kill us." Scott rarely spit, but he did now into the lake. "My survival instincts may have been bred out," he said.

Errol looked aghast.

"It happens!" Scott said. "Farm turkeys'll look up at the rain until they drown."

"*I* told you that," Errol said. "Turns out it isn't true."

Scott snorted. "If Nazis marched into my bedroom, I'd probably hide under the sheets and squawk 'No fair!' as they garroted me."

Errol shook his head vehemently no. "You'd fight back. I know *you*."

Had Errol forgotten? Slammed into his car, Scott hadn't fought back. He'd cowered on the ground until his "friend" had stalked away. His defeat and shame had been complete. But if Errol wanted to forget that, so did he.

"You're right," he said. "Mess with me, they'd be picking teeth out of their Wiener schnitzel."

Errol laughed approval. "Damn straight!" His brow unfurrowed, his eyes lit up and, quickly as it had come, his bad mood was gone.

"So, Wolverine," he said, "what else you been up to? Besides thinking yourself catatonic."

Scott started to say *karate*. But Errol had trounced a black belt in the District Tavern, and scorned *those little senseis in their judo suits*. Cutting his sentence off at "Ka," Scott made a sound like a man throwing up his epiglottis.

"Speech therapy?" Errol said.

Scott ripped line off his reel as if it disgusted him. "Three months back, I got a gig with a band called Lyinhart. Top management, a rich backer, record contract guaranteed. Trouble was, Glen, the singer, couldn't sing. And wouldn't let *me*. One demo, and our management quit. The backer, who was Glen's uncle, backed out. Four days ago, I found out Glen was set to ax me. So I packed my truck and drove up here."

"Your name'll be doo-doo in town."

"Could be," Scott said. "But if I stay in music, I'm moving to LA. Or maybe I'll delight my dad and go to law school. Make crime pay."

"What's Sara think?"

"We broke up." He hesitated, then spilled the truth. "Actually, she dumped me."

For a guy who'd grown up without a father, Errol did a great Disapproving Dad. "You two went out for a long time."

"It's not like I asked to get dumped," Scott said. Though he *had* asked in a way, telling her father, "Sorry, Sir, I'm not for sale." He watched a white moth dip too near the water, then spin on the surface of the lake.

Which would come first, trout or drowning? he wondered as Errol said, "You should've married her."

Sara'd thought so too. "Your *values* are just ego," she'd screamed toward the end of their last fight. "You dumped on *us* so you could feel above it all."

Scott took pride in his moral sense. Most people he knew had shaky values, or none. Still, would it have been so bad to manage a newspaper that Sara's father owned? Had her judgment been accurate? Were his values *just ego*, even now?

"I met a honey on the Ave the other day," he said, and forced a rakish grin. "Maybe I'll ask her to move in."

"Marriage is different. You commit to someone absolutely," Errol said, and hawked a huge loogie into the lake. A distance shot. "How's songwriting?"

Scott expelled a *Pfff!*: half-hiss, half-sigh. "Nobody wants original songs from a bar band," he said. "I've sent my stuff to publishers. No go." He shrugged as if to move the spotlight off of him. "How 'bout you? Still burning up the stage?"

Errol gave a sigh, then raised his hand to shade his eyes. "In the words of John Lennon, 'I just had to drop it. On my toe.'"

"Now, that's a drag," Scott said. "You're the real McCoy."

"Life's not a Woody Allen flick where everyone lives in Manhattan and makes big money in the arts," Errol said, and spit again. "I miss the theater every day. But it's not practical. Also, you may have noticed, I'm not gay."

Liking girls hadn't kept Errol from being a Drama Department star, as Scott recalled.

"Even if I *were* gay, actors starve. And I'm not the starving type," Errol said, and whacked his belly: not Thor-tight anymore. "Being married, maybe having kids . . ." He shrugged. "I've got to go for the green."

Errol was rationalizing, any fool could see. But Scott had no wish to call him on it. And no right.

"How'd you meet Claire?" he said.

Errol played out line and settled back. "I was still working weekends at the boathouse . . ." He didn't have to add, *after our fight*. He rubbed his forehead, scratched his chin, and yawned. "Life drags along like nothing's gonna happen. Then wham!—something cracks you on the head."

Scott raised his hands to protect his skull. "I'm waiting."

"Claire and Katie—that's her best friend—they showed up with two wimps to rent canoes." Errol repositioned his rod, and checked the drag. "Remember in *Gatsby* how Daisy *smells of money*. Claire smelled of *class*. You oughta see her in a bikini." He paused. "Second thought, maybe you'd shouldn't, Cathouse."

Scott dodged Errol's poke, but returned his grin. Errol had dubbed him "Cathouse" when his band backed strippers at The Kitty Club.

"You know me," Errol went on. "I whispered, 'Come back at eight'. When she did, I took her for a moonlight ride. In a *boat*, sinner." He Groucho Marxed his eyebrows: up-down, up-down. "Two months later, we got married and moved to Spokane."

"You don't waste time," Scott said, and hoped it sounded like a compliment. After the fight, he'd thought that Errol might come by to apologize.

That, or they'd run into each other and patch things up. Now he knew why that hadn't occurred.

"When you hook a world-class trout, why mess around?" Errol said. "Get her in the net, and don't let go."

At the word *go*, Errol's reel screamed. He grabbed his rod just as a fair-sized rainbow vaulted into the air behind their boat.

"All *right*," Scott said as Errol killed the engine, thrust his rod tip high, and reeled as fast as he could to take up slack.

"About time," Errol said, then "Whoa Nelly!" as line ripped off his reel.

Two minutes later, as Errol grinned ear to ear, Scott netted a fat eighteen-incher with dark black spots and a blood-red line running down its side.

"That's more like it," Errol said.

"Let's get some more," Scott said.

But after ten minutes and no hits, his excitement died down.

"What do you do in Spokane?" he asked Errol. "Besides bask in marital bliss?"

Errol hesitated, then said, "I work for Claire's dad."

Scott winced inside. If he'd gone to work for Sara's dad, his whole life would have changed.

"What's Claire's dad do?"

Errol scanned the shore as if he felt a watcher, too. "Land development," he said, and didn't look at Scott.

What could Scott say? The old Errol had damned land-developers to the tenth circle of hell every time a high-rise or Vacation Village sprouted on a favorite steelhead run.

"Mostly I wine and dine rich assholes, and sell 'em on investing," Errol went on. "I've gotten pretty good."

"You always could sell saltpeter in a whorehouse," Scott said.

Errol's response was interrupted by a *whap!*

Scott dropped onto the boat's floor. "What was that?!"

"Wasn't a gun," Errol said from beside him on the floor. "That old man got me spooked."

Steering one-handed, he lifted his head to peer over the gunwale as the boat chugged ahead.

Another, louder *whap!* Close by.

The men turned toward the sound and saw rings fanning out as if the king of all ghost trout had breached.

"Was that a fish?!"

"Kill the motor. Let's see."

Their goal, barely five feet from shore, was a clearing in a solid sea of lily pads. "Maybe a deep hole," Errol said as the boat slithered through the pads.

Poised to cast, Scott felt dizzy. He'd thought the movement in his head was from the boat. Now, with the boat almost stopped, his head continued to spin.

Thirty feet from the hole, Errol stopped rowing. Scott made two false casts, then dropped his fly on target, and let it sink in the black water.

Willing his head to stay still, he twitched his fly. When it stopped cold, he set the hook. His rod bent double, something heavy on the line.

"Lordy! Hold him!" Errol roared.

When Scott's rod didn't buck, he reset the hook even as the truth sank in. "A fucking snag!" He yanked again, then groaned. "Shithouse mouse! Row me in."

"This lake's turned into a turdburger," Errol said as, like some giant water bug, the boat wallowed on oar-legs through the sea of pads.

"There's good fish here," Scott said. "That old man proved that."

The "deep hole," when they reached it, went down barely two feet. The bottom was a snarl of roots that stretched like shaggy tentacles out from the trees on shore.

As Scott's fingers followed his leader to where it disappeared in green-black moss, the spinning in his head increased. He felt light-headed, the way he had with the dying deer. Shadows danced on the water. Weird shapes flickered out and in. A tightness clamped down on his chest.

Is this a heart attack? he wondered, fighting panic. *A stroke?*

Don't be a wuss, he thought. *You just need a nap.*

The moss looked like it could hide some knife-toothed North Woods eel. Poking through slime, he felt his fly, and tried to twist it free.

As if he'd turned a switch, the water in the hole began to glow. A woman's corpse lay tangled in the moss and roots. Her head was gone. Ribbons of gray skin waved in an underwater breeze.

The rotting tube of her neck rose like a trout, gaped, and slurped his hand inside. He tried to yank it back. His hand went numb. Then his arm. Then all of him. He felt like a convict immobilized by one drug while another sank its teeth into his heart.

The monster's throat felt like cold mud. Something rough as a cat's tongue scraped his skin. His hand burned as if stomach acids were digesting his flesh. Some force was trying to pull him out of the boat. It could not be happening. And yet it was.

Then the neck-tube let go. Scott's hand shot from the water, gripping his fly: slimy, but unharmed.

He looked around as if wakened from deep sleep. "Jesus!"

"You called?" Errol said just as another *whap!* rang out.

Thirty yards off, a geyser dropped back in the lake. Close by, a brown head dragged a V-shaped wake.

"Beaver!" Scott said. His head was clear; the water-monster, gone. *Was it a vision or a waking dream?*

"Give me beaver, or give me death!" Errol proclaimed, grabbed the oars, and went splashing and thrashing across the pads.

The beaver had disappeared as completely as the monster. But twenty yards away, another broad tail spanked alarm.

"Did you see that?" Errol said. "Exceeding cool!"

Beyond the lily pads, the lake was clear but for a slight green tinge. The sun had climbed straight overhead. Even the dullest trout would take cover and be uncatchable until shadows restored its confidence.

Scott wanted to tell Errol about the monster. But the image was fading. And the fear. He'd spent the morning whining like a world-class wimp. Why reinforce the notion? Dr. Z said that a strong imagination "heightens PTSD." His mind had crossed the murdered girl with the notion of a dead lake. The same way he'd produced a "vision" of being a deer, he'd called up a monstrous Spirit-of-the-Lake. He and the wilderness effect.

As their boat broke into open water, Errol pulled in the oars and grabbed the starter cord. One quick tug started the motor. "I'm hungry," he said. "Ready to head in?"

"Don't mention *head*," Scott said. "Let's go."

8

The summer she turned ten, on the second day of a family vacation in Yellowstone, Claire's parents had left her with a cheese sandwich while they ducked behind a park restroom to have one of their fights. Before she knew it, she was ringed by bears.

Her screams brought her parents running, and routed the begging bears. But she'd never been so scared until today. She'd been only a few yards from the truck, but it had felt like miles as, clothes clutched in her right hand, she ran for her life. She'd dropped her socks, but once inside the camper, she locked the door and yanked her pants and sweatshirt on. Dressed, she'd felt a little safer, but not much as she endured a fearful hour, unarmed and helpless against any assault the woods might send.

She watched, now, with relief bordering on joy as Errol and Scott putt-putted leisurely in. She'd seen *Killer Grizzly* twice on TV. And what other animal was huge, brown, bad-smelling, and likely to lurk in the woods around a lake whose name, in Spanish, meant *bear*?

But had those yellow eyes and that brown bulk been real? she asked herself as the men clambered ashore. More likely, her skittish brain had conjured them. Not only had nothing shambled from the woods to rip the cab open like a sardine can; not so much as a squirrel had approached Errol's truck.

Rather than tell the men her "adventure" and see them smirk, she hopped from the truck and called cheerfully, "How'd it go?"

◆ ◆ ◆

Scott jumped out of the boat and, as Errol beached it, held up their two fish. "No world records," he said. "But we'll eat."

Claire wore the same sweatshirt and pants as yesterday, but her hair was straighter. More natural.

"We'll feast," Errol said, and gave Claire a lusty kiss while Scott, feeling out of place, headed off to clean the fish.

Skirting the campfire ring, he wondered what expression a severed head would have. Better, he decided, not to know.

At the lake's edge, he peered into the water—Spirit-free—and knelt to clean the fish. His was already three-fourths gutted, so he started with Errol's, trying not to think as he slit the fish vent-to-gills, ripped out the viscera in one squishy mess, cut away the stomach, and tossed the rest as far as he could into the lake. Some creature would find them there, and feast.

He swirled both trout in cold lake-water, then used his knife to scrape out the rest of the insides, plus the channels of thick blood that ran along the backbones and could spoil the fish's taste. He swirled each fish a few more times, cut off the heads, and laid the pair out neatly on a bed of weeds.

Placing the stomach of Errol's fish on a stump, he pressed it with the flat of his knife. Two green insect larvae squirted out, along with a yellow jelly that, spread with his knife, proved to be a mass of tiny, near-transparent . . . things.

"Hey," Scott called to Errol, "look what these guys were eating."

Errol came on the run. "Baby scuds," he pronounced, bending to see. "Let's try to match 'em," he said, scooped up both fish, and headed for his truck. "I'll ice these down," he called over his shoulder.

Scott, cleaning his knife in the lake, thought again of the dead girl and the bones that he and Errol had thrown. Maybe he should find them, and take a closer look.

He stood, walked to the campfire pit, then stepped cautiously into the trees. Even with fishing knife in hand, he felt uneasy. Leaves seemed to glare. Limbs and brambles raked him as he forced his way in the direction he thought the bones had gone. How many people had been buried here, he wondered, over how many thousands of years? How many graves had he walked on since he arrived? Who was he walking on right now?

A lake as beautiful as this must have been a gathering place. Sacred, probably. A place for visions. Maybe his Spirit-of-the-Lake was a vision that, somehow, got left behind. Maybe that girl's death had spoiled Oso's "medicine," and spawned a monster.

Back home, such thoughts would seem ridiculous. Out here, they seemed more than possible.

Off to his left, something gray-white caught his eye. Not bone, he saw as he came near. Paper. A magazine.

Kneeling, he pulled his find from beneath the brown needles that almost hid it. The cover was gone; the paper, curled and stiff; the pages, fused. Still, several pulled apart. Enough to prove this was pornography.

Scott glanced around, on high alert. Nothing moved. Thick woods blocked the campsite from view.

He stared at a floppy blonde kneeling to straddle a cucumber, then realized with a jolt, she wasn't kneeling. Both legs ended at the knee. The magazine, when he flipped through it, was full of amputees.

He dropped the thing in disgust onto the ground, then felt compelled to pick it back up. Estimating where the centerfold would be, he pulled. The pages ripped apart, revealing a thick, red-brown stain.

Again, he dropped the magazine. This time, he kicked pine needles over it. *Like a cat*, he thought, heading back the way he'd come. The stain, if it was blood, most likely came from a fish. Even if not—even if yesterday's bones had been the beheaded girl's, the perv who'd chopped her up was dead. There was no danger now, Scott told himself as he rushed past the campfire pit. No need to find the bones.

Back at his camper, he set up his fly tying vise, found a boulder-seat, and started tying. Right away, he felt calmer. So many times he and Errol had consigned studying to the suckies of the world, uncorked some Old Smiley Fortified Wine, and stayed up half the night—Errol the teacher, Scott the eager pupil—tying flies and regaling each other with tales of trophy trout and eager women past, present, and sure to come.

He tied two green Carey Specials—the easiest fly he knew—then got up to check on Errol.

Three flawless green scuds lay on his tying board. A tiny green nymph was pinched into his vice.

"That your famous Dandy Green?"

"The same," Errol said, not looking up.

Returning to his own vise, Scott tied three Dandy Greens: their bodies more like beach balls than the cigar shape they were supposed to be.

On a hunch, he wrapped his smallest hook, a #20, with leader material. The resultant fly was a light blue, and bigger than the jelly-things. It *was* translucent, though.

"Hokey," Errol said when Scott showed what he'd made. "But it might work."

Bent over his vise, Errol was painting lacquer on a tiny hook, building an amber body which, Scott had to admit, looked a lot like the baby scuds. The process, though, looked tedious. He'd stick to "leaderbugs," for now.

◆ ◆ ◆

The bear-scare had been a good thing, Claire told herself, gathering up her socks from where she'd dropped them ten yards from Errol's truck. Her fear had hammered home how much she loved Errol and counted on him. She already had one divorce. Two would condemn her utterly.

With this in mind, she walked to where Errol hunched over his flies. "Want to take a walk?" she said, loading the phrase with possibilities.

Errol glanced up, then down. "Sure. Give me a few minutes."

Claire sighed. That could mean hours. She pictured the days of their vacation stretching out: awkward, uncomfortable, unendingly dull. If she'd known Errol would meet a friend . . .

But how could she have known? How could Errol? Her job was to amuse herself so that she didn't turn bitchy with boredom, and ruin everything.

Opening their camper, she pulled out a sketchbook and, reluctantly, her curlers, then strolled to the lake. With the sun bright and the men a few feet away, who could believe in killer grizzlies? Still, she stayed near the boat, where the shore was clear.

Curlers seemed moronic on a fishing trip. But Errol liked her hair curled. Win a man with beauty, and you were beauty's slave.

Wetting her hair with lake water, she wrapped the curlers, then cheered herself by playing with bugs in the shallows at her feet. Wiggling a stick in the lake bottom scattered swarms, their frenzy comical until she realized they were swimming for their lives.

She tossed the stick away and tried a few quick sketches while her hair dried. But making art was just so *hard*—hard to start, hard to finish, hard to enjoy what she had done. Peter had called it *Art Historian's Disease*: Rembrandt's taste without his skill.

She jumped when, to her right, something moved in a tree. Not a squirrel. A gray, robin-sized bird, watching from a limb.

Another joined it, scrutinizing her.

When both birds flew into the woods, Claire followed until they stopped. Perched on low limbs, they glared with fierce obsidian eyes. As if they knew what she was about to do. Or were commanding her to do it.

"Wait here," she said, and trotted to the truck.

She'd thought the men might laugh at her curlers. No chance. Engrossed in fly tying, they barely looked up.

She dropped her sketchbook in the camper, took three slices of bread, and jogged back to the birds. They'd moved deeper into the woods, drawing her in like witches in a fairy tale. She liked the shadows. They no longer threatened her.

"Come closer," the birds seemed to say. "Come play."

A new bird joined the pair as Claire tore off three chunks of bread, placed them on the ground, and walked five steps away.

The birds eyed the food, fluttered down to perch above it, then, suspicious, flapped back up to where they'd been.

One rasped a loud complaint. Another joined in.

The largest found, at last, the nerve to land beside the bread. He glared at Claire, snatched a piece, flapped back to his tree and, ten feet up, gulped down his prize. Before the other birds could act, he was back on the ground, then in his tree, both remaining pieces in his beak.

As the loud bird rasped outrage, a fourth bird joined the group.

"Glutton," Claire told the bold bird. She tore the bread in four pieces and, hoping she didn't call up some Native demon, tossed them in the four directions—north, south, east, west—the way, in movies, she'd seen medicine men do.

The bold bird fluttered to the ground, plucked up a piece of bread, and eyed her quizzically. Another bird mustered the courage to sail down and nab a piece. The new arrival did the same while, high in the tree, the loud bird continued scolding as the largest bird beaked the last piece.

"Is that all you can do? Complain?" Claire asked the loud bird, which continued to berate the universe.

The other birds fluttered near Claire, or perched just out of reach.

She tore a piece of bread and held it high.

The birds eyed it greedily.

Another joined the loud one, denouncing Claire's cruelty. Then the big one left his perch. A brush of feathers, a tug, and the bird had another prize.

Choosing a spot where needles covered the damp earth, Claire tore the remaining bread into four chunks, and was about to offer it to the four directions when, on a whim, she sat, then stretched out on the ground. The curlers jabbed her, but she didn't stand back up. She adjusted the curlers, placed two pieces of bread on her stomach, one on each breast, then shut her eyes. This morning's sexy feeling had returned: a pelvic glow. She was an offering: bride of the god-with-yellow-eyes.

That thought opened *her* eyes. Even the loud bird had stopped screeching and joined the rest in gliding tree to tree, eyes on the fallen giant and her bounty. Birds were dinosaurs, she remembered. Feathered, flying dinosaurs.

She shut her eyes again, and settled into the cool earth. Wings swished across her breasts as birds swooshed and fluttered by. She felt warm and swimmy-headed, like after smoking pot. Unlike last night, she *wanted* to make love.

A whir of wings. Then, something soft brushed her right breast.

Cracking her eyelids, she saw a bird flap off with a hunk of bread.

Again she shut her eyes. What if she hadn't imagined that brown shape, that yellow eye, that smell? What if a bear were watching, looming over her? Could a bear smell a woman, like dogs do? Would it thrust its nose between her legs?

She crossed her legs and squeezed her thighs, like when she was a girl and didn't know why it felt good. She moved her hips: a sexy grind.

Then a stick cracked. A voice barked, "Claire?!"

She'd leapt off the ground and scrambled to her feet before her brain recognized Errol.

He rushed to her. "Are you okay?"

"I'm fine," she said, her face on fire. The birds were gone. Had they really been there?

"What were you doing?!"

"Being ravaged by bread-people," she said: the first thing that came to mind.

Errol looked so stunned, she had to laugh. Here he was: the answer to her horny prayers. "I was just feeding some birds," she said.

Errol pointed to a tree. "Those Camp Robbers?"

Claire looked, and nodded. There the birds sat, watching her.

"Don't lie too still," Errol said. "They'll think you're dead, and eat your eyes."

Claire felt her sexy glow flare into irritation. Errol loved to catastrophize. And even if he were right about the birds, why make everything ugly? In the old days, he would have felt her mood, and capitalized.

She knew that she should take his hand as they walked back to camp, but she withheld it and they walked back like strangers.

9

Errol wanted to crush more than the plants that blocked his path as he stomped back to camp with Claire. His fear at finding her gone had turned to panic when he saw her on the ground. He stomped that fear underfoot now.

The sight of Scott chomping a sandwich, cheeks puffed like a hamster, made Errol smile, and calmed him down. He let Claire catch up, then wrapped his arm around her waist. "Feel like a snack?" he said. "I'll make coffee."

"Okay," she said with a smile that, if not eager, was still a smile.

He lit the Coleman stove—he couldn't bring himself to use the campfire pit—and put a pan of bottled water on to boil. He would have liked to use lake water. More hardcore. But he didn't want to catch Giardia or some other nasty stomach-bug out here.

"There's no more tuna," Claire called from beside the cooler. "Hope you like peanut butter."

Errol knew Claire hated peanut butter. Her not griping made him want to please her. "Don't worry," he said. "We'll go to town soon."

"That'd be good," she said; then, "Excuse me," and ducked into the camper.

Moments later, her hair falling in loose curls, she glided toward him, holding out a sandwich like an offering.

"Thanks, Babe," he said, and kissed her. "You'd shame Aphrodite, I swear."

Wherever Claire was, she radiated class. She was like her mom that way. Not at all like *his*, rushing from her job as a bank teller to play Willy Loman's wife in some thirty-seat community theater. Sheila Gunn's affectations were legion, but her act was tight.

Lunch over, Errol collected cups and plates, grabbed soap and steel wool, and strolled to the lake. He gave the plates a good scrub, rinsed the coffee cups, and strolled back, warm and sleepy in the midday sun.

Opening his ice chest, he drained the bag of melting ice, dumped the ice into the chest, and slid the trout—Scott's barely half the size of his—into the empty bag. Pouring his jug of Tang into the bag, he tied it tight, dropped the bag into the chest, placed the chest in the cab of his truck in case of bears, hid the chest under his parka, and locked the doors.

The temperature felt close to seventy: perfect for an outdoor nap. But he wasn't spending enough time with Claire. To compensate, he sat beside her in the camper, and tried to chat. He was too sleepy, though, to think of much to say, and was glad when Scott walked up and asked, "Feel like exploring?"

"Sure," Errol said. "Come on, Claire. Let's see some sights."

"More trees?" she said, but followed with, "I'll get my coat."

"Errol, I've got a problem," she said when she came back, fly rod in her left hand, coat sleeve extended in her right.

Errol had to smile, seeing a Dandy Green stuck in the sleeve. "I hook myself all the time," he said, showed her two rips in his own parka, then clipped her leader, and handed her coat back with the fly still attached. "Call it a merit badge," he said.

"A merit badge in klutziness," she said, shrugged on the coat, and took his hand as, Scott following close behind, Errol led her onto a faint trail into the woods. A few feet in, she released Errol's hand and fell into step behind him and in front of Scott.

The sight of Scott bringing up the rear sent a guilt-pang through Errol's heart. In the old days, he and Scott were equals: equal talent, intelligence, attractiveness to women—equal in all but physical strength. Errol had liked knowing he had that edge. But by shoving Scott to the ground on that cold day four years ago, he'd made the edge overt, and destroyed their friendship's equilibrium. Could they get it back? And without it, could they be friends?

The air was cold under the trees, and got colder the farther in they walked. Spring might be halfway to summer on the lake, but winter held on in the woods. Among the evergreens and deciduous buds, enough gray stalks and naked limbs remained to show how deadly-cold this place could be.

Deadly, but clean, pure, and beautiful, Errol told himself, watching a green-and-yellow warbler flash by. This was the perfect place to recharge his spirit and clear his mind. If he could just catch up on sleep.

"Know how to tell spruce from fir?" he asked Scott, just as Claire, who'd lagged behind, called, "Hey, guys! Look at this!"

Errol first, then Scott hurried back to where Claire stood beside a hollow stump ringed by shelf fungi. Inside the stump: two large, yellow, absurdly phallic mushrooms.

"Missed anything lately?" Scott asked Errol, who had to squelch an urge to kick the mushrooms down. For some reason, Claire's staring at them bothered him.

"I thought you'd found more bones," he said, and resumed walking, the others falling in behind.

Had last fall's murder made this place feel dangerous? As the trail narrowed, Errol ripped through the greenery until the scent of wounded plants clotted the air. He pictured himself lost and floundering, vines and creepers pulling him down while every tree called out, "Yes, you've seen me. No, you haven't. Yes, you have."

With a lunge, he threw off the vine-tangle that had snared him, and the fear. He couldn't possibly get lost. Not with the lake's topaz-blue glittering through the trees. Five years ago, he could have confidently hiked to the Yukon from here.

"Why are we rushing?" Claire called from the rear. "Let's rest," she said, and plopped down on a fallen tree.

◆ ◆ ◆

As Errol clomped back to sit with Claire, Scott dropped down in a patch of sunlight several feet away. "Is this fabulous, or what?" he said, trying to show he didn't feel like what he felt like: a third wheel.

"A place like this can add years to your life," Errol proclaimed.

"Too bad there's no market for scouts anymore," Claire said. "Except the boy kind."

"No future in Injun-fighting," Errol threw in.

"*Pioneer*'s gone the way of *cave-painter*," Scott said, and liked it when Claire laughed.

"Oh well," she said. "We can start a woodsy commune, and wait for the Apocalypse."

"I joined a commune for a week," Scott said. "Fun times. We pooled our self-righteousness, and shared it equally."

Errol snorted. "Being a rich bum's fine. Play *Don't-Have-Shit* until you're ready to go back to living high." He plucked up a stick, and rolled it in his hands. "There's great stuff out there"—he gestured at the world—"but no one's handing it to me. So . . ." He snapped the stick, and flung it. "Back to the rat race."

"You know," Claire said, as if she'd pondered rat races for decades, "win enough races, and you can pay other rats to race for you."

Errol looked at Scott. "She means her dad," he said. "He's the Rat King."

Claire's eyes narrowed, but she spoke softly. "I'm sure it's hard admitting all he's done for you."

Scott leapt in to calm the waters. "Errol just means that out here, with the birds and trees and odd mushrooms . . ." He looked at Claire, then Errol, who had to smile. "It makes city life look kind of bleak."

"Win your rat race, and you won't have to look at it," Claire said. She stood and, as if to show that the subject was closed, started back the way they'd come.

Errol took a breath to reply, then sighed, and started after her.

Scott clambered up, and saw a huge brown toad—the biggest toad he'd ever seen—hop behind a patch of ferns. "Hey, check this out," he called, moved in for a closer look, then yelled "Aaah!" and jumped back.

Errol rushed up. "What's wrong?"

Scott pointed toward a thick green bush ten feet away. The toad was gone. But behind the bush, something big lay on the ground. A low buzz grew audible as, with Errol beside him, Scott moved in.

The shape resolved from dead woman, to dead deer, to what it was: a dead calf.

Flies, disturbed by their approach, settled back down. Maggots like fat grains of white rice writhed and wriggled across the rotting flesh. Up close, the thing stank bad enough "to gag a maggot," Scott would have said, except it clearly wasn't true. The eye sockets were stuffed with wrigglers. Chunks had been ripped off the trunk, baring the spine. The bottom halves of both back legs were gone.

The thing had settled on its stomach, haunches raised. As if waiting to be entered from the rear.

"Christ on a crumbcake! That's nasty," Errol said.

"Thank God it's not the girl," Scott said.

Errol touched his lips and rolled his eyes in Claire's direction. "Stay back, Babe. You don't want to see this."

"Think that's where those bones came from?" Scott whispered.

"Could be. People let their cattle graze out here."

Now Claire had seen, or smelled, and was backing away. "Errol, that's enough sights for today."

Scott stepped back, eyes on the carcass as if it might follow him. Then he noticed the fir tree beside the calf. Ten feet off the ground, bark hung in shreds, the white tree-flesh laid bare. He'd seen similar marks, though lower down, on a pine in the Cascades. A forest ranger had called them "territorial claw-marks of a bear."

"We should get out of here," Scott said. But Errol and Claire were already heading campward, triple-time.

10

With Scott and Claire close behind, Errol burst out of the woods into the sharply slanting midafternoon sun. The calf had killed his appetite, but it made sense to eat now, instead of in the dark, tired and famished after fishing the night bite.

"Want to build a campfire?" Scott sounded tentative.

"Naw, use my Coleman," Errol said, and tried to will himself into a better mood. While Scott readied the little stove, Errol pulled the Tang-marinated trout from his ice chest. Unable to stop yawning, he rolled the bodies in corn meal, stuck a pat of butter inside each, melted more butter in the hot frying pan, and dropped the fish in.

"Stay awake a few more hours," he told himself, "and you'll sleep like a log."

◆ ◆ ◆

Scott couldn't help thinking that Claire, sipping Diet Coke on the hood of Errol's truck, looked like a model set to bare it all. Instead of staring, he focused on his leader, checking it for kinks and frays while Errol extolled the wonders of "fresh trout, rolled in corn meal and fried golden-brown."

"You sound like a menu," Scott said.

This encouraged Errol to use "golden-brown" in every sentence.

Slipping his spool of 5X tippet back into his fishing vest, Scott wadded his parka up, stuffed it under his shirt to make a hump the way he'd done in the old days, then shambled toward Errol.

"How'd you'd like a *golden-brown* hump-in-the-cajoonies?" he croaked.

Errol backed away. "Avaunt, Quasi-Dodo," he roared, then ducked into his camper. Moments later, he popped back out. "Hey, Scott!" he called, and gaped his mouth to show a yellow mush of crackers and Cheez Whiz.

Scott staggered back, shielding his eyes. "Sanctuary!" he cried. "He's showing food!"

In the course of many fishing trips, he and Errol had decided that the funniest humor was the adolescent kind. At twelve, it was funny in its own right. At eighteen, it was funny in its own right, and because it was funny that something so stupid should be funny. The older you got, they had predicted, the funnier it would be that stupid things still made you laugh.

Scott thought, now, that their theory was wrong. Today's *Hunchback of Notre Dame* routine felt strained. Embarrassing. Claire didn't know their history. And even if she did, she might think their games were stupid. Which they were.

Errol, on the other hand, was laughing so hard that he spewed cracker, inhaled it, and dropped, thrashing, to the ground. He seemed torn between death by suffocation and hilarity until, gasping, "Oh no! My fish," he jumped up and scuttled to the stove.

"We're not crazy," Scott told Claire, who looked wary. "Men are like chimps. We like to throw our crap and hoot."

Before she could reply, Errol called, "Come and get it!" He didn't wait for them to come, but shoveled the smaller trout onto Scott's plate, walked to Claire, and dropped half of the larger fish onto hers.

"Hot damn," he said, speared a chunk of meat, stuffed it in his mouth, and with an expression of stage-bliss, began to chew.

The bliss changed to stage-dismay. "Muddy!"

"Does taste kind of like boiled mudpuppy," Scott said.

Claire said, "I think it needs a pinch more . . . fish."

Errol twisted his face into a tragedian's mask. "My trout dinner," he wailed. "I bragged about it to my friends. Fresh trout, golden-brown, prepared my special way." He paused, took a breath, then raised his hands to the sky and squealed, "Humiliated!"

The sudden squeal startled Scott into a laugh that shot Tang up his nose, out his mouth, and all over his clothes.

"Shit!" he said. "You made me nose it! Shit! That stings!"

Errol's most recent mouthful of fish spewed out, and he dropped to the ground, kicking his feet and howling with laughter.

The sight was too much for Scott. All strength left his legs just as it used to, and he fell to the ground, shrieking. Yet even as Errol gasped, "Stop! I can't take it," and Scott tried unsuccessfully to stand, he had the sense that they were struggling to call back a happier time. A time before he'd rolled on the ground at Errol's feet.

Claire, when Scott could finally stand, looked incredulous. Or appalled.

He tried to stop laughing long enough to explain. "See, this clown you're married to announced in poetry class . . ." He cracked up here, but forged ahead. "'The main theme in modern literature, as in life, is the humiliation of the protagonist.'"

The memory of Dr. Cartwright's pinched red face overcame Scott's wish not to look ridiculous, and stretched him back on the ground, howling.

Maybe their theory of humor was right after all, he thought as he dusted off his pants. "Anyway, this trout's better than a cherry bomb suppository," he told Errol. "I'll fight anyone who says it's not."

◆ ◆ ◆

"It's better than a Big Mac, any day," Errol said, wobbling to his feet. How a trout pulled from a crystal lake in Canada could taste like Mississippi muck, he couldn't say. Still, the trout was golden brown. He'd caught it himself. He was hundreds of miles from Pop Gunn and Land Development. Claire was smiling and Scott was his friend again. That made things better than okay.

Gulping the last chunk of muddy fish, he pitched the skin into the lake for birds, ducked inside the camper, and emerged with a bottle of "The Black Sheep of Canadian Whiskey," Yukon Jack. He felt like Yukon Jack himself as he swaggered up to Scott. "Hey, Wolverine, care for a little hair-of-the-malamute?"

"Sure thing, Fieldmouse." Scott dodged a punch, grabbed the bottle, and took a healthy swig.

Errol reclaimed the bottle, sucked his own long swig, and let the spirits light a sun in his belly as shadows stretched out around them. He gave an "Aahh" of satisfaction, and stuck out his hand to Scott, who gripped it tight.

"God damn, it's good to see you," Errol said, then turned to Claire. "Come on, troops. Let's get some ghosties!"

II

Thirty yards beyond their bay, something big attacked Claire's fly: three sharp tugs that rattled her rod and sent shocks through Scott's spine where he sat in the middle of the boat. One quick run, and the fish was gone. A few more yards, though, and Errol snagged and landed a hard-fighting three-pounder.

Was the middle seat a bad place to be?

When, a minute later, Claire hooked a fish as big as Errol's, Scott told himself, "Your time will come." Yet gloom was starting to descend. The trout loved Errol's Dandy Greens. They'd never eat his pathetic leaderbugs.

In his hurry to change flies, he muffed his clinch knot twice before he could tie on his own slop-version of a Dandy Green.

Errol had just released Claire's fish, and was casually swishing his net through the water, washing off fish-slime.

"Could we get moving?" Scott said.

Errol frowned, then—recognizing, probably, the pained look of the fish-less—nodded. "Okay. Sure."

Two quick tugs, the motor roared, and they were off.

Scott let out his line, and prayed. It was one thing if the whole party got skunked. But to be The Wretch, the only one not catching fish, was agony. He was too old to feel this way. But he still did.

He should have tied his flies like Errol's. He'd half-assed the job. Now he was doomed. He remembered, as a child, watching men with giant surf rigs haul fish after fish up on the beach while he, with his kid-rod, cast twenty feet, got a backlash bigger than his reel, and fled to his parents, crying his eyes out.

He felt the same way now. When Errol hauled in another fish, the despair that swallowed him was the same he felt back home: "Everybody's making it but me." Including Errol, with his rich wife and *land development*. Not only was Errol bigger and stronger, he'd become richer and more successful, too. Five years before, he and Errol had declared balance-of-power "the secret of friendship." That balance had been, on many fronts, destroyed.

Setting his rod down, Scott braced it with his knee. Keyed up as he was, if a fish hit, he'd yank the fly out of its mouth. Better to let the boat set the hook. Besides, good things came unexpectedly. Setting down his rod was telling Fate, "I'm not prepared!"

For two long minutes, nothing happened. Four minutes. Six. The sun slammed down on a hard slant. The woods stared balefully. Whatever-in-the-hell *bale* was.

Pretending not to look, Scott watched his rod tip like a cat until, attention flagging, he gave up. Powerless again.

He was half-dozing, wrapped in hopelessness, when his reel suddenly screeched like a macaw. He grabbed his rod just as, thirty yards behind the boat, two feet of silver torpedoed up out of the lake as line scorched off his reel. This was it: the kind of fish he'd driven deep into the wilderness to find.

He reeled in line. The fish tore it back out while Claire looked on, Errol babbled encouragement, and Scott prayed silently, *Don't get away. Please. Don't get away.*

The fish came in, ran, came in, ran, jumped, dived, jumped, and ran for five more minutes before Scott could get it moving toward the boat where Errol waited, net already in the lake.

The big fish surged and splashed. Scott fought to stay calm. Almost there…

The trout rolled on its side and slid, a silver slab, toward the boat. The fly barely clung to its lip!

"Skin-hooked," Errol warned, reached out as far as he could, and lifted the net.

Scott felt the fly pull free and hit him in the face.

Errol yanked the net out of the water. "Got 'im!"

The lake echoed back Scott's shouted, "Yeah!" A world of failure slid off his shoulders as he pumped Errol's hand, grinning so wide he felt his mouth would split.

Shiny and fat, with gray-green back, black spots, and just a hint of pink slashing its flank, the big hen Kamloops—five pounds if she was an ounce—lay wrapped in net at the bottom of the boat.

"Poor fish," Claire said.

Errol found his scale, and was about to weigh the fish when Scott said, "We've got a fish to eat. Let's let her go."

"She deserves it," Errol said.

"You look at that fish like you're in love with it," Claire teased.

"You're right. I love a good fish," Errol said, and kissed behind Claire's ear.

To limit damage to the trout's protective slime, Scott dipped his hands in the water before untangling the fish from the net. He lifted her in both hands like an offering, then lowered her into the lake.

On her own, she would have bellied up. Scott moved her gently back and forth, forcing water through her gills.

When she flipped feebly, he opened his hands. One wave of her tail, and she was free, diving down into a patch of tall weeds where, nose down, she stayed, clearly visible some twenty feet below.

"She'll be okay," Errol said.

Scott dried his hands and radiated love-of-life. With The Skunk vanquished in a big way, he could relax and be magnanimous. "Your turn, Claire," he said.

The smile she sent back made his breath feel jiggly. Then they were off, letting their lines out into water turning gray under the lowering sun.

◆ ◆ ◆

Within a minute, Claire hooked a two-pounder which, despite a lot of thrashing, fumbling, and line-snarling, Errol managed to net.

"I want to let him go," she said. And with Errol's help, she did, her face flushed, breath coming fast. No doubt about it: there'd be hot sex tonight. Assuming he could stay awake.

Paralleling shore fifty yards out, Errol scanned for rises or a hatch. But nothing marred the gray-glass surface of the lake. To his right: water and woods. To his left, set back in a small cove, he saw a mound of sticks near shore.

"Look!" he said. "A beaver-lodge!"

Scott clapped his sunglasses on. "It is!"

"Where?" Claire said.

"Sight down my arm," Errol told her. "See?"

"I think," she said without conviction.

"Reel in," Errol said. "Let's check it out."

"I thought beavers were industrious," Scott said as they neared the egg-shaped mass of jumbled sticks. "This thing's a mess."

Errol killed the motor and sculled with the oars. "They put most of the work inside," he said. "There's tunnels, rooms, stored food . . . hold on!"

The lodge top was collapsed. Its sticks were old, cracked, dry.

"Abandoned," Errol said, and turned to Claire. "Want to check out the floor plan?"

"You sure they're gone?"

"I'm sure," he said, then couldn't resist adding, "Almost."

Scott reached past the boat's nose, grabbed a protruding stick, and pulled them alongside. The lodge was as long as the boat, and rose two feet above the lake.

"Will it hold us?" Scott asked.

"I wouldn't chance it," Errol said, happy to don the Expert robe. "Those sticks are sharp. You might wind up shish kabobbed."

"It's all caved in," Claire said.

"That's how I know it's empty," Errol said. "Beavers would fix it."

"No wonder these things are called *sticks*. They're stuck in tight," Claire said as, with a grunt, she pulled one out.

"Beavers are mud-masons," Scott said.

"Watch your hands," Errol said. "Who knows what's in there."

Claire dropped the stick she was holding, and jerked back. "Snakes?"

"Ice can trap beavers in their lodges," Errol said. "You might grab a fistful of rot."

Claire sat on her hands. "No thanks."

Scott pulled on his wool gloves. "Would beavers do the Donner thing?"

"They're supposed to be strict vegans," Errol said, and tossed a loose stick onto shore. "But you never know . . ."

◆ ◆ ◆

"Look," Claire said. "A room!" Pleased to have seen it first, she pointed at a hole in the lodge through which a partly collapsed space was visible.

"Wait," Scott said. "Something's in there."

Claire jerked back, making the boat pitch. Errol grabbed the lodge and steadied them, then squinted into the hole. "That's no dead beaver."

He and Scott removed more sticks as Claire's heart climbed into her throat.

"Aw no! It's a dead baby!" Errol said. With a long stick, he started working the thing toward the mouth of the dark hole.

Claire made herself peer into the hole. "It's not . . . no . . . thank God! It's just a doll," she said, and gave an embarrassing giggle of relief.

"Oh. Good," Scott said as Errol reached in and pulled the object out: a nude figure, carved crudely from a foot-long chunk of wood.

Its long hair dripped, mud-matted, as Errol held it up.

"She's got a rack," he said, and—typical Errol—thumped the jutting bust with his forefinger.

"Like some fertility fetish," Scott said.

"Her legs are really short," Claire said. Those short legs made her scarier.

"Venus of Oso Lake," Errol said. "Except for this." He tapped a rusty nail that had cracked the wood between the figure's thighs. "Half Barbie, half Ken."

"That's a penis," Claire said. "But not hers." She touched a carved slit that reached above the spike. Her insides clenched in sympathy.

Scott glanced at Errol. "Her hair looks red!"

"Wash it off," Errol said with more urgency than Claire thought was warranted. Watching Scott grasp the figure by its stubby legs, then swirl it, head down, in the water, she wondered why the interest in red hair?

"Damn!" Scott said, lifting the figure from the lake. "The hair fell off."

"It wasn't hair," Errol said. "Looked more like moss."

Claire freed a stick from the lodge, and used it to poke deeper into the hole. "Errol," she said. "There's something else."

Using their sticks in tandem, they dragged out a sweatshirt, then a pair of jeans: muddy and wet, but folded neatly.

"Hell of a chest of drawers," Scott said.

"I've never seen a beaver in blue jeans," Errol said; then, after a pause, "You have to take 'em off."

The joke hung like a beer-belch in the air. Claire nearly said something snide, but Scott's failure to laugh was chastisement enough.

Against her better judgment, she unfolded the jeans. *Women's* jeans.

Her left knee, which she'd hurt playing tennis in college, had begun to throb. For one panicked instant, she couldn't breathe. Then she could, but still said, "Errol, I want to go."

"Me too," he said. "I'm getting splinters."

"I mean leave here," she said. "Leave this lake."

"Leave Oso?" Errol's voice was an injured whine. "Why?"

"Something's wrong," she said. And knew that it was true.

"I know another lake," Scott said.

Errol spun to face him: Innocence Betrayed. "What about the ghost trout?"

"Other lakes have big trout," Scott said. But sounded apologetic.

"We haven't *seen* them," Errol shot back. "We could waste days learning to fish some other lake. I don't *have* days." He spun toward Claire. "I work my balls off all year. Now we're starting to catch fish . . ." He seemed incredulous. "You really want to leave?"

Claire stared at the metal boat-bottom. The last thing she wanted was to be the scaredy girl.

"If it means that much to you," she said, "I'll stay."

Errol brightened instantly. "Leave the clothes here. Somebody might've left 'em for . . . who the hell knows why? As for this . . ."

Gripping the doll by its short legs, he pulled. The doll broke like a wishbone where the nail had cracked her.

"I hate folk art," Errol said, and flung one half in the lake, the other in the woods. "So much for that." He looked at Claire. "Okay?"

"Okay," she lied.

Scott jabbed his finger at the lake. "Look there!"

Twenty yards out, in the direction Errol had heaved the doll, fish dimpled the water like rain.

"All *right*," Errol yelled, and yanked the motor cord. His motor chugged and died. "Goddamn it! Start!"

Claire still wanted to leave. But she'd have to sneak up on the subject, now.

"Errol . . ." Her voice sounded childish in her ears. "Did Spaniards make it this far north?"

"I don't know. Why?" he grunted between yanks. "Come on, you prick," he told the motor.

"The word *Oso*..." When handsome Dr. Velasquez pronounced the word *otho* in her freshman year, she had assumed that he was gay. She had been wrong.

"Tomorrow we take your boat, or my arm gets a raise," Errol told Scott as the motor sputtered, sputtered, caught, then died.

"Deal," Scott said.

"*Oso* means *bear* in Spanish," Claire said. She'd just taken a breath to tell about the brown bear-shape and the yellow eyes when Errol gave the motor cord a vicious yank. His fist, arms-length behind, struck her in the face as the motor roared to life.

"Damn it, Errol," she yelped. Despite herself, tears filled her eyes.

Errol, fiddling with his engine, called over his shoulder, "Watch it, Babe." As if the blow had been a tap. "What'd you say about Oso?"

"Oh, forget it, Errol," she said.

◆ ◆ ◆

In the next hour, Scott caught two fish, Errol caught three, and Claire hooked and landed four trout over three pounds. And despite her reel's falling off, and twice getting her feet wrapped in line, she didn't lose a fish. Or smile.

She didn't want to stay at Oso. And Scott understood why. That red-haired doll hadn't just had short legs; she was an amputee. Carved, most likely by the crazyman who'd left the magazine, beheaded the girl, and maybe cooked and eaten her. That he had hanged himself didn't make Scott feel much better about staying here.

A pale moon had climbed overhead. Coyotes gibbered and yipped. The sun had slipped behind the trees, night starting to rush in as Errol killed the motor and rowed into their bay.

Scott stared hard into the lake. *See*, he told himself. *No monster-in-a-fish-suit's tracking me.*

Then a sunken log moved. Another. And another. They were gliding past a school of yard-long fish!

"Errol," he whispered, "look down!"

Errol stopped rowing, and peered into the lake. "Christ on a chalupa," he hissed. "It's them!"

Scott counted nine trout, patrolling like sharks. "They *are* like ghosts," he said as softly as he could.

"Get down, Babe," Errol hissed to Claire, and she obeyed.

"Maybe they're spawning," Scott whispered, readying to cast.

A whistling overhead said Errol had beaten him to it. Then his own fly was *whish*ing into the near-dark.

When something tugged, Scott set the hook so hard his fly flew out of the water and smacked him in the face.

"Damn spinach," he said, and hoped Claire hadn't seen.

A few more casts, and the trout had merged like ghosts into the darkness of the lake. Too dark now even to clean the spinach Scott's fly picked up, coming in. And what if he hooked something horrible—a dead body, or worse—in this black soup?

"Maybe the old man's right," Scott said. "Maybe they won't eat."

"I'm not leaving till they do," Errol said, and picked up the oars.

Only their creaking broke the silence as he rowed to shore. The coyotes had gone mute. It was too cold for frogs and bugs. The only sounds were human-made as the boat grated ashore and the party stowed their gear, flashlights groping like feelers in the dark.

A wind had sprung up, dropping the chill factor below the forty-six on Scott's thermometer. He was glad they'd eaten early. Now he could go straight to bed.

He wasn't glad, when he came back from the bushes, to find his eyes drawn to Errol's camper. Usually, his sex drive took a holiday on fishing trips. Those trips, though, had been all male. No wonder, in the old days, a woman on a ship was considered bad luck.

As he watched, Claire came to the camper door and sat, feet dangling. He feared she might undress and cause a new moral dilemma. Instead, she said—he heard this clearly—"Errol, have you seen my UW ring?"

"Not in a while," Errol said.

Claire said something too quietly for Scott to hear.

"I'm sorry. It was an accident," Errol said.

Claire spoke again. At length.

"We'll look tomorrow," Errol said when she was finished. "Come inside. I need to sleep."

With a shoulder-heaving sigh, Claire stood and shut the camper door.

Scott knew he should sleep, too. Still, despite the cold, he stayed outside, sipping Tang. Was *he* the reason Claire wanted to leave? While she and Errol were still awake, he could rise to the role of gentleman: say goodbye and drive away.

But that doll had really scared her. The North Woods were clearly not her cup of tea. His being gone wouldn't make her want to stay.

To flee from Oso when he had a shot at those huge trout would be a huge failure-of-nerve. Also, he was reconnecting with Errol. If he left now, a lot of great times might never occur.

In any case, he'd never find his way out in the dark. For tonight at least, he had to stay.

That settled, he climbed into his camper, washed, and trying to ignore what happened when he thought of Claire, wriggled into his down bag. He could ease his horniness himself. But how sick would that be, getting off on his friend's wife?

No sounds intruded from next door as, fighting to overlay Sara with Julie and not Claire, Scott fell asleep.

◆ ◆ ◆

He wakened once, to pee. No dreams of the "Spirit," Unconscious be praised. Easing out of the camper, he rushed to drain his bladder before his equipment froze.

The wind had died, but had blown clouds across the stars. In front of him, the lake spread out like a dark stain. Like blood, feeding the forest: unchanged since time began. No wonder humans, so small and weak, heard supernatural powers in the wind. No wonder they imagined headless girls, wendigos striding through the trees, and demons dropping from the sky.

On the north shore, where the forest began its long, unbroken march to the Yukon, a light flickered. It disappeared, flickered, shone brightly, then went out. The old man must be camped out there. Him, or some other fisherman. This wasn't Lake Scott-&-Errol. With the world growing more crowded by the day, they were lucky any solitude survived.

Goosebumped and shivering, Scott climbed back in his camper, locked his door, then snuggled down into his bag to watch his thoughts blip away, one by one by one.

THIRD DAY

12

Errol woke at first light, fuming. Claire had gone to sleep last night with barely a "Goodnight." He'd lain awake for hours, his stomach burning. No question, his ulcer had returned.

Was Claire sabotaging this trip because it wasn't Hawaii? He wanted to wake her and demand to know. But anger gave way to pain, which yielded at last to fitful sleep. Now, despite the cold, Errol wanted only to break out of the camper, which seemed brimming with Claire's spite.

She'd slept well, and was still at it. Her face, which she swore he'd "punched," looked fine. It would serve her right if he left without a word, and fished with Scott. That would mean war, though. So he bumbled and banged around until she looked at him.

"Rise and shine, Babe!" he said, and tried to sound enthusiastic.

She rubbed her eyes. As always in the morning, she looked girlish and vulnerable. "I'll get up," she said, her spirits seemingly restored.

His anger melted. "Put your fish-catchin' hat on. We're gonna knock 'em dead," he said, and stepped out of the camper into a gray dawn.

The sky looked ready to rain. But fish often bit better in the rain. The temperature wasn't too cold: maybe sixty, with no wind.

Scott was already up, chowing down on bread, Instant Breakfast, and Tang. "Ready for 'em, Grizz?" he called. "I fought one of those ghosties half the night."

"Let's take both boats," Errol said, and tried to sound hearty. "More room to cast."

Scott was pulling out his motor as Errol spoke. "At Old Man's Bay?"

"You got it. Let's hope he's not there," Errol said, then helped Scott lift his boat off his camper-top and lug it to the lake.

As they walked back, Claire bounced up with a cup of Tang and a bright, "Good morning, boys!"

"Better dress for rain," Errol said, expecting complaints.

Instead, she said cheerfully, "It shall be done," and bounced off to get rain gear.

Ten minutes later, the two boats were speeding side by side toward Old Man's Bay.

Rain began almost at once: light at first, then heavier, fat drops peppering the lake. Errol liked being safe and dry as the elements tried to soak him. His right hand, though, had to steer the boat. Despite warm gloves, his fingers were soon soaked and chilled.

In any case, the rain helped wake him up. As cold drops dribbled down his face, he killed his motor near the mouth of Old Man's Bay. No old man. Good!

"Want me to rig you, Babe?" he asked.

Face half-hidden by her rain jacket's hood, Claire looked cozy as a cat. "No thanks," she said. "I'll sit here and keep warm."

Near shore, a forty-foot ring of drowned trees showed how the lake's level had gone up. That ring could be a fish-magnet.

Sure enough, Scott's rod was doubled and pumping.

Errol cast toward shore, trying not to envy Scott when—wham!—a two-pounder smashed his fly, and blew out of the water.

Twenty minutes later, as Errol released his third fish, a hazy sun squeezed through the thinning clouds. The fishing slackened with the rain. When the pocked lake-surface cleared, Errol saw only sandy bottom. Not so much as a minnow.

"Want to hear a joke?" Scott called across the fifteen yards between the boats.

"Sure, if it's good," Errol said in his normal voice. Sound carried well across water.

Claire, huddled in the prow, didn't look up. Or seem to hear. Sulking again?

"Okay. A city guy buys a summer home in the country," Scott began. "He's working on the house when a big country boy walks up. 'Gon' be a party this Sa'urday night,' the country boy says. 'Yer invited.'"

Errol snickered. From his time in Texas, Scott could do a first-rate redneck twang.

"'That's very kind,' the city fellow says. 'But I've got so much work, I doubt I can make it.'"

"Sounds like Claire's father," Errol said. "The work part. Not the accent."

He set down his rod as Scott went on.

"' 's gon' be drinkin',' the country boy says.

"'Well, I'd like to try the local spirits,' the city fellow says. 'But I've got so much to do.'"

Errol snickered louder. Claire, he saw, had turned to listen.

"The country boy leans closer. 's gonna be fightin'.'

"'A wild party? You're tempting me,' the city boy says. 'But I've got so much to do.'

"The country boy leans closer still. 's gonna be fuckin'.'"

Errol was fizzing like a pressure cooker. Scott raised his hand for silence.

"'That *is* enticing,' the city guy says. 'But I've got mountains of work.'

"'Well, you change your mind, this here's ma number,' the country boy says, and hands the city guy a scrap of paper."

Claire had pulled down her rain hood, the better to hear. Errol hoped the joke wasn't *too* obscene. He hoped Scott showed Claire that respect.

"Well," Scott said, "the weekend comes, and the city fellow's bored. He thinks maybe he'll try the local culture before his wife and kids come from New York."

"Typical," Claire said under her breath.

"So," Scott went on, "he calls the country boy. 'I can come to your party after all,' he says. 'What should I wear?'

"'Don't matter much,' the country boy says. 'Jes gon' be you'n me.'"

Errol thought the joke was too long for its punch line, but laughed anyway. Claire, on the other hand, gave something close to a shriek, then cackled like a manic loon. She actually had to wipe tears from her eyes.

How long since she'd laughed that way for him?

"Hey, *I've* got one," he said.

"I'll vouch for that," Claire said. "But do you have a joke?"

Before he could respond, she said, "I heard this one from Nyla." She turned to Scott. "She's half Paiute Indian."

"Let's hear the joke," Errol said.

She took a breath. "Okay. A Paiute and a Navajo are drinking in a bar."

"Sounds reasonable," Errol said.

"The Paiute says, 'You know, I can get in my car and drive across my reservation in fifteen minutes.'

"The Navajo puffs himself up. 'Well,' he says, 'if I get in my car and drive all day and night, I still won't be off my reservation.'"

"'Yeah,' the Paiute says. 'I had a car like that.'"

Claire's face, already pink from cold, pinked more as both men's laughter rang out across the lake. She poured herself a shot of Tang and knocked it back.

"You're a hit, Babe," Errol said, and had to battle down a yawn.

"I've got to remember that one," Scott said; then, "I'm gonna try in close to shore."

His anchor, coming up, shed dense, fish-spooking gray clouds into the water. *Muddy as Claire's motives*, Errol thought. She'd told her joke for Scott. Meaning she was still pissed from last night. And probably still wanted to leave.

"Fuckin' mud," he growled, raised his own anchor, dumped it in his boat, and followed Scott through a bottleneck into a small, sandy bay.

A big one splashed in the drowned trees. And off to the right . . .

"Scott," he called, pointing. "Another beaver lodge."

Scott shot him a thumbs up just as Claire said, "Errol, could you take me to shore?"

"What's wrong?" Errol asked.

"My period." She spoke softly, so Scott wouldn't hear.

"Already?"

"Those new pills have mixed my hormones up."

"Stop taking 'em," Errol said. When she didn't answer, he asked gloomily, "Want to go back to camp?"

She shook her head no. "Here's fine."

"Okay," he said and, sure he was spooking fish every inch of the way, squeezed through the drowned trees and rowed for shore.

"You're gonna be okay?" he asked as the boat touched land.

She unzipped her rain jacket. "I'm fine."

Fumbling in his dry-bag, he extracted a pair of rubber boots. "Wear these," he said. "Keep your feet dry."

"Thanks." She took the boots, then rolled up the blanket she'd been sitting on. "I'll bring this too."

"Don't go too far," he said. "If you need help, holler."

"Can you have half my period?"

Errol felt his face go red. "I mean, if you . . . I don't know . . ." He gave her a playful nudge. "Aw hell, take off!"

"Careful," he said as she stepped into the water. It was only inches deep, but lake bottoms were tricky. Sometimes what looked rock-solid would turn to slush.

"You good?" he said when she reached shore.

"I'm good."

A rush of tenderness choked him as he watched her waddle, unsteady in his too-big boots, into the woods. She'd been a good sport to come here. From now on, he'd be extra nice. He swore he would.

◆ ◆ ◆

"Don't be morning sickness. Please," Claire prayed as she trudged from the water onto more-or-less dry land. Her head ached. Her stomach felt queasy and tight.

At least the woods would stop the sun's drilling her eyes. She felt its greenness open for her, then squeeze shut as if she'd entered Nature's womb.

Seen as female, the woods felt friendlier. Or was it that, with the air warming up and the men near, she could relax and tease her fears. Like touching a snake's cage at the zoo, enjoying her revulsion as the thing slid by.

Dead leaves and twigs cracked as she walked. Could Indians, Native Americans, whatever, slip soundlessly through woods like these, the way kid-books said they could?

Things were less brushy farther in, but just as loud. She could see nothing of the men, and only small bits of the lake: a Peter Max, psychedelic blue that shimmered through the trees as vapor exhaled from the ground.

"You okay, Claire?"

Errol's voice sounded muffled, but near.

"I'm fine," she called back. "The ground's not too wet. I may take a nap."

She bent to spread the blanket, then winced as a cramp grabbed her insides like a fist. *Please God*, she thought, *let it be my period*. She feared uterine cancer only slightly less than breast cancer, which she feared more than anything. Except, maybe, pregnancy.

Straightening, she felt the tell-tale movement: like something pulling loose inside and trickling, slow and sticky, down her birth canal. Well-screened by trees, she stepped out of Errol's boots, then her sweatpants, then her panties. Seeing them stained like the ones they'd found in camp, she felt a surge of relief that flowered into a happiness so extreme it almost scared her. All of her emotions seemed more extreme in these woods. More extreme and volatile. One minute she hated the place and wanted to leave; the next, she loved it and wanted to stay. Was this what Errol called "the wilderness effect?"

Stretched out on the blanket, she felt the same pelvic glow she had felt with the birds. But more intense. She touched where it felt the best, and sighed. Having the men so near felt sneaky and exciting, like when she was sixteen, making out with Dave McGinnis in the broom closet at St. James Methodist while the whole congregation milled outside.

She shut her eyes and seemed to drift. Her hand moved with more purpose. Her breath came faster. Could that doll yesterday have brought on her period, and this ultra-horniness? Some sort of voodoo effect?

"The woods remind me I'm an animal," Errol liked to say.

She wanted to roll on the ground and feel soft dirt against her skin.

Instead, she stood, pulled Errol's boots back on and, almost floating, walked deeper into the woods,

This is crazy, she told herself. *This isn't me.*

Or maybe it was. A more interesting *me*, who did as she pleased, and didn't care what others thought.

A few yards to her left, a huge tree struggled up from tangled brush. Its half-dead top looked demonic: living green mixed with dead brown. *Like me*, she thought, *after teaching for three years.*

What would her students think if they saw her now? And their parents, in their nice houses in what seemed, from here, a different universe?

"Fuck 'em," she said as, brush clawing her bare legs, she pushed through to the tree.

In front of its trunk: a whole family of phallic mushrooms!

She walked forward, unsure what she meant to do. There were six mushrooms: four small, one medium, one large. She kicked the small ones away, then bent and plucked the medium. Except for its yellow-orange color and the spore-filled slits under the head, it looked like a sex toy.

As a joke, she kissed its tip, then hoped it wasn't poisonous.

Christa, her college roommate, had owned a porno CD that she called "My rainy day man." In Claire's favorite scene, a brown-haired girl sucked a man while doing herself with a dildo. The girl had brown hair, small, saggy breasts, and a plain face. ("Must be the producer's daughter," Christa'd joked.) Not only wasn't the girl a bleached blonde with a boob job like her co-stars; she didn't pout, give ear-splitting moans, or purr, "Oh, yeah!" Her excitement was real, apparently. And contagious.

Claire slid the mushroom-head into her mouth, tasting mildew, rain, and earth.

A gout of blood dripped down her thigh. She touched where it had come from, shuddering. These 'shrooms might be the psychedelic kind. But would they act this fast, and in this way? She felt *so* spacey. Excited, but panicked, too, like the first time she smoked weed.

Errol said the woods could "do a number on your brain."

"Not just my brain," she told herself as she knelt, one knee on each side of the big mushroom. She seemed to be observing from a height, thinking,

"This is sick," while—one hand on the ground for support—she lowered herself toward the thing.

A drop of blood painted the yellow mushroom-cap. Then she was guiding it inside.

It felt smooth and weirdly warm—absurd and yet erotic as it thrust up from the ground, and she slid down toward the earth.

Could the men hear?

She shut her eyes, and pictured blinking yellow lights: animal eyes. Yesterday's bad smell had returned. But it was sexy, now. *Everything* was.

She held back until her groin pressed the ground—as if the earth were fucking her even as she gave birth to it. A cry burst out of her as she pitched forward, spitting one mushroom from her mouth and snapping off the other as she ground out her orgasm in the mud.

No telling how long she lay there, letting her senses drift back. As if she'd wakened from a dream.

"Claire?!" Errol's voice powered through the trees.

She scrambled up, away from the mushrooms. "I'm here, Errol. Where are you?"

"In the boat. What's going on?"

"Nothing," she called. Thank God, he wasn't on shore. "I fell asleep."

"You weren't crying?"

"No." Damn his good ears! "I had a dream. I think."

"You sound funny."

"You do too. I like it here. I'll come back soon."

"Take your time," he said. "As long as you're okay."

She squatted, trying to think rationally. What had come over her? What should she do? If she couldn't remove the mushroom, she'd die of embarrassment. Or worse.

She had to pee, so she did, then felt inside. A little grit, but nothing else. The mushroom must have slipped out.

The head, of course, contained the spores. She might have enough potential mushrooms in her for a million pizzas. Still, her period would wash them away. If they were there. If this hadn't been an X-rated *Alice in Wonderland* fantasy.

The thought of being watched wasn't sexy now. The woods didn't feel friendly any more.

Her blanket was just a few steps away. She rushed to it, pulled a tampon from her sweatpants—be prepared!—and, mushroom or no mushroom, pushed it in. Then she dressed, and started toward the lake.

Which way? Her mind seemed tangled in the underbrush. Her usually good sense of direction was gone. She couldn't see one hint of blue.

She looked around, and gasped. A deer was staring through the trees.

Deer weren't violent, she knew. But this one had the start of horns.

"Errol," she called, fighting terror. "Where are you?"

The deer turned. Gone.

"I'm over here," Errol called.

She grabbed onto his voice like a life preserver: close, and to the right. She scrambled toward it, crashing through the brush until she saw Peter Max blue.

"Errol!" she called, and wallowed toward him through the mud.

13

"What the hell're you using?" Errol growled as Scott tied into his fourth fish.

"One of my leaderbugs," Scott said. Anchored forty feet away, he sounded as if he were sitting in Errol's boat.

"I'll be goddamned," Errol said. Almost too sleepy to see, he tied on a Lacquer Special. Result: Scott landed two more big trout before Errol could coax a strike—from a ten-incher that jumped once, threw the hook, and left Errol an angry man.

The moment Claire had burst out of the woods, trout began to rise. Now, a half-hour later, they had stopped.

"Try a leaderbug," Scott said.

"My fly's not the problem," Errol said, and doggedly cast on. The problem was that he was casting to no fish. His sunglasses, which let him see to the lake-bottom, showed a fishless waste in front of him.

Scott, by contrast, had hogged the beaver lodge, where there'd be deep holes and more cover. Using the double-haul that Errol had taught him, he dropped his fly onto the sticks, then, with a quick twitch, into blue water.

A swirl, a splash, and Scott yelled, "Yeah!"

The big trout could have dived back to its lair, wrapped Scott's line around a log, and improved Errol's mood in a big way. But fear drove it to open water, where Scott could steer it clear of snags, wear it down, and after five long minutes—in which Errol kept casting frantically—bring it to the net.

He hefted the four-pounder for approval.

"He's beautiful," Claire called from her spot on Errol's prow.

"She," Errol corrected. His smile felt forced out by pliers. "No need to yell. Voices carry on a lake."

◆ ◆ ◆

"Thumbs up or down?" Scott called, hefting his fish for all to see.

"Up!" Claire called from the front of Errol's boat. With her hair a gorgeous mess, she seemed fresh out of bed, ready to jump back in. "Let her go," she urged.

"Done," Scott said, lowered the fish into the lake, and steadied her until she flicked her tail and swam away.

"How did you know it's female?" Claire said.

Errol, already back to casting, didn't speak, so Scott replied. "Hens have smaller heads and more graceful bodies. They usually fight better, too."

"Gyno power," she said.

"You got it," Scott said. "I mean, you're right. Not that you've got . . ." He stopped speaking. His foot seemed drawn irresistibly toward his mouth.

"Could you two shout a little louder? Scare off a few more fish?" Errol said, and kept casting, grim as death.

Scott, triumphant, felt no rush to recast right away. He rowed his net through the water to clean it, then slid out of his raincoat. Condensation had slicked his parka, but the sun would dry it soon.

He glanced at Claire again, and saw her glance away.

"Caught you looking," his friend Tommy Tanner used to say, to the embarrassment of high school girls. But why would Claire look at him: clearly a lesser man that Errol?

Scott remembered a night, years ago, when he'd beaten three guys in a row arm-wrestling in The District Tav. The vanquished had set up a chorus: "Take him, Errol." And Errol, arms thick as Scott's thighs, had laughed. "Not a chance. He might kick my ass," he'd said. And preserved their equality.

"Enough of that," Scott said, as if to the blood knot he was tying. This afternoon might be the time, after a good half-day's fishing, to drive away. He could exchange information with Errol, suggest they plan some future trips, then head out: a good man and a good friend, not the interloper he was now. With any luck, Ursula Lake—assuming he could find it—would make Oso's trout look like fingerlings.

Okay, he thought, *that's what I'll do.*

Too bad Julie wasn't here to keep him company. But it would have been presumptuous to ask, after one kiss. She was a buyer for Nordstrom's. She couldn't just take off.

Anyway, he'd come here partly to be on his own. In the woods, superfluous things fell away, leaving what mattered: Did you eat? Sleep? Shit? Were you warm? Dry? Healthy? Happy? Safe? What did you *need*?

Even now, the wilderness was working on him. Damned, though, if he could guess what it would do.

◆ ◆ ◆

An hour later, with the score Scott nine, Errol two, Errol's patience snapped.

"Gimme one of those leaderbugs, willya," he demanded, as if Scott had been holding out. Errol knew he wasn't, but it felt as if he was.

To reach Errol's boat, Scott had to raise anchor. He *didn't* have to cause an underwater silt-storm.

"Christ on the crapper," Errol groaned as the chalky silt-cloud spread. He pictured trout fleeing in droves, like his hopes for this vacation. And all the while, Scott grinned: the unencumbered rock-god-wannabe, loving that he had the upper hand.

Scot's boat nudged into Errol's as he offered his flies. "Take two or three."

Errol took two, with a grudging, "Thanks."

Scott checked his watch. "It's 12:15. Think I'll head in for lunch."

"Fine with me." Errol's shrug said he was staying, and that nothing was fine.

"I'll go too, if that's okay," Claire chimed. "I'm starved."

Errol drilled her with his eyes. "Do what you like."

"Do you mind, Scott?" she asked. "Can I ride in with you?"

"Sure," Scott said, but looked at Errol. "Is that cool?"

"It's cool," Errol said, and tried to mean it. But some imp of the perverse made him whistle a false cast past Claire's head as, with Scott holding his boat next to Errol's, she half-climbed, half-toppled aboard.

Her too-quick movement tipped Errol's boat, and nearly dumped him in the lake.

"Christ on a styrofoam crutch," he sighed, and kept mechanically casting and stripping, casting and stripping while Scott, whom he'd started to wish had stayed in Seattle, first rowed, then motored Claire out of the bay, onto the open lake, and out of sight.

14

Perched far forward in Scott's boat, Claire stared into the lake—so clear, she could see rocks, white sand, and weed-beds shimmery as a mirage. She felt light-headed, still half-high. Had the mushrooms done something to her brain? Or was it this lake, these woods, that made her feel life's normal rules did not apply?

The boat seemed on a liquid treadmill. Only by watching the shore pass could she see they were moving.

She dipped a hand into the water. Cold as snow! She was a good swimmer, but the cold would finish her long before she could reach land.

Strange to be gliding over what could be her death. Strange, but not scary. Even the burned bones and the beaver lodge clothes seemed, in hindsight, no big deal. Odd things were to be expected in the wild. That's why people went there: to escape the tame and usual.

"Look! Deer!" Scott called over the boat's roar.

Claire followed his pointing hand, and saw three deer standing nearly in the lake. Unlike the one she'd seen after the mushroom "incident," these were does: antlerless heads raised, ears high, listening. To what? The boat?

"A buck's probably watching from the woods," Scott said. "They let the does break cover first. Make sure the coast is clear."

"How intrepid," she said. Which stopped the conversation.

She wished, now, that she had stayed with Errol. He'd make a scene when he came in. Also, she felt nervous with Scott. You never could tell about men. And she had mixed feelings about this one. A gentleman would have gone elsewhere to fish.

Back in their bay, Scott killed the engine and let the boat coast in. Claire, still wearing Errol's spare boots, hopped into the shallow water and held the boat's nose while Scott jumped out after her.

"Thanks," he said, and dragged the boat, scraping and grinding, high up on shore.

While he busied himself with fishing gear, she grabbed toilet paper and slipped into the woods. Its power hit her instantly: not female or friendly anymore. Killer grizzlies loomed. Eyes glowed in every shadow. And there was nothing *but* shadow.

She felt so vulnerable in her stupid squat! Men could simply haul it out. For women, Nature's call, in Nature, was a chore.

She felt some grit where none should be, but no mushroom. Had the sex-thing been her imagination, run amuck? Was that possible? Either way, it had been supremely strange.

Also strange: her "period" had stopped. That worried her, but she refused to think about it now. She cleaned herself as well as she could, yanked up her pants, and dashed back into the sun.

At the clearing's edge, she stopped to pick a few of the white daisies that must have bloomed overnight. Bathrooms, tampons, toilet paper—they all tried to link themselves with flowers. Now she did too, reentering Scott's presence as if she'd been gathering nosegays.

He stood beside his camper, faced away, eating. Oblivious to her.

She could retreat to her camper, and stay there until Errol returned. Having braved the woods, though, she should be able to face Scott!

She tossed away the stupid daisies, walked toward him, and said, "What's for lunch?"

Turning, he held up a slice of peanut-buttered bread. "You tell me."

"Yuck."

"Exactly." Folding the bread, he shoved half in his mouth, gulped it down, shoved in the other half, then poised his knife above the peanut butter jar. "Want one?"

She'd never liked peanut butter, but she said, "Okay," then added, "I'll make my own."

"Fine by me." Placing the knife in the peanut butter jar, Scott handed it to her, along with a slice of bread.

She realized, taking the bread, that she hadn't washed her hands. *Oh well*, she thought, spread peanut butter smoothly and evenly, then looked for a clean place to cut the bread in two. Not finding one, she folded the bread as Scott had done and gulped it down.

"Would you like another . . . sandwich?" she asked.

"That'd be great."

She pulled out a fresh slice of bread, spread the peanut butter, folded the bread, handed it to Scott, then made another for herself.

Scott swallowed his in two quick gulps. "Thanks," he said. "Food someone else makes always tastes better to me." He wiped his mouth with his sleeve, then said, "You must think I'm a colossal turd."

She felt herself blush even as she chewed. He'd read her mind. Yet, as soon as she had swallowed and could speak, she asked, "Why do you say that?"

"I've wrecked your romantic holiday."

She hesitated, then said, "Errol's not a romantic man." This sounded so bitchy, she tacked on, "He used to be."

Scott re-wiped his mouth, and shook his head in disbelief. "Errol's practically a second Keats," he said. "He's the most romantic guy I know."

"Your friends must all be CPAs." She smiled to show it was a joke.

Scott pulled a fly from the wool patch on his fishing vest and placed it back in his fly box. "He'll do better when I'm gone."

To her surprise, she felt a pang. "You're leaving?"

He nodded. "Before it gets too dark."

"Don't leave because of me."

He shrugged. "This country's full of lakes."

Her resentment, which she'd been struggling to hide, turned—poof!—to gratitude. "That's very considerate," she said. His generosity made *her* feel generous. "But you should stay. Errol's so glad you two met up. *I'd* be a turd to ruin that."

"I still think . . ."

"That's a bad habit." She smiled, then turned her head to look across the lake. "Any problems Errol and I have . . . we'll have them whether you're here or not."

On impulse, she took his hand—softer than she'd expected—pressed it once, then, dismayed by what she'd done, let it go. "Maybe you could talk to Errol." She swallowed wrong, and coughed. "Say . . . I don't know . . . say he should be nicer to me. Let him know he's blowing it."

To hear aloud what she'd been thinking added to her dismay. So did Scott's answer: "You don't leave much room for doubt."

She started to take offense, then let it go. "You're probably right."

"Anyway," Scott said, "I can't just walk up and say, 'Here's some advice.'"

She nodded. "Stay anyway. I need an ally with more brains than a vibrator."

He looked as discomfited as she felt. Of all comparisons to make! She felt light-headed, like with the mushroom. Out of control.

Crossing her eyes, she sucked in her cheeks to make her famous cross-eyed fish.

Luckily, he laughed.

"When bombing verbally," she said, and plopped down on the tailgate of his truck, "go for the gross-out."

He laughed again. "Want another 'sandwich'? Before I put everything away?"

She thought a moment. "Okay. Sure."

"You want to make it?"

She shook her head no. "I trust you."

"Big mistake." He took a piece of bread, spread it with peanut butter, folded it, and held it out.

"Thanks," she said, and started to eat while he poured her a cup of water.

"Want some Tang in this?" he asked.

"No thanks. That stuff tastes worse every day."

"It does," he said, and handed her the Tang-free cup.

The water was warm but welcome. When she'd drained her cup, Scott refilled it, then pulled a sugar cookie from a brown sack and held it out. "Dessert?"

She seldom ate cookies. But she accepted this one, nipped off a corner, and liked it.

Her next action started as politeness, but felt less virtuous by the time, holding the cookie in mouth range, she asked, "Want a bite?"

Scott hesitated, then said, "Okay."

She felt a quick thrill as his lips touched her U-shaped mouth-mark. She knew as surely as she knew her name that she should head straight for her camper. But she finished the cookie. And she stayed.

"Why do men work so hard to catch overgrown anchovies?" she said, to say something.

"Fishing's fun. Believe it or not."

"Errol's obsessed with it," she said. "I don't see the attraction."

"This may sound horrible," he said. "But when you hook a fish, you steal its energy. The more it runs and jumps, the more you steal."

"You're right. It sounds horrible."

"It's instinctive," Scott said. "A fisherman who's catching fish feels *viable*. Like a cougar that's caught a deer."

"So right now, Errol feels less viable than you?"

Scott looked surprised. "Errol's caught fish."

"Less than you. And he hates it."

Scott opened his cooler, and put the bread, peanut butter, and bag of cookies inside. "When fishing's bad, you can feel cursed," he said. "Like Fate hates you. We call it being *the wretch*. The fishless one."

"The wretch," she said. "That's serious."

"It is."

She felt cookie crumbs on her lips, and brushed them away. "Don't you feel sorry for the fish?"

Hefting his cooler, Scott shoved it into his camper and shut the door. "You sound like my mom," he said.

"Naïve?"

"Tenderhearted."

At least he hadn't said *old*.

"Errol tells me you take care of her," she said.

"*Took* care. She died."

Claire made an *I goofed* face. "I'm sorry."

"I'm not," Scott said. "There wasn't a lot left of her."

"What was her . . . trouble? If you don't mind my asking."

"Brain damage. A drunk driver."

"Oh *no*!" She pictured a woman her mother's age, but with a shaved head and empty eyes. "I hope the driver had insurance."

Scott shook his head no. "He wasn't even in the country legally." He tightened his lips and scrutinized the ground. "Mom had insurance, but bills still wiped her out. I had some money my grandmother left me. That went, too."

"That's terrible!"

The glistening in his eyes made her heart go out to him.

"It makes me crazy when I think of it," he said. "I try *not* to."

"Let's drop it, then."

A big bird with a white head—an eagle?—flapped out from the trees, and swooped down over the lake. Gliding a few inches above the surface, it seemed to slap the water with its feet, then fought its way back into the air, a large fish flipping in its grip.

Nature wrote the book on cruelty, Errol liked to say.

"You didn't answer my question," Claire said. "Do you feel sorry for the fish?"

♦ ♦ ♦

"If I let myself, I would," Scott said. "That's what we get for being conscious animals."

A straight *Yes* would have scored big points, he knew. But he didn't want big points. Feeling a pine needle drop into his hair, he plucked it out and sailed it away.

"Fish aren't smart," he said. "They've got good instincts, but no sense of the future. No, 'Shit, I've failed.'" He smiled. "No *I* at all."

"The hook has to hurt," she said.

"Me and de Sade," he shot back. "Pleasure out of pain."

"Don't get defensive."

Her tone was teasing. But thinking of his mom's fate always made him furious. More reason to detest the *system*—of "justice," and everything else.

"Look . . ." His voice had come out hard. He tried to soften it. "I could say, 'Pain's part of life. I'm doing Nature's Will.' But Nature doesn't have a will. Nature's just there. Hooked fish are frightened. They're in pain. And instinct makes their thrashing fun for me."

Her face said he was still hitting too hard. Her face, that was making him giddy.

He swept his gaze across the lake. In the direction Errol must be. "I don't usually think of this," he said. "Who thinks *slaughterhouse* when he scarfs a steak?"

She seemed to follow his gaze across the lake. "Well," she said, "we've had our first fight. And we aren't even dating."

How respond to that? Scott was still searching when she said, with her most magnetic smile, "Errol says you play guitar. He says you're great."

He shrugged. "I'm okay."

"You play professionally? In bands?"

Scott nodded. "Guilty as charged."

"That's exciting." Her eyes widened. As if she were flirting.

"It *can* be." Scott hoped he wasn't turning red. "Good rock-and-roll is right up there with fly fishing and sex."

He wished he hadn't added *sex*.

"You're lucky," she said. "Not many people can make money doing art."

"*Art* is stretching it," he said. "Nose-picking's more artistic than a copy band playing bars."

"That's . . . vivid."

She smiled, so he did too. He wanted to say more. But would she understand? And if she did, would that be good?

"I played a concert a year ago at Volunteer Park," he said. "At least a thousand people came. I was singing our version of that old Zeppelin song. 'Dazed and Confused.'"

She hummed the opening riff.

"You got it," he said, and had to smile. He pictured the park: emerald grass and trees, the audience unrolling like a multi-colored carpet down the hill. He heard his band, the late, lamented Odin's Eye, thundering behind him. He heard his guitar, his voice rising from some depth he hadn't known was there.

"I felt on fire. Like I was Prometheus, passing flames to everyone," he said. "A voice in my head told me—I swear, I heard it—'This is where you belong.'"

"Like Paul on the road to Damascus," she said. "God wants you to be a star. So you can help people forget their boring lives."

Scott tried not to grin stupidly. "To be even a small asteroid, you've got to write songs. And market them," he said. "I'm more like a bricklayer, busting my buns six nights a week. When I get home, I'm too tired to write. All I want to do is sleep."

Claire stretched her arms high. Which pushed out her chest. "British bands work out their own songs on the job," she said. "Couldn't you do that?"

He shook his head no. "In Seattle, bar bands have to play *the hits*, or people don't show up, and the band gets axed. So we play the hits. And people come, and bitch about the boring band."

"If it's so bad, why not do something else?"

"I need to eat." Scott stepped back to keep a safe distance between them. "Rock-and-roll's wearing out. I want to change that, like the Beatles did. And Zeppelin. And Queen." He realized he was twisting his cowlick, and dropped his hand. "Most people never know what they were born to do. I *know*. I just can't get to first base doing it!"

"I don't see you stopping at first base," she said, then blushed crimson. "Errol raves about your poetry. You could do *that*. Be the nose-picking Lord Byron."

That made him laugh. "I might," he said, "if I had a trust fund."

"Those are dangerous," she said. "Take it from me."

"I'd chance it," he said. "Poetry's about as saleable as ear mites." He sounded like a pouty child, he knew. And pouted on. "Anyway, music's what I really want to do.

Her nod told him she understood. "Theater's what Errol really wants to do. You're a purist. Like him."

"A pure downer," he said. "Let's talk about you. Tell me something interesting."

She thought a moment. "Well, my first husband was gay. How's that to start?"

He had to smile. "It got my interest."

"He was a London art critic. A lot older than me. And my professor. I thought he was a superior being. The great Peter Langford. Above demands of the flesh."

She was wearing a purple Pendleton shirt, open at the neck. Scott's gaze kept drifting toward the flesh between her throat and breasts. Drifting, then jerking away.

She seemed to know, and closed her shirt with her left hand. "Ask me something else."

"You don't like fishing," he said. "What *do* you like?"

"I like dance. And theater." Her eyes shifted up. "And visual arts, of course. After UW, I studied painting in London for two years."

She dropped her hand. Her shirt fell open again.

"That explains the accent," he said.

"I've still got it?"

"A little bit."

"I'm a chameleon with things I like. Another hour, and I'll sound like you."

It seemed churlish not to say, "I like you too." But he focused on the lake, its surface flashing with diamonds. "Visual arts," he said, as if testing the term. "The only thing I ever drew well was a bow."

"A violin bow?"

"A bow and arrow." He pantomimed. "You know, you pull one back. It's called *drawing*."

Her look said, *What are you babbling about?*

"Okay, *Saturday Night Live* won't be calling," he said, with a funny (he hoped) grimace of chagrin. "Do you still paint?"

"Off and on," she said. "I'm good enough to know that I'm not good enough." She sighed and, for some reason, tightened her belt a notch. "I've studied Oriental medicine, computer programming, counseling—I always start off strong, then quit. I *have* a trust fund, so I can pull my nose off the grindstone when it hurts." She sighed again. "I teach school now."

Scott stopped shifting foot-to-foot, and sat down next to her on his tailgate. "What grade?" he asked, and realized that he'd sat too close. And that she didn't edge away.

"Sixth," she said. "Some of them are adolescents, some are children. Most are some of each."

Their heads moved closer. He barely knew what he was saying, rambling about "a difficult age," his lips inches from hers. The gap between their mouths kept shrinking. It was about to disappear when, as if he'd dozed off at the wheel, his head snapped back.

Her head did too. "I think I'll take a bath," she said.

Scott pointed at the lake. "In there? You'll freeze your . . . you'll freeze."

"I won't go *in*. I've got a washcloth."

The image of her brushing her hair in Errol's camper flashed to mind.

"So," she said, "would you hang around here till I get back? Preserve my modesty, and such."

He felt as if he'd been caught looking up her dress. "Oh. Sure. I'll tie some flies," he said and, his face flaming, started digging out his gear. All the same, he noticed the way she moved under her baggy pants, heading for the lake.

"That stuff can make you nuts," he told himself. If he *did* stay at Oso, he'd stay far away from Claire.

15

Hurrying toward the lake, Claire felt her face cool as her composure fell back into place. For months, she'd toyed with the idea of an affair. If Scott wasn't Errol's friend, he would have been a candidate. Especially after their talk. He had a sweetness and vulnerability that Errol lacked. She hated the thought of cheating. But *Till death do us part* only made sense when death came before thirty. Who, except for Nyla and her, believed in it these days?

What were you supposed to do when the man you married wasn't the man you wound up married to?

Her mother'd had affairs. Katie'd had two. Affairs, Claire had read somewhere, could take the heat off marriage problems. Unless, like Katie, you got caught, and your life blew to smithereens. Mom, though, was still married to Dad. For what that was worth.

She knew that Errol had been a player. She'd liked being the woman who made him change his ways. For all she knew, though, he was cheating now. Men took screwing around as their phallic due.

Was she drawn to Scott out of anger at Errol? The way he'd smacked her in the face and kept fishing spoke volumes. Now, he was pouting over his failure to catch some stupid trout. Pouting and feeling less *viable* because he couldn't *steal their energy.*

Face facts, she told herself. *He was never right for me.*

"Theater is not a job. It's an affliction," her mother had warned. "The boy has no money, and no prospects except for you. He's a big, good-looking nobody, going nowhere. And he'll take you with him."

"The ride down's got to beat being like you," Claire had screamed. Then, in the best Hollywood tradition, they'd both had a good cry. Two weeks later, she was Mrs. Wolfe. Four years after that, Prince Charming had lost his charm. Her coach-and-six looked more and more like a pumpkin.

She passed the place where she had "seen" the yellow eye. It took an act of will, but she kept walking until she came to a small inlet almost completely wrapped by woods. If something grabbed her here, she might never be found. Mrs. Wolfe, sixth-grade teacher at Pine Hills Elementary, would simply disappear.

She could skip bathing and head back to camp. But how pathetic would that be? Anyway, she wasn't ready to face Scott. And she wanted to wash away all traces of "the incident."

She tried to quell her fears as, hanging her towel on a bare bush, she stripped, and draped her clothes next to the towel. For speed's sake, she only unbuttoned her Pendleton halfway, then pulled it off like a sweatshirt. She had no wish to dance or pose today.

She washed her lower half thoroughly, pulled her jeans back on, then unsnapped her bra, scrubbed her chest, and started on her neck.

Errol loved to see her in jeans with no top. She wondered what Scott would say, then aborted the thought. Scott was off limits. Period.

Something—squirrels? camp robbers?—rustled. Things were always rustling here.

She looked around. Seeing nothing to fear, she finished washing, quickly toweled dry, put on her bra, then pulled her shirt over her head. Except one arm went into the head-hole. She pulled it out, then, twisting like a contortionist, thrust it right back into the head-hole.

"Damn!"

She could have unbuttoned the shirt. But she refused. Carefully, she fitted one arm, then the other, into their proper sleeves. Then she fitted her head into the neck-hole, and pulled down.

As her head emerged, she caught a rotten smell and heard loud rustling behind.

She whirled, and saw a monster with one yellow eye.

◆ ◆ ◆

Scott was already dashing toward Claire's scream when he realized he had no weapon to face . . . anything.

A new scream—"GET AWAY FROM ME!"—routed those concerns. Still, he was relieved when the only thing that burst out of the woods was a small man who, rather than attacking, was hobbling away.

Three bounding strides, and Scott was on him, wrapping his chest in a bear-hug and bulldogging him to the ground. The man barely struggled, only groaned and squirmed, demanding in a hoarse voice, "Fuckin' white fucker, let me go!"

Unsure what else to do, Scott sat on his captive's back to hold him down. Any sense of heroism fled as he saw matted gray braids—oh hell, an Indian—and registered the stench. Worse than a skid row derelict.

"What the fuck is going on?" he yelled as Claire burst from the woods.

"That's him!" she screamed.

"That's who?" Scott said. "What's going on?" It better have been something bad, or he could wind up jailed. Assault, battery, sitting on a First Nation—the possibilities, he'd learned from Dad, were as endless as lawyerly greed.

Claire was literally dancing with outrage. "This creep was watching me," she said. "Yesterday too!"

"Yesterday?! What happened yesterday?"

Scott got up off his captive, hoping there were no "actionable injuries."

The man stood slowly. An inch or two shorter than Scott. Less old, maybe, than his body seemed: forty-five or fifty, with a big nose, and the right side of his face puckered and seared. The same burn-scar pulled down the corner of his right eye, which was yellow like a cat's. The other eye was dark brown verging on black.

He wore jeans shiny with grime, and a gray-and-red plaid button-down he must have bought at a thrift shop. Once fully upright, he offered Scott a look of boundless hate, then turned and began to limp away.

"Hold it!" Scott grabbed the man's shoulder, and spun him around. He smelled like a dumpster on a hot day.

"Let me go, white man!" he wheezed.

He was white-skinned for an Indian. As white as Scott. His voice rasped as if he had some lung disease. "Turn me loose," he croaked. "Or you'll be sorry."

The scarred face and the look in those mismatched eyes made Scott let go. "You *are* loose." He tried to sound like a seasoned crisis-handler. "What's this about?"

"He was *watching* me!" Claire jabbed her finger at the man. "Yesterday too. I thought he was a bear."

"She's full of shit," the man growled. "I was walkin' in the woods. Indians *own* the goddamn woods. Anywhere you look, our ghosts are there."

"Take that up with the Prime Minister," Scott said.

By all rights, this scene should have been funny. But it wasn't to Claire.

"He was spying on me, Scott!" she said, almost in tears.

"A guy's out walkin' in his own woods and sees a nekkid woman—what's he s'posed to do?" the captive growled. "You'da looked too." He leered at Scott. "It's Nature's Law."

Scott looked away, not wanting to concede the point.

"Were you *out walking* yesterday?" demanded Claire.

"I don't walk much since white men fucked up my leg. I wasn't nowhere near here. Prove I was!" The look he turned on Claire seemed meant to incinerate. Instead, she took a step toward him.

Scott jumped between them. "What's your name?" he demanded.

"Jim Bearclaw," the man proclaimed. Reaching inside his shirt, he pulled out a long yellow claw hung on a leather thong. "That's a magic claw," he said, and flourished it. "No white man's got nothin' like it. I'm chief of the Bear Clan."

Looking as if he'd tomahawked Scott down to size, Jim Bearclaw dropped the claw back down his shirt.

"Chief pervert," Claire said.

Bearclaw wheeled. "The Bear God gave me that claw, bitch. I'll send him to tear off your fat *tits*!"

As he spat the last word, Bearclaw yanked out his claw and slashed it down his palm. Scott saw a line of blood appear as, palm outstretched, Bearclaw lunged at Claire as if to brand her.

Scott's shove caught him mid-lunge, and nearly knocked him down. As Bearclaw straightened slowly, Scott took his *shito ryu* ready stance. "Be cool, man," he warned. "If you like having teeth."

His dialogue seemed lifted from a movie. As Bearclaw himself could have been. An old and very stupid one.

"Where do you live?" Scott demanded.

"The woods," Bearclaw said, blood dripping from his palm onto the ground.

"*Where* in the woods?"

"Everywhere, white man. The woods is an Indian's mother."

"Well, *I'm* not," Scott said. "No chicken soup from me. If I see you again . . ." He groped for a blood-curdling threat, but settled for "your ass is grass." He gave Bearclaw another shove. "Get out of here. And don't come back."

"Don't let him leave!" Claire was dancing with outrage again. "He'll sneak back and kill us all."

She might be right, Scott realized. But what could he do? Drive the guy to town? Press charges? For what? He could wind up jailed himself. In Canada.

"You want to guard him for a week?" he asked Claire.

"Let Errol decide. He'll know how to handle this wanker!" She tightened her jaw the same way Errol would have done. The same disgusted, superior air.

"My eyes are on you!" Bearclaw croaked like some giant bird of prey. He'd stopped at the clearing's edge to wave his claw. "You cripple everything you touch," he croaked. "Expect the bear, white devils!"

Scott, ready to prove that he could be as tough as Errol, took a step toward the man. But he had already slipped between the trees.

"Your name sounds like a sweet roll, you fucking...pastry!" Scott yelled. And let him go.

16

An hour later, tired, hungry, and fishless, Errol was back. He heard the Bearclaw tale in silence, forehead furrowed, eyes narrowed to slits.

"Good thing I wasn't here," he said. "I'd have killed the bastard."

"I don't think he's dangerous," Scott said. "Kind of a backwoods bag-man."

"His cart-pushing ass better stay away from me," Errol muttered. "Sure you're okay?" he asked Claire.

"I'm fine," she said, then turned to Scott. "Sorry I barked."

"No problem," he said. "Just don't bring home any more weird friends."

"Okay, Dad."

They both smiled. Errol wasn't smiling, though, as he retired to the bushes. The Indian's threat, the mutilated calf, and that fir tree they'd seen the other day, claw-slashed ten feet above the ground—all of this made him think a grizzly could be near. And grizzlies, unlike black bears, attacked people.

The safest course would be to leave. BC had lots of other lakes.

But what if none of them panned out?

Those claw-marks *could* have come from a big black—shy, and by now, miles from here. As for 'Bearclaw,' Scott was right: the guy was probably a harmless loony tune. Crippled, to boot. "Fuck him," Errol said aloud. No way he'd let a clown like that chase him away. Not when he might've found the source of those ghost trout!

"I tried to nap in my boat," he told Scott while they fried up the fish they'd kept. "I couldn't sleep, so I rowed back into the trees.

"Beavers have dammed up a creek. And there's a trail beside it, which I took. Half a mile in, there's another lake. Not clear like Oso. Almost black." He paused for effect. "Mosquitos were hatching. Bathtub-sized rises everywhere!"

"Did you fish?!"

Errol made a doleful face. "I left my gear in the boat."

"Presto Humiliation," Scott said, and both men offered a grimace to that deflating god.

"How big's the lake?" Scott said.

"Smaller than Oso, but big enough. And *not* on our maps."

"So only locals know it! Hey, next time Oso craps out . . ."

Errol gave Scott a playful jab. "You're a genius. You think like me."

Tonight's fish tasted as muddy as yesterday's, so dinner went fast, ending with sugar cookies all around. Scott washed the dishes, Errol rinsed, Claire put away.

"Better lock anything stealable in the campers," Errol said. "In case ol' Bares-His-Ass comes back."

When that was done, they climbed into the boats and, Errol leading, headed out.

The loons were back: two black-and-white shapes in the center of the lake. From time to time, their demented laughter was returned from somewhere too far off to see.

The temperature hung near sixty as the sun rolled down a blue sky wisped with gray. Errol had seen a few ducks on the water, and heard their quacks and whistles overhead. Now, suddenly, ducks were everywhere—mallards, pintails, goldeneyes, a widgeon, a cinnamon teal—swimming, diving, chasing each other across the lake. In a few weeks, the marshes and bays would be full of peeping babies tagging after quacking moms.

Old Man's Bay was easy to find. Today, though, the only action came when Claire snagged bottom and lost her fly.

"Don't bother with a new one," she told Errol. "I'll just watch you."

"I'll rig you up, just in case," Errol said, and tied on a Dandy Green.

"Think I'll try closer in," Scott announced, and motored away.

Errol finished with Claire's rig, then roared after his friend, who'd made it through the shallow channel and stopped thirty feet from the beaver lodge. The likeliest spot in the little bay.

"Anything?" Errol whispered, dropping anchor twenty feet away.

"Not yet," Scott said—and reared back into a nice one.

"Leaderbug?" Errol called, trying to stay calm.

"Sure enough."

Scott had given him two. Claire had lost one. Errol plucked the other from his fly box, snipped off his Dandy Green, whipped the leaderbug onto his tippet and, too rushed even to check his knot, hurried to cast while Claire resumed her morning posture in the prow.

Errol relaxed when Scott's fish jumped and threw the hook. He didn't wish Scott bad luck. Just no better luck than *his*.

He laid a perfect cast beside a submerged stump, then saw a small brown head moving among the drowned trees. "Scott," he hissed. "Beaver."

◆ ◆ ◆

Claire saw the beaver, too—though Errol had pointed it out to Scott, not her. She sighed. This was Tuesday. They'd drive home Sunday and be back to work on Monday. Four more days of 'vacation.' With, now, a dirty old native in the mix.

She sighed again, then heard a noise. Three green-headed male mallards and a smaller brown female were splashing near the shore. It looked like play until one greenhead flapped its way on top of the female, then used his beak to force her head under water.

The other greenheads circled, pecking at the pair.

"Errol, what're they doing?" she asked as the female thrashed and the greenhead held her down.

"Mating, Babe. He'll let her up if she cooperates."

Apparently, she did. The greenhead hopped off. The small brown head came up. Then the other males moved in.

"Leave her alone," Claire said under her breath. She wanted to throw something, but couldn't spare a shoe.

The mallard hen dodged her new suitors, then leapt into the air. The spurned drakes took off in pursuit, leaving the successful male to swim around quacking, puffed with success, before—horny again?—he leapt into the air and sped toward where the winged dots were diminishing.

"Those males mean business," Errol said, as if she might have missed the fact. "Next time we're at the park, check for bald spots on the females' heads."

Was he implying that she could stand to lose some feathers, too?

"Golly gee," she chirped. "I thought duckies were all sweet and cuddly."

"'Nature, red in tooth and claw,'" Scott offered from across the water.

Errol nodded. "Ever see geese barge?"

When Claire declined to answer, Scott piped up, "What's that?"

"If two males want the same female, each one tries to grab the other's neck and force it under . . . *there's* one!" Errol lifted his rod to set the hook, then held on as a two pounder tail-walked across the bay.

"You've earned your freedom," Errol said when the fish came in.

Claire saw the hook snaked through its eye at the same time Errol did.

"Aw Jeez. No wonder you fought hard," he said, and broke the fish's neck. Extracting his fly pulled the eye out, too.

Claire felt sick, but couldn't look away until Scott shouted, "There's one!"

She turned. His rod was bent in two.

"Big one?" Errol called.

"Feels huge. Jesus!" The trout shot into the air: two feet long, and bright as a silver tray.

◆ ◆ ◆

Fishing etiquette forbade casting near somebody fighting a big fish. Sapped by lack of sleep, though, Errol's courtesy ran out fast. His fishing days were leaking away. And there stood Scott, once again hogging the best spot.

"Takes his sweet time," he muttered to Claire, then started casting close enough that Scott's fish could potentially cross his line.

Like a yellow beachball on a bed of nails, the sun sat balanced on the pointed tops of evergreens. Errol half-expected it to pop and rocket across the sky. The bay was filling with shadows as he filled with bitterness. He'd loved fishing ever since, as a boy, he'd racked up strings of yellow perch with worm and bobber. All last year, slaving and chafing at his desk, he'd dreamed of Oso. Now Scott, who hadn't known a fly rod from a pea pod when they'd met, was catching all the biggest fish!

"Five pounds, easy," Scott called, radiating glee.

With a mighty double-haul, Errol dropped his fly where Scott's had been. He did this just to prove he could. The odds were slim another big trout would be there.

Scott released his fish, then, having roiled the water in front of him, moved his boat a few feet to the right, and cast in front of a wicked-looking snag that poked out of the beaver lodge. Errol watched Scott's line lay out like a green scratch on the water, then spring tight.

"Got 'im!" Scott sang.

This made Errol rush his next cast, which slapped water behind him, whizzed by half-an-inch from his own ear, provoked an "Oh!" from Claire, and nearly wrapped one of the drowned trees. "Sasquatch shit," he groaned, just as Scott yelled,

"Crap! Came unpinned."

Errol turned to get a look at Scott's chagrin, and saw, on his left, three huge trout swimming maybe two feet deep, on a course to pass under his line.

He stripped in fast, to put his fly right in their path. But Scott's leaderbug was too small, too transparent, too blue. The ghosties would ignore it, just as the old man had said.

The take, when it came, was too light to feel. His line simply began to move through the water, heading leisurely toward shore.

With a smooth, two-handed motion—line pulled down with his left hand, rod raised with his right—Errol set the hook.

A salmon-sized trout porpoised out of the water as line shrieked off his reel.

"Shithouse mouse!" Scott yelled.

"Oh Jesus God!" Errol howled. "I'm using 6X."

Instead of making a long, sizzling run, the fish cruised back and forth twenty feet from the boat, as if unsure what had occurred. It was so big, it must barely feel the fly.

"That's twenty pounds," Scott called. "Don't pressure him."

All the fish had to do was swim a few feet into the drowned trees. The line would snag, and that would be that.

"Lead him out of the bay," Scott called. "Wear him down in open water!"

Scott was right. But that meant Claire would have to row.

"God *damn* it!" Errol wailed as the fish cruised toward the trees, and the injustice of everything sank in. "Claire"—his voice came hard and tight—"Do exactly as I say."

He kept his eyes on his line as it sliced across the bay.

"Pull up anchor," he commanded. "Don't splash. Lift it in the boat, and gently set it down."

◆ ◆ ◆

Claire gripped the anchor rope and pulled. For one awful instant, the rope wouldn't budge. Then up the anchor came: like a sea creature shedding clouds of sand. Its weight, when it broke water, nearly yanked her overboard.

Errol groaned. "Christ on . . ." His voice trailed off as Claire regained her balance and, with both hands, heaved the anchor into the boat.

It hit the metal bottom with a thunderous *clunk!*

"Quiet!" Errol's voice shook with desperation. "Move to the center of the boat. Careful!" He groaned as her movement rocked him. "Take the oars, and row us *slowly* out of this bay."

"I haven't rowed since Girl Scout camp," Claire protested. "You said you'd teach me." Her resentment warred with fear that she would botch the job and bear the blame.

"We have no choice." Errol's soft, precise voice chilled her. "Do it. Carefully. Slow, even strokes."

Half of her wanted to drop the oars and whine, "This isn't fair." The other half wanted to help Errol catch this fish.

"Help her, Scott," he pleaded as the boat began to swing.

The fish made a short run toward the trees, then miraculously stopped.

"More with your left oar," Scott called. "Claire! Left oar. Take your right out of the water. Stroke. That's it. Now use both oars. Slowly. Evenly."

Errol's boat crept toward the open lake.

"Lead him, Errol. No pressure. Claire, right oar. Right oar. *Right*!"

Claire stroked with her left. Again, the boat began to swing.

"Claire! Both oars out of the water!"

"I can't do this," she wailed. But Scott's voice was calm. And she obeyed.

"You're doing great," Scott called. "Row with your right oar. Gently. Now both oars."

To her amazement, the boat straightened, then began to creep toward the mouth of the bay.

Stiff and silent, Errol stood by his motor, a figurehead-in-reverse, coaxing the fish along. A few yards, and it would be in the bottleneck.

Claire had found a rhythm now. The boat moved jerkily but steadily forward as Scott called commands.

She entered the bottleneck as the fish followed like a bull with a ring through its nose. The channel was fifteen feet long, three or four deep, with five feet of open water down the middle, and ten feet of weeds on either side. This would be the hardest part.

Night was closing, but there was still enough light. She could do this. She'd be okay.

"Almost there. Steady. Evenly," Scott coached. "Who says ghost trout won't bite?" he said as the boat nosed into open water.

◆ ◆ ◆

Whether the fish saw the weeds or simply tired of being led, without warning, it made a rush toward the trees.

"Oh shit! Don't row!" Errol barked at Claire. Line tore off his reel, burning his fingers when they tried to slow it down. Ten yards. Twenty. Thirty.

Into the backing. When his drag didn't slow the fish at all, he used his left palm to slow the reel, its handle a spinning blur. If that handle hit a finger, it could break bone.

Fifteen yards into the backing, and ten feet from the trees, the fish slowed, then stopped. Errol reeled as fast as he could. To his amazement, the fish swam leisurely back toward his boat.

Scott had ceased directing Claire, and sat motionless in his boat, quiet except for an occasional, "Holy shit!"

Errol relaxed a little. First runs were the worst. The boat was now in open water. Keep the fish there, and he could wear it down. He'd hang it in his living room where Pop Gunn would see. 20 lb Kamloops Trout Taken on 6X Tippet by Errol Wolfe. So much for *uncatchable*!

Fifteen yards away, his trophy made short, erratic runs, letting itself be coaxed gradually toward the boat.

Closer. Closer.

Errol's rod tip dove as the fish bulled back toward the beaver lodge. As Errol tried to maintain an ounce less pressure than the line could take, the fish surged forward into the backing again. Then, inches from the lodge, it stopped, and let itself be cranked toward the boat where Claire sat, oars flapping, as Scott called, "Steady. Steady . . ."

The fish could plunge into the weeds and snap the line at any time. But it did not.

Groping blind, Errol's hand closed on his landing net. He pictured how he'd lead the fish into the net, clamp the rod under his arm, slip his right hand under the mesh in case it broke, and lift his prize, dripping glory. Glory and vindication.

"He's tired!" Scott called. "He's three feet long!"

Working delicately, with patience and skill, Errol worked the ghost trout in. Not ghostly any more.

Closer. Closer.

The line went slack.

"Oh no!" Panic surged through Errol as he reeled frantically, praying the giant would pull back. Praying for a miracle.

"The fucker's gone," he wailed, feeling the life drain out of him. "For no damned reason. It's gone!"

"Son of a bitch!" Scott said.

Alone, Errol might have cried. Instead, he dropped onto the seat, face and body sagging, rod dangling from his hand.

Claire rushed to hug him. "Errol, I'm sorry. I tried. Errol, I tried."

The thought that this could be Claire's fault roused Errol enough to reel in.

His leader was intact. At the very end, a pig's-tail of curled monofilament showed where the fly had pulled off. His knot had failed. The knot which, he remembered now, he'd been too rushed to test.

"MOTHERFUCKER!"

Claire jumped back, looking terrified. Errol didn't care.

"Fifty-one weeks!" he roared. "Fifty-one cocksucking weeks I worked my balls off. For THIS!"

He seized his starter-handle like a python's neck, and yanked as if to rip off its head. The motor coughed, then roared as Claire scrambled to pull in the oars.

They shot through the bottleneck, out onto open lake. Errol saw the loons, and steered for them. They took to the air as, face frozen in despair, he closed in on camp like a kamikaze.

◆ ◆ ◆

Left alone, Scott fished mechanically. The ghost trout seemed to have spooked the other fish. Scott didn't care. He made a desultory cast toward the beaver lodge, and thought he glimpsed a human shape among the trees.

Then it was gone.

"Shadows," he said aloud. But thought, *Bearclaw*.

Alone in a small boat twenty yards from shore, Scott would be a sitting duck for anyone with a gun.

He reeled in fast, started his motor, and roared out of the bay. If Errol was leaving, he'd leave too, darkness be damned. The place would be too creepy with his friends gone, and Old Yellow-Eye lurking.

The dusk was thick when, minutes later, Scott rowed into their bay. A light in Errol's camper showed he was still here.

The light went out as Scott beached his boat. But the truck stayed.

Errol's boat was full of gear, just waiting for Bearclaw to steal. Right after he killed them in their sleep.

Trying not to scare himself, Scott grabbed an armful of Errol's gear and stowed it in his own cab. Losing that fish had to be tough. Errol's luck all day had been so bad, it was no wonder he'd acted like a tool.

When all the gear was safely stowed, Scott dragged both boats high up on shore. If someone moved them now, the noise should wake him.

Errol had brought along a shotgun, a pistol, and a full-sized ax. Scott's only weapons were his hatchet and fishing knife. He carried these to his camper, then locked himself inside. After a quick once-over with his wash-cloth, he climbed into his sleeping bag, placed the hatchet and knife in easy reach, and flicked off the light.

No love-cries came from his neighbors' truck that night.

FOURTH DAY

17

First light's chill gray had filled the camper when, groggy after another night's bad sleep, Errol came awake. Footsteps outside ...

He let his right hand slide from his sleeping bag into the boot he'd placed beside his head. His fingers touched cold steel.

Barely breathing, he eased his .22 pistol, then its loaded clip, out of his boot. Muffling the click under his sleeping bag, he inserted the clip.

The steps got closer. More than one person. That Indian and his friends? Or maybe worse.

Something shoved his camper, hard.

Gun raised, he burst out of his bag, yanked open the curtain, saw a monstrous snout, jerked back and, even as his brain registered "Cow," fell over Claire. Scrambling to get off of her, he rapped his head on a steel lantern and yelled, "Shit," just as—KA-WHAM!—a blast hit from all sides.

Claire screamed, thrashing under him.

"Oh Christ, are you hurt?" he wailed, rolling away onto his back.

"What's going on?" she squawked. Not hurt, apparently.

"It's okay," he said and, feeling no pain in his own body, realized it was true.

"Errol, what the fuck?" Scott yelled from outside. "All these cows ..."

Errol sat up, pistol in hand. "My fucking gun went off," he yelled. "It's okay."

Claire popped upright. "Your *gun*?!"

"Come on, Claire. It's no big deal."

"You left a loaded gun in here?!"

"You were worried about that nut-job. Bares-All. Anyway, the clip was out."

"Look at these cows," Scott yelled, outside. "Beat it, Bossy. This ain't the OK Corral."

Except for a small hole through the window screen, nothing was harmed. Errol had left the glass window open to let in air. Amazing luck.

Which Claire, of course, refused to see. "Jesus, Errol, you could've killed us," she said, glaring at him, then out the window.

"There's a million cows outside," he said.

"More like *six* cows." She turned from the window and offered a wry smile. "Well, I'm up."

He made a face of Brobdingnagian chagrin and hugged her, feeling his heart and hers both beating hard. "Sorry," he said. "I sucked the mop on that one."

Claire seemed inclined to drop the matter, thank the Lord. "Brrr. It's *cold*," she said, crawled back into her bag, and curled up tight.

As his heartbeat normalized, Errol realized he was shivering. "'s cold enough to freeze the nuts off a steel bridge," he said in an old-hillbilly voice as he pulled his long underwear on. Strange how perspective shifted with the time of day. Last night, losing the ghostie had meant the death of hope for his whole life. This morning, hope had clambered back. The giant trout were here, and they would bite. If he'd hooked one, he could hook more.

Even without them, he loved Oso Lake. Out here, he barely thought of work and Pop Gunn. Once-overs with his washcloth kept him cleaner than long showers in Spokane, where business greased his skin, and worry gave his sweat an acrid stink.

Chief Seattle'd said it all: White men must learn to live "in harmony with the Earth," or die of "spiritual starvation."

He'd felt starved for a long time.

Catching Claire's eye, he said, "Let's start over," then leaned down to kiss her. "Mornin', Babe."

"Mornin', Deadeye . . . Richard," she said; then, "Would you mind if I drove into town? We're out of things, I feel grungy . . ." She trailed off to indicate a list of woes.

Errol did *not* want her driving to town alone. She could get lost, or hurt, or in some other mess, with no way to contact him. Say that, though, and—especially after the gun thing—she'd be irate.

He could drive her, and wreck his fishing day. But forcing her to fish would also wreck the day. And she couldn't stay in camp alone. Not with that backwoods bag-man slinking around.

If she went to town, they wouldn't fight. She'd be pleased with him. They could have a sexy night.

"Okay," he told her. "Take the ax. Mark some trees, so you can find your way back."

"Good idea. Thanks," she said, and kissed him.

"You won't be lonely?" he asked as she snuggled up.

"If I am, I'll sketch. Or read a book."

"Come back by five. We'll be here by then," he said. "You want the pistol? Just in case?"

"The shotgun's behind the seat, right?"

He nodded.

"That's enough firepower." She smiled. "Don't worry. I'll be fine."

She looked so pretty in her down cocoon, he had to kiss her again. "I love you, Claire."

The brightness of her smile reminded him that he should tell her more. He would, he swore.

"I love you too, Errol," she said.

"Don't lose these, if you want to make it home." Extracting the truck keys from his parka, he pressed them into her hand, then pulled his orange sweatshirt over his head, kissed her again, and jumped out into the chilly dawn.

The cows, five grown ones and a calf, were wandering back up the road that must have led them into camp. With luck, they'd wander off into the woods, so Claire wouldn't need to squeeze past them.

"I love a shoot-out in the morning," Scott said over a cup of Tang.

Guilt flashed through Errol, remembering how he'd cast into Scott's fishing spots. The guilt increased when Scott told how he'd stowed their gear.

"You're a pal," Errol said. Then, more softly, "Jesus, I could've killed Claire."

"Were you shooting at those cows?"

Errol shook his head no. "I thought they were that Indian. Hairball, or whatever his name is. I got my gun out, and the fucking thing went off."

"You'd have smelled him before you heard him," Scott said. "He stinks like a mummy's bum."

Errol gave a snort. "Claire'll shoot *me* if I sleep with that gun again. But one of us should have it ready."

Scott shrugged. "Give it to me."

"Hold on," Errol said.

Claire was naked when he gaped the camper door. She made a show of covering with the sleeping bag. "Can't a girl have *any* privacy?"

Errol squelched an urge to jump her on the spot. But Scott was waiting. Not to mention the ghost trout. Which were as solid as *he* was.

Leaning to kiss her, he squeezed a breast, then grabbed his pistol and the extra box of shells. "There'll only be one gun in here tonight," he said, kissed her again, and climbed outside.

"Here you go," he said, and handed Scott the pistol, muzzle up.

Removing the clip, Scott placed the shells in his glove box, and shoved the pistol and clip under his seat. "They'll be right here," he said, and locked his truck.

"Here. I tied some more of these," he said, offering three leaderbugs to Errol.

He took them gladly. "Thanks, Wolverine."

"No problem, Grizz."

Errol placed the flies carefully in his fly box. Then, pulling the ice chest from his cab, he wolfed four slices of bread and a handful of high protein cereal, washing it down with water from one of his plastic jugs. He'd just finished making peanut butter sandwiches to bring for lunch when Claire popped out of the camper, truck keys twirling on one finger.

He trusted her, of course. And Winoma was no hotbed of Lotharios.

Still, he was glad she'd worn her old green sweatpants and a gray sweatshirt, and hadn't curled her hair.

"Got what you need out of the truck?" she called.

"Think so," he said. "Be sure and come back right at five. I don't want you waiting here alone. Or trying to find this place at night."

She nodded, hopped into the truck, and fired it up. "I'm off," she said, blew Errol a kiss, and bounced away.

"Bring back some tuna. And honey. And ice," Errol called. "And don't get lost!"

But she was gone.

"Big City calls," he told Scott. "Got to exercise that shopping gene."

Scott snorted a laugh as the two lugged their gear to their boats.

"I packed this in case we fish Secret Lake." Errol coined the name as he dumped a deflated rubber boat into the bow of his aluminum one.

"Should I bring mine?"

"We'll fit in one," Errol said. "Why lug more crap?" A moment later, he shoved off, then yanked his motor into life. "Come on, Wolverine. The bite is on!"

"Anchors away," Scott called as his own motor roared.

"Hurrah, hurrah, hurrah for the lowly fish!" Errol boomed.

Scott joined the song as the boats chugged off into a morning mist already lifting to reveal a blue, pink, and silver mother-of-pearl sky.

The lake felt, now, like an old friend: the crystal water, the silt bottom, the scribbled tracks of the big snails, or whatever they were. Errol could marvel and enjoy these things even as he motored straight to Old Man's Bay.

No old man. Also, no hatching insects. And no fish.

The same proved true for Beaver Bay, site of last night's ghost trout debacle.

"Ready to try Secret Lake?" Errol said after a fishless half-hour.

"Hell yes," Scott said. "I'm pinin' for a ghostie."

"Pack it in then, Tex," Errol said.

They raised their anchors and, Errol in the lead, rowed past the beaver lodge and into the drowned trees.

18

Scott picked his way carefully, dodging most branches, but smacking into some. Oars would be sure to hang up here, so he pulled them into his boat and used his hands, moving tree-to-tree like an amphibious monkey as, Errol still in the lead, they squeezed into a shallow slough.

"There's the dam." Errol pointed to a wall of sticks, water surging through in spots. As if, Scott thought, the beavers had tried to keep something out. Tried, and failed.

Shaded by dead and dying trees, this place made Scott think of a colder Everglades. Any second a cottonmouth might slide into his boat, or a hat-sized spider drop out of the trees.

The water here was barely three feet deep, the bottom covered with the green-black goo from which the Spirit-of-the-Lake had floated up—the same way, Scott recalled, it had floated into last night's dreams. The dying deer had been there, too. And Sara.

And Claire. He remembered too well how she had slid into his bag, her bare backside hot against him. He'd wakened like a panicked thirteen-year-old, stripping off his boxers in the dark, trying to minimize the mess.

For better and worse, Mom wasn't there to check his sheets.

Good thing Errol didn't know about the dream, Scott thought as they neared the beaver dam.

"We walk from here," Errol called, and with Scott following behind, half-pushed, half-poled toward the edge of the slough.

Scott waited in his aluminum boat while Errol stuffed his inflatable boat into a backpack, shouldered it, scooped up his rod and collapsible plastic oars, then, wearing the same kind of calf-high pac boots as Scott, stepped from his boat into a foot of brown water.

"Hope you wore your rubbers, son," Errol said. Tying his boat to a leafless bush on shore, he raised his foot to shake one muddy boot at Scott. "Wait! Not there!" he yelled just as Scott stepped from his boat and plunged into deep muck.

"Shit!" Scott's scream was instinctive. So was grabbing his boat, though his struggles to get back in nearly tipped it. His legs had gone instantly numb, as if something had sucked out all their heat. His body shuddered like a rat bit by a snake: strength draining fast.

"Errol . . ." A membrane had dropped between him and the world. He couldn't breathe. Could barely hear Errol yell, "Relax. Let your legs float up. Hold on!"

The Spirit-of-the-Lake had him, its dead weight dragging him down.

Errol clattered to his own boat and jumped in. Arms held out like a tight-rope walker, he ran the length of his boat, then leapt into Scott's.

The impact jarred Scott's grip loose from his boat. Arms flailing free, he felt himself pulled toward some underwater hell.

"Kick!" Errol yelled, stretching out his hand. "Let your legs float up and *kick*!"

Somehow, Scott caught or was caught by Errol's big hand. His legs waved feebly while Errol, leaning back as if to beach a battleship, hauled him—squirming, shimmying, worming painfully—back into his boat.

Dripping black ooze from the armpits down, Scott lay panting, feeling the Spirit's world retreat like a snail into its shell.

"Something grabbed me," he gasped, shivering. "I swear."

"I know," Errol said. "Freezing-ass cold, sucking muck."

Scott lay a moment, letting the truth sink in: *That's all it was.*

"Pieces of feces." Trying to stop his teeth from chattering, he sat. "That's twice you've saved my ass."

The other time, he'd tripped while wading the Snoqualmie River. Help-less in chest waders, he'd felt the current dragging him away. But Errol was there. Errol, braced like a boulder. Errol, risking his life and his favorite steelhead rod, stretching it out as far as it would reach. Scott vividly recalled grabbing the rod tip, feeling his feet touch bottom and his death-drift stop.

That was the first time his teeth actually chattered. This was the second as, with Errol's help, he dragged his boat to drier ground, and tied it to the limb of a short, sturdy tree.

Always carry extra clothes, Errol had preached from the first time they fished together. Now Scott opened his dry-bag and, standing in his boat, began to change.

His shaking hands could barely peel off his wet things. But once his spare sweatshirt was on, the shivers started to subside.

"Is that a penis, or a strawberry on a toothpick?" Errol jeered.

"Tip of the iceberg," Scott said as he squirmed into old longjohns ripped in the crotch, but mercifully dry.

"More like ice *sliver*," Errol shot back, giving Scott a shove that nearly knocked him down as he tried to pull up his pants.

Scott recalled that other shove that had slammed him into his crippled Ford, and down onto the street.

Errol had just made amends for that, and a lot more!

Upending his boots, Scott watched black water squizzle onto blacker mud. Good thing he'd dressed to hike. If he'd worn waders, they'd have filled. Errol might not have been able to pull him out.

"I've got spare everything but boots," he said, pulling his wet ones back onto his dry-socked feet. Standing, he tugged his stocking cap down on his head, stamped his feet to get blood flowing, and stepped carefully out of the boat. He felt good. No, better than good. What was an adventure without peril to spice things up?

"Okay," he said. "Ready to rock"

Errol gestured like a maître d'—"Right this way, Sir"—and led the way around a smaller, shallower slough until they came to a yard-wide creek with, as Errol had said, a deer trail following it.

Scott looked for *his* deer. Which, of course, wasn't there.

"Was that quicksand back there?" he said.

"More like mud slurry," Errol said. "But it could suck you down as fast as Vicki Lee."

"Ah, Vicki of the Velvet Tonsils," Scott said.

"Wonder what happened to her," Errol said.

"Last time I saw her, she'd found Jesus."

"You're kidding!" Errol looked back at Scott, theatrically appalled. "Where'd she find *him*?"

"Dunkin' Donuts, from the look of her," Scott said.

Errol shook his head mournfully as he trudged forward. "What a waste. Like a strip show at the Braille Institute."

Dr. Zepeda would have called that joke "insensitive"—which it would have been, if a blind person had been there to hear. Since one had not, the bad taste made Scott laugh more as the trail entered thick woods. The creek was maybe five feet wide now, choked with weeds that waved in the current like mermaid hair.

"Damn these wet boots," Scott said. "You could crush my feet and ice your lemonade."

"That's a grim thought," Errol said. "Spoil good lemonade." After a few steps, he announced, "Good thing you've got your hat. If your brain gets cold: presto hypothermia."

Scott snickered as they walked. "*Brain*'s a funny word," he said.

"Claire and I checked into a motel one time as Reverend and Mrs. Brain," Errol said.

Scott knew the story. But he laughed, and Errol went on. "I hate a cold brain. Guys have been found dead in the snow, right outside warm cabins. Their brains got too cold to work, so they sat down and died."

"Lots of people's brains don't work, and they don't die," Scott said.

"Does seem unfair," Errol said. "Hey! I've got a joke."

"Two inches isn't funny."

"No," Errol said. "But a foot-and-a-half *is*."

Scott laughed, then Errol joined in. The good old days were surging back.

"Come on, Shitheap Son of Colon," Scott commanded, "Tell the joke."

"Okay." Errol paused to build anticipation. "Why did Helen Keller masturbate with her left hand?"

"Got me."

"She used the right to moan."

The joke was old, but Scott laughed anyway. Following Errol through the woods, he was trying to remember a joke about a Catholic, a Muslim, and a Jew in a whorehouse when Errol said, "There she is! Secret Lake!"

Sure enough, water was glinting through the trees.

"Swarming with twenty-pounders, I hope," Scott said.

Errol picked up speed. "That was a nice fish last night."

Now that Errol had broached the subject, Scott could comment. "Nice is right. I've never hooked a trout half that big."

"Ghost my ass. I nearly had him."

"You played him perfectly," Scott said. "Claire looked ready to shit-hem-orrhage. But she did okay."

Scott found that, after last night's dream, he felt slimy saying Claire's name.

Errol, never guessing, sighed like a man sipping fine wine. "She did better than okay." He slowed his pace, so Scott and he were side-by-side. "She's got it all," he said. "Looks, brains, money, great in bed. If she only wanted kids!"

Was this one of the *problems* Claire had mentioned?

"Pregnancy's tough on a woman's body," Scott said.

"That's what *she* says!" Errol pulled off his stocking cap, and jammed it in his coat pocket. "Hell, you exercise and get your figure back."

"When did you start wanting kids?"

"When I was in theater, I couldn't afford 'em," Errol said. "Now I've got a good job, a little cash . . ."

"Claire says no?"

"She says she's *not ready*. Which I'm pretty sure means *not in this life-time*. She's an only child, like us. Not big on self-sacrifice." He squinched his mouth as if he'd swallowed a bug. "Doctors call a thirty-five-year-old pregnant woman *elderly*. Claire's almost thirty-three." Errol seemed about to stop and launch a tirade, then walked on. "She's an *artiste manqué* like my mom."

"Maybe I'm a troglodyte," he said after a few more strides. "But I think it's sick to give up motherhood for a few less stretch marks on a body that'll crap out anyway."

"She must love hearing that," Scott said.

Errol turned his head back to display a rueful face. "Like a hot-coffee enema. I'm a genius at pissing her off."

"The biological clock bongs pretty loud," Scott said. "Maybe she'll hear it, if you back off."

"I'll do that," Errol said. "Once I get a personality transplant."

The closer they got to the lake, the more branches had grown across the trail. Errol had to bend each one back, then hold it so as not to whack Scott's face. "You were always good with women," he said, bending a spruce limb. "I nailed 'em, but you made 'em want to stay."

Scott thought of Sara. "I kinda lost the knack."

Errol gave a snort. "Women!"

"One thing I've learned," Scott said. "Women who know they're beautiful"—he almost said *like Claire*—"want to be more."

"Claire *is* more. She knows I think she is."

"Errol," Scott said with a warmth that startled him, "she's in town, and you're with *me*! If I had a woman like her, I don't care if she didn't know a fly line from an airline, I'd be with *her*."

Errol shook his head no. Emphatically. "You *think* you would," he said. "I spend fifty-one weeks a year doing what Claire wants. She can spend a week . . . Christ chloroformed, look at those rises!"

The creek flowed out of a small inlet, maybe fifty yards across. And all fifty were boiling with fish.

Errol ran the last few yards, and danced on the shore. "Just like yesterday!"

Dumping his pack on the ground, he yanked out his inflatable boat and a plastic pump. "I'd suggest a Mosquito," he deadpanned. "Any size."

"Why a Mosquito?" Scott deadpanned back as he smashed one on his face. He pulled his stocking cap down as far as it would go, zipped his parka and, fanning his face to keep the little vampires at bay, tried to rig up while the air around him whined.

Watching Errol's right arm piston as he pumped his boat, Scott felt a surge of admiration that was close to love. Sweat, sunburn, matted hair, and stubble worked like makeup on his friend. He was the All-American superstud Scott had always wanted to be. There was more life in Errol, more talent and more drive than in ten "regular" guys. That's why their fight had hurt so much. A beatdown by cops who didn't know you was one thing. A beatdown by your best friend was something else.

"Want me to rig you, Grizz?" Scott asked.

"Yeah. Thanks," Errol said, huffing as he pumped.

The lake's surface was boiling like a Jacuzzi when Errol stood up. "Ready to rock!"

Scott nodded. "I gave you a #18 Mosquito. Check the knot."

"I trust you," Errol said, tossed his boat in the water, the oars and pump in the boat, then jumped in himself. He tied the oars into their oarlocks and took the rods from Scott. "Anchors away."

Scott placed both hands beside the oarlocks, then gave a shove that propelled him into the boat, and the boat away from shore. Errol flailed the oars, and they were off.

"*Two-man boat* my hefty ass," Errol said. "More like two zygotes."

"It's okay," Scott said. "We've done it before."

Errol, though, had been thinner, before. Even sitting cross-legged, Scott could barely squeeze into the boat. Soon their legs would require "stretching" in each other's laps, faces, chests and, if they weren't careful, groins. Casting would be one-at-a-time, the non-caster's face pressed to his knees to avoid a scalp ornament.

Still, these problems paled next to the advantage of fishing from a boat. Errol's fly had barely touched water when a fish sucked it down. Scott's fly bounced twice among the boils before a trout engulfed it with a splash.

"A double!" Errol crowed as both fish jumped and ran, both men twisting, turning, fighting not to foul each other until, with enough shouting, splashing, cursing, and laughing for ten men, each brought his fish in.

These were darker than Oso's fish, their backs gray-black, not green. A bright pink stripe swept down their sides.

"Marked like my ghostie," Errol said, and threw his fish back with a splash.

Leaving his catch in the lake, Scott gripped his fly, gave a quick twist, and the freed trout flashed away.

There was, technically, a five trout catch limit per day. That limit, though, was for bumblers who couldn't release a fish without killing it. Scott and Errol caught and released at least a dozen one-to-two-pounders until, abruptly, bites from fish and mosquitoes both stopped.

"Not too shabby," Scott said as, legs in one another's laps, the men sat grinning.

"Now we're warmed up, how 'bout we try for ghosties?" Errol said.

"One of us needs to fish deep."

"I'm rowing," Errol said. "*You* change lines."

Scott's grimace acknowledged this as painful but fair. A breeze was making his fly dance, agile as a real mosquito, out of reach. It was a feat to catch it without hooking Errol, the oars, or worst of all, the boat, which it could pop.

Once Scott had seized his fly and clipped it off, he had to remove his spool of floating line. Then, as the boat bounced in heavier waves, he had to lock his spool of sinking line onto his reel without stabbing Errol in the eye. To feed the new line through all eight guides on his rod, he had to shove his rod butt out over the water. This plunged his reel into the lake so that, pulled back into the boat, it dripped all over Errol, who swore at Scott, who laughed and dropped the leader at the final guide, and had to redo everything as Errol jeered.

Finally, Scott said, "There! Let's go."

Errol positioned his own reel in his lap, settled his rod on Scott's knees, and started to row around the shore of Secret Lake.

19

Watching camp give way to forest in her rear view mirrors, Claire wished that she had stayed with the men. The cratered road felt ready to jolt the truck apart. The woods looked eager to overrun the road and swallow her. Yet she wasn't sad to leave the maleness of the camp. Half the time the guys seemed to be thinking, "Yuck, a girl." *Sophomoric* was being generous.

On the other hand, that's how men were. Egyptian workmen had carved dirty pictures when not building pyramids. It was good for Errol to play sophomore again. These days, he barely played at all.

Thinking of Errol, her mind felt like a tennis ball. She adored him; she couldn't stand him. They'd make it; there was no hope. Back and forth. Back and forth.

Her heart jumped as something cat-like flashed across the road.

"I'm safer here than sleeping with Errol's gun," she told herself. But she had to stay alert. These roads were a maze. Fail to make good mental notes, and she might not find her way back.

Lucky she had a good sense of direction and a great eye for detail. She had no trouble finding unusual rocks, trees, or stumps to mark her route— no trouble until, when she thought she should have reached the highway, she came to a junction with no special mark at all.

She hated to leave the safety of the truck. But she put it in neutral, engaged the emergency brake, pulled out Errol's ax, and hacked a big chunk from a tree a few feet into what she prayed was the right road.

She viewed the tree from several angles, making sure the white tree-flesh was obvious from both directions. Then, as she turned back to the truck, something flashed yellow in the trees.

She raised her ax, fighting to hold it steady in her shaking hands. When nothing charged at her, she backed up to the truck, scrambled in, and floored it.

The truck lunged ahead, then died.

"Oh no," she moaned. Hands shaking harder, she released the emergency brake. Errol scorned automatic transmissions, so she had to push the clutch in and turn the key.

The engine coughed, coughed, started up.

"Come *on*," she prayed, popped the clutch, and roared away.

A minute later, except for the jolting of the truck, she'd stopped shaking. She could laugh at herself now. If Bearclaw had been there, he would have jumped her.

If Errol had been there, he would have laughed.

These woods would make anyone feel fearful and frail. Shapes seemed to glide among the trees. Rodents, not all tiny, zipped across the road. A deer with short, spike-horns nearly ran into the truck, and then was gone.

Fear of hitting a cow or deer made sense. But Bearclaw, with his bad leg, couldn't glide or zip or bound. Scott was right: he was a backwoods bagman, with a smell that made your standard derelict seem drenched in Chanel.

Maybe *that's* what scared her most: not the power of a Vampire King, but the death-stink of Nosferatu.

Her whole body sighed with relief when, up ahead, she saw her dirt road turn to gravel, then in half a mile, blacktop. She stopped the truck, then made herself get out and mark another tree. Done with that, she walked calmly back to the truck and drove for town.

In thirty minutes, she was there.

She'd never heard of *Sunoco*. But it was a gas station, so she pulled in. Errol would be pleased if she gassed up.

One other car was at the pump, two attendants bending over it. Or rather, she saw as she pulled in, one attendant—Native, with a Sunoco hat—and the car's pimple-faced white owner.

She pulled up opposite the other car, popped open her gas flap, and pulled her keys from the ignition. She felt, as she stepped out of the truck, much the way she'd felt leaving the plane at Heathrow in London, on her own for the first time in her life.

"Is this self-service?" she asked the attendant.

"I'll take care of it," he said.

"Thank you. Fill it with Premium, please."

The man gave an impudent, gap-toothed smile and a two-fingered salute.

"Is the ladies room open?" she asked.

"Yes, ma'am," came the reply, with a smirk from pimple-face.

She walked toward the restrooms, willing herself to ignore rustic lechery. That didn't stop her from feeling the men's eyes, and flushing with embarrassment.

The restroom was dingy, but smelled clean. The soap dispenser worked. There was a stack of paper towels and a full roll of toilet tissue. The hot water was hot. All things considered, the place was a godsend.

She wet a paper towel, soaped it, and washed her face and neck. She would have liked a longer scrub, but feared to leave the truck too long. The attendant could flatten her tires, start an oil leak, or do something else that would cost money and get Errol on her case. She could wash more thoroughly at Howdy Do's.

Working carefully, she made a tissue toilet seat, then sat. Nothing like camping to make a girl appreciate a real commode.

It still amazed her how men—excluding her dad—seemed obsessed with bathroom functions. "Rejection of socialization and the Rule of Mom," Dr. Lindner had labeled the phenomenon back in Psych 101. Claire and her friends joked that males had a *disgusting gene* at least as potent as females' *shopping* one.

She smiled at this, and was just ready to stand when something thudded against the restroom wall, followed by a muffled laugh.

She made herself sit still, eyes scrutinizing the chipped yellow wall. Behind a knothole above her head and to the right, something moved!

Yanking up her pants, she dashed outside. Pimple-face's car was still there, neither he nor the attendant in sight. A gas nozzle stuck out of her tank.

She stormed to the truck, and had just yanked the nozzle out when, not even trying to suppress their grins, the two men ambled toward her.

She placed the nozzle back onto the pump, screwed on her gas cap, jumped in the truck, and turned it on.

"That's $37.68," the Native said, ambling up while his friend stopped a few steps back, and smirked.

"I usually charge more. Run and whack off while the memory's fresh," she said, and roared from the station into the street.

Her heart was thudding. Excitement, not fear. This was the Claire she liked: a proper daughter of Bob Gunn. She felt so good that, after stocking up on supplies at Big Value, which should have been called Big Larceny, she decided to eat breakfast, then have a drink before attempting Serious Art.

Locking her two overpriced sacks in the camper, she drove to Howdy Do's.

The place was busy. Careful not to scratch Errol's truck, she squeezed into the last spot in the parking lot, locked the truck, and walked into the eatery. While people jostled in and out, she spied a just-freed-up table, and sat down. When the same waitress she'd asked about the phone said, "Know what you want, hon?" Claire managed to say, with a straight face, "I'll have the Log Master, please."

Two huge pancakes, two scrambled eggs, plus bacon, sausages, and toast with strawberry jam, the Log Master contained more fat than she normally ate in a week. But what were vacations for, if not to overeat?

She chewed slowly, savoring the pancakes, eggs, and bacon—delectable, compared to camping fare—but steering clear of the gray-green sausages. Leaving them to seep grease onto her plate, she wiped her mouth with her napkin, and allowed herself a satiated sigh.

The morning rush had died, leaving only her and, at a table across the room, an old couple hissing like adders back and forth. Claire ordered a refill of coffee, then sat back, sipping happily as she read the book she'd brought from home, *The Joy of Dogs*. Errol had claimed, "Dogs are substitute babies." But he'd agreed they would get one when they got home.

"Maybe it'll kick-start your mothering instincts," he'd said.

She'd forced a smile, and said, "You never know."

Her watch read 11:19 when she stood to go. Five seemed a long ways away. But if she got too bored, she could drive back to camp, and when the men came in, pretend she'd just arrived. If by some chance Bearclaw showed up, she'd drive away. Or run him down.

That idea shocked her. And made her smile. She'd never have thought *that* in Spokane.

She would have sold her soul for a hot shower, but settled for a full-body soap-on-paper-towel wipe-down inside a toilet stall at Howdy Do's. Feeling cleaner than she had since leaving home, she walked to her truck, climbed in the camper, and changed into jeans and her purple Pendleton. After applying just enough makeup for self-respect, she locked the camper door and drove to Trixie's Bar.

Errol would have a mental hernia if he knew she'd gone alone into a logger bar. But she refused to be controlled by his unreasonableness. One drink would clear her system long before she got to camp.

The beat-up cars and pickups parked outside Trixie's weren't the wheels of Beautiful People. No problem. Even Canadian chainsaw-murderers were probably polite. In any case, she could take care of herself.

As she pulled open Trixie's door, a stale-tobacco stench hit simultaneously with the jukebox whining of some country swain. When the door slapped shut behind her, the room went so dark, she nearly fled. Instead, she steeled her nerves and, once she could see, picked her way toward the bar.

On the far left, two logger-types huddled with the bartender.

She chose a stool on the far right.

One of the loggers said something she couldn't hear. All three men laughed. Then the bartender clomped toward her: a short, heavyset man with a thin beard that failed to strengthen his weak chin.

"What can I do you for?" he asked, voice sounding tired and gentle, not the Popeye-gravel she'd expected.

"An apple martini would be nice."

The man shook his head wearily. "Sorry. We're fresh out of those."

Had she embarrassed him? Was he sneering at the pretentious Yank? *It doesn't matter*, she thought, but said aloud, "How 'bout a Tequila sunrise?"

She feared he'd be fresh out of them, too. But he nodded, and moved off to pour the drink.

She opened her wallet when he set down the glass. "What do I owe?"

"Fellows over there took care of it," he said, looking down to wipe the bar in front of her.

Claire couldn't help glancing the *fellows'* way. This gave both men license to wave.

She wished, now, that she'd skipped the makeup. Still, in a slutty way, the attention felt good.

"Tell them 'thank you,'" she said. "But I'd rather pay. How much, please?"

The bartender looked disconcerted. "Four fifty."

Claire laid a five-dollar bill, US, on the bar, picked up her drink, and let her eyes explore the room.

In one corner, lit by a dim red candle in the middle of their table, a middle-aged couple kissed. The man's hand, she saw, was underneath the woman's skirt. *There's a painting*, she thought, and tried to memorize the scene.

Maybe she *should* quit Pine Hills. Shoot for a job teaching art at a high school . . .

The only other people in the bar were three men drinking longneck beers at a table by the wall. They were staring at her, so she looked away, then nearly jumped off her stool when a voice said, almost in her ear, "What's the matter, Beautiful? Don't like to drink with Indians, eh?"

One of the two men from the bar had crept up and was standing much too close. His hair was dark, but his features were European.

He mistook fear for anger, because he said, "Don't get mad. I just hate to see a lady drink alone."

"That's nice of you," she said as calmly as she could. "But I'm fine."

"I can see that," the man said with a leer that made her want to kick him where it hurt. "Hey, Jerry." He looked at the bartender. "Tell her about folks who drink alone."

The way he said *aboot* was pure Canadian.

"Give it a rest, Nick," the bartender said. "She's not your type."

"Sure she is." Nick moved closer and, breathing fumes of alcohol, snaked his arm around her waist. She wanted to yank away, but she was frozen. Petrified.

"Back off, Nick."

The deep voice, coming from right beside her, restored her power of movement.

No need for it now. Nick's arm was gone.

"I was just horsin' around, Ted," Nick told the man who'd spoken. Where had he come from? With his work boots, jeans, and red plaid shirt—did men up here wear anything but plaid?—the new man looked like a Central Casting Lumberjack. And not the Monty Python kind. He was almost as tall as Errol. Broad in the chest and slim-waisted like Errol used to be. Handsome in a bearded, Paul Bunyan way.

"He's harmless," *Ted* said in his deep voice as Nick slunk back to his friends. "Don't see many women like you in here."

She was tempted to shoot back an irate, "In what way *like me*?" But that would just encourage him. She was trying to decide what she *should* say when the door let in a blast of sun. In its center, like a fire demon: Jim Bearclaw.

"You!" She jumped up, pointed, and with no idea what she'd do if she caught him, lunged his way.

He jumped back. The door slammed shut.

Claire yanked it open and rushed outside.

The man was halfway down the block, sprinting away. No limp that she could see.

Behind her, the door opened and Ted strode out. "Whatcha want with Tom Tworivers?"

"His name's not Bearclaw?!"

"Not hardly," Ted said. "Where'd you hear about Bearclaw?"

Coming from Ted, *aboot* was cute.

"Where does this *Tom Tworivers* live?" Claire demanded.

Ted pointed down the shabby street. "Couple of blocks that way." He flashed a waggish, lady-killer grin. "If you're interested, I gotta warn you, he's a little weak upstairs."

Claire felt a jingly fool's cap settle on her head. "Bearclaw was older," she said.

"A *lot* older. Bearclaw was an old-time medicine man."

"You're kidding."

Ted shook his head no. "With a wooden leg, people say."

"Was he . . ." Claire tried to seem unfazed. "Dangerous?"

"He chopped up a few white women. Claimed some Bear God ate 'em."

"I'd call that dangerous," she said. Jim Bearclaw had talked of a Bear God.

"Don't worry," Ted said. "That was a hundred years ago."

Claire made a stab at humor. "He must've had mother issues."

Ted shrugged. "He hated whites. And women were, you know, the source. He thought we wrecked things for his people." Raising half of his top lip, Ted gave an Elvis sneer-grin. "Why would he think that?"

"What happened to him?"

Ted looked about to spit, then caught Claire's eye and swallowed instead. "He said no rope could hang him. Bad call." Cocking his head to one side, he caricatured a hanged-man face. "Somebody told you he's Bearclaw?"

Claire nodded, trying to stay calm. "I thought your friend Tom was him."

"All First Nations look alike?"

"No!" Protesting too much? "I'm sorry I scared him."

"He'll get over it. Prob'ly tellin' all his friends this smokin' white-eyes tried to rape him."

Claire didn't like the sound of *rape* on this man's tongue.

"Did your guy have a scarred-up face?" Ted asked. "And stink?"

"He did!"

"That's Jim McGee!" He said it like the punch line of a joke.

"Who's Jim McGee?"

"A full-on head case." Ted made the finger-rotating-around-his-ear crazy sign. "He dragged his ass up from the States two, three years back. He wanted logging work, but he's all crippled up. Truck-driving accident, he says."

Ted inched closer to Claire, and lowered his voice. "He also says Bearclaw was his great-great-grampa."

Claire inched away. "Is he . . . violent?"

"Only to your nose." Ted thrust his hands in his back pockets, then yanked them out. "Another thing—that fool's as white as you and me. First Nations here just laugh at him. 'Specially since he started greasin' his hair." The way Ted pinched his nose and squinched his face made him look like a little boy. "Bear grease is hard to come by, so he uses bacon fat."

Claire was starting to feel better. Not good, but better. "He should've picked a different name. Grizzly Claw's got a nice ring."

Ted looked confused.

"A bearclaw's a kind of sweetroll in the States," she explained. "It's like naming yourself Apple Fritter."

Ted shrugged amiably. "Whatever you say." He held out his hand. "I'm Ted Brumley, speakin' of names."

Brumley's hand was as big as Errol's, but calloused and hard. She took it briefly, then let go. "Claire Wolfe," she said. "Thanks for saving me in there."

"Any time." Ted Brumley grinned. "You still thirsty?"

Claire teetered on a precipice. Errol would see what she was doing as virtual adultery. On the other hand, she still had hours to kill. Was it better to have a drink with Ted, or spend the time resenting Errol?

"I left my drink in the bar," she finally said.

"Let's find it, eh?"

"Canadians *do* say 'eh' a lot, eh?" she said, startled by her own effrontery.

Ted didn't seem to mind. "If we only had one word, it would be 'eh,'" he said, and pushed open Trixie's door.

Claire hesitated for a microsecond, then walked inside, feeling Ted close behind. In Washington, loggers ranked with musicians in disreputableness. She assumed it was the same in Canada. This logger, though, seemed nice enough. And he *had* rescued her.

Seeing Nick still at the bar, she felt ashamed: caught on a movie date by the boy she'd told, *I have to study.* He probably was thinking, *Racist bitch.* All she could do now was avoid his eyes.

Her drink, naturally, was gone.

"She'll have another," Ted told the bartender.

She started to protest, but let it go.

"How'd you meet McGee?" Ted asked.

"My husband and I met him in the woods." She was glad to establish the *husband*.

"Will your *husband* mind you drinkin' with me?"

"Not one drink," she said, then added, "I've got to meet him in an hour."

"Fisherman?"

She nodded.

"Where you stayin'?"

She balked, then told the truth. "Oso Lake."

The look on his face said, *Not good.*

"What's wrong with Oso Lake?" she said. Maybe he knew a better place. Errol would love some insider information.

"Fishin's great out there," Ted said.

"But what?"

"Nothin'," he said, then threw in, "A girl got killed at the campground last fall."

"Killed?!" Claire's head felt light, as if a doctor had said *Cancer.* "Killed how?"

"Boyfriend." Ted seemed ready to say more, then stopped.

"That's terrible," Claire said. But she thought, *Not Bearclaw. Good.*

"He hanged himself in jail," Ted went on.

She tried to sound implacable. Like Errol. "That's good. I guess."

"It would've been. Except he got away."

"Oh . . ." She almost said *shit*, but stopped herself. Maintain some class.

"My brother-in-law's RCMP. Royal Canadian Mounted Police," Ted explained. "He said the guy played possum when they cut him down, then knocked a guard over the head and ran away." He lowered his voice and moved closer. "They hushed that up. Anyway, it was twenty below outside. He probably hid somewhere, and turned into a popsicle."

The thought of that was less awful than the thought of him hiding near the Oso Lake campground.

The drink, Claire knew, was going to her head. Ted was starting to look good.

"Like a refill?" he said.

He wasn't smooth or educated. And he didn't brush his teeth, she decided as his breath assailed her face. But he seemed confident. The local ladies' man.

"No thanks," she said. "One more, I won't be able stand up."

"That's okay," he said. "I'd like you just fine lyin' down."

20

"Secret Lake" proved a lot bigger than it looked. Bays bordered bays that led to other bays. Coves led to shallows that bled into swamps. The water, which was almost black, struck Scott as perfect for "ghost" trout.

The black color came, apparently, from algae: rod-shaped, like bacillus bacteria, Scott discovered when he scooped up a handful. If Oso Lake was sick, *this* lake might be why. The fact that it wasn't on his map made him feel it could have leapt out of nowhere, like the ghost trout.

That was impossible. Still, he was trying to isolate one of the rod-shaped algae when a screech made him spill his specimens. His head shot up just in time to see Errol's rod buck, and relax.

"God *damn* it! Caught my reel handle on my fucking knee," Errol said, and pulled in a flyless leader.

"Fish or snag?" Scott asked.

"Felt like another ghostie."

"Jesus!"

"He ain't exactly smiling on me," Errol said, and tied on another leader-bug.

The next strike came from the wind. Errol had been rowing into the same breeze that had routed the mosquitoes. Now that breeze was joined by its big brother. Then the whole family swept in. Two-foot swells rolled across the lake. Errol's most energetic rowing couldn't keep the boat from blowing back.

"Lay down, wind, in the name of Jaysus!" he yelled, oars attacking each wave like a new enemy. But when a big one broke over his bow, he yelled, "Wet ass! Wet ass! Bring her about," then, oars flailing, sprinted with the wind toward shore.

As the boat neared land, a large bird burst from the evergreens.

"An osprey! No . . . cool! A bald eagle!" Scott proclaimed as the white-head-ed raptor flapped up and, on the high wind, soared away.

"Not many of *them* left in the States," Errol said, still rowing hard.

Scott watched the bird grow small above what looked like endless woods. "The American Bird," he said. "Gone with the American Dream."

"Gimme a break, Pompus Poeticus," Errol said. "No, gimme a hand."

Dropping the oars—Scott hoped they were tied on tight—Errol grabbed a pine sapling that jutted from the shore. Scott seized the oars and, flailing them like awkward legs, pushed, splashed, and thrust the boat aground. As fast as his cramped thighs would allow, he scrambled out of the boat, gripped the trailing painter-line, then pulled everything, including Errol, out of the water and onto solid ground.

Errol unfolded his legs slowly, then half-stepped, half-fell out of the boat and stood with Scott, groaning and stretching. Luckily, the wind wasn't cold. Errol made a show of feeling his wet rear, then plopped down in a bare spot on the bank. Scott, whose rear was also wet, tied the boat to a small tree, placed a large, flat rock inside to help anchor it, then dropped down beside his friend, two feet from the forest's wall of trees.

Waves had begun to whitecap on the lake.

"Wouldn't want to sink in that," Errol said.

Scott locked his hands behind his head, and stared up at the sky: a purple blue, streaked with high clouds. "Douchebag wind," he said. "You think you're on the verge of something great, and a wind pops up. 'Sorry, not for you.'"

"Yeah," Errol said, "a guy catches a lot of bowfins."

When Scott didn't comment, Errol tried again. "Life's full of bowfins."

"Okay, okay," Scott groaned. "What's a 'bowfin'?"

Errol rubbed his hands, miming *delighted to say*. "Many miles north of Chicago lies a land of lakes teeming with walleye, pike, pickerel, and as you've seen, muskellunge."

Scott thought of the huge stuffed musky that had hung on Errol's apart-ment wall.

"These lakes have muddy bottoms. Oozy, festering places full of foulness and fish shit. Therein the bowfin abides."

Big as he was, Errol seemed to swell: half Roman orator, half quiz show host.

"These so-called *fish* have an eel's body, a long dorsal fin, and a great, hideous head," Errol went on. "You think you've got a musky, then crank in humiliation."

Now Scott remembered about bowfins. He and Errol had had this same talk years before.

"It's like a toadfish," Scott said. "I caught one in Galveston. They live in muck and eat whatever loathsomeness rains down."

"Like oceanic congressmen," Errol said.

Scott snickered. "I caught a toadfish the day Dad took me fishing," he said. "The *only* day."

"At least you had a dad."

"At least your sperm-source was a Rhodes scholar."

"Mom *says* he was a Rhodes Scholar. She only knew him for a night."

"She should have married that guy who took you musky fishing," Scott said.

"That would've meant moving east. No more equity waiver stardom in Bellingham," Errol said, then hawked, and spit into the woods.

"Debonair," Scott said.

"Eloquent," Errol fired back. "That trip with *Uncle* Dave was once-in-a-lifetime luck."

"My dad considered fishing unpaid work," Scott said. "He wasn't big on fun."

Scott had been twelve the day his father came home early from "the office," reeking of alcohol. He'd dropped his short, muscular body into his chair, and announced, "I guess that's that."

"What happened, Frank?" his mom said, hurrying out of the kitchen.

"Metzger bawled me out in front of everyone. For something *he* screwed up."

Scott had seen his father's boss, Frank Metzger: a beefy, red-faced man who smoked stinking cigars, and laughed combatively.

Scott's mom was always fretful. Now her voice shook as she asked, "What did you do?"

"I told him to stuff it," Dad said in his most matter-of-fact voice. "Then I flattened the fat prick."

Three years later, Dad was sober, divorced, remarried, and studying Law in a third-tier school in Houston, his paternal input reduced to occasional checks and once-a-year phone calls. That was the extent of his and Scott's relationship until Scott was accepted to Rice University and, amazingly, his dad offered to pay.

He stared out at the lake, wave-tossed as a stygian sea. If the wind didn't die down, they'd have trouble getting back.

"What *I* need," he said, "is a big pile of cash."

Errol ran his hand through his thick hair. "Don't we all. "

"At least you've started piling."

"I do all right," Errol said, like a man who could downplay his success.

"I'm guessing Claire's dad's pretty rich?" Scott hated how he liked the feel of Claire's name on his tongue.

"Thirty mil, at least," Errol said.

Sara's dad was worth fifty, Scott thought, then thrust the thought away. "You're in *great* shape," he told Errol.

"If I survive," Errol said. "Pop Gunn's a slave driver."

"Still, when he croaks . . ."

"He's only sixty. Doesn't smoke, doesn't drink, doesn't do jack shit but ride my ass and make money. He could outlast western civ."

"That's what fries me," Scott said. "I can't afford a six-month break to write some songs, but guys like him can piss a fortune away and never miss it." He reached down, plucked a reed, and shredded it. "I wish somebody'd piss even a couple grand my way."

"Do what *I* do, you can make a couple grand a *day*," Errol said. "People are so desperate and dumb—hand 'em shears, and they'll fleece themselves."

Scott plucked a fresh reed, and hurled it at the lake. Sara's father would have thrown a lot of cash his way.

"Maybe my dad's right," Scott said. "I should go to law school."

"Then fucking go!"

Was the heat in Errol's voice support or scorn?

"If I'm going to get screwed," Scott said, "I might as well sell myself dearly."

"Cheap!" Errol seemed, for an instant, on the verge of tears. "Money's cheap. And easy. Music, theater—*that's* hard."

"Every time I turn around, someone else I knew in school's a Big Success," Scott said. "They'd crap their pants laughing if they saw me."

"Fuck 'em with a totem pole," Errol said.

"Why can't talent rise, like people said it would?"

"Who said *that*?"

"Besides my mom?" Scott rolled his eyes in self-mockery. "Charles Dickens said it. Excellence, plus kindness, decency, and self-denial lead to wealth and happiness."

"And the Mounties always get their man." Errol plucked up a twig, snapped it, and tossed a piece at Scott. "You've got to stop thinking you're too noble to win."

Scott picked up the twig and studied it. "I don't think that."

Errol shrugged. "Ask yourself, 'What would I stoop to, to succeed?' In music, or anything."

Scott snapped his twig. "What do you mean by *stoop*?"

"Anything you think's beneath you."

"My drenched ass is beneath me," Scott said. "And it's cold." He shifted from cross-legged to knees-against-his-chest. "Nice guys don't just finish last. They don't even get to play."

"You don't mean *nice*," Errol said. "You mean *saintly*. No deception, no hurting anyone, or you're a bastard."

You think you're Sir Frickin' Galahad, Sara had sobbed.

"I'm a long way from saintly," Scott said, as much to Sara as to Errol. "But I hate winning at other people's expense. I see their side, and I feel *bad*."

Errol's blue eyes sparked. "Never see your opponent's side, unless you use it against him." He grabbed a baseball-sized rock as if to use it on an opponent's head. "Dostoyevsky said: 'If there's no God, everything is permitted.' Think of your enemy enjoying things you're dying for and could have *had*." He tossed the rock hand to hand to hand, then set it down. "Scruples are great—once you can afford them."

Scott crossed his legs again. "I'm sure the real Robin Hood stole from the rich, and kept it. I just . . . it's not reasonable to think . . ."

"Fuck being reasonable! A man needs things to *hate*!" Errol grabbed the baseball-rock, and flung it at the waves breaking on shore. The breath he took to say more, morphed into a yawn. "Axolotl ovaries!" he yelled. "Bad sleep makes me *crabby*!"

He raised his arms over his head and stretched elaborately. "Look," he said. "Our generation knows that life's one long dead-baby joke. We suffer and decay and die. Everything's futile in the end. But the world keeps tossing acid in our face. Something's got to pay for that. If one thing's not absurd, it's self-interest."

Scott bowed his head. "No argument. I sour-grape when I can't cut it."

"*I* can," Errol said, and expelled a thunderclap.

Scott scrambled away. "Aw, man! Nietzsche said, 'Because people fart, there is no god.'"

"Lucky I brought toilet paper," Errol said, and pulled a wad from his parka. "Leaves give me a painful rash."

Scott had to laugh.

"You want something to sit on? I'll bring you a stool," Errol called, wading into the woods.

Scott gave him thirty seconds, then followed.

Five years back, this would have been spontaneous. Now it felt scripted. Obligatory. Another try at recapturing what still hovered out of reach.

A swatch of white skin led Scott's eyes to Errol: pants around his ankles, butt hung over a downed tree.

Scott found a pine cone, lobbed it in a high arc, and heard it rattle through thick branches to thump down inches from Errol.

"What the shit?!" Errol barked. "To coin a phrase."

Scott moved closer, and lobbed another cone.

Errol started pulling up his pants.

Scott lobbed four cones in quick succession.

Errol was fumbling with his belt when the last cone conked him. "Dammit, Scott!"

Scampering back to the boat, Scott sat down as if he'd been there all along.

"Goddammit, Scott," Errol said, boiling out of the woods. "I wiped too fast. Now I *will* get a painful rash."

"A man looks his best taking a dump," Scott observed. "God's image all the way."

"Michelangelo should've sculpted David on the pot," Errol said.

"Two steps out of Eden, Adam had to *make*," Scott said. "That was the First Humiliation."

"Want to hear the Quintillionth?" Errol didn't wait. "When I was twelve, I had a paper route."

Scott laughed. "Say no more."

"One day I also had the stomach flu."

Scott nodded sagely. "I like a man who grasps the humor of the simple turd."

Errol made a woeful face. "I'm not talking *simple* turd."

"Spill it," Scott prodded. "So to speak."

"I was delivering papers when the cramps hit," Errol began. "The closest crapper was at a Shell station six blocks away. I pedaled as fast as I could, jumped off my bike, and raced inside." Errol made a tragic face. "Too late."

Scott fizzed through his nose.

"I'd been goosing for half a block," Errol said as Scott fizzed louder. "When I got in the restroom and tried to unbuckle my belt, I swear, the blast would have flattened Pompey. Diarrhea ran down my pants, over my socks, and onto my new Nikes."

"Humiliated," Scott squealed, and rolled onto his side. Was Errol making this up? Or had he been too embarrassed to tell it, before?

"My bowels were empty by the time I could sit down," Errol said. "Then I realized there was no toilet paper."

Shrieks from Scott. His limbs thrashed in the pine needles and leaves.

"I kept repeating, 'What am I going to do?' My legs were covered with shit. The floor was covered. My shoes and socks were covered. My jeans and underwear were full. And I still had to deliver fifty papers, eat breakfast, and get to school.

"Then I found out the water faucet didn't work!"

Scott was wallowing on the ground. Nothing forced about *this* laughter. The Good Times had returned.

"I stripped from the waist down, and stepped into the stinking crapper," Errol went on. "Then I washed my legs, one at a time, and flushed. Then I stepped back in, and stood, one legged like a stork, and washed my butt. Somebody opened the door, but shut it fast. I jumped out and locked it. Then I flushed. And washed my jeans and tennis shoes. And flushed. And washed some more.

"Some grownup started yelling, 'Hurry up,' and banging on the door. I stood there whimpering, 'What am I going to do?'"

"No more!" Scott squealed.

Errol forged ahead. "I left my shit-drenched socks and jockeys in the sink, and pulled on my soaked pants and shoes. Then—squishing, and tracking shit-water with every step—I marched my pinched little face out of the can, past a fat guy and his fat, squirming kid, and jumped on my bike and rode away."

Scott felt bad for the guy who'd had to clean up Errol's mess. But picturing that woeful face made him laugh more.

The wind had calmed during Errol's story. As if some lake god had unplugged a giant fan. The lake surface was settling into black glass.

As Scott stopped laughing and tried to catch his breath, Errol untied his rubber boat, lifted the rock out of the bottom, and dropped it, with a thunk, onto the ground. "Once more into the breach," he said. "Your turn to row."

Scott stood slowly, wrung out from laughing. The smart move would be to head for camp before the wind kicked back up. But that was also the wimpy move, so he didn't suggest it.

To his left, a large brown feather stuck, spear-like, out of the lakeshore mud. "An eagle feather!" he proclaimed, and plucked it up.

"That's a wing-feather," Errol said. "Indians thought they stood for strength. Or bravery. Or good luck." He did his tongue-out imitation of a Greek comedian's mask. "Hell, how do *I* know what they thought?"

Scott ran his finger down the feather's sleekness the way, as a boy, he'd stroke the turkey feathers in his "Indian headdress."

"*Nerve*," Scott said, tucking the feather in his vest. "It stands for *nerve*."

21

They'd gone less than a mile when, rounding a point, Errol saw what looked like an old motel set back in a large bay.

"Looks like an old-time fishing lodge," Errol said.

"Let's troll in and see," Scott said.

"Let's row in," Errol said: more a command than a suggestion. Scott had caught three trout, including a three-pounder. *He*, even after a change to sinking line, had eked out one paltry tap.

Scott rowed faster, but didn't reel in. Thirty oar strokes, and he'd slowed back to trolling speed.

Errol recognized his own technique for dealing with idiots: Agree completely, but don't change. If the idiot complains, look hurt. Thank him for his suggestions. Do what he asks until his attention wanes. Then do what you like.

Errol was about to call Scott on his bullshit when the bullshitter snagged up. Unable to admit to trolling, he had to break off his fly and keep rowing as if nothing had occurred. This mollified Errol. And the old lodge positively cheered him.

It was deserted, and seemed to have been that way for a long time. Once, there had been three docks. Today, only a few planks dangled from pilings soft with rot. As Scott rowed harder, threshing through the black water, the blow-up boat passed over sunken trees that writhed like surfacing sea monsters.

"I half expect a plesiosaur," Scott huffed between strokes.

"A T-Rex would feel at home here," Errol agreed.

Dead pines mixed with live ones at the water's edge, their gray, jagged nakedness stark against the forest's green. The trees seemed larger than those around Oso. As if these woods were older. Maybe by a lot.

The shore was spiked with toppled trunks that angled into the black lake. What had been the lodge's front yard was overgrown with trees: shorter and thinner than the surrounding woods, but still good-sized. A gravel path led from the ruined docks to the buildings, which were made of rough-hewn logs.

Errol beached the rubber boat and held it while Scott climbed out. Then, with a sense of high adventure mixed with a pleasurable touch of fear, he led Scott crunching up the gravel path.

There were nine buildings in all: a big one that faced the lake, and behind that, two rows of four cabins each. All nine buildings had faded brown sides topped by faded red roofs. The main building had a wooden porch and two doors: one front, one back, both padlocked shut. A mummified rat—poisoned?—lay by the back door. Blue drapes, faded to near-white, masked six windows, all locked tight.

A wooden sign above the front door was too weathered to read.

"Probably said something like 'Land-a-Lunker Lake,'" Scott offered. Picking a hand-sized rock off the ground, he turned it over in his hands.

"There's no road in, but the path looks used," Errol said. "*Somebody* comes here."

Pressing his forehead against a window, he strained to see through a crack in the drapes. Too dark inside . . .

"Maybe a caretaker," Scott said. "Once a month."

"He'd have to fly," Errol said. "A pontoon plane!"

"That's it! I'll bet fishermen flew in here," Scott said. "So why'd they stop?"

Errol's first thought was, *Some evil force moved in.* But that was horror movie bullshit. "Maybe the owner died," he said. "And the property got tangled up in court."

"Could be," Scott said. "Want to check it out?"

"Hell, yeah!"

To Errol's surprise, Scott raised the stone he'd picked up and dealt the front door lock a blow that shattered it and left the room at their mercy.

◆ ◆ ◆

"That's how the hoods in high school did it," Scott declared, pushed open the door and, trying to hide how much he'd shocked himself, stepped inside.

Light from the open door showed three long dining tables with chairs, an open cupboard full of dishes, and an open drawer of tarnished utensils.

Behind this room was a dim kitchen with a sink, a black wood stove, and a spider that Scott thought, at first, was a rat as it skimmed across the floor.

"I like spiders on a par with penile cancer," he said, as much to himself as to Errol as he backed out of the kitchen.

The dining room was full of cobwebs. Having seen one of the architects, Scott took a stance barely inside the door, and left the rummaging to Errol, who had once plucked a fat spider from its web and crushed it between thumb and forefinger in front of Scott's astonished eyes.

Errol lifted a stack of yellowed *Vancouver Sun*s off a wooden chair. "These things are forty years old," he said.

Scott, taking a paper from Errol, was tempted to plop down on the porch and read. But a spider might fall from the pages, or crawl from some crack between the weathered boards.

"Think they're worth money?" Errol asked.

"I doubt it." Scott dropped the paper on a table. "One sneeze would turn 'em into dust."

"Let's check out the cabins," Errol said, and led the way outside.

The cabins weren't padlocked, but the doors of the first two were locked from inside. Ditto the third.

"Want to break down the door?" Scott asked, and was about to ram it with his shoulder when Errol said, "Let's try the others first."

Scott was glad to spare his shoulder. But the wilderness effect was raging. He felt fired up to the point of recklessness. No failure-of-nerve now!

He followed Errol past the fourth cabin, also locked, then across ten yards of gravel to the last cabin, second row.

As the men drew near, a huge toad hopped into their path. As big as the one they'd seen by the dead calf, it stopped and stared, then squeezed under the cabin.

"Did you see that?" Scott said.

Errol grimaced. "I hate a big toad."

"It looked like it was watching us," Scott said. And thought, *My eyes are on you.*

"Maybe it's a gay prince checking you out," Errol said, and gave Scott a poke. "Come on, Wolverine. Try the door."

Scott gripped the metal knob, and turned. To his surprise, the door opened to reveal a filthy bed.

Scott jumped back as if it were a moose-sized spider. "Somebody lives here!" he said. And he knew who.

Errol rapped hard on the open door. "Anybody home?"

Getting no answer, he strode into the room.

Scott, fearing to be sniped from the woods, slipped inside too.

Beer cans littered the floor. A small sink was clogged with dishes: unwashed and crusty, though a drip from the spigot proved the place had running water. There must be some kind of pump . . .

The bathroom door, open, revealed a flush commode.

On a table by the unmade single bed, a half-full whisky bottle camped next to a pile of porno mags. One, open to its centerfold, lay on stained, incongruously mauve sheets where its owner must have wished the real woman—a huge-breasted, freckle-faced gargoyle—could be. She lay spread-eagled, mouth forming an "O," eyes attempting a come-hither look as her fingers spread something the color and texture of rare roast beef.

Her legs had been scissored off at the knees.

"Christ chloroformed, what's dead in here?!" Errol said.

The reek of dirty clothes, unwashed skin, and worse, made Scott want to retch. His eyes fastened on a heap of clothes by the far wall. He pointed to the gray-and-red shirt on top. "That's his. Bearclaw's."

"You sure?"

Scott nodded. "This place stinks like him."

"Think he's a squatter? Or the caretaker?" Errol asked.

"Could be."

The cobwebbed corners of the room implied that Bearclaw shared Errol's indifference to spiders. And the two guns on the wall—a rusty rifle, and an old single-shot twelve-gauge—declared their owner was no pacifist.

Worse, the rack was built to hold three guns.

"We should go," Scott said.

Errol wavered, then dashed across the room, tore open the battered dresser, and drawer by drawer, flung its contents at the wall.

A pile of centerfolds fluttered to the floor. Errol held one up: a brunette with her legs scissored off.

He pounced on a brown leather wallet on the floor beside the bed. "Let's see who this asswipe really is."

"He's bad news. Look." Scott pointed to a yellowed clipping tacked to the pine-log wall. The clipping, from *The Athabaskan*, seemed excerpted from a speech. A shaky hand had underlined two sentences in red: *The white man's sickness lames our spirit. It chokes off our power and makes us doubt our sacred ways.* Under the text, in the same red ink, two words were printed in block letters: NO MERCY.

"I'll 'no mercy' his perverted ass," Errol snarled, and yanked open the wallet.

The ID holder was empty. But the bill compartment held three blue-and-yellow Canadian fivers, plus a laminated card.

"A trucker's license! From Montana," Errol crowed. *"Jim McGee.* Looks like old Hairball drove big rigs." He thrust the card at Scott. "This him?"

The license showed a younger, unscarred "Bearclaw." His decidedly pale face, topped by the square bristles of a crew cut, looked less fierce than deeply chagrined. Both of his eyes looked brown. Whatever scarred him had injured his eye, too.

Scott plucked a pill bottle off the floor. Prescribed for James McGee. "Haloperidol," he said. "Schizophrenics take that."

He jumped as Errol kicked the emptied dresser, and sent it crashing into the wall. "This psycho better stay real clear of Claire." He grabbed the open porno mag, and flung it, pages flapping, across the room.

Scott's earlier recklessness had disappeared. His nerve was failing fast. "Let's go," he urged. "We're trespassing."

"This guy's a zero. A backwoods meat-beater."

"He's crazy. And he has a gun." Scott pictured Bearclaw/McGee stepping through the door. What would it feel like to be shot, he wondered, then assured the gods he didn't want to know.

"The guys who threaten never act," Errol said.

"Let's not chance it." Scott edged toward the door. The cluttered, stinking cabin made him gag. Those cut-off legs . . .

Errol gave the bedstead a parting kick, yelled, "Fucking shit," hopped on one foot, then limped behind Scott back into daylight.

The sun, blazing as it slid down the sky, made the scene less threatening. Scott checked his watch—2:49—and slipped his sunglasses on as he followed Errol toward their boat.

For some time now, his bowels had been grumbling. He'd ignored them, knowing Errol would pay him back for earlier. Now, danger or not—maybe *because* of danger—he could ignore no more.

To his right, in a small aspen grove, he saw an outhouse. Talk about good luck! *Probably for the groundskeepers*, he thought, rushing toward it. Luckier still: its door had a thick latch. Errol, who had almost reached their boat, couldn't get to him in there.

"Pause for the cause," Scott called, then ducked into the outhouse and latched the door before Errol could react.

Instantly, Scott regretted his haste. The place made McGee's den seem perfumed. The only light and air came from a slit below the roof. Flies buzzed inside, making the place perfect for spiders. And what better web-spot than across the hole?

Scott stuffed his sunglasses into his shirt pocket, and peered into the reeking pit.

Nothing but blackness.

He wanted to bolt outside. But if he did, Errol's paper route disaster would become his own. And he had no more dry clothes.

Pulling his stash of toilet paper from his pocket, he yanked down his pants, making sure his butt stayed a safe distance from the wooden seat.

He was rebuckling his belt when the first rock hit.

"Too late!" he yelled.

As pebbles rained on the roof, a lightness in his back pocket made him grope for his wallet.

Oh no. The back-pocket button on his spare pants had come off. His wallet was gone!

A fresh hail of pebbles clattered down the outhouse roof as Scott squinted desperately at the floor. There! A dark rectangle near the back!

Relief flooding through him, Scott bent and grasped the wallet, still damp from his dunking in the muck.

A sudden BANG! made him flinch so forcefully that his sunglasses slid out of his shirt pocket, past his clutching fingers, and down toward the dark hole.

"Shit!" Thrusting his wallet into his front pants pocket, he threw the outhouse door open to get more light. Let his glasses be on the floor. Please . . .

No such luck.

"Aw Jesus goddamn bloody *hump*," he wailed. "Miserable!"

Errol dropped the rocks he was carrying. "What's wrong?" he asked, all innocence.

"I dropped my sunglasses down the shithole," Scott wailed. "Shit and double shit. Those glasses cost me eighty bucks."

"Humiliated," Errol squealed, then, as if he were safe in camp, dropped to the ground, howling.

Scott had to smile. Away from Bearclaw's lair, his nerve was bubbling back. "I need those glasses," he said. "I'll get headaches without 'em."

The news made Errol shriek. "Stop," he gasped. "I can't breathe . . ."

"Think we can push this thing over?" Scott said. He wanted to leave fast, but wanted his sunglasses, too.

"You're going into the *shithole*?" Errol shrieked and, Bearclaw or no Bearclaw, doubled up again.

"It's better than a bunch of headaches," Scott said. Placing both hands on the rough wood, he braced and shoved.

The outhouse tilted a tiny bit.

Scott shoved again. The outhouse tilted more. Time had pressed it deep into the dirt. But it would fall.

"I'll help you," Errol said, getting to his feet. "But *you* do the spelunking."

He placed his big hands next to Scott's, and both men pushed. The wooden box leaned, leaned some more, made a ripping sound, and toppled with a crash.

Errol gave a strangled scream, and fell back as if he'd been shot.

Scott stared. "Oh holy shit!"

At the bottom of a four-foot hole, his sunglasses lay on top of a shit-splattered skeleton. Chunks of dried flesh clung to the gray bones. No clothes. No skull.

"The legs!" Errol said. "They're cut off at the knee."

"Oh shit!" Scott said. "Those bones we found . . ."

"Thank God Claire's in town," Errol said.

Scott's glasses stared up at him. All he had to do was take them. But he could not face climbing down into the hole.

"Let's split," he said. "If McGee comes back, we're fucked."

"We've got to report this."

"Okay, we will. Let's *go*," Scott said, and set off for the boat.

"Wait! We've got to put this back!" Errol gestured at the outhouse. "He'll move the body, and we can't prove a thing."

Scott turned to face Errol from thirty feet away. "The dirt's torn up. He's gonna know. Come on, let's go!"

One more glance at the corpse and—imagining a rifle's *Crack*, a sharp pain in his back—Scott ran.

✦ ✦ ✦

"We can't just leave her!" Errol yelled after the fleeing Scott. He tried to right the outhouse by himself. Too heavy. It, or he, might fall and crush the body. What was left of it.

He backed away. Scott's panic infecting him, he began to walk fast, then run toward his boat. Would his friend leave him behind?

No. Oars-in-hand, Scott sat waiting in the boat.

He started rowing the instant Errol shoved off and jumped in.

Leaning down to present a smaller target, Errol counted Scott's oar strokes. One. Two. Three. Four. Each stroke meant that much more distance a slug would have to fly. That much less impact. That much better shot McGee would have to be.

If he so much as nicked the boat, it would sink in the bone-chilling lake, and they would drown.

Scott's oar strokes were weak. The boat seemed barely to move as it labored around a wooded point. Errol wanted to grab the oars. But changing rowers might waste more time than his rowing would gain.

When, finally, the lodge was out of sight, Scott stopped rowing and wiped his forehead as they bounced in wind-chop a hundred yards offshore. "We should be out of range," he said.

Errol glared at the boat's rubber bottom, undulating underfoot. He wanted to smack Scott for panicking him. Making him run. The knowledge that his anger was unjust angered him more. To fear being shot made sense. But in spite of all reason, he'd been sure the corpse would leap out of its hole and rattle after him, headless and wailing.

22

However hard Scott rowed, the boat would not move fast. And finding the way back proved a problem. One bay looked like the next. And there were lots of bays.

Eyes shut, Errol had been kneading his temples with both hands. Now his eyes flew open. "What if Claire's early? McGee could be there." He glanced around, as if enraged not to be farther along. "Row faster!" he barked. "Or let me."

"Be my guest," Scott said, and handed him the oars.

In a perverse way, he felt glad when, minutes later, Errol had to concede that he'd rowed into the wrong bay.

Their next choice, a joint effort after backtracking, proved correct. There was the creek, and yes, the trail.

Errol took the lead: jogging, his backpack clattering. Scott jogged behind, trying to formulate a plan that didn't involve meeting cops. He remembered the flashing red light rushing up as he drove home from his gig at Delaney's. When he pulled over, two meaty Houston cops jerked him from his car, and slammed him against their blue-and-white . . .

"We could kill him," Scott blurted on the run.

Panting, Errol slowed to a walk. "Kill McGee?"

Scott had spoken more from frustration than real intent. But the idea was easy to justify.

"No one would find him here," he said. "Or even look."

Errol trudged a few more paces, then, chest heaving, stopped and stared as if Scott had dropped to earth from Pluto. "That's murder," he said.

"It's justice," Scott said. "Why give the Law a chance to let him go. Like that drunk who hit my mom!" The idea's audacity, plus the fact that he wasn't panting, fueled his sense of righteousness. "Freaky porn, cut-off body parts—that's serial killer stuff. The guy's done it before."

"Jesus!" Errol couldn't seem to catch his breath. "Claire . . ."

"You told her to come back at five?"

Errol nodded.

"She won't be early," Scott pronounced with more confidence than he felt. "McGee freaked her out."

"I hope you're right."

"Let's do the world a favor. Off the bastard," Scott said. "That, or go and fish some other lake."

Errol looked incredulous. "Let him get away?!"

"He'll be long gone before the Mounties show," Scott said. "Besides, they *got* their man. Think they'll admit they blew it now?"

Errol started trudging again. "We've got to tell them," he flung over his shoulder.

Scott dogged his heels. "We could end up suspects. They might not let us leave."

Errol started a slow jog. "That makes no sense," he gasped. "She's been dead for months."

"You want to trust the Law to get it right?" Scott demanded. "The Law planted cocaine on me. I'm pretty sure Dad bribed someone to get me off. And I *still* got a year's probation. The Law's a cluster-fuck!"

"*Scott*," one cop had mocked, squinting at the driver's license he'd demanded to see. "Like Scott-*free*?"

"I guess," Scott had said.

"That's fixin' to change," the cop said, then, to his partner. "Don't he look like a woman with that hair?"

The other nodded. "Put a beard on him, knock his teeth out, and I'd fuck him."

The cops, who seemed straight out of some 1960s *Easy Rider* clone, frisked him as if he were a punching bag.

"Where's your dope, Rolling Stone?" the *Scott-free* cop demanded, then pulled from his blue uniform a cellophane baggie holding white powder and a crack pipe. "Whaddaya know?"

Scott recalled a rush of panic, a nightstick's blur, a blinding flash of pain. Next thing he knew, he was being thrown—with two cracked ribs and a concussion—into a cell full of criminals, charged with resisting arrest and possession of cocaine. Him, who'd never done coke in his life. Rice University scholarship or not, he couldn't stay in Houston after that.

"Scott!" Errol stopped so quickly, Scott ran into him. "We're not killing McGee!"

Face tomato-red, chest and belly heaving, Errol looked middle-aged and near collapse. "Listen, man . . ." He bent over, hands on his knees, fighting for breath. "I know I said I'd kill him. I'd like to. But Christ . . ." His voice half-pleaded, half-attacked. "Remember *gigolos in the Bahamas*?"

Another time, Scott would have smiled. That had been his and Errol's favorite fantasy.

"We never got there," Scott said.

"I never *will*," Errol said. "I've got a wife now. And a job. And monthly payments, life insurance, the whole bit. Laugh if you want, I've got responsibilities." He straightened his back. "One of them's reporting this. You want out, leave. I won't mention you were here. You can fish and fuck around all you like. Just not with me."

His wind returning, Errol seemed spoiling for a fight.

Scott wanted to oblige. But why? So he could lose again?

"Hell," he sighed. "I can't let you take all this crap on by yourself."

Errol took a breath as if to launch an attack, then deflated with a loud sigh. "I appreciate that," he said, and resumed walking.

Scott followed, glad Errol couldn't see his face. Killing McGee might be a bad idea. Okay, it *was*. But Errol's sanctimony galled. This Errol was a far cry from his old friend, who'd bit off life in giant chunks, and let nothing interfere with a good time. *That* Errol's brash spirit and contempt for convention had inspired Scott. Now Mr. Untamed had become Family Values Man.

As for the Errol who'd said, "Fish all you like, just not with me," Scott had seen *him* before—sneering, with all the considerable scorn that he could muster, "Either drive us, or you don't fish with me!"

Out of consideration for Errol's feelings, Scott hadn't told him what Horst at Foreign Car Repair had said: "Brakes all shot. Need everyt'ing replace." Instead, he'd fired back, "If I want to fish with a prick, I'll use my own."

Next thing he knew, he was bouncing off his car's hood, down onto the cold concrete. Errol had stepped forward, ready to mop the street with him. Instead, he'd spat, "You're too damn puny to punch out," then spun and stalked away, leaving Scott dazed, and their friendship dead in the street.

◆ ◆ ◆

Blasting down the trail, Errol remembered that fight, too. Scott's brakes had failed, and he had no money to fix them. As a Christmas present for his friend, he, Errol, had worked three days in the December cold to replace the things. He'd rented special tools to wrestle with Scott's pathetic Ford Escort: so corroded and old, junking was too good for it. He'd done all this to help a guy who kept whining, "Are you *sure* you can do this?" Then, when the work was done and Errol asked him to drive thirty miles to where steelhead were stacking up on the Snoqualmie, Scott had claimed, "I don't dare drive at all."

By the time they reached their boats, Errol felt half-dead, and fully furious. "It's 5:02!" he gasped, as if it were Scott's fault.

With no apology, Scott stepping-stoned over Errol's boat into his own, leaving muddy footprints on both seats.

"Don't mention this to Claire," Errol said between gasps. "She'd want to drive straight home."

"My lips are zipped," Scott said, barely panting.

"I'm gonna tell her we're reporting poachers," Errol said, more to himself than to Scott as they rowed and poled their boats to open water.

Their motors roared in unison. Then they were churning campward, neck-in-neck. After a few moments, Errol realized that he was racing Scott. And not just to reach Claire sooner. To show him who was number one.

He'd begun to pull ahead when, above the motors' drone, he heard a *Boom!*

"Come on," he yelled at Scott, and full-throttled for camp.

Bug-sized in the distance, Claire ran into view. Waving his shotgun, she scrambled to the water's edge, then turned from the lake to face the woods.

"Hold on, Babe!" Errol yelled, though he knew she couldn't hear.

Two frantic minutes later, he splashed ashore and ran to where she stood, staring at the woods.

He grabbed the shotgun from her hands. "What happened?"

"A bear," she said, and wouldn't look at him. "I shot it."

"Where?!"

She pointed toward a thicket. "In there."

"You're sure you hit it?"

She nodded. Unnaturally calm. In shock.

"She wounded a bear," Errol said as Scott pounded up.

"Oh shit!"

"We've got to find it." Shotgun hip-high, Errol advanced on the thicket.

"Wait! I'll throw something," Scott said.

♦ ♦ ♦

Grabbing a fist-sized rock, Scott underhanded it in a high arc over Errol's head and into the thicket. Had McGee sent the bear? Or dressed up as a bear? Crazy thoughts. But not impossible, out here.

Something thrashed in the thicket. The next moment, with a piteous, near-human bawl, a small black bear charged from the underbrush, straight into a tree.

This was no man-in-a-bear-suit. Blood added gloss to its black fur.

"I hit its eyes," Claire said. "It's blind."

"It's just a cub." Errol raised his gun. "I'll finish it."

The shotgun roared. The little bear fell, then staggered back up, mewling: *Ooh uh! Ooh uh!*

Errol shot again. The cub fell back, then made a crippled charge across the camp. Running broadside into Errol's truck, it bounced off and dropped to the ground, thrashing and bawling.

"Fucking bird shot!" Errol raged.

The bear's agony seared Scott's bones. He saw Errol's ax against a tree, and seized it. Screaming like a berserker, he charged the bear, and brought the ax down hard.

The bear squalled, its shoulder crushed.

With a cry of anguish and disgust, Scott swung again, clipping the head.

Again, again, again he swung, smashing the skull, crushing the doglike muzzle, dodging the claws that raked earth and the air as the small bear thrashed and thrashed and finally lay still.

Errol walked over and, looking sick, stared at the dead animal. "Jesus," he said. "We're in way over our heads."

Blood had splashed Scott's face, hands, clothes. Red smears streaked Errol's truck. The bear, Scott realized, had hit exactly where he'd left the ding. He saw it underneath the blood. Next to the bear's dent, it was nothing.

He felt like vomiting, but tried to joke. "You think it's dead?"

"Naw. It's sleeping," Errol replied.

Claire walked to Errol and took his hand. "It looked bigger. I'm sorry."

"It's not your fault," Errol said without conviction.

"It's no one's fault. This place is snake-bit," Scott said, scanning the trees. The cub's mother had to be near . . .

"Fuck it," Errol said. "We're leaving anyway."

"We are?" Claire's relief was clear.

"Right away," Errol said. "Before momma shows up."

In ten minutes, the trucks were packed. While Claire waited in Errol's cab, the men dragged the bloody pile of baby bear into the woods.

"Far enough," Errol said after a few steps. Then they both ran.

23

"Bullshit, Errol. You report poachers to the Game Department, not the police," Claire said as the two trucks banged over the road she'd driven down an hour before. The woods became a different world at dusk. She felt trapped in some huge stomach, villi waving, eager to digest their trucks.

She deserved it, for shooting the little bear.

"Show me a Fish and Game office," Errol was saying, "and I'll go there."

"Bearclaw's mixed up in this," she said. "Did you see him?"

She wanted to announce that Bearclaw's name was Jim McGee. *That* would get Errol's attention. But it might also lead to talk of Ted Brumley.

"No. We didn't see *Bearclaw*," Errol said, his condescension thick enough to spread on toast. "Fuck that looney tune."

"Did you know a woman was killed where we camped?" Claire said, and heard the challenge in her voice.

"Who told you *that*?"

She had a whole story prepared: A chatty woman at the Howdy Do, etc. Instead she slapped him with the truth. "Some guy in town."

"*What* guy?"

Errol's voice was hard: his jealous tone. Why had she opened her big mouth? "I don't know his name," she said.

"Where'd you meet this *guy*?"

Here comes trouble, she thought. *Well, let it come.* "I had a drink," she said.

Even in the dark, she felt his glare. "At Trixie's?!"

"Is there a Sofitel in town?"

"You went to Trixie's by *yourself*?!"

His voice rocked the small cab. She kept hers down. "Errol, I spent eight hours in a half-horse town. There's not a lot to do."

"Come on, Claire. A logger bar?" He spoke like an exasperated dad. *Her* dad. "I'd say that's asking for trouble. At the least."

"Errol, if I wanted to cheat. . ." She heard her mother to her father: total ice. "I wouldn't pick Trixie's to do it."

"That's comforting."

The way he moved from anger to sulking irony said she'd hurt him. Which made her sad and cooled her down.

"Baby . . ." She put both hands on his shoulder, and leaned across the cab to kiss his cheek. "I wish you'd trust me. Tell me what's going on."

"I trust you, Babe," he said. "Trust *me*."

She scooched away from him, anger surging back. "Barefoot and pregnant, I can't get in trouble, right?"

"Christ on a cruller," Errol groaned. "Contemporary Woman speaks."

"Oh Jesus, Errol!" Moving as far away from him as she could get, she tried to wipe him and his assholery out of her mind. It would have served him right if she'd screwed Ted Brumley, instead of reading trashy novels in BIG VALUE.

Despite its cover blurb—"Love on a moose-hunt"—she'd enjoyed *Passion in the Pines.* Candace was the trophy wife of Sidney, a rich brain surgeon twice her age. Pierre was the handsome French-Canadian guide. Their soft-porn scene on Lookout Mountain had stayed with her all the way back to camp.

She could never have played it out with Ted. He'd taken her "No thank you" like a three-year-old—called her a *cock tease* and tantrummed away. Being with him would've been like screwing an orangutan.

Still, if she'd spent more time with him, she might not have crossed paths with the little bear.

She forced that picture from her mind, replacing it with handsome Pierre. For some reason, he'd made her think of Scott.

Behind them, Scott's headlights flamed on. A minute later, Errol clicked his on, too.

Night beat them by twenty minutes into town.

◆ ◆ ◆

The RCMP station was dark when Errol pulled up. The drugstore, too. Even the Laundromat was closed. A sign on the station door gave a number IN CASE OF EMERGENCIE.

An ancient pay phone stood nearby. Errol fed it with Canadian coins he'd brought along just in case, then dialed the number.

"No answer," he said after seven rings. "No voicemail," he added as he hung up and his coins jingled back.

"Oh no," Claire said. "What if the *poachers* get away?"

Errol wished to hell he'd just told Claire about the body. Tell her now, and she'd ream him a new one. She wouldn't care that he'd been trying not to scare her, and to save their vacation.

"Errol," Scott called. Through luck or foresight, he'd parked ten yards away—out of earshot of Claire, Errol realized as he walked to his friend's little truck.

"What do you think?" Scott said.

"Hell, *I* don't know," he said. "Nobody's here. And nobody answered the phone."

"Fucking cops," Scott said. "Lord knows when they'll be back."

"Tomorrow morning. If we're lucky," Errol said. "This thing'll cost us the whole day!" Errol knew he should feel differently. Someone had died. But he'd come here to fish, not to wait around for cops. Nothing he did now would help the headless girl.

"Here's a thought," Scott said. "A guy I met at Brewster Lake—'Old Hodges,' they call him—he told me about a lake maybe eighty miles from here. It's full of food, and really deep. Old Hodges says the average trout's three pounds. And some go thirty."

Despite himself, lights started flashing in Errol's brain. Was policing a part-time job in Winoma? Could he count on these absent amateurs not to muck things up? Scott might be right. The jerk-offs might arrest *them*!

"This lake's so far back in the mountains, no one goes there," Scott said. "Ursula Lake. Even the name's seductive. And . . ." He paused for effect. "Old Hodges drew a map."

Reaching into his glove compartment, Scott handed Errol a folded hunk of paper bag. "We could fish there a couple days, then report the girl on our way home."

"You've got to report a body right away."

"This one's been dead for months," Scott said. "We could send a letter. Anonymous. Or leave a note. Stay out of the mess. If the Law's involved, I guarantee there'll be a mess."

"It's an idea," Errol had to admit. Claire would be there for any face-to-face with Mounties. His poachers story and his ass would both be fried.

He pictured a thirty-pound Kamloops: twice as big as those ghost trout.

One fish like that would nullify all his bad luck. The Mounties, on the other hand, were already causing *more*.

"Good citizens have a call-the-cops reflex," Scott said. "But cops aren't super-sleuths who set everything right. Sometimes they shoot the one who made the call."

Errol couldn't argue. Newspapers were full of that. "This lake. Ursula . . ." He looked at Scott for reassurance. "Nobody goes there?"

"That's what Old Hodges said."

"I don't trust these *Mounties* any more'n you do," Errol said. "Assholes can't spell *emergency*." He sighed, and pulled his keys from his pocket. "I tried to do the right thing. Hell with it. Let's go."

He started toward his truck, then stopped. "No, shit, I can't. McGee might kill another girl."

"That's why I said we should kill *him*."

"I'm not . . ." Errol started to say "a criminal," then stopped. He felt physically off balance, pulled a dozen ways. "Let me think about this," he said.

"While you think, I'll go to the store. I'm in the mood for a *Big Value*," Scott said, started his truck, and drove away as Errol walked back to Claire, stewing.

"Where's Scott going?" she demanded.

"Big Value. He'll be right back," Errol said, but wondered if he would. Scott could wash his hands of this whole thing. Drive away to fish Lake Ursula, kill Jim McGee, whatever. End of friendship. Again.

Damn these local cops for being gone. And damn himself, for lying to Claire. All he needed was an Inquisition now.

"Pause for the cause," he said and, not waiting for an answer, walked behind the strip mall, unzipped in the chilly dark and, to the sound of his own splashing, tried to untangle his thoughts.

The more he peed, the more Scott's idea made sense. They could leave a note for the cops: say where the body was, and tip them off about McGee. No need to meet them in-person to do that.

He zipped his fly and started for the parking lot, then stopped, still wavering. No wonder his ulcer was wrecking his sleep. This vacation, like his life, had come unglued.

"I've got to talk to 'em myself," he said aloud, *call-the-cops reflex* or not. As for looking bad to Claire, he'd bite the bullet and confess.

He'd started for the parking lot again, when an angry male voice brought him up short.

Claire's voice responded. Sounding scared!

In four steps, Errol rounded the corner, charging toward his truck.

A bearded hulk, in complete lumberjack drag, stood by Claire's door. She'd rolled her window up.

"I'd tear this truck apart as soon as look at it," the man was shouting—obviously smashed. Hearing Errol's footfall, he turned. "You're hubbie, eh?"

Errol slowed, assessing the stranger. For once, he lacked the edge in size.

"I don't know what you're doing, friend, but do it elsewhere," Errol said in a measured voice. "Unlock my door, Claire," he ordered, and walked to the driver's side.

The beard moved around the truck toward him. "Your wife's a cock tease, *friend.*"

Errol's brain burst into flame. "I'd suggest you leave," he told the man. "While you can walk."

Claire scrambled out the driver's door and grabbed him. Putting herself between him and the lumberjack. "It's okay, Errol. This is Ted."

"Soon to be the late Ted," Errol said.

Ted stopped, half of the truck's hood between them. "Twenty-four carat cock tease," he said. "With a pot-gutted husband I'm bettin' she don't fuck anymore."

As always before a fight, Errol felt his mind leave his body and look down from above. "We should walk over to Trixie's," he told Ted. "So your friends won't have to look for your remains."

Claire gripped his arm. "Errol, please!"

He flung her off. "I know you started this," he said. "I'm almost sorry for this clown."

"Don't sweat the RCMPs," Ted advised. "My brother-in-law's the chief. He loves it when I kick some Yankee ass."

Doubt flickered in Errol as he moved toward Ted. The guy seemed fit and confident, while *he* was out of shape. He'd proved that already today. Still, he'd whipped bigger men. When they weren't drunk!

Errol circled in a half-crouch, arms wide, wrestler-style. Ten years since he'd been in a ring, but it felt like yesterday.

The lumberjack mimicked his stance. He shuffled three steps to the left, then charged.

Errol nailed him with a glancing right and a knee to the face. But Ted slammed his shoulder into Errol's gut, wrapped thick arms around his legs, and—the guy must have wrestled, too—took him down.

They landed hard, kicking and flailing. Ted rolled on top, and bounced a punch off Errol's chin. Errol's body convulsed with rage. Ted flew back, sprawling on his butt. Errol jumped on him, snarling—fingers in his throat, thumbs digging deep.

With a spit-flecked growl and a hand in Errol's face, Ted broke the hold, rolled away, and scrambled to his feet. He ran a few steps to evade pursuit, then turned to face Errol, who was struggling to get up.

"That's enough, please, no more!" Claire implored. But stayed out of the way.

The men ignored her, glaring across fifteen feet.

Errol was panting. And Ted saw it. "That gut'll cost ya, Pudge," he jeered.

Errol was ready when Ted charged. But his movements were slow. Ted ducked a right, and rammed Errol back into his truck. His head slammed the windshield. Stunned, he kicked and clawed, groping for eye, groin, any soft thing. But Ted was on him, heavy as death, pressing him back and back and back.

Why had he let himself get out of shape?

Ted's fingers bored into Errol's windpipe, shutting off the air. Errol gagged, tugging at Ted's hands as the pain and pressure increased. Fear gripped him hard. Then, magically, Ted moved back, thumbs gouging grooves into Errol's throat. Errol gave a shove to free himself, rolled off the truck's hood onto his feet, and pasted Ted with a right elbow to the jaw that nearly spun the bearded head off the thick neck.

Ted sagged back into Scott's arms. Scott—who, Errol realized now, had grabbed big Ted—let him drop to the concrete. Out cold.

162 • URSULA LAKE

"Where'd *you* come from?" Errol gasped.

"Big Value's closed."

"Is he all right?" Claire said. Meaning, clearly, Ted.

"Hope not," Errol said. And didn't look at her.

"I thought you needed help." Scott sounded apologetic as he stepped away from where the big logger sprawled.

"I didn't *need* . . ." Errol felt his neck, which hurt like hell. "Fucker crushed my windpipe . . ."

Claire knelt by the motionless man. "Errol, is he dead?"

"I'm touched by your concern." Errol's mind was clearing, thoughts flash-flooding back. He'd been beaten in front of Claire. Humiliated. "Were you gonna let him strangle me?" he said.

"No."

Something odd about Claire's voice turned Errol's head. She had stood up. In her right hand, she held his hunting knife: a foot of unsheathed steel.

"Christ on a crudité!" His energy surged back. He felt like dancing around Ted, hooting, "You lose!"

Scott knelt beside the fallen man. "He's breathing. Who the hell is he?"

"Police chief's brother-in-law," Errol said.

Scott started to smile, then stopped. "You serious?"

"Unfortunately."

"That's fucked up."

Errol nodded. "Come over here. In case he's listening."

They moved as a group to the other side of Errol's truck, forty feet from Ted.

"We should get out of Canada," Errol said. "We could fish in the States. Say, Brewster Lake."

"It's four hours to the border," Scott said. "If the Mounties are looking for us, they'll catch us going through. We should lay low for a while."

Errol frowned. "That might be true." He turned to Claire. "What do you think?"

"I think I should have held out for Hawaii." She gave a wry smile, then said, "Scott's probably right. If we stay out of sight, and go back at different times, we're less likely to get caught. Assuming they look for us. I doubt if this is Ted's first fight."

"They sure as hell won't find us at Ursula Lake," Scott said.

Errol sighed. He thought a moment, then turned to Scott. "Think you can find it in the dark?"

"I can try."

"Okay," Errol said. "Let's go."

Opening his truck, Errol climbed in. Then Claire did too.

"What about *him*?" Scott said. "He'll call his brother-in-law when he comes to."

Errol climbed back out of his truck. "Okay," he said, his mind speeding. "We'll drop him out of town. Make sure he's got a long walk back." He looked around, expecting cop cars to roar up. "Can you drive, Claire?"

She nodded, still holding the knife.

"I'll ride in back, in case he wakes up," Errol said. "You follow Scott."

"Okay," she said.

"I've got his arms," Scott said. "You grab his feet."

Errol got a grip above Ted's thick ankles, then counted: "One, two, *three*!"

"Fucker weighs a ton," Scott grunted as Ted's body left the ground.

Claire opened the camper's door. The men two wrestled Ted in.

"You lead," Errol told Scott. "Stop in a mile or so," he added, then, already sore and shaky from the fight, half-rolled, half-fell into the camper next to Ted.

◆ ◆ ◆

Claire climbed into the cab alone, started it up, and followed Scott as he pulled out. She'd set Errol's knife down on the seat. She sheathed it, now, by feel. Eyes fixed on the road, she slid it back under the seat.

Would she really have stabbed Ted? Back in Spokane, the idea would have seemed absurd. But when she'd seen Errol bent backward, Ted's hands at his throat, the force of her feelings had startled her. No halitosised tree-hacker was going to kill her man!

She glanced at her side mirror, and saw headlights far behind. Was someone following? Police? Bearclaw/McGee?

As she watched, pulse thudding, the lights disappeared.

Scott's truck was pulling away. She pressed the gas to catch up, but didn't floor it. All she needed was to get pulled over now.

Every instinct in her body screamed, "Run!" But Scott was right about the border. And if they left, *she* would have wrecked their trip: she and her stupid flirtation. She didn't want the blame for that.

And there was something else. Something surprising. She'd begun to like this place: the lakes, the mountains, the woods. Even the fishing. How much of this was due to Scott, she wasn't sure. The way he looked at her made her shivery and hot. First Ted, now Scott. Had that mushroom clicked a sex-switch in her brain? She'd never act on any feelings she might have. But her general excitement level was way up.

Thank God, Scott's lights had moved to the shoulder. The distance between them shrank. Then she was pulling in behind.

She checked her mirror. No following lights.

Putting the truck in neutral, she set the brake, but kept the engine running, primed for getaway.

"He's really out," she heard Scott say. The fear in his voice frightened her. If Ted died, Errol might go to jail. In Canada! She might be charged as an accessory. Which, morally, she *was*.

"He showed up drunk on his ass," Errol said. "Lean him on this tree, so he won't choke on his own puke. This shithead doesn't get to die like a rock star."

"I get his legs this time," Scott said.

Ted mumbled something unintelligible.

"He's coming to," Errol said. "Come on. One, two, *three*!"

Claire heard shuffling. Cursing. But Ted was alive.

"That should do it," Scott said.

Errol said, "Yep." Then the men crunched back toward her.

"Old Hodges said, don't drive the mountain roads at night," Scott said. "We'll find a logging road, and park off the highway."

Errol opened the truck's door. "Move over, Babe. I'll drive."

Claire resented the way he took command—as if he hadn't lost his fight and almost gotten killed. Still, she squirmed into the passenger's seat.

She checked her side mirror, but couldn't see Ted.

"Poachers'll have to wait," Errol said, and pulled out after Scott.

Just like that, she was fuming. Did Errol think she was a fool?! Why had she ever married him?

Even the fight was an outrage. Fights over women were fights over property. She'd moved from keeper to keeper all her life. In the process, she'd gained respectability, security, privilege. And paid with . . . everything else.

But what was the alternative? Double down on art? Risk getting not only too old to have kids, but so old that, if she fell on her face, no one worth having would pick her up?

Maybe she *should* work for her father. Learn his business, please him, and nail down her inheritance. Mom, the alcoholic, would likely die before Dad. Some young trophy wife could drain his cash. That couldn't happen if she, Claire, controlled the business.

She pictured herself at fifty, fending off gold-diggers while she steered a multi-million-dollar corporation. Rich. Powerful. Alone.

If this truck's lights went out, she thought, *I'd be blind as the little bear.*

She shut her eyes as a test, then quickly reopened them. Scott's taillights were a red beacon showing the way.

She checked again for headlights following. Saw none.

Despite herself, she let her body ease toward Errol's. They might be finished, but old habits died hard. Errol meant well, and loved her unconditionally. Loved her enough to fight for her. To *die* for her.

The cab was warm. She'd wakened early.

Almost against her will, her head settled onto Errol's shoulder, which eased her into sleep.

FIFTH DAY

24

Sunrise saw the two trucks jolting down a pitted dirt road that led, Scott hoped fervently, to Ursula Lake. He'd passed a long night parked behind Errol on a narrower and more pitted dirt road. Fearing cops, log trucks, or worse, he'd barely slept. Mostly he'd fretted about "Ted." Had someone found him? Had he walked back to town? Had he gotten Errol's license number? Had he seen *him*?

His odometer showed twelve miles since the highway, but it felt like fifty as he lurched and rattled through forests much like those surrounding Oso, though the ground looked rockier, and the trees less green. Old Hodges had said you didn't need a four-wheel drive. Scott prayed that this was true, and that his truck's suspension would survive these jolts.

Killing the little bear felt like the worst kind of bad luck. The girl's corpse had seemed more Halloween prop than person. But the bear had been so real: its crushed skull and blood and awful, bawling groans. Any spiritual credits he'd earned with the roadside deer had been forfeited, plus a lot more.

Should they have run for the border? Hard to say. And what if Old Hodges's map was wrong? Scott was ready to stop and confer with Errol when, just before he signaled to pull over, the road forked and he saw two hand-lettered signs nailed to a tree. One pointed right to Dick's Dude Ranch; the other, left to Ursula Lake.

Honking in triumph, Scott veered left, with Errol following close behind.

Right away, the road began to twist and climb. The two trucks wound around and up, up and around, lurching over half-buried boulders, splashing through chugholes filled with snowmelt. Scott feared that he might have to turn around and scrap their plans. He couldn't risk getting stuck here.

But the road stayed passable.

As they climbed, patches of snow appeared, ringing the bases of huge conifers. Wildflowers—white, yellow, red, purple, blue—speckled the roadside. Chipmunks and ground squirrels blurred across the road. When he and Errol got out to test a split-log bridge before trusting their trucks to it, they heard a scream.

"Cool!" Errol said. "That's a lynx."

Once past the bridge, they kept climbing: twenty miles from the highway, clinging like bighorns to the road as it wound beside two-hundred-foot cliffs with no safety rails, no warning signs, nothing but space to fall into. Each turn of their wheels took them farther from help, but also from The Law and Jim McGee. No one would look for them up here.

Scott blessed Old Hodges for warning not to try the road at night. With luck, his fishing tips would prove as accurate.

By six thirty, the sun had climbed above the mountains, night's chill retreating before a warm, cloudless day. They hadn't passed a dude ranch. Still, what if some joker had reversed the signs?

He wished he'd plucked his sunglasses out of that hole. Could they be traced, and used as evidence? Could they—this was ridiculous, he knew—be used in magic against him?

At mile twenty-six, as his truck labored up a long, steep rise, he spooked a deer. He just had time to see how much it looked like "his" before it bounced into the woods. When he topped the rise a moment later—yes!—he saw the glint of water through the trees.

"All right!" he yelled, mashed his horn, and bounced down the rock-strewn road until, with Errol hot on his tail, he skidded to a stop in front of a large lake, not blue like Oso, but jade-green. Ten feet away, the road flowed into the water and civilization stopped. There was no campfire pit, no picnic tables, no trashcans, just a clearing with barely enough room for their two trucks. On all sides, wooded mountains hemmed them in.

◆ ◆ ◆

Errol whooped and leapt out of his cab. "Call me Paracelsus!" he proclaimed. "My luck's about to turn from shit to gold!"

Claire, climbing out on the other side of his truck, seemed to have forgotten "poachers." Or just let it go. Gazing out over the lake, she was smiling. This was already shit-to-gold.

Only a slight breeze stirred the lake's green surface, but heaps of thick foam on the bank showed that, last night, waves had crashed against the shore, which wasn't sand, but small gray rocks. Errol kicked the foam, and a big chunk flew away. Beneath the foam, the pebbly gray-black ground quivered like some gigantic creature's skin.

Bending for a closer look, Errol realized that the shore between the rocks was crawling, literally, with fingernail-sized, gray-black baby frogs. Some were squirming toward the lake. Others lay like tiny zombies, waiting for the sun to warm them into life.

"Check out the ground!" Errol called. Everywhere he looked: more tiny frogs. He'd just ended the life cycles of several, he observed, lifting his boot.

"Careful. You'll squash 'em," he warned as Scott and Claire clomped up.

"The tadpoles must have been the size of sperm," Scott said.

"Ick," Claire said.

"Frogs or sperm?" Errol asked.

"Both," Claire replied, but with a smile.

"Ready to fish?" Scott asked.

"Ready to *catch*," Errol said.

◆ ◆ ◆

Forty minutes later, with Errol in the middle and Claire in the prow, Scott was piloting his boat across Ursula Lake. The water was less clear than Oso's, but more clear than Secret Lake, its green tint darkening as the depth increased. No Spirit-of-the-Lake lived here. Not that Oso's had been real . . .

"I'm using 4X tippet," Errol said. "I don't want to hook another giant on 6X."

"Great minds think alike," Scott said. Old Hodges claimed to have "killed 'em" with a black woolly bugger, so Scott had tied one on when he changed his leader. He would have shared his tip, if asked. But he liked, for once, outfishing Errol.

An hour later, he'd caught two high-jumping trout over three pounds while Errol and Claire fished on without a hit.

Seeing Errol sunk in gloom, Scott handed him his last black bugger. "Try this," he said. Once back in camp, they could tie more.

Looking too miserable for pride, Errol tied on the fly. Almost at once, he hooked a brute that made two jumps, and—"God DAMN it!"—came unpinned. He recast in such a hurry that his line slapped water behind him, then his fly slammed into his right sleeve, and stuck.

While Errol extracted the fly, cursing as his parka tore, Scott asked Claire, "Want to trade rods? Mine's got a killer fly."

"All right," she said. "Thank you."

She'd started the day in a red windbreaker zipped to the neck. As the air warmed, she'd unzipped, exposing a blue blouse and no bra underneath. Now, exchanging rods with Scott, her hand brushed his. This, plus the movement of her breasts under her blouse, sent a thrill from Scott's groin to his head and back again.

The thrill increased when she tied into a bruiser, laughing and shrieking like a girl, her nipples poking through her shirt so forcefully that, by the time Errol netted her prize, Scott's pants were tighter than the smile on Errol's face.

"Let's let him go," she said.

When Errol said nothing, Scott said, "Want me to help her?"

Errol, hurrying to cast again, said, "Go for it. You've got the magic touch."

Three-pounds-plus, the big rainbow lay in the net, frilly red gills opening and closing uselessly.

"Wet your hands," Scott said. "Now, up!" He cradled the fish and, Claire's hands beneath his, lowered it into the lake.

"Back and forth," Scott said. "Force water through his gills."

Claire's hands gripped his as the fish fought for balance.

Stabbed by guilt, Scott glanced at Errol, who fished on grimly, eyes grilling the lake as, with a flip of its tail, Claire's fish swam down and down and then was lost in green.

"It feels good to let them live," she said, wiping her hands on her jeans, and giving Scott her most magnetic smile.

"It does," Scott said.

Errol raised his head. "We won't get more if we sit here yammering."

The trout, though, seemed suddenly to have sworn off flies. After an hour without a hit, Errol barked, "Fuck a woodchipper! Let's eat."

"I'm ready," Claire said, and opened Errol's cooler, which held their lunch.

◆ ◆ ◆

"We can troll while we eat," Errol said before Scott turned his motor off. "Hope springs eternal," he added, and flashed Scott a mouthful of Cheeze Whiz behind Claire's back.

"How suave," Scott said, and passed him a cup of Tang.

Two mallards flew past, quacking. Their short wings whistled, pumping hard.

"I had a nightmare about ducks." Claire said between spoonfuls of yogurt.

"I had a nightmare about not catching fish," Errol said as the boat chugged on, dragging his line behind. He stopped himself from adding, "I wish I'd wake up."

Claire, sexy as always, adjusted her butt on the metal seat. "I was hostessing at Denny's when a duck family waddled in," she said—aiming her words, Errol thought, squarely at Scott. "They were all dressed like Puss 'n Boots: plumed hats, ruffled shirts, and boots that looked ridiculous on their thin legs."

"You ought to paint that," Errol said.

"Maybe I will," Claire said. Dismissively? "They were so cute, I patted one. My leg started to hurt, so I looked down." She looked down at her leg as she spoke. "A duck with shark teeth was biting me. Then all the ducks started to bite, and I woke up."

"It's good we wake up when things get really bad," Scott said.

"If we're asleep," Errol said. Getting no comment, he added, "I dreamed a tsunami washed me out to sea."

Claire shut her eyes, trailed her hand in the water, and sighed.

Errol knew he shouldn't comment, even as his mouth said, "Am I boring you, Claire?"

"Not at all."

Before he could decide how to respond, Claire's reel screeched and her rod banged across the boat.

"Jesus!" Errol yelled, and grabbed Scott's rig just before it went overboard. He let the fish run once to make sure it was hooked, then dutifully handed the rig to Claire.

Five minutes later, she landed and released a four-pound buck.

"*Now* you've got the hang!" Scott said.

"Here's your rod," Claire told Scott, handing it back with a wide grin.

When, minutes later, Scott tied into a hen that weighed five pounds but fought like ten, Errol fished through the whole fight, feeling his face twist like a Kwakiutl demon. Once the fish was landed, and he still hadn't had a hit, he reeled in furiously.

"I slept for shit last night," he growled. "I need a nap."

"Try my rod," Scott offered. "Seems like it's hot."

Errol's first impulse was, *Fuck your rod*. But Scott was trying to help. Even if he relished having to.

"I need to sleep," Errol said.

"Want to head in?" Scott asked.

"For now. Sun's too high, anyway," Errol said and, with a vicious snap, popped Scott's wooly bugger off his line. He had an impulse to thrust it back at Scott, but stuck it in his own fly box and mashed the box shut.

♦ ♦ ♦

Scott kicked himself all the way back to camp. He should have traded rods with Errol instead of Claire. Once in a bad mood, Errol tended to stay that way.

The big man jumped out of the boat and seized the painter-line the instant they touched land.

"Don't beach me," Scott said. "I think I'll fish a little more."

"Suit yourself," Errol said, and was stalking away when Claire called, "Errol—do you mind if I fish, too?"

Errol kept walking. "Would it matter if I did?"

Scott winced inside. The last place he wanted to be was between Errol and his wife. But there he was. He couldn't *order* Claire ashore.

He could decide not to go back out. But he hated to quit when he had a hot hand.

"We'll likely get skunked, this time of day," he said, hoping to discourage Claire. But she stayed put.

"Don't wake me, comin' in," Errol growled over his broad, retreating back.

"What a snot," Claire said as her husband ducked into their camper and, against his better judgment, Scott started back across the lake.

"Hell is being The Wretch," Scott said. "Especially on your one trip of the year."

Claire re-zipped her windbreaker to her neck. "He's acting like a two-year-old," she said.

"I'd probably act the same if it were me."

"I'll bet you'd act at least three," she said, stretched forward, and patted Scott's knee. The pat was more maternal than sexy. But it felt sexy anyway.

The force of her smile nearly winched him across the boat.

◆ ◆ ◆

Claire watched the green lake swallow her black fly, then sat still, hands strangling her rod. Lose Errol's gear, and she'd never live it down. For that matter, she might not live down fishing with Scott. Still, it served Errol right. Whatever had made him leave Oso, it wasn't to report "poachers." His lie was infuriating. And *so* depressing. How could she stay married to a man who didn't trust her?

All the same, she liked being out on the water. She felt like part of a

Japanese screen: a tiny figure in the middle of a lake ringed by snow-capped mountains.

"You were right," she told Scott, forcing her voice to rise above the motor's drone. "Fishing *is* pleasure out of pain."

He looked at her as if surprised that she could speak. "So I'm acquitted of perversion?"

"No, I'm *convicted.*" She started to unzip her windbreaker, then zipped it back. She should have worn a bra. "When I hook a fish, I feel like some cavewoman who can feed her family, have lots of babies, and go with any man I like."

She moved to the boat's middle seat so she wouldn't have to shout. But Scott stopped talking. With their knees almost touching, he looked everywhere except at her.

"Errol says you might move to LA," she said after a long pause.

"I might." He yanked out another pull of line. "My friends who tried it came back beaten black and blue."

"That won't happen to you."

"I'm glad *somebody* thinks so."

As if it had moved on its own, her hand patted his knee. Again. "Whatever happens, you're an artist. That's a great thing to be."

"A *rich* artist is great to be," Scott allowed. "A poor one is a hobbyist who should get a job."

"Spoken like a true American." She brushed back her hair in a way she knew was flirty, then wished she could take the motion back. "The trouble with rich is, you don't need to excel," she said. "I'd give anything to be really good at something."

"When the world says, 'Your majesty,' why disagree?" Scott said. "Anyway, I'm sure you're good at things."

The same kind of blush colored Scott's face that she could feel heating up hers. "I've failed at everything that matters to me. Even my marriage," she said, and looked away toward the shore. Before Scott could reply, she said, "Sorry if that's too much information."

◆ ◆ ◆

"I admire your honesty," Scott said, and trying not to seem flustered, fiddled with his reel. His body felt robotic: responding to commands he knew Claire didn't mean to give.

"Remember in *The Brothers K*? The Karamazovs' *vital energy*?" she said. "You have that."

The Brothers K was the greatest novel he had ever read. He loved that she could reference it. To compliment him!

"Errol has it too," she said. "He used to have more."

She stared at the bottom of the boat where, Scott noticed, half an inch of water sloshed. Was his boat leaking?

"Don't quit music," she said, and for the third time, touched his knee.

"I don't *want* to."

When he looked up, her eyes were on him: blue-green irises nearly swallowed by black pupils that looked as deep as the lake. He tried to think of Julie, but her image wouldn't coalesce.

"What guitarists do you like?" Claire said.

"The great ones. Clapton. Page. Beck. Ritchie Blackmore. Brian May," he said. "Hendrix was the king."

"He had all *kinds* of Karamazov energy," she said. "And look how well he did."

"He was a great player, but he made it on hype." Scott hated to sound negative, but truth was truth. "Hendrix was a black hippie who burned his guitar and humped the air until some bigshot said, 'Hey, I can use that boy.'"

"Hype *yourself*," Claire suggested. "Meet the right people. Schmooze 'em up . . ."

"I'm bad at that," he said, and yanked two more pulls off his reel. "The *right people* are lawyer-slash-executives who think D minor's an eighth-grader with big breasts."

Scott hoped that he seemed nobly outraged, not whiny and ineffectual. But the gates of self-pity were open wide. The fact that Claire was beautiful, sympathetic, and out-of-the-question made matters worse.

"Saint Disney preaches, 'Follow your heart,'" he said. "That's a highway to depression. To make it in music, you've got to either be lucky or ruthless beyond belief. Forget the rules. Forget fairness, and standing in line. Everyone and thing exists to advance *you*." He twitched his fly three times. No bite. And no response from Claire.

"I had one chance to jump the line." He almost told her about Sara's dad. But considering Errol's deal with *her* dad, she might take it wrong. So he only said, "I turned it down."

◆ ◆ ◆

A flutey birdcall pulled Claire's eyes away from Scott. She would have sworn she saw someone step from the woods and point at their boat. At the same instant, she smelled smoke.

Terror surged into her chest. If these woods caught fire, they'd be trapped!

"I . . ." she began. But the smell was gone. The person, too. Her brain was playing tricks. Again.

"People who *make it big* sell themselves so often they could supposit the Empire State Building, and not feel a thing," Scott was saying.

"If you understand the system," she said, "you can beat it."

Scott shook his head sadly. "When dumb people get kicked, they think it's an exception, and keep trying. It's worse when you know kicking's the rule."

"Isn't it worse not to try?" Claire found herself losing patience. Just a little, but enough to cool things down.

"You're right," Scott said as their boat chugged forward and the fish refused to bite. "Not trying is the worst."

She saw a chance to dial things down another notch. "Speaking of trying," she said, "can you teach me to cast?"

◆ ◆ ◆

"Errol taught *me*," Scott said, glad to pull his friend back into the picture. "He's a great teacher."

"He's too impatient. With me, anyway."

What was he supposed to do—say *No, you're wrong*? His only choice was to kill his motor and say, "Okay. I'll try."

"We'll have to stand," he added, "Careful. We don't want to swim."

He stripped his line in, and got to his feet. If they practiced on land, she'd snag up right away.

"Stay on my left, so I don't hook you," he said as she pulled off her windbreaker, and stood. "Keep your wrist straight. Your arm moves from the shoulder. Up and down." He demonstrated. "Stop your backcast at one o'clock. Feel your line uncurl . . . then, pull your elbow down, and stop at ten. Like so!"

He made one cast, then several more to demonstrate.

"You're more graceful than Errol," Claire said.

"He gets more distance. And accuracy," Scott felt obliged to say. He laid out one more cast, reeled in, and set down his rod.

Scott scanned the lake as Claire inched closer. If only Errol would motor out and break the mood. The boat kept tilting him toward Claire. His own voice seemed small and far away: "We should switch sides. So you don't hook *me*."

Rod in her right hand, she took a step. The boat lurched. Then she was in his arms, rod clattering on the boat's floor, which was wobbling like a tightrope.

"Sit down," he warned. Then he was falling, yelling "SHIT," the boat pitching like a bronco, throwing him. He heard Claire scream as ice-water engulfed his head.

He surfaced, sculling, dragged down by his boots' weight. His lungs refused to take in air. His heart stopped beating.

But his legs were moving. Nothing had grabbed them.

His boat floated calmly several yards away. Claire was thrashing toward it. Clutching a side. Struggling to get in.

Scott's heart started back up. He seized a breath. "Claire," he yelled. "Don't move. You'll tip the boat."

He fought his way to the side opposite her. One hand on the gunwale, he managed to tug his boots off and drop them, one by one, into the boat.

There was no Spirit-of-the-Lake here, but simple cold was sucking out his strength. Internal flotation would keep his boat from sinking. If it swamped, though, they'd die of hypothermia before they got to shore.

"We'll be fine," he said, and tried to believe it. "Pull down hard. Balance me."

The boat wobbled and tipped. Scott's gunwale was two inches from going under, but Claire's weight was just enough. Hooking one numb leg over the side, Scott heaved himself up and, with a painful, scraping, shoulder-wrenching thud, into the boat.

"Scott, hurry, please, it's cold," Claire begged, her teeth chattering like dice.

Scott picked himself up, grasped her hands, and pulled—the way, at Secret Lake, Errol had pulled *him*.

He was not as strong as Errol. Not even close. If Claire pulled him out of the boat, he might not have the strength to get back in.

"Claire," he yelled. "Kick! Like you're swimming!"

Slowly, squirming and flapping her feet as he pulled, she wriggled her upper half into the boat, then hung jackknifed across the side until Scott reached over and dragged her legs, immobilized by cold, over the gunwales, one by one.

Limp as a soaked towel, she lay next to Scott on the wet floor of the boat, both of them panting and shivering in the sun.

She sat up finally. "Thank you," she said and, looking down, twined her fingers between his. Her wet blouse was clear as cellophane, her nipples pink and tight. Hair dripping down her back, she could have been a water nymph in jeans.

"You're welcome . . ." What started as a nervous laugh came out of Scott's mouth like a last gasp.

Claire crawled across the seat and pressed her mouth to his. The Last Commandment reared between them: a locked door, all Nature on the other side. For one long instant, he held it back. Then, with a crack, the door was down. He met Claire's kiss, passive at first, then matching her heat with his own.

His shaking hands found her cold breasts through her blouse, then under it. Her tongue warmed his lips as she gave soft, encouraging sighs.

"It's freezing," he said as his shivering intensified.

"We need to take off these wet clothes," Claire said. Her eyes, become the same green as the lake, were shining and huge.

He cast a stricken glance toward camp and Errol. Then, feeling like he'd lost his bearings in the universe, he started his boat and sped for the far shore.

25

Errol had planned to crawl into his camper, pull the curtains, and catch up on his sleep. But his ulcer burned. Fighting that Canadian asshole hadn't helped. His whole body felt like a bruise.

His mind hurt just as bad. For all he knew, the RCMP were searching for his truck. His description might be all over Canada.

Or maybe not. No point in second-guessing, now. He had to stop worrying, he told himself as he lay in the half-dark, deep-breathing the way he and Claire had learned when they took Beginning Meditation at The Learning Company. Even then, he'd had the ulcer: earned, in tandem with his Top Salesman prize, by hawking insurance while taking fifteen units and directing plays at UW. He'd vowed never to sell out like those potbellied managers he'd seen sneaking shots of bourbon at their desks. But that vow had vanished as completely as the mantra toad-like little "Vishnu," as white as *he* was, had been "inspired" to give him. His personal Cosmic Noise.

"Fuck you," he said. To Vishnu, Claire, Scott, Pop Gunn, and the whole world, including and especially himself. That was his true mantra: "Fuck you!"

His bottle of Yukon Jack was nearly empty, but he downed the rest to spite his ulcer, then lay back. The pain in his gut, naturally, got worse. Every nerve in his body seemed glazed with itching powder. He should have reported that girl's corpse, cut his losses, and gone home. He would have done it, but for "Ted."

Just the thought of being beaten by that oaf made his guts burn. The thought that Scott had had to save him was beyond humiliation.

Then there was Claire. Ted had called her a cock tease, and it was true. Take that shirt she'd worn today. Her nipples had bugged out more than

Scott's eyes. Which was a lot. Any time he thought his *cojones* were gone, Claire found a way to slice off more.

A groan that was more like a roar surged out of his mouth. Leaping up, he tore out of his camper and, in his sock-feet, flung himself into a dance of rage. He stomped the ground, rained punches at the air, whirled and howled as if he'd gone berserk. Ever since his mom's breakdown, he'd been afraid of losing it like her. Even as he flailed, he wondered, "Now?"

But his fit exhausted itself with his breath. He dealt the air a few more crotch-kicks, then dropped, panting, onto the ground.

Shame followed relief. He hoped to hell the woods had swallowed up his sounds.

Claire had been trouble this whole trip. As for Scott—it was like getting back with an old girlfriend: great at first, then you started to recall why you broke up. Errol saw, plain as day, what had kept Scott from the Big Time. Too much self-pity. Too little drive. Post-traumatic stress disorder was a smokescreen for failure-of-nerve.

Yet Scott saw *him* as a sellout!

He envied Scott's freedom to bed anyone he chose. But there was more to life than sex. Claire understood him. She knew how hard he'd worked to escape his scrimp-and-save childhood, his mom playing Eternal Ingenue, forcing him to be her plumber, electrician, carpenter, roofer, gardener, mechanic, plus personal manager and confidant. He'd vowed to obliterate that life—never again to worry about money or a reaming from the Powers That Be. He'd willingly exchanged Artist Wannabe for Young Executive, fighting to give Claire the life they both deserved.

Ironic, though. Before him, Claire had been engaged to, count 'em, *four* Rising Young Executives, and found them all, as she'd told him in those first fantastic weeks, "ball-less and dull." So she married him, then teamed with Daddy to make him a eunuch, too. Now she swooned over guys like Ted, and maybe even Scott, for the very traits she'd pounded out of *him*.

Rage swelled again. He had too much fire inside. Theater had channeled it. Working for Pop Gunn, he had to tamp it down. *Way* down. Okay, he could do that: tamp and tamp until he rose so high no one could tell him not to burn. When that happened, watch out, world!

He'd started pacing. Like a grizzly in a cage. Fishing alone, he knew he'd score. Scott's success had wrecked his rhythm, and made him try too hard. That, plus lack of sleep, had made him frantic, impatient, careless. Had made him The Wretch.

It was midday, now: the worst time to fish. (What if Scott caught a thirty-pounder? Or Claire? Don't think of that.) He needed to relax, have fun, then hit the water fresh. Once he got home, he'd sic the cops on Jim McGee. As for Claire, let her flirt. Neither she nor Scott would dare do more than bat their eyes.

"What a fantastic place," he said to reinforce the fact. This was the most remote, unspoiled lake he'd ever fished. Trout could grow huge in its depths: thirty-pounders he had a real chance to catch. Thanks to Scott. He shouldn't forget that.

All he needed was one pat on the back from Fate—one trophy trout to say, "You've still got what it takes." In the coming months of hard-sell, soft-sell, bullying, fawning, lying, mangling his better nature, and brassing it out in Land Development, that fish would tell him, "Greatness is still possible for you."

He made himself drink in the scent of evergreens and deep, clean water; the lapping of the lake; the kiss of sun and a light breeze, everything framed by old-growth woods and godlike mountains.

One peak in particular, capped with snow, rose straight out of the far shore. As if the lake had slid, otter-style, down the mountain. "Climb me, little man," the mountain called. "Climb me, and I'll change your life."

He guessed the summit was three thousand feet above the lake. Allow thirty minutes to reach the foot, two hours up, two hours down . . . he'd still be back in time for the night bite.

Thoughts of the mountain dialed down his stomach pain. His socks were muddy, so he pulled on fresh ones, then his boots as he hummed Fats Wallers's "Your Feet's Too Big." Trust old Fats, with tongue in cheek and stride piano pumping, to ease him back into a better mood.

He kept humming, then singing as he bolted his motor to his boat and loaded his gear. At the last minute, he left a note for Claire in the camper.

"Gone exploring. Back when I'm done." It was brusque, but more consideration than she'd given him.

His motor started right away. He backed carefully from shore, then turned the boat to face the mountain, and gunned it.

"Your feet's . . . too . . . big," he blared as he roared off across the lake, trying to simulate piano and four horns with just one mouth and assorted gyrations.

To his left, a tiny flash in the sunlight would be Scott's boat. It was too far away to see its shape, much less to pick out Scott or Claire. *Screw 'em both*, he thought, and motored on, glad when a point of land blotted them out, and only the mountain loomed.

In twenty minutes, he was beaching his boat at the mountain's foot. He thought about hiding the boat. But who was here to steal it? A wendigo?

He stuffed a flashlight, his hatchet, and a coil of rope into his pack, gazed around to get his bearings, then started to climb.

The grade was steep. But spring hadn't yet filled in the underbrush. He could use tree trunks for leverage, when and if he needed it.

At times, the lake would disappear, then reappear farther below, blue-green as Navajo turquoise. Birds flitted, twittering, through the trees and brush. Squirrels leapt branch to branch, or preached from pulpit-limbs. Chipmunks scooted here and there, popping in and out of holes, shrilling bird-like whistles while, far out on the lake, a pair of ospreys, or maybe eagles, soared.

A tawny, long-bodied, short-legged creature slipped behind a fallen tree. Marten or weasel, probably. In Washington, Errol knew most birds and animals by sight and sound. Less so, up here.

Maybe because he'd left his boat exposed, he couldn't shake the sense that something—cougar? bear? human?—was stalking him. He back-tracked twice, sure he heard footsteps, but found nothing.

Loud cawing jerked his gaze to where three crows—big birds themselves—harried the flight of a hulking, shag-headed, purple-black raven. This bird of ill omen made him think of Jim McGee. That creepazoid could have rehidden the girl's body and be in the Yukon by now.

Did grizzlies live in these mountains? He checked over his shoulder, glad to see only the glint of water through the trees. Up here, there were so many ways to die.

"My wind's for shit," he mumbled as he stopped to rest. Five years ago, this incline would've been no sweat. Lack of exercise, not drunken "Ted," had kicked his ass. He'd join a gym as soon as he got home. Work fewer hours. Maybe join a community theatre. If Claire saw him in his element, she might remember why she'd married him. *He* might remember who he was.

First, though, he had to have a showdown with Pop Gunn.

Taking a long swig from his water bottle full of Tang, he stood, and resumed climbing.

What was the altitude here? Eight thousand feet? Breathing was brutal. Yet the summit still seemed far away.

The higher he climbed, the more snow there was. Any bare ground was wet from runoff. Rills of snowmelt sparkled everywhere: the elixir of life.

Several hard-breathing minutes more, and he was crunching through the slick snowpack of spring, when sunlight changed soft powder to glittering ice. He blessed his pac boots' gripping soles, and the bare trees, which often saved him from a fall.

From this height, he could see a long ways behind. No one or thing was following.

The thin oxygen had made him weak as that old man at Oso. His heart beat triple-time. Even standing still, he couldn't catch his breath.

His watch said 1:50, and he wasn't near the top. Even worse, he'd lost the lake. It was only a trick of trees and angles, but it worried him. There was no 911 up here.

He brushed snow off a fallen log, and sat again. His altitude-headache felt like an ax thunking into his brain. Yet, louder than blood drumming in his ears, he heard a distant roar. Like what a wendigo might make.

Shoving down the urge to flee, he gripped his hatchet, stood, and climbed.

At first, his loud breathing and the crunch of snow muffled the roar. As he climbed higher, the roar returned. The wind blew stronger, colder, less broken by trees. Still he climbed. He wouldn't quit. No goddamned way.

The vegetation had grown sparse; the trees, gnomelike and bent. Up here, the soil became too rocky, and the climate too harsh to sustain thick woods. Still he followed the roar: up and to his left.

The view was like something Lewis and Clark might have seen. Monumental. Snowy peaks and wooded valleys stretched unbroken to the horizon.

But no lake.

"It couldn't disappear," he told the blue sky, ignoring a voice that hissed, "It could."

His feet had left a trail in the thin snow. But even without that, if he walked to the right and down, he'd find the lake.

Once, hiking the Cascades with cousin Joshie, he'd gotten lost in a freak June storm. One minute the wind had been their friend; the next, their deadly enemy. They'd walked and walked while snow blotted out the world—walked until Joshie, just turned thirteen, lay down and, in the most melodramatic movie style, told Errol, "Finish me."

Errol remembered how he'd yanked little "Fieldmouse" up, threatening to drag him by his prick if he had to. The boy had stood and followed meekly as Errol trudged on and on until, at last, they'd lucked into an empty cabin. There, huddled in summer sleeping bags, they spent the night. Then, in the morning, with the sun bright and the snow melting, they'd found themselves barely fifty feet from the trail.

Now, as the howling increased, Errol called on the courage and tenacity that had saved him then.

"Sounds like wind," he told himself. "Wind blowing through something."

2:40. The sky was flawless blue: no clouds, much less snow-clouds, in the sky. He'd give himself until 3:10.

His eyes swept the snowy grade above, then stopped. Backtracked. Forty-five degrees up and to the left, he saw what looked like a black bullseye in the snow. A cave. The sound seemed to come from there.

The wind, picking up chill from the snow, drove ice-needles through his parka as he climbed. Tearing past the open mouth of the cave, that same wind made it bellow like a titanic organ pipe. Forget the Phantom of the Opera. Every wendigo in the world seemed to be howling.

"Christ on a crabcake," Errol said. "The Mouth of Hell."

He bet the Indians called it that. And had legends to explain it. Maybe even held sacrifices there.

One time when Scott had ribbed him for attracting "trainloads of shit," Errol had said, "If you go outside, you're sure to step in something." Now, while Scott stuck to the safe and easy, *he* had heard the mountain's call. He'd taken a chance, and found something ancient and wonderful.

Fatigue gone, he hurried toward the gaping mouth.

Just outside the cave, he stopped, letting the roar swirl around him.

He pulled his flashlight and hatchet from his backpack. Then, hatchet in right hand, light in left, he stepped into the cave.

The roar became a rumble instantly. Glowing in his flashlight's beams, the stone walls seemed smooth and wet, as if a giant worm had tunneled out the cave, and retreated moments before.

Fifty feet inside, the cave bent to the right, blocking the white circle of day.

Errol halted. First the lake had disappeared. Now, the daylight. What if his flashlight failed?

He dared himself, "Turn it off and see."

More like don't see, he thought as darkness slammed down like a fist. He stood a moment, gripping his flashlight until, as if a projector were warming up, a pile of skulls emerged out of the dark. Glowing pale white, they seemed to sense him. They turned, aiming their empty eye-sockets his way, then started rolling toward him, pale jaws clacking as they howled.

A headless girl floated his way. A scar-faced Indian raised a bloody knife.

This must be caused by altitude. Reverse nitrogen narcosis, or some such. Errol shook his head, and flicked the flashlight on.

The visions disappeared. All the same, he started jogging toward the entrance to the cave.

A pale shape loomed in front of him: nine feet tall, with a skull-head. Errol didn't stop. He ploughed right through.

No impact. Only cold.

He ran faster, flashlight groping at stone walls like a hand in a coffin. Seeing light, he sprinted for it, the wendigo's chill breath chasing him until he stumbled, gasping, into open air.

The monster roared its disappointment from the cave as Errol staggered down the mountain. All he wanted was to be back in camp. To tell his wife and friend of his adventure, bask in their praise, and ridicule his fears. Maybe tomorrow they'd all explore this place.

He looked back to be sure it was still there.

It was. Roaring.

He hurried on, turning every few steps to check the cave over his shoulder. His right foot kicked something: a log under the snow. His feet attacked each other. In a snarl of arms and legs, he fell.

His flashlight and hatchet flew out of his hands as, feet first, he began to slide. He gave a little laugh, lightheaded and drunk, grabbing at trees and bushes barely out of reach. *Beats walking down*, he thought.

He was on his side now, moving too fast when, with an effort, he reached for a scrub pine. His right hand cupped it as his body slid by. Then his feet ran out of snow, and dropped.

<h2 style="text-align:center">26</h2>

"This trip was supposed to save my marriage," Claire said, resting her head on Scott's chest. "I knew it was hopeless," she told his collarbone. "I just couldn't admit it."

She wanted to tell him, *Stop fidgeting.* But the rocky ground and weeds under his bare back had to be uncomfortable.

"Now I know how Judas felt," he said, and stroked her hair.

Screened by thick foliage, they lay in a small clearing a few feet from the lake. Their fishing rods leaned against a tree beside Scott's sack of extra clothes. Their wet clothes hung on bushes, drying in the sun.

"We'll hear his motor if he comes looking," Scott said.

She noticed that he didn't say Errol's name. She said it for them both. "Errol sleeps like the dead. He'll be out for hours."

With any luck, that would prove true. Still, it was good their boat was fifty yards away. If Errol appeared, they'd throw on their wet clothes, say they'd fallen overboard, and gone ashore to warm up and dry off.

"I can't believe . . ." Scott raised his arms waist-high, then let them drop. "Any of this."

"It's like I was baptized," Claire said with a wan smile. "Full immersion. Born again." She did a feeble *cross-eyed fish*. "More like possessed."

"*I* am, for sure," Scott said. "By you."

She almost told about the mushroom. But he'd think she was perverted. Or worse. Anyway, *possessed* was just a shifting of responsibility. She'd had sex with Scott because she wanted to.

She sat up, bent back down to kiss him on the lips, then said, "I've made such a mess of my life. No real career, and now my second marriage . . ." Her eyes brimmed. "Trail of ants."

"Trail of ants?"

She nodded. "My friends and I say that when something's dead."

"'Trail of ants.' That's good."

"Speaking of trail of ants," she said, "Do you know how old I am?"

He made a show of scrutinizing. "Don't tell me you're underage."

She gave his face the softest slap. "I'm thirty-two. Almost thirty-three."

Did she see surprise? Disappointment?

He cupped her left breast as if weighing it. "You could've fooled me," he said. "Anyway, thirty's the new thirteen."

"I can fool the world about my age," she said. "But not my 'biological clock'. As Errol likes to say."

Scott squirmed, adjusting his position on the ground. "Errol," he said. As if recalling a dead friend.

"I'm terrified of getting old," Claire said. "Middle-aged women get ignored."

"I could never ignore you." Like any man with a hard-on, Scott sounded eager as a pup.

She kissed him lightly, then deeper. He settled back. She straddled, guiding him inside.

"I'd never do this," he said, "if I wasn't . . ." *A traitor* jumped into Claire's mind, even as Scott said, "Crazy for you."

"Tell me how to please you," she breathed, sliding slowly down on him. She loved the feel of him. Loved knowing he was at her mercy. In her power zone.

"Tell me what you like," she breathed, shutting her eyes and leaning back in the way that drove Errol wild.

"You're doing great," Scott said, one hand on each breast. "Keep doing it."

"Tell me . . . how you . . . like it." Her words came in short bursts as she moved: a languid belly dance. Let him think he was running this sexual show.

He moved one hand to her waist, and forced her back so he was less than half inside. "Tease me," he said. "Just barely. There."

After a few seconds, she moved to slide down all the way. He stopped her.

"Please," she said, as if he'd roused the nymphomaniac in her. Which he had, in a way. But she knew, too, that men loved hearing women beg.

"Let me," she said. "Please."

"Not yet," he said as if completely in command. "Not now. Not yet."

◆ ◆ ◆

Scott used both hands to hold her back. With her eyes closed and head thrown back, she looked like St. Theresa in Ecstasy. He had to wonder, could Errol work her up like this?

The thought of Errol made guilt shoot through him. Every part but one.

"Bend down," he said. When she obeyed, he took a nipple in his lips as she made cooing noises that were almost song.

When she was ready, he moved his hand back to her breasts, and let her wet fire surround him.

"Get on top," she whispered. "Please."

He rolled her onto her back and let himself go, her cries fast and hot in his ear: the cries he'd heard on that first night. He tried to shove that thought away, and focused on her flawless face as she wrung out the last spasming drops from both of them. Then they lay still, side by side on a carpet of pine needles and fern, making sounds of contentment and congratulation.

As his heart slowed and pine needles jabbed his skin, thoughts of Errol crowded back. They made him want to push away from Claire. To tell himself, *This never happened*. Yet he felt too drained and comfortable to move.

She sat up first. "If you gave up music," she said, "what would you do?"

Flat on his back, he thrust his arms overhead and stretched. "*There's* a segue."

"Sorry," she said, and lay back down beside him. "I'm just curious if you have a Plan B."

"Not business. I'd be too bored to get out of bed," he said, then remembered that her father was in business. A hateful one.

"Duly noted," she said, nuzzling his neck.

He stared up at the cloudless sky: bright Giotto-blue. It was good that she wanted to understand him. All the same, he felt like she was sneaking up. Like Dad pushing for law school. Was she already planning to run his life?

"I'm interested in physics," he said. "Einstein changed the world." Shutting his eyes, he ran both hands through Claire's damp hair. It smelled of lake, now, and shampoo. "Too bad I don't have his IQ."

"*You* don't aim high," she said. "How about something mere mortals can do?"

"I had a philosophy prof at Rice. Dr. Mansfield," he said. "I wanted to be like him: a modern Socrates, in search of Right, Justice, and Truth. With shaggy silver hair and no hemlock."

He pushed his arms overhead, and stretched. It felt great to be naked, physically and psychologically, with a woman as bright as she was beautiful. Women he met in clubs made him feel like a star. But he doubted his future wife hung out in bars. Claire was a leap back into the world where people got what they went after. Losing Sara, he'd lost that world. With Claire, he might get it back again.

She's Errol's wife. The thought had pumped its poison before he could thrust it away.

He spoke more fervently, to compensate. "I took a course from Mansfield. Philosophy in Action," he said. "The *action* turned out to be, mostly, praising *The Workers.* I doubt if Mansfield ever met a real worker, but we all got *A*s because grades were oppressive. And the next year, Mansfield converted to Scientology."

He'd hoped to get a laugh. But the story sounded sour, coming out.

Close by, a hammering began.

Claire sat up straight. "What's that?"

Scott's first thought—war drums—was idiotic. "Just a woodpecker," he said.

"It's loud." She swept her gaze around the lake, then back to him. "These woods are . . . uncanny."

"That's a good word for 'em."

She took his left hand in hers, seemed to scrutinize it like a palm reader, then let it go. "Do you believe in the supernatural?" she said.

"I think people need it sometimes. To make sense of things."

She nodded. "Death, for sure."

"Think of the Indians who lived here," he said. "Not only would they go stir-crazy, stuck in their lodges for months of every year. Sometimes food must've run out."

She pursed her lips and shook her head as if to say, "Too horrible to think about."

"Better to imagine twelve-foot cannibals roaming through the snow than to think of your own family eating you," he said.

"Do you think the supernatural is ever *real*?"

Normally, Scott loved this part of a new relationship: sharing mental *and* physical intimacies. Now, because of Errol, his feelings kept shifting. Good, bad, good, bad . . .

"The supernatural's probably natural," he said. "We just don't know how it works." He caught himself pulling his cowlick, and lowered his right hand. "Think how early humans must have looked at fire."

She looked out across the lake. Scanning for Errol? "You know about dark matter and dark energy, right?"

"I know most of the universe is made of it."

"Ninety percent," she said. "And we can't find it. We only know it exists because of math." She took his hand again, as if not sure whether to keep or let it go. "What if ghosts and demons are dark energy? Or something like it."

Scott pointed at a big spruce to their left. "That tree looks solid, but it's mostly empty space. Who knows what else we don't perceive?"

"Some of the thoughts I have out here . . . they don't seem to come from me." She looked around as if the woods were listening. "I wonder if brains can leave their energy behind."

"Sometimes I think the woods are conscious," Scott said. "And lakes. And animals. If they were, what kind of thoughts would they have? And how would their thoughts feel to *us*?"

"I wonder too," she said, then turned to face Scott squarely. "Why did Errol go to the police?"

Blindsided, all Scott could think to say was, "You should ask *him*."

If she'd wheedled, gone tearful, or simply said, "Okay," he might have come clean. Instead, her eyes narrowed. "Is there some dark secret here?"

"I don't like to talk behind Errol's back."

"But it's okay to bonk his wife?"

Scott sat up, stung. "If he won't tell you, I will, once we're home. Right now, I take the fifth."

Her look wasn't angry, but it wasn't pleased. "If music doesn't work," she said, "you should try Law."

He made a face. "I'd rather shake down widows for the mafia."

"You disapprove of the justice system, too?"

No missing the edge in that.

"Law's a game," he said. "Lawyers play and clients pay. So says Jim Murray." Realizing Claire had never heard of him, he added, "That's my dad. He's a lawyer."

"Complex societies can't function without lawyers," Claire said, as if quoting a text.

"They can't function *with* as many as we've got. All those suits looking to be tycoons—they suck the life out of the country. Name a problem, and lawyers make it worse."

"*You're* Mr. Positive." Claire's voice sounded sharp, the way it had when she defended the *rat race*. "What *does* pass muster with you?"

He thought at first that she had said *pass mustard*. Then he felt as if she'd stuck an ice-pick in his gut. His dreams of love and understanding instantly went flat. He'd wanted to confess, "I'm scared of LA. I'm scared I'll fail at music, and have to take a job that sucks the life out of me." Instead, he said, "The woods pass muster. Lakes and rivers do. Until land-developers get at 'em."

She took a moment to respond. When she did, her voice was cold. "It must be tough to live up to your high standards."

Change *standards* to *values*, and Sara had returned.

"Standards can be concrete overshoes," he said. "But without them, people are just . . . depraved. Life is chaos and ugliness."

He yanked his jeans on, trying to think what else to say. But she had turned away, her shoulders shaking.

He felt like a size six thousand heel. "Claire? Did I upset you?"

Not the brightest question. Still, it—or his arms around her—had the right effect.

"I just want things to be okay," she said. "I want us to be happy. Errol too. I care for him. Just not the way I *did*." She sighed, and looked near tears. "You're right. My life is ugliness and chaos."

"Don't listen to me," he said. "I exaggerate. A bird craps on my head, and I think a pterodactyl strafed me."

She looked up as if to ask, *Say what?*

"I failed third-grade math. I multiplied the answers by one hundred."

He'd used these lines before, but never to such good effect.

He used one finger under her chin to raise her head. She shut her eyes. Opened her lips.

A moment later, everything was fine.

◆ ◆ ◆

The tree that Errol clung to was very small. His right wrist, which had absorbed the shock of his fall, felt dislocated; but his left relieved some pressure as his legs fought for a foothold in the rock wall they had slammed into.

The tree was barely four feet tall, two inches thick. It couldn't hold his weight for long.

Slowly, carefully, he chinned upward. Muscles straining, he angled his body left, sliding his right leg up, struggling to hook it over the cliff's edge. If he only weighed less. Or worked out more. Two more inches. Just two. And it wouldn't go.

He groaned with pain and fear as his thigh cramped. All he could do was hang on till the cramp released. That, or his grip gave out and he fell.

Somehow, he forced his leg up another inch. Another half-inch.

192 • URSULA LAKE

His arms were weakening. The ledge was crumbling. The wind sounded like the laughter of ghosts.

He thought of letting go. The swoosh of falling. The horrendous smack.

With a last, gut-wrenching groan, he forced his knee up and up until it scraped over the edge. Using that edge as a fulcrum, he levered his body up and up until, at last, all of him was on solid ground.

He lay there panting, afraid the least movement would make him slide.

Ever so slowly, he wormed forward on his belly. His hand left red smears on the snow as he reached for another tree. Grasping that, he pulled, clawed, slithered his way onto its uphill side. Only then, with its three-inch trunk between him and the downhill slide, did he look to see what he'd escaped.

It was a freak drop-off, barely ten feet wide. The mountain's normal incline continued on both sides—and sixty feet below. Not much of a cliff, but "'twas enough; 'twould serve."

He shivered violently. Black dots danced in his eyes. His stomach heaved, and he was retching his guts out—lying, braced against the tree, watching breakfast, lunch, Tang, and Yukon Jack roll down the slope. His ulcer raged as he spasmed with dry heaves.

Thank God there was no blood.

He lay a few more moments, mustering his strength. A toxic cloud that had wrapped him began to dissipate. As if he'd just purged poison.

He resumed wriggling, keeping the little tree behind him as he clawed upward toward the howling cave. A few more yards, and he was on his hands and knees, then shambling gorilla-style until he reached the cave mouth, and his footprints that would lead him to his boat.

He stood upright. His watch said three thirty. Lots of daylight left.

His wrist hurt, but didn't seem dislocated. All of his fingers worked.

"That was close," he said, turned from the cave, and started back to camp. His legs were rubber, his arms heavy as anvils.

A hundred yards, and he remembered he had left his flashlight and hatchet in the snow.

"Damn," he said, his voice so weak, it scared him. He didn't dare go back. He had to hurry—reach his boat, get back to camp, get food, get warm.

His sweat-drenched skin was losing heat. And there was no food in his stomach to make more. He zipped his parka to his neck and pulled his stocking cap over his ears, but kept shivering. Hypothermia was calling, loud and clear.

He walked faster, following his footprints in the thinning snow. His mind jumped back to eighth-grade gym, the day Coach Simmons made him box Nicky Monczuk. He pictured Monczuk's sneering mouth, his slick black hair, his cruel, confident eyes as he moved in.

Errol could still feel Monczuk's first punch to his face. They wore twenty-ounce gloves, soft as pillows, but Monczuk's bony fist bored through. The pain popped something in Errol's brain. He threw a flailing right that glanced off Monczuk's arm, but knocked him back. If he lived to be a thousand, he'd never forget seeing fear leap onto Monczuk's cocky, big-jawed face.

Another right drove Monczuk across the ring. Pride forgotten, the school badass fought only to survive as Errol rained punches on him. Even the other badasses cheered as Coach Simmons rushed in to rescue Nicky: bleeding and senseless on the ropes.

He was Monczuk, now—staggering, falling, floundering, fighting to hold off a total rout. He'd tried to bluff the woods, and it had called his hand.

A million trees loomed, each identical to the rest. The snow was patchy. His footprints were gone. He could be lost. He could die here.

Branches lashed his face and tore his clothes as he plunged blindly downhill. His thoughts were garbled. He could not hold down his fear.

Then, through the trees, a sparkling! Like a miracle, the lake stretched out below.

4:35. Plenty of time. He'd be down inside an hour.

Forcing himself to stand up straight, he turned and raised his middle finger solemnly. "Up your ass!" he told the mountain. "I survived!"

27

To Scott's relief, Errol was not raging on shore when they got back.

"The nematode returns," Scott said, tying his boat to a small tree. He spoke softly, though Errol's boat was gone. What if he'd watched them from the lake? What if he was hiding, ready for revenge?

"If you're a nematode, I'm a tapeworm. Twenty feet long," Claire said. "But the heart wants what it wants. Assuming tapeworms have hearts."

Jumping ashore, she hurried to Errol's camper, and ducked inside. A minute later, she was hurrying back to Scott.

"He left a note. He's off exploring," she said. "He didn't say when he'll be back."

Still speaking softly, Scott said, "How'll we face him?"

"Like nothing's happened," Claire said with conviction.

"Things *have* happened. Several times."

"This is *not* the place to hash things out," Claire said. "We need to act normal. For now."

"You should take off my pants," Scott said.

He'd meant his spares, which he'd loaned her. But she pulled him behind his truck, and began unbuckling his belt. "Since you asked . . ."

"They'll be a mite loose in the crotch if Errol finds us," Scott said, pulling away. How could she goof around, after what they'd done? And how could he?

"Put on your own clothes," he said. "Don't mention falling in."

"Bad boy," she breathed, coming back into his arms. "You've got me all worked up."

"When can you come to Seattle?" he asked as she molded herself to him.

"Soon!" She stepped back, then pirouetted like a happy child. "I feel bad. Really. But I'm *crazy* about you."

"Crazy's the word. This feels like Lancelot and Guinevere."

"Which one am I?"

Scott tried to laugh, but managed only a weak croak.

"It's like I swallowed a love potion," Claire said. "Though that would make us Tristan and Isolde."

He loved that she knew *Tristan*. Though that meant she knew how it turned out.

"Being here's the potion," he said. "The woods simplifies things."

"Hold that thought!" Claire kissed his cheek, and ducked into her camper.

The thought he held—*How did I let this happen?*—was answered when she stepped out of the camper, intoxicating even in the baggy sweatsuit she'd worn that first day in Howdy Do's. He saw it all now: he'd never stood a chance.

"Thanks for the loan," she said, and tossed him his spare pants.

He caught the pants, and transferred them to his camper. "What'd you do with your wet stuff?"

She shot him a knowing look before she said, "Oh, *that* wet stuff. I hung it up. Just a girl washing her clothes."

She motioned Scott behind his truck, opened his shirt, and tongued his nipples, one by one.

He squirmed away. "You want to drive me wild?"

"Turnabout's fair play." She wrapped her arms around him, tight. "Sex is so *serious* with Errol. It's fun with you."

Scott moved her mane of hair and kissed her neck. She dropped to her knees, nuzzled his inner thigh, and was unbuckling his belt again when, in the distance, an outboard motor chugged.

She stood quickly. "I'll pretend to be asleep."

"I'll cook a fish," Scott said. To himself. Claire was already gone.

He had to face Errol sometime. Might as well be now.

◆ ◆ ◆

Now proved the perfect time. Errol was too full of his roaring cave to question anyone, or even lament missing the night bite.

"I'm too tired to fish," he said as Scott helped beach his boat.

"Me too," Scott said, and prayed Errol never found out why. "I'm cooking dinner. Want some?"

"Sure. Thanks," Errol said. "Give me a minute."

It took less time than that for him to duck into his camper, and duck back out again.

"Claire's asleep," he said, taking the plate of fish Scott offered, with two slices of protein bread.

While they ate, Errol rattled on about the cave. He dismissed his injuries—a wrenched right wrist, and the start of a black eye—as "no big deal."

"It sounds cool," Scott said. "And very strange."

"It is," Errol said. "We should go back before we leave." Finished eating, he washed his plate off in the lake, and gave it back to Scott. "Thanks for the food," he said; then, as if in passing, "You and Claire do any good?"

"Not a bit." Scott tried to look chagrined, as if to say, "I went against your judgment, and I paid." He hoped that Claire could hear, and would corroborate.

"She give you trouble?" Errol asked.

Scott waited to see what else would come. When nothing did, he shook his head no. "She barely said two words."

Errol nodded. "She flirts with you to get at me." Before Scott could think how to respond, Errol said, "Let's leave her here tomorrow. I've got a score to settle with you."

Scott's stomach flipped before he realized what was meant. "Oh. Yeah. You *are* due for a bonanza."

"Tomorrow," Errol said. "Pack a lunch, and we'll stay out all day. I can't believe it's Thursday. My thirty-pounder's calling, 'Come and get me!'"

"Let's not disappoint him," Scott said, and forced a grin as, with a parting wave, Errol stomped toward his camper.

"Pieces of feces," Scott said under his breath. Being with Errol made him feel like the World's Most Contemptible Man. But he couldn't drive out of here this late in the day. And now he'd promised to stay tomorrow, too.

He plopped his butt down on his bumper, and sat to watch night settle on the lake. Now that Claire had won his heart, he could admit how much Sara had wounded it. He'd felt so certain of her love. Then—talk about feeling helpless—she was gone.

Had the void she'd left caused him to fall for Claire? Had Claire's money and class, so much like Sara's, played a part? Was she as perfect for him as she seemed right now? Or was the wilderness coloring his view?

Time would tell. Assuming they *had* time.

On the one hand, his nerve hadn't failed. Offered what he wanted—he only now realized how desperately—he'd taken it. On the other hand, he'd lacked the courage to uphold his Last Commandment.

So much for *values* and being Sir Galahad. The next question was, *What now?*

Friendship with Errol was impossible, that was sure. He was crazy for Claire; that was sure, too. He felt like he loved her. But how much of this "higher" feeling sprang from lower down? What would happen back in the civilized world?

With Claire gone, Errol would quit working for her dad. If he moved back to Seattle, Scott might be forced down to LA. It would be too slimy to be with Claire under Errol's nose.

Would she move with him? If she did, would they get along?

Errol's camper door was shut. But Scott could hear him telling Claire about the cave.

The start of a song popped into his head: "Enchantress, enchantress, / you've got your fire burning through my brain." He'd written the song after his lunch with Julie. Had it been a premonition of Claire?

In the dying light, Ursula Lake gleamed like a vast pool of mercury dulling to lead as the sun squeezed behind the trees. Back at Oso, Jim McGee could be waiting like a trapdoor spider for another girl. Scott hated that.

"File a report," Mom would have said. "Even if it's bad for you." Beneath all his sophomoric philosophizing, *she* was the source of his values. To her, self-interest had equaled selfishness, which equaled sin.

But life was messy. Everyone was compromised. To be happy, you had to stop quibbling, and grab the things that made life good. For instance, Claire.

If there's no God, everything is permitted.

Hearing Errol still going on about the cave, Scott put his hands over his ears, then let them fall. Next to adultery, eavesdropping was no big deal.

Claire spoke softly, as if she knew that he might hear. Errol had lowered his voice too. Unable to make out half their words, Scott was ready to retreat to his camper when he heard a sleeping bag unzip, then, to his dismay, the familiar thrashing.

Claire was now cheating on *him*.

As Scott's emotions writhed, Errol exploded, "What do you mean, 'Don't?'"

Scott felt stricken for his friend. He also felt like cheering.

"You've been a bitch this whole trip," Errol yelled. "Don't cock tease *me*!"

Scott squatted down beside the lake, hands over his ears in a posture of grief. He had caused this.

"Go ahead, Errol." Claire's voice cut through the night: icy and clear. "If you want sex so much, rape me!"

When, seconds later, the thrashing resumed, Scott was torn between running for his camper and running to help Claire. "Never come between a fighting couple," Dad had said. "They'll turn on you." But how could he sit still while Claire was brutalized?

"Fucking cunt!" Errol roared. Something slammed against the camper's wall. Scott leapt to his feet. One more loud sound, and he'd intervene.

But only silence came.

Had Errol hurt Claire? Had he *killed* her? No. She'd make noise if she were hurt. Errol would make noise if she were dead. More likely, they'd turned their backs and now lay in the dark seething, the way he and Sara had after he turned her father's offer down. The longer the silence, the more likely this was true.

Whether from emotion or cold, Scott was shivering. He zipped his parka, then pulled his flashlight from his camper and walked down to the lake to pee. Better to escape the sordidness until he could change it.

Remembering the little frogs, he shined his light ahead. But if the frogs were there, he couldn't see them.

With two steps to the shore, his flashlight died. Two hard shakes brought it back. Cheap piece-of-crap. If he ever had money, he'd never buy bottom-of-the-line again.

While he peed, he shone the flashlight up and down the shore. A few feet to his right, something long and white was floating in the lake.

A severed leg?!

No, he saw as he zipped up and moved closer. It was a dead fish. A really *big* fish. How had he missed it before?

Errol's boat was closest, so Scott pulled out an oar and used it to nudge the fish to shore: a giant trout, thicker than his thigh, and close to three feet long.

Old Hodges hadn't lied.

Dropping the oar, Scott knelt beside the fish. Both eyes were intact, so it hadn't been dead long. What could have killed it?

Again, his flashlight died. When shaking didn't help, Scott stood to go back to his camper.

As if by magic, the flashlight came on. The fish glowed ghost-white in its beam. Then, behind it, two red eyes poked from the lake.

Scott caught his breath, then understood: a giant toad. Did the tiny ones grow into these monsters?

The toad sat, frozen. Watching him.

"My eyes are on you," Jim McGee had said. But giant toads were common in these woods. McGee was many miles away.

The toad's eyes burned in the flashlight beam. Seeming to accuse.

Scott waved his hand to take in the whole lake. "All yours," he said, replaced Errol's oar in his boat, turned, and double-timed toward his camper, leaving the fish to rot, the toad to stare.

SIXTH DAY

28

Errol stood on a glittering Hawaiian beach, cool water lapping at his feet. The sun warmed his bare shoulders. Kids splashed through gentle waves, squealing.

Claire called his name. He turned, and saw her in the purple bikini she'd worn the day they'd met. She stood a few yards out, waving, *Come in!*

He could have cried with relief. He'd been sure she hated him.

"Coming, Babe," he called, and ran toward her.

A small wave rolled in. He laughed as she lost her footing and fell in a foot of water. Fell, and lay facedown.

"Claire?"

She started moving out to sea, arms and legs feebly sloshing.

"Claire!" He high-stepped through waves like a running back. "Claire! Lift your head!"

Ten feet away from her, he couldn't close the gap. The water, now waist-deep, swirled with current. The too-soft sand sucked at his feet.

"Claire!" he yelled. "Lift your head!"

Her sloshing stopped.

"This is real," he told himself, starting to swim.

A few strokes, and he'd seized her foot. His feet touched bottom: firm sand, water still waist-deep.

Her hair looked like red seaweed. He grabbed it, then lifted her head, dripping, from the sea.

Only her head. Its features dripped like candle wax.

Floundering away, he dropped the head. Something wrapped his arms and legs.

◆ ◆ ◆

He woke, thrashing in his sleeping bag. Outside, it was dark. His ulcer burned. Claire was asleep, as far from him as she could get.

He groaned, remembering her "rape me" dare.

His bladder was tight, but he shrank from crawling out into the cold. He ached to hold Claire, and have things be okay. If she rebuffed him, though, he feared what he might do. Rather than risk it, he burrowed down into his bag, pulled the hood over his head, and dozed fitfully until gray light signaled dawn.

Feeling drugged from lack of sleep, he eased out of his sleeping bag and forced himself to dress. Finished, he kissed Claire: still asleep, or pretending to be. "Scott and I are going fishing," he said. "Want to come?"

No response.

"I won't go if you don't want me to." He paused. "I'm really sorry . . ."

When she didn't speak or open her eyes, he climbed out of the camper, took a long leak, and ate breakfast. He felt anything but rested, anything but confident. Still, he told the open air, "This is my day." He and Claire had always fought a lot. And always made up.

The weather had been perfect since they'd left Spokane. Now it mirrored his unsettled mood. The sun hadn't topped the pines, but the sky seemed darker than yesterday, more glowering.

He wished he could see a weather report. A serious storm could knock down trees, wash out the road, and trap them here. Sometimes, though, fish bit best before a storm. With luck, that would happen today, and they'd be on the highway before major weather hit.

In any case, this would be his last day here. He needed to get home, report the corpse, and work things out with Claire. And Pop Gunn, too. One trophy trout or twelve noon, whichever came first; then he and Claire were gone. If Scott wanted to stay, that was on him.

A muffled buzz was Scott's alarm. Moments later, the man himself poked his head out like a suspicious tortoise. Errol had to smile at Scott's face: unshaven, ringed with bristling hair.

"Your head looks like an explosion."

"Yours ain't exactly the answer to a maiden's prayer."

"Not to Claire's," Errol said, moving closer to Scott. "We had a bad fight."

If Scott had heard anything, he didn't let on. "That's no good," he said, and dumped an envelope of Instant Breakfast in a glass of water.

"What I need now is a thirty-pounder," Errol said, lugging his bag of spare clothes to his boat.

"You deserve two," Scott called after him. "Or three."

◆ ◆ ◆

Thirty-pounder reminded Scott of the dead fish last night. While he gulped down a stomach-turning mango Instant Breakfast, he walked down to the lake to take a look.

The fish was gone. Some creature must have scavenged it. Something smaller, Scott hoped, than a bear.

Claire hadn't emerged from the camper. Still sleeping, or pretending, Scott was sure. Not dead.

He'd hoped to see her before he and Errol set out—to catch her eye, and show her she was on his mind. Two different times last night, he'd jerked awake, sure Errol had killed her. Between fretful dreams—all vanished, now—he'd made a plan. He'd fish a little while with Errol, then fake an attack of kidney stones. He'd seen his dad have one, so he knew what to do. Needless to say, he'd have to leave. Once out of the mountains, he'd head either for Brewster Lake or home. The border should be easy, if he crossed alone. Claire would come to Seattle when she could. They'd see how things unspooled from there.

Errol's voice, unexpected as an air horn, made Scott jump. "Let's use my boat. It'll bring me luck," he said.

Was this a joke? The only luck Errol's boat had brought him had been bad. For all Scott knew, Errol planned to throw him overboard. But what could he say except, "Okay"?

Minutes later, as he'd done so many times, he shoved them off, then jumped in the boat. Errol yanked his motor into life, and they set out across the lake.

Scott pointed at a bank of darkness to the north. "I don't like that sky."

"Most of it's blue. Maybe the blue will keep the heathen hordes away," Errol said, then added, "Fucking Claire!"

Scott tensed. But *fucking* was only an adjective.

"What's wrong with her?" he asked as casually as he could.

Errol sighed. "Last night, she shut me down cold."

"You mean in bed?"

"No, butt-wipe, she snubbed me at The Club!" Errol finished tying on a fly—Scott's woolly bugger—and clipped off the excess leader as if it were someone's head.

"Bummer," Scott said, disgusted by how well he lied.

"Claire's the first woman I've met who likes sex as much as me," Errol said, then shook his head sadly. "Not last night."

"Maybe she's got an infection." Scott almost mentioned a pain in his side that might be kidney stones, then stopped himself. Best not to overexplain.

"She did get something once," Errol said. "They gave her some cream."

"Wasn't the clap." Scott made a face and rubbed his rear.

"You'd know," Errol said. "Cathouse Murray, Moral Diving Bell!"

Scott's laugh, meant to be bawdy, sounded weak.

"If my own wife gave me the clap, I hate to think what I might do," Errol said.

"You never fool around?"

"No. I don't." Errol pulled off his stocking cap, scratched his head, then stuffed the hat in his pocket. "Things look different when you're married. You swear you'll be faithful. Besides . . ." He glared at his rod as if daring it not to dive. "This is the closest I've come to a good family life. I won't let my idiot dick wreck it for me."

Scott was spared an awkward pause by a reel's screech.

"Yeah!" Errol roared, grabbed his rod, and reared back into something big. But it fought strangely. A few seconds, and it ceased to fight at all.

Cursing, Errol pumped in a five-foot, trailing gob of weeds.

Scott's own black bugger came up looking clean. Just to be sure, he started to lift it into the boat when—wham!—a flash of silver shot up from green depths and seized the fly.

Line screamed off his reel. "Jesus!" Scott screamed. "It's a beast!"

◆ ◆ ◆

Errol watched in misery as the trout tore up the lake and Scott howled with glee. Ten minutes later, it took all of Errol's self control not to muff netting the fish: eight pounds of shimmering Kamloops trout. The biggest of the trip.

He tight-lipped, "Nice fish," then, as Scott released his trophy, rushed to cast. He let his line sink for a count of ten, eyes focused on his mountain. For a second, he'd have sworn he heard the cave. But the roar, if any, was inside his head.

Except for those clouds to the north, the sun had risen on another perfect day. A few cumulus puffs drifted, white as snow, in a sky like bright blue tile. Soon it would be time to shed his parka, but not yet. Not while every breeze carried a nighttime chill.

The water was glassy, camouflage-green. Sometimes, though, a patch of lake took on a corrugated, washboard look. Sometimes one of those washboards—"cat's paws," sailors called them—sped toward the boat. Errol would feel a puff of breeze as corrugations and cold surrounded him. Then the breeze would die and warmer air flow back as the cat's paw sped away.

Through it all, skillfully, methodically, triple-checking every knot, Errol fished and fished and caught nothing.

Scott had a hit. But the fish, as if in answer to Errol's prayers, broke off Scott's fly.

"Didn't even feel that big," Scott griped, poking through his fly box. "I should've tied more black buggers."

Errol was thinking the same thing. He should have tied his own.

Scott, to his credit, didn't ask for his fly back. And Errol didn't offer.

"A black Carey ought to work," Scott said, and tied one on while Errol cast the last black bugger. Uselessly.

Ten fishless minutes, and he snarled, "This spot's a shitburger. Let's troll."

◆ ◆ ◆

Claire had watched from the camper as the men readied to leave. To her surprise, she wasn't angry at Errol. She just felt cold.

Her arm hurt where it had slammed the camper wall. She turned it over. Sure enough, a bruise ran down from her elbow. Errol would feel awful. And she would make him pay.

That Errol hadn't *meant* to hurt her almost made it worse. She'd displeased him; he'd flicked her away like a gnat. That's what it meant to be a woman: to have your thoughts, opinions, wishes flicked away. Not because they were worth less than a man's. Because you were weaker physically.

To steal time off for this trip, she'd had to claim that her Grampa Jim, dead for three years, had died again. When she got back to school, she'd face well-meaning inquiries that would make her feel anxious and contemptible: the same way she'd felt leaving town as Errol guffawed and she shrank down in her seat, afraid of being seen.

No wonder the men screamed *humiliation!* It made them feel what women felt every day, hemmed in by beings who could overpower them. She, daughter of the overpowering Bob Gunn, had naturally married Errol, who made other men feel weak and small.

She was so used to feeling overpowered, she'd been almost grateful when Errol didn't rape her last night. He could have, though. To be raped or not to be raped—that, like every other question, was decided by men. Fuckers all!

She'd hoped that Scott would find some way to stay behind. If he had offered, she would have said "too risky," and loved him for it. But the men's talk made it clear: Scott wasn't just going, he was glad to go.

How, after yesterday, could he pal around with Errol? Just seeing the men together made her stomach roil. All the same, she didn't like being alone in this place that seemed remote as Mars.

Errol's motor gave its angry roar, and the boys were off, Scott's red stocking cap making him look like a rapper Santa. One longing glance would have redeemed him. But his grin proclaimed, "There's nowhere else I'd rather be."

"Fuckers all," she said again, and wormed back into her bag. Still, even in his hat, with a week's stubble, Scott looked good. Remembering the feel of him inside her, she murmured, "Mmmm," as if he were listening.

She'd thought the "wilderness" had revved up her sex drive. But it had been Scott all along. She was still young enough to restart life with him. Maybe have a baby, too. He *must* love her, to give up Errol as a friend.

On the other hand, what kind of man fucked his friend's wife?

A man in love with a woman who loves him back, she told herself. The man/woman bond trumped everything. *That* was Nature's Law. Even if the term made her think, *Nature's Way*, which made her think, *granola bar*.

To trade her husband in on a new model, though . . . it made her insides writhe. Talk about cold. And desperate.

One day when she was ten, Daddy away "on business," her mother had flopped beside her on their big blue sofa, breathed bourbon in her face, and said, "Claire honey, men have their jobs and cars and boats and ballgames. All women have is men."

She'd told herself that she'd do better than her mom. She'd have her own career, her own interests. And she had started well. A month after gradua-tion from the U, ultra-posh Wetherford Gallery—housed in a building her father happened to own—asked to host her first one woman show.

"Stan Wetherford went nuts for your slides," Daddy assured.

She showed her best stuff: watercolors, pen-and-inks, charcoals, temper-as, oils. She also brought things dating back to childhood, since Daddy said, "People love to chart an artist's growth." And her stuff sold! She stood in a fuchsia evening dress, answering questions like the young genius she was supposed to be. "How do you get your ideas?" "Who are your influences?" "Where do you see yourself evolving?"

Everything was perfect until she overheard two women in the restroom.

"Isn't this the worst?"

"The liver worst. Has Richard bought anything?"

"Just one. A horse, or tree, or something in between."

"Dan says we'll hang ours in 'a suitable spot'—the closet. Or the fireplace."

"Oh well, Rich says it's cheaper than call girls for Bob Gunn."

"Someone should tell the poor girl she's wasting her time."

Claire stayed hunched in her stall until she could stop crying. Then she went out and received more accolades, smiling sweetly until the show was done. A year later, one rainy winter afternoon at the London Academy of Art, Professor Peter Langford had declared she had "the eye of a painter, but not the soul."

"Not to worry," he'd soothed. "Critics live better than artists, and need neither eye nor soul."

"If things go well between us," he added, "I'll get you on at *The Times*."

She'd left Peter—his arrogance and wheezy laugh and saggy old man's body—before she could build a "career" as his beard. She'd left him for brilliant, young, dope-addled sculptor Paul. Then Andy came along. Paris was fabulous—until Georges stole Andy from her. And on and on. Now here she was staring down the barrel of middle-age, and all she had was men.

Her stomach's growling made her realize she was starved. Falling in love always made her ravenous just when she was most conscious of her weight. But was she really in love, or did she have to think that to justify what she had done?

Taking a granola bar from the ice chest, she unwrapped it, ate it in three bites, then poured a glass of Tang from the half-full pitcher Errol had left behind. The thought of last night made her cringe. She'd hoped to be a free-spirited woman, jumping lover-to-lover with no false sentiment. Instead, she'd been repulsed by Errol's touch.

On the plus side, his violence had eased her guilt. And opened options. Last night, she'd felt her only choice was to leave Errol. This morning, she wasn't sure. Errol loved her, and she doubted that would change. He was a known quantity. Scott, on the other hand, was a question mark. He seemed angry and depressed. And didn't even have a job. All he risked to be with her was a butt-kicking from Errol. To be with *him*, she'd have to give up life-as-she-knew-it.

At least for now, part-time might be the way to go.

She hated to be so calculating, but she owed it to herself to "optimize her opportunities," as Daddy liked to say. Anything less, for him, defined *failure-of-nerve.* If she exercised and ate right, she had some good years left. There was a limit, though. And it hinged on looks, as long as she defined herself through men.

Why do it, then? Why not stop teaching, and paint seriously again? She was a long way from the girl who'd taken Peter's word as Law. Ten years of living could create a lot of "soul."

But could she buckle down and do the necessary work without approval from men? It would be like having a stroke, needing to relearn everything. Still, it didn't have to happen instantly. Also, artists had lovers. Everyone knew that.

She pulled her sketch book from her duffel bag, jumped from the camper, and began to draw the lake. The work went well. Her eye saw, and her hand took it down: the shore, the water with its shimmer and bounce, the snow-topped mountain, the dark bruise of clouds that thrust against the sky's unfathomable blue.

Her talent was a genie waiting to be freed. No wonder she resisted normal, practical things. The genie always stopped her, begging, "Notice me!"

Turning her back on the lake, she drew the trucks, with their campers like turtle-shells; the green-furred woods; the road like a tentacle reaching back toward civilization's Cthulhu-head. She watched Errol's face appear magically on her page. Peter had called her visual memory "eidetic." He'd granted her that much while, spiritual vampire that he was, he kept her dependent, and sucked the artistic life out of her.

She closed her eyes, called up Scott's image, opened her eyes, and drew.

"This is good," she said, surveying what she'd done. "It's really good."

Her mind told her she'd worked a few minutes. Her watch said an hour. She felt breathless, as if she'd won a marathon.

She'd lost control briefly with Scott. Not unlike with the mushroom. (What did *that* say?) Now, with Scott away, it seemed clear that they should take a long step back. Until Seattle, anyway. That was the decent, adult thing to do. The smart thing, too.

Yet even as she made this resolution, she felt it slip like a badly-tied knot. She'd been dying of thirst, but hadn't known until she took a drink. The thought of losing that drink, even briefly, made her crazed.

Good thing drawing had tired her eyes. Climbing back into the camper, she locked the door, burrowed into her down bag, and fell asleep thinking of Scott's face.

29

"Goddamn it, what is *wrong* with me?!" Errol stared in disbelief as Scott's second big fish flapped on the bottom of the boat. "I swear, I'm cursed."

"It's just bad luck," Scott said. "Yours'll turn around."

"There's no *time* for it to turn around," Errol practically wailed. "I fish without a touch, we trade rods, and bang! Mine gets a fish."

"I *said* you could fight it." Scott lifted the big trout, brandished it, then lowered it into the lake. One tail-flick, and it was gone.

"That's not the same. You know it's not."

"Fish with both rods," Scott said. "I've caught enough."

"For Chrissake, stop babying me!" Errol felt torn between a wish to wring Scott's self-satisfied neck, and to burst into tears. He knew too well that a good fish would make his outburst laughable. If he still had Scott to laugh with.

He couldn't think straight. Lack-of-sleep had wrapped cotton around his brain. "What am I doing *wrong*?!" he said, and shook his head in baffled misery.

"You're a lot better fisherman than I am." Scott spoke as if explaining math to a slow child. "What could you be doing wrong?"

"If I knew, I could fix it!"

"Fishing's like everything else," Scott said. "Perfect your cast, tie better flies, fish the right spots—what matters most is still dumb luck."

Errol felt something blow in his brain, a pool of resentment surging up. He pictured Scott on the ground, playing victim: the poor nice boy bullied by the big bad man.

"No wonder you're still playing shithole bars," he said. "You didn't get discovered right away, so instead of fighting harder, you whine, 'My luck's bad. Life's so mean,' and hide under a diagnosis."

Scott's face looked like he he'd bitten off a mouthful of spoiled meat. "I know," he said with weary condescension. "You too can become President.

Drag yourself up by your bootstraps—or your wife's—so you can hoot, 'Look Ma, I'm a self-made man!'"

It took all of Errol's self-control not to knock Scott out of the boat. "At least I *have* a wife," he said.

♦ ♦ ♦

Errol's narrowed eyes told Scott that he had crossed a line. Once again, he had to gag down the humiliating truth: Errol was too big and too strong. Any time he wanted to impose his power, he could. Still, Scott had taken vengeance in advance. Errol's humiliation was that much worse because he didn't know.

Scott took a breath, and let it out. "Come on, Errol. Let's just fish."

"Suits me," Errol said. A moment later, in a conciliatory voice, he said, "That's a big caddis."

A lone, very large caddis fly had fluttered down onto Scott's leg. Its lacey wings gave it a graceful, feminine air, comically offset by antennae that trailed like body-length mustachios.

"Know what the national bird of Iraq is?" Errol asked.

He was extending an olive branch, so Scott took it. "No," he said. "What's the national bird of Iraq?"

"The fly."

Scott had to laugh. Angry men looked like angry chimps. And it was hard to take a chimp seriously. Even himself.

"Hey," he said, "let's get you a monster."

"I'll second that," Errol said.

They were trolling close to shore, watching for inlets, beaver dams, any place fish might collect.

"There's a rise!" Errol hissed. "Another!"

He cut the engine and they drifted into the shadow of a cloud. There, in darker water, thousands of midges sat like fly specks on the surface film while others disappeared into huge swirls.

The lake was less than five feet deep here, full of weeds.

"A zebra midge ought to work," Errol said.

"I've got one somewhere," Scott said, but was still looking when Errol made his first cast.

As if by magic, the cloud overhead dispersed. The midges vanished. And the rises stopped.

◆ ◆ ◆

"God *damn* it!" Errol wailed. "Even Canada's gone to hell." He cast desperately, feeling the last of his vacation running out. Scott, meanwhile, sat with his rod lowered, looking smug. He didn't even deign to fish as Errol cast and cast and caught nothing.

"Remember last time?" Errol said. "We couldn't keep 'em off our hooks." He hawked a gob into the green water, watched it float, then made his cast. "Five more years, guys'll be lucky to catch an eight-incher a week. Might as well put up some condos, while there's something left to sell."

"I wondered when you'd get to that," Scott said.

"In twenty years, there won't be shit for anyone," Errol said. "Better to cash in while you can." He scanned the lake for rises, and saw none. "Americans'll pay plenty for a Trout Fishing Paradise. Even if it's ex-paradise when they arrive," he said, and laid out a perfect roll cast to a perfect spot. "Promote a few lakes up here, I can afford some *real* fishing." He lifted his line and, in one smooth motion, cast again. "How'd you like to catch Atlantic Salmon in Iceland?"

Scott stood, and promptly muffed his cast. "I'd like it. Sure," he said, readying to cast again.

"Try paying for it with your noble heart," Errol said, and capped his statement with another flawless cast just as a three-pounder grabbed Scott's fly and tail-walked like a tarpon.

Errol kept casting through the fight, didn't offer to net the fish, and when Scott brought it aboard, didn't so much as look.

"I'll keep this for dinner," Scott said—pleased, Errol could see, to rub his triumph in. He found his pliers, and rapped the fish sharply on the head while Errol sat rigid as a sphinx.

Half a minute later, when Scott muffed another cast and draped line over them both, Errol blew. "Christ on a corncob! You're as bad as Claire!"

"I told you," Scott said. "My fish were all dumb luck."

Errol fought the urge, again, to smack him one. "You're a sneaky little prick," he said.

◆ ◆ ◆

Fear hit Scott like ice water—where he'd soon be swimming, if Errol knew about him and Claire.

"You're the kind of chickenshit who'd ding a guy's truck for being better than yours," Errol said.

"What do you mean?" Scott offered feebly.

"I saw my paint on your door that first day," Errol said. "I let it go, I was so damned glad to see you."

Scott knew he should apologize. Explain he hadn't known it was Errol's truck. He knew this, even as his mouth was saying, "It's just like you to hog three spots."

Errol shook his head in a stage-worthy display of disbelief. "You're the same self-righteous asshole I dumped in the street."

"I may be," Scott said. "But you're not the guy who dumped me."

Scott words were phrased not as a challenge, but a fact. No need to fake kidney stones now. "Look," he said, "Just take me back to camp. I'm ready to head home."

"That's good," Errol said. "I'm ready for you to go."

He cast another five minutes—to prove, Scott knew, that he'd only move when he damn well pleased. Then he yanked up his anchor and roared away.

He stayed in camp just long enough to slosh ashore and ask Claire, with a show of great good cheer, "Hey, Babe, ready to try your luck?"

"I'm not in a fishing mood," Scott heard her say as he lugged his gear, plus the three-pounder he'd saved to eat, back to his truck.

"Scott's taking off," Errol said, practically pleading. "Come on, Claire. Just you and me."

Scott couldn't hear what she said back. But he heard Errol say, "Thanks for the great company," before he snatched Claire's rod from where it leaned against a tree, then stalked back to his boat and roared away.

30

"Double ick. Another toad!" Claire said, and yanked up the green blanket she'd spread behind Scott's truck. "I dreamed about a toad," she said. "I don't remember what."

Scott peered under his truck. The toad's big eyes, yellow with black pupils, stared back. Not Bearclaw's eyes. Just a big amphibian looking for shade.

"Begone, toad," he said, and poked it with a stick

Grudgingly, the toad hopped into the sunlight.

"Away, away!" Scott poked some more, herding the thing toward the lake. The little toads were back in force. But, cruel as Yahweh, the big one seemed indifferent to how many it crushed.

Scott left it in the shallows, a few feet from where he'd seen the dead fish and, for all he knew, this same toad. Toads were poor swimmers, so Scott didn't drive it in over its head.

He'd planned to drive himself straight out of here. But Claire had vaporized those plans. "Stay a little while," she'd begged. And like a fool, bewitched and scared to seem a wuss, he had obeyed.

Returning to Claire, he found her lolling on her blanket, arms winged out behind her head in *Naked Maja* style. Wearing pink panties and nothing else, she would've given Goya heart failure.

Scott's breath quickened even as he said, "This isn't safe."

"Could you see me from the lake?" Standing, she twined her arms around his neck and pressed her breasts against his chest.

He couldn't speak.

"We'll hear his motor miles away," she said. Avoiding, he noticed, using Errol's name. "Besides . . ." Her baby-doll pout was meant to be funny, but was still sexy as hell. "The woods are cold."

"Not with you around." He kissed her mouth first, then both breasts, then knelt to kiss her stomach as he rolled her panties down. One quickie for the road. And an extra smack across the face for Errol.

◆ ◆ ◆

The dark band of clouds on the horizon had taken on a crazed orange glow. Still, as far as Errol could tell, blue sky was holding bad weather at bay. They could drive out at one or even two and still be fine. That gave him three hours to fish.

To spite the clouds, he drove straight at them until he reached a likely spot, and slowed to troll. He took pride in never cheating when he fished. But wardens were less likely than white rhinos out here. He'd use two rods— Scott's woolly bugger on his, an orange scud on Claire's. Once he saw what worked, he'd go back to one rod.

Fifteen minutes later, two rods had proved useless as one.

Those little frogs he'd seen in camp might make good bait. But camp was a long away. He didn't have the time to spare. Anyway, he didn't want to re-enter Claire's bullshit zone. Or, if Scott were still around, to watch him leave.

His eye shifted from Claire's rod to his, which had begun to twitch.

He picked it up. Very carefully.

It twitched again: a big trout bumping, trying to make up its mind.

"Take it," he whispered. "Take it. Please."

A heavy tug! He killed the engine, double-set the hook. And felt the life-less drag of spinach.

"Fucking SHIT!"

He reeled in and started ripping off the green weed-streamers that had wrapped his leader. As he did, he saw that the butt-end was kinked. It wasn't much—just the slight hint of a spiral. But it was there.

Now he remembered: last September, at the end of a great day on Brew-ster Lake, his propeller had wrapped his leader and a little bit of line. He'd already racked up a twenty fish day, so he'd unwrapped leader and line, driven home, and put his gear away for winter. That little spiral could have spooked fish!

Why hadn't he changed his leader before he left home? "Stupidity," he said aloud as he clipped off the old leader and tied a new one on. Still, if he hadn't been so tired, desperate, and distracted by Scott, he'd have seen the spiral right away. *And* checked the knot that cost him his ghostie.

He reeled Claire's line in, stripped off goo, then cast both lines back out and trolled.

Another hundred yards, and his rod dove. He grabbed the rod, killed his engine—and his line went slack.

He swore, started to reel in, then felt a heavy tug. He set the hook, and a fish made itself known with three wild leaps. At two pounds, it was no giant. But it was a start, he told himself as he lifted it from his net and broke its neck.

The fish's stomach, when he opened it, was stuffed with small black snails. Ha! Without Scott, he was starting to get somewhere.

Reeling in Claire's line, he stood and, with his own rod, cast Scott's woolly bugger toward the shore. He let the bugger sink. One. Two . . .

Before he got to *Three*, a fish hit hard.

Minutes later, heart thumping, he netted and released a gorgeous five-pound hen: not a trophy, but his best fish so far.

Watching the trout fin down and disappear in the lake's depths, he felt a surge of confidence. Starting now, things were going to change. He and Claire would go to counseling. He'd set things straight with Pop Gunn. As for Scott—he'd been a dick, but he, Errol, had been one too. If Scott was still in camp when he got back, he'd plop a fat crow on a plastic plate, and eat. If not, he'd find him in Seattle and apologize.

When ten minutes of casting yielded no more hits, Errol set the throttle for its slowest troll, cast out both lines, and settled back to wait for the last-minute trophy he deserved.

His heart jumped when his motor coughed.

It coughed again, recovered, chugged smoothly for fifty more yards, then choked, spat, wheezed, spat, sputtered, spat, and died.

"What now?" Errol moaned. A quick check showed no problem with the engine or the prop.

The gas tank, when he picked it up, felt light. There was no slopping when he shook it. No gas at all.

God fucking damn! He'd had a half-tank when he checked last night. Or had that been the night before? Either way, he should have checked when he let Scott out. He'd been so pissed that he forgot.

Oh, well. Rowing might work *better*. Big trout liked a slow troll.

He bent to grab his oars, and saw that there was only one!

He sat a moment, staring as the truth sank in. It would take hours to hike back to camp, then back to his boat. The storm might hit and trap them here. In any case, his fishing time was done.

"SON OF A FUCKING BITCH!"

The snow-capped mountain that he'd "conquered" bounced his voice back in his face. He was thirty yards from shore. Over a mile's wet, miserable hike to camp.

Flailing like a maniac, he canoe-paddled to shore and beached the boat.

The fish he'd gutted was a problem. He didn't want to lug it all the way back to camp. Left in the sun, though, it would spoil.

"Shit. SHIT!" he yelled, and heaved the fish underhand, in a high arc, as far as he could out onto the lake. He watched it splash down forty feet from shore, then picked up his empty gas tank and started to slog.

31

The sun was straight up overhead, and hot. The dark clouds' assault on the blue sky seemed to have stopped.

Claire lay on her stomach, trying for a full-body tan. Scott, naked too, sat cross-legged beside her. The woods looked like a Zen screen behind them.

From time to time, at Claire's direction, Scott rubbed lotion on her legs and back. His truck was packed to go. He'd gutted his trout and placed it in his ice chest. He had no ice, but he'd stop to cook the fish once he was out of these mountains.

It was crazy to still be here. But Claire had begged. "He'll stay out all day. Anyway, we'll hear his boat."

He didn't dare look cowardly and rush away. But why, he wondered, would she take this kind of risk? Because, he realized, she'd been humiliated, too. This was revenge.

"Did you read about that man with the prosthetic leg?" Claire asked out of nowhere. She had raised up on her elbows, showing her breasts to full effect.

Scott tried to focus on her face. "What man?"

"Some disabled vet took off his leg to go swimming. When he came back, it was gone. Somebody stole it."

This seemed a strange subject, but Scott tried to be polite. "That sucks," he said.

"That's what the man thought," Claire said. "He was hopping mad."

It took a moment for the joke to register. When it did, Scott had to laugh. "That's the stupidest punch line I've heard since kindergarten," he said. "Insensitive, too."

"I made it up. Just now." Claire's deadpan was distressingly like Errol's.

"Stupid's good," he said. "Stupid and insensitive's the best."

♦ ♦ ♦

"Glad you think so," Claire said, and lay back down.

Motionless under a hot sun, the forest breathed a greenhouse scent that made her think of summers at her Grandma's in Georgia. She was tempting fate and didn't care. Her life with Errol seemed far away. She felt lithe and warm and sensuous: Cleopatra, attended by her faithful lover-slave. She knew she should be hustling Scott away. But she felt euphoric and invincible. Exhilaratingly out-of-her-mind.

Scott stretched out lazily beside her. "Did you and Errol hit it off well sexually?" he said.

"So-so," she said, glad her face was turned away. Men asked these questions not to learn the truth, but to be reassured. You either had to change the subject, or lie.

"Women are strange. Even to us," she said. "We latch onto a wild man, then try to tame him. If he resists, we give him hell. If he accepts, we lose respect. And passion. Either way, we lose."

Two feet away, a lone blue flower had enticed a honeybee. The bee would crawl inside the flower's bell, rummage around, back out, take off, helicopter above the flower, then re-land and crawl back in. With no other blue flowers in sight, the bee seemed reluctant to trade its sure thing for the unknown.

Scott stroked her rear. "My dear," he said in a horrific British accent, "you are truly callipygian."

It jolted her to hear Errol's favorite word coming from Scott. Maybe he'd taught it to Errol. And used it on how many other women?

"It means *beautiful-buttocked* in Greek," he was saying.

Men always had to teach.

"For all I know," Scott said, "the Greeks used it for boys."

She laughed at that. When his hand changed position, she relaxed and let him guide her legs apart. She raised her hips, and gave the kind of soft moan that drove men wild.

"I love you, Claire," he said, and slid inside.

She gave another moan, then heard a roar as something huge came crashing toward them. *Bear!* she thought, her body electric with fear. She felt Scott floundering across her back as she screamed and rolled away. Then she saw Errol.

Face turned monstrous, he charged at Scott, howling, "I'll kill you!"

He hammered a fist into Scott's head. Scott dropped and tried to crawl away. Errol grabbed his leg.

Thrashing like a sprinter chained to the block, Scott broke free and staggered to his feet. "Wait! Errol! Hold it! Please!" he begged, and tried to run.

Errol leapt forward, caught Scott's shoulders from behind, and dragged him down. But the power of Errol's leap carried him beyond his prey, and let Scott claw back to his feet.

Claire grabbed her clothes and ran behind their truck. Struggling to dress, she kept moaning, "Oh no. Oh no." If she lived, her life would never be the same.

Paralyzed, she saw her husband charge at Scott again, roaring like a bear. Would he kill *her* after Scott? What should she do? His knife was in their truck . . .

Scott looked half the size of Errol. He dodged one of Errol's punches, then caught one in the stomach, doubled up with a grunt, and fell, rolling onto his side.

Errol roared again, raised his hands like claws, and moved in to tear out Scott's heart.

Scott's foot flashed up from the ground. Errol jackknifed and fell, clutching his groin.

Scott staggered up. Bent double, he stumbled toward Claire. His face was twisted like Daddy's after the Wetherford disaster, when he'd smashed a chair and she knew she'd pushed too far.

She backed away, certain Scott would turn on her. Instead, he staggered past and flung himself at his truck. He yanked the door open. But he didn't jump in and tear away. Didn't leave her to Errol's rage, as she had feared. He thrust his hands under the seat.

Errol was on his feet, starting to charge when Scott whirled. "Hold it, Errol!" he gasped, and raised a gun.

◆ ◆ ◆

If Errol's mood was foul when he started back to camp, it was fetid by the time he spied his camper shining through the trees. He could almost hear trout giggling.

"King of the Wretches," he muttered. "I crown me."

His clothes were soaked and muddy. He was gushing sweat. The sun had roused squads of mosquitoes, hot to breakfast on his blood. Just as he'd feared, the sky was clouding up for real. He felt dead on his feet, and would have to ask Scott, if he hadn't already left, to motor him back to his boat. That, or repeat this miserable trek.

It was beyond humiliation.

Mosquitoes seemed hungriest near shore, so he'd retreated fifty feet into the woods, and was deciding how to skirt a large, tangled, and bloodthirsty thicket when he heard a woman's laugh. Throaty and sexual.

Suspicion, which he had refused to countenance, sprang up, squealing.

He picked his way around the thicket toward the truck. Glimpsing Scott's white torso through the brush, he stopped, temples banging. He had an urge to run—back to the woods, to his boat, the roaring cave, anywhere. If he didn't see Claire, he might choke down his fears, and live in spite of them.

Claire's next laugh pulverized that hope. Forty feet away, naked in the sun, there they were: his wife and his best friend. The corniest story of all time.

He shook his head hard, holding back a scream as Scott stroked Claire's pale, perfect flank. As she raised her rear and opened like an oyster, he felt his life shrivel and turn black.

"I love you, Claire," Scott said. And began to hump her like a dog.

When she moaned exactly as she did with him, Errol's brain boiled over in a roar. He threw his gas tank down and charged.

Before Scott could squirm away, Errol drove a fist into his head. He felt a thrill as the puny traitor reeled, slimy dick flopping. Errol could hear some-one—himself—bellow, "I'll kill you!" as he caught Scott's leg from behind.

His fingers sunk into the flesh. But Scott broke free, gasping, "Wait! Er-rol! Hold it! Please!"

He turned to run, but Errol seized him and flung him down before the force of his own rush swept him beyond Scott, who staggered up and squirmed away.

Not fast enough. Errol was on him, smashing resistance, knowing his enemy was weak and would be his. He threw Scott crashing to the ground. Again, the little Judas squirmed away. Errol stunned him with a glancing blow, then drove a fist into his gut, trying to break through his bowels to the other side.

Scott collapsed onto his back. Errol roared triumph. He raised his hands, ready to rip Scott into shreds. Then Scott's foot drove into his groin.

Grunting in agony, Errol fell.

For a moment, he couldn't move. By the time he'd dragged himself up-right, Scott had reached his truck.

Ready to retch his insides out, Errol stumbled forward just as Scott yelled, "Errol, hold it! Please!"

32

It seemed to Scott, as he clambered over Claire, that he had dreamed this many times. Then Errol's fist smashed that thought like a clay pigeon, leav-ing only one: Escape!

Errol's huge hands grabbed him. He fought free. Errol pulled him down. Again he broke free and clambered toward his truck.

Errol seized him from behind. Scott went down, got up, went down, spun away, blocked a vicious haymaker—pleased, somewhere in his brain, that karate worked. Then Errol connected.

As his breath whooshed out and pain rushed in, Scott knew that he would die. Still, thudding to the ground, he tried to roll. His body stalled. Petrified, he saw Errol lift his hands as if to hurl a thunderbolt.

Scott's leg flashed out instinctively: a perfect side kick into Errol's unguarded groin.

Errol's face turned tragic as he fell.

Scott urged his body up. His torso wouldn't straighten, but his legs jolted him toward his truck. His keys were in his jeans beside Claire's blanket. His driver door, though, was unlocked.

Flinging it open, he thrust his hands under his seat. Errol's pistol was there. And the loaded clip. He slammed this home, whirled, saw Errol charging, and screamed, "Errol, hold it! Please!"

Errol was ten feet away when the firing pin struck an empty chamber, five feet when it struck again, finding the rim of the .22 long rifle shell the clip had fed.

The pistol barked. Errol stopped and clutched his stomach, eyes gone wide.

A witch-scream shrilled behind Scott. "No!"

Witch-arms grabbed him. He wrenched free. His elbow speared Claire, flinging her away. Backpedaling, he kicked a rock, sprawled on the ground, scrambled up and stood, panting, pistol extended at arm's length. "Errol, stay back!"

Errol's mouth gaped, but no sound came. His eyes met Scott's with no sign of recognition.

"Stay back! Please!"

To Scott's horror, Errol stretched out both arms and, like the Frankenstein monster, lurched toward him.

Scott aimed above the red bullseye on Errol's gut. Millions of volts raced through his arm as he shot—once, twice, three times, as fast as he could pull.

Errol kept coming.

Scott turned to run. Errol's truck blocked him, so he spun toward the woods.

Again, Errol caught him. A thick forearm levered up his chin, grinding his Adam's apple, cutting off his wind. He kicked and clawed, gagging. Errol held him, his arms a thick garrote.

Scott dropped the .22. His hands, windmilling, grabbed Errol's hair and tore. Errol's grip tightened, his breath a wheezing moan behind Scott's ear.

Scott kept gagging. He felt himself leaving the fight, arms and legs heavy, fear and frenzy clotting into resignation. *This is dying*, he thought, and barely cared.

"Stop it! Stop it!"

Claire's voice reached him from far away. Something slapped against Errol's head. The big man groaned, loosening his grip.

Scott's legs sagged, and he dropped to the ground. Struggling to roll, he made it to his hands and knees, but couldn't stand. Couldn't breathe.

In the background, Claire moaned, "Oh God, he's hurt. There's so much blood. Oh Jesus, Errol . . ."

She stood above Errol, clutching the .22. Somehow she'd put on panties and a shirt.

Errol lay on his back, arms and legs moving like a wind-up soldier, running down. His sweatshirt was soaked with blood. Blood leaked from his mouth and nose. His breath coughed out in raspy chunks. His mouth gaped, but no words came out.

"Oh God, Scott, help him," Claire moaned, rocking back and forth above her husband. "Oh God, he's hurt so bad."

Snake-quick, Errol's hand snared her calf. She screamed, trying to kick free. Errol held on. Opening his bloody mouth, he pulled her foot toward him as if to chew it off.

The .22 barked in her hand. Blood flew from Errol's head. His body jerked. His head lolled.

Claire stared down, then up, as if uncertain where she was. Raising the pistol, she pointed it at Scott, who had just gotten to his feet. As he dived behind Errol's truck, she turned the thing toward her own head and stared into the barrel, oblivious to Scott as he circled behind her. She didn't resist when he seized her arm and pried the gun out of her hand.

"Don't hurt me," she begged, cringing back. "I won't tell anyone. I swear."

Scott aimed the gun down and flipped the Safety on. "No one'll hurt you. It's okay," he said. Though *okay* was light-years from what it was.

"I tried to help." Claire's voice was toneless, flat. "I hit him. To save you both."

Scott saw blond hairs caught between the pistol's plastic handgrips and its metal stock. Claire had hit Errol with his own gun. Very likely, she had saved Scott's life.

"I didn't mean to shoot," she said. "The gun went off. He scared me." As if these words had snapped a spell, she launched herself like a demon at Scott. "It's your fault!" she shrieked. "God damn you!"

He stepped back, fending off her fists until her face contracted and released a sob.

A torrent followed. Scott caught her arms and held them at her sides. When she stopped struggling, he released her arms, which grabbed him and held tight.

Still unsteady on his feet, he could only repeat, "It'll be okay."

"Help me, Scott," she wailed. "Don't leave me."

He stroked her hair, soothing. "I won't." His voice sounded mechanical. He couldn't think. His body wouldn't stop shaking.

He tried to lead her away from Errol. What had been Errol. "Over here," he urged.

She held back. "No. I . . ." Instead of finishing, she sat, picked up Errol's hand, and held it in her lap.

Scott wavered, then limped toward his truck. The door was open, just as he'd left it before things turned . . . irreversible. He climbed in, closed the door, and sat behind the wheel, head in his hands.

"He's dead," he said aloud. "What should I do?"

His mind was a stalled motor. He pulled and pulled the cord. It wouldn't roar.

Through the windshield, he saw Errol's body, Claire beside it like some wailing widow in the Middle East. What if he wasn't dead, but mute and suffering? What if the body rose and charged toward him, gushing blood?

Not only Scott's hands, but his whole body shook as, round by round, he reloaded the .22. *I should kill Claire* flashed into his brain, and out again.

Kill the one who'd saved him? The one he'd told *I love you* just minutes before?

He was still naked, he realized. Easy prey.

Placing the pistol on his seat, he jumped out of his truck and limped to where he'd left his clothes.

The sight of Claire's blue bra on the green blanket started him shaking again. "What should I do?" circled in his head. The same answer kept barking like a dog locked in a room: the stupid reflex, "Call the cops."

"Concentrate." His voice seemed not to come from him. "Concentrate."

He kicked the bra and blanket into a heap, then dressed, still shaking, all of his senses cranked up to ten. Evergreen-smell hit with air-freshener strength. Birdcalls came at him from all sides. *Chip chip chip chip. Wick wick wick wick. Caw caw caw caw.* As he walked back to his truck, some songbird trilled an aria while a rising wind hummed, swished, and rattled through the trees.

Seeing Claire sitting in his truck, he feared she might have grabbed the .22. But it lay where he'd left it on his seat.

He moved the gun onto the floor, then sat beside Claire. "Is Errol's shotgun in your camper?"

"No. I looked."

That was bad. Bad that the gun was gone, *and* that she had looked for it.

"We've got to get rid of his body," she said. Her voice was calm. Scarily so.

"If we hide things," he said, "it looks like murder. This was self-defense."

"For you. Not me."

"I saw him grab you!"

"He needed help. So I shot him in the head?" Tears oozed out of her eyes as if her brain was a squeezed sponge.

"It was self-defense," Scott said again.

"We can't prove that."

She was right. The RCMPs would separate them. They'd promise one immunity to nail the other. And who seemed the more likely murderer?

Not beautiful Claire.

"We could say someone attacked us," he offered. "Jim McGee."

"Killers always shift the blame." Claire spoke as if addressing a problem in logic. "Police always suspect the wife."

"Or the lover."

She half-smiled, as if he'd uttered a mildly good *bon mot*. Could he trust this change of mood? Could he trust *her*? He looked around as if answers hid in the woods.

"Okay," he said, "what should we do?"

"Pretend this never happened," she said. "Hide the body, all the evidence. Then fly to England. I'll wire Daddy for money. I'll say Errol left me. Or I left him. I don't know . . ."

"It looks bad if we go together."

"I'm not letting you out of my sight." She took his hand as she said this. But more than love quivered in her words.

"Won't your father think something's . . . off?"

She shook her head sadly. "He knows Errol was dying to get away." She gave a sickly smile. "Dying."

Her eyes looked like the little deer's at the moment it died. Beyond shock. Empty.

"What about Errol's mom?" he said.

"They don't talk much. If she finds me, I'll say he left me, and I don't know where he went." She shook her head as if there were flies in her skull. "It's not perfect. But it's a chance."

Another sponge-full of tears tracked down her face.

"Let's do it," Scott finally said. "I'd never trust the Law to get things right." He kissed her cheek as she stared straight ahead. "You rest here. I'll clean up," he said, then walked to his camper, struggling to think.

If anyone showed up now, he'd either kill them or give up. He'd decide which when the time came. *If*, however, no one came and they hid *all* evidence, they might get out of this. Few people had seen them in Canada. And no one had seen them at Ursula Lake. Errol hadn't known the lake existed. No one would look for him here.

So—how to make his body disappear?

A man his size would be hard to drag through woods. He'd leave a trail.

Plus, the ground was rocky. Digging would take forever, even with a full-sized shovel, which they didn't have.

Also, animals dug bodies out of graves.

Ursula Lake was deep and not much visited. They could wrap Errol in a blanket, weight it with rocks, and sink him. That might work. If Scott could stand to touch the corpse.

It lay on its back, eyes staring blindly at the sky.

Walking up to it—his second; Mom had been his first—Scott stretched out his foot and poked.

No movement. Dead. All that brash, Rabelasian vitality gone. Not into heaven, or the earth, or anywhere. Just gone.

Errol had shit himself, just as Scott's mom had done. Trying to ignore the smell, Scott unfastened Errol's backpack and pulled it off without looking at Errol's face. Next, he emptied Errol's pockets, dropping wallet, keys, and loose change into the pack.

It felt criminal to be rifling Errol's pockets. Almost more criminal than killing him.

A moment's thought made him retrieve Errol's keys from the backpack. He wasn't thinking right. He'd almost screwed up big.

Claire had laid her head down on his dashboard. He'd get no help from her.

He walked to pick up her green blanket, tossed it toward Errol's corpse, then stuffed her bra in Errol's backpack.

He kept thinking he heard cars. Each time, he started shivering, desperate to jump into his truck and run. But he made himself stay still, repeating, "Concentrate," until either the cars came—they didn't—or the shivering stopped.

Inside Errol's camper, he found a roll of cord and a coil of rope. "Never go anywhere without rope," Errol used to say.

A noise outside the camper made Scott jump.

Claire stood in the doorway. Fully dressed but vacant-eyed, she said quietly, "Get rid of my things. All of them. Please." Then she shuffled away. Still in shock.

What if she stayed that way? A loose cannon. Unpredictable.

He forced the thought out of his mind, digging around until he found Errol's bag of extra clothes. He started filling it, realized that Errol had way too many things, and tossed the bag onto the ground.

Maybe he should strip the body. But the thought of seeing Errol's wounds appalled him. If Errol were found, his teeth would identify him, clothes or not. The best plan was to make sure he wasn't found.

He spread the green blanket, and tried to roll Errol's body with his feet. It was too heavy. He'd need to get down on his knees and shove. Like he'd done with that dead deer, eons ago.

The shit-stink made him gag, which turned into sobbing as he rolled the body in the blanket. Like a burrito, he couldn't help but think.

He slid three good-sized, flattened rocks inside the blanket, then used Errol's cord to tie off the ends. That done, he used half of Errol's rope to wind the blanket tight. Feeling his friend, limp and squishy under the cloth, was horrible. But he hummed the "Dazed and Confused" riff, and the job got done.

He dropped a few rocks into the clothes sack, lugged it to his boat, then returned for the corpse.

Claire was still in his truck, head on his dashboard. Leaving everything to him.

Scott lifted Errol's tree-trunk legs and, groaning with the effort, dragged. This was much harder than dragging the dead deer. He should have put the rocks in last. His strength, though, was coming back. The power of necessity.

Three rest stops later, Errol's body lay beside the boat.

Scott got the legs inside without a problem. But the torso wasn't halfway in when, with a loud scrape, the boat lurched away from shore, and the corpse slid into the lake. Scott had to wade through clouds of freezing red water to stop the boat from drifting away.

Soaked and shivering, he dragged, first boat, then body—soaked, and even heavier—back to shore.

"Concentrate," he said, and tensed his muscles, trying to generate heat.

It didn't help. Still, if a desperate hundred-pound mom could lift a truck, he should be able to lift Errol. An army of moms couldn't be more desperate.

He hauled the boat completely out of the water. With it stabilized on land, he managed somehow, limb by limb, to shove/wrestle/heave Errol's limpness inside.

His watch said 1:29. He kept thinking he heard cars, though none drove up. He launched his boat, climbed in, and was about to start the motor when he realized he'd left Errol's pistol in the truck with Claire. She might shoot herself. Or him.

Leaping from the boat, he beached it again, and rushed to her. "Come on, Claire." He took her hand. "Come with me."

She looked uneasy as he plucked the .22 from the truck's floor, but followed meekly as he placed her in the prow and relaunched the boat.

The motor started on the first try, and drove them swiftly toward the center of the lake—two hundred feet deep, Old Hodges had said.

The bank of dark clouds to the north had thickened, taking on a surreal orange glow. The whole sky was turning gray. The lake sloshed in a rising wind.

"Hurry," he told himself. "Hurry."

Ten minutes more, and he cut the engine, letting the boat glide. A million eyes seemed focused on him from the trees. Car after phantom car pulled into camp, then disappeared as he squinted at the clearing and their two tiny trucks.

He tried a few tentative grips on Errol's blanket. None worked. He'd have to wrap it with his arms.

"I'll help," Claire said, and without warning, stood up.

"Sit down!" Scott yelled.

She dropped instantly, looking terrified.

"You'll tip us," he said more gently. "Sit still. Let the boat stabilize."

As Claire froze and the boat slowly stopped rocking, Scott fought down thoughts of the dunking that had started this nightmare. "Okay," he said. Heart more nearly shuddering than beating, he began to lift and push Errol's corpse over the side.

The shit-smell seemed inconsequential, now.

The boat pitched and heeled as Errol's feet touched water. Scott was glad, now, that he'd brought Claire. This could not have worked alone.

"Go to the edge of the boat. Lean way back and balance me," he told her as he shoved and tugged at Errol, who seemed bigger than ever, dead.

Oh fuck, Scott thought. *We're going to swamp.* This far from shore, they'd die. But what was the alternative? All he could do was, inch by inch, force Errol's body into the lake.

He shoved more desperately as water slopped over the gunwale, the boat tilting toward the perpendicular.

"Lean *way* back, Claire," he shouted. "Out over the edge!"

Water was pouring in when, with a scraping sigh, Errol's body slithered out of the boat.

The craft rocked crazily, then gradually stopped. Two inches of water sloshed in the bottom of the boat, but there was no risk of sinking.

"You poor, sad man."

Scott looked up, thinking Claire meant him. But she was staring at the water, whispering, "Why'd you marry a rich bitch like me?"

Errol's body kept shrinking smaller and smaller until the green blanket flickered like a fish and merged with the green depths.

Restarting his engine, Scott motored a hundred yards away before he jettisoned the weighted clothes sack. He made a stab at bailing with his hands, then gave it up and, with Claire sitting silent, roared back to face the problem of Errol's truck.

The water in front of camp was too shallow to sink it. Better to drive it off one of the cliffs they'd passed coming in. If he could find the right one.

"Wait here," he told Claire when they were back on shore. Then, .22 under his belt, he went to work.

First, he unscrewed Errol's license plates and stuffed them into Errol's backpack. He used Errol's ax, stained with dry blood from the bear, to crack Errol's windshield. After pulling off the small VIN plate, he cleaned out Errol's glove box and side-pockets, swept up everything under the seats, and stuffed it all in the backpack.

Ransacking Errol's camper for traceable things, he found Claire's sketchbook, full of pictures of Errol, their trucks, their two campsites, and three sketches of *him*. The likenesses were startling. And incriminating. He almost asked Claire if she wanted them, then changed his mind and stuffed them in Errol's backpack, too.

The shotgun was not to be found. Errol must have set it down after he shot the bear at Oso Lake. Set it down and left it there.

That wasn't good. Still, anyone who found the gun would likely keep it. Unlikely it would be traced back to Errol, much less to him.

Climbing out of Errol's camper, Scott started toward his own, then stopped, heart shuddering. Errol's boat! How in flaming hell had he forgotten *that*?

Errol must have stashed the boat, then walked back to take them by surprise, Scott thought as he raced for his own boat.

Claire sat beside it, plucking at the ground. *What's she doing?* Scott wondered, then saw that she was crushing little toads with her fingers. Crushing them, then flipping the bodies away.

"Oh no," she moaned, hearing about Errol's boat. She looked like a madwoman, fingers red with toad blood.

"We've got to find it," Scott said.

"Don't leave me," she begged, scrambled into his boat, and sat down in the prow, leaning forward as she had on that first happy, hopeful day.

33

The next hour felt like the longest of Scott's life. He hugged the shore, hoping Errol hadn't stashed the boat in the woods. It would take hours to circle the lake. He'd search an hour to the left, he decided, then speed back to camp and search an hour to the right. Search and pray.

Fifty-eight minutes later, he saw a white thing floating in the lake. It looked like a severed arm. But moving closer, he saw that it was a dead fish: much smaller than the one last night. And gutted, too.

His first thought—*Another fisherman is here*—vanished when he saw the fish's bent-back head, its neck broken "Indian-style." He scanned the shore, saw a silver wedge, and pointed. "There!"

Errol's boat was pulled up in a tiny cove they might have motored by, except for this: Errol's last fish.

Scott beached his boat next to Errol's, and jumped ashore just as a huge eagle flapped out of a stand of tall weeds, up and away. As Claire sat useless as a figurehead and the eagle soared, Scott shoved Errol's boat into the water, relaunched his own boat and, with Errol's painter-line in hand, chugged back out onto the lake.

Internal flotation would make Errol's boat hard to sink. Better to drive it, along with his truck, off a cliff.

As if rejecting this idea, the boat began to fight—veering off course, refusing to be easily towed. The stiffening breeze made matters worse.

Claire could have helped by steering. But she was no use even for that, still sitting, staring straight ahead. She was a problem, no doubt about it: prime to raise suspicions, and/or to break down and confess. It was almost suicide to let her live.

That was his reason speaking, though. Or was it failure-of-nerve? *I won't hurt her,* he told himself as, two hundred yards from shore, where the lake was deepest green, he eased Errol's stuffed-tight backpack over the side.

Twenty minutes later, they chugged back into camp, Errol's balky boat dragging behind. Scott beached both boats, opened Errol's camper, and started to stow the loose gear from Errol's boat inside. As he worked, he saw that Errol's gas tank was gone. Had he run out of gas? Was that, and not suspicion, why he'd come back to camp on foot?

The tank was bright red. If Errol had dropped it close-by, it should be easy to spot. But a quick look turned up nothing. And he didn't have time for a long search. An anonymous gas tank wouldn't lead the law to him.

Using his hundred-pound-mom strength, he managed, after several tries and some damage to Errol's truck, to get Errol's boat up on its rack. How insignificant that little side-ding appeared now.

Claire was still sitting in his boat, feet half-submerged in the water that had nearly swamped them.

"I've got to get rid of Errol's truck," he said, unscrewing his boat's drain plug.

"I'll help," she said as water gushed out onto the rocky ground.

He needed help desperately, but didn't trust Claire to give it. "I've got it handled," he said.

She didn't argue. "Come right back," she said. "Promise."

"I will." He gave her a quick kiss on the forehead and, securing the pistol in his belt, walked to Errol's truck.

He half-expected it to be dead as its owner. That would screw them royally. But no, it started right away.

Good thing Dad had taught him how to drive a stick, he thought as he eased the truck out of the campsite, then lurched and rattled up the dirt road leading out.

The road hugged cliffs in several spots. Scott rejected three before he found a long, straight drop that ended in thick woods he hoped would hide the truck from view.

Aiming the truck toward the cliff, Scott put it in neutral, emergency brake on. Motor idling, he searched for the right-sized rock.

He found one quickly, lugged it to the truck, and used it to hold the accelerator down.

The truck roared as if enraged.

A sense of tragic waste caught in Scott's throat. Errol had sold his soul to buy this rig. A few things might be saved to make the loss less total. Spools of fly line. Errol's Sage rod and reel. Untraceable things.

"No," Scott said aloud. "Make a clean break."

Reaching his right foot into the cab, he pushed the clutch to the floor. Move too slowly when he let it out, he could be yanked over the cliff, too.

He put the truck in first gear, released the brake, then popped the clutch, jumped back, lost his footing, and fell.

The truck lurched forward and died.

"Shit!" Scott yelled from where he lay, sprawled painfully on the rocky ground.

The truck sat so close to the edge, Scott felt like a cliff-diver as, slowly, cautiously, he eased back inside the cab. The drop into the trees seemed infinite. It would be easy to fall—no guilt, no hiding, every problem solved.

"No," he told himself. "Concentrate!"

He moved the rock off the accelerator, reengaged the emergency brake, put the truck in neutral, and turned the key.

The engine started up again.

If anyone comes down the road, I'm screwed, he thought, then forced the thought out of his mind. Thought was the death of action. Enemy of nerve.

He eased out of the truck, then, kneeling on the ground, used the rock to press the accelerator to the floor. He let the truck roar for a moment. Then he stood and, leaning as far back as he could, reached with his right leg into the cab.

Depressing the clutch, he shifted the truck into first gear and released the brake with his left hand. Slowly, very slowly, he let out the clutch.

The instant that it caught, he yanked his leg out of the truck and threw himself backward onto the ground. The roaring truck lunged forward and, topped by its huge camper and rowboat-party-hat, dropped off the cliff.

It didn't hang like a diver in the air. It nosed straight down, struck the rock wall, then slowly rolled: a swan dive out of control. With less noise than he'd imagined and no movie-fireball, it slammed through the trees and, miraculously, out of sight.

He'd feared the truck would leave a hole in the woods that would lead all eyes to it. Instead, the trees had swallowed it as completely as the lake had swallowed Errol. Lacking plates and VIN number, the truck would be hard to trace and, like the shotgun, harder still to link with *him*. The finder, if there was one, might salvage what he could and go away.

"It's done," Scott said, and started back to camp at a quick jog.

Luckily, the road ran mostly downhill, and his lungs had begun adjusting to the altitude. He blessed Sensei Mishikawa for the wind sprints that ended each karate class. Errol's .22 seemed to weigh twenty-two pounds, but when it bounced out of his belt, Scott scooped it up and jogged on with it clutched in his right hand.

A minute more, and he topped the last rise and stumbled, gasping, down the hundred-yard incline into camp.

Claire sat exactly where he'd left her, hunched over in his boat.

Rain was holding off, but the blue sky had gone solid gray. The dark cloud bank had thickened more.

"Come on," he told Claire. "We've got to go."

She gave the .22 a frightened look. But when, after making sure the safety was on, he shoved the pistol in his belt and held his hand out, she took it.

"I'm better," she said, and climbed awkwardly from the boat. "I can help."

"Good," he said. "Let's get my boat up on its rack."

Obediently, she gripped the back end of his boat and, shuffling behind, helped him lug it to his truck and hoist it up.

"Thanks," he said when everything was clamped down tight. He hated looking weak, but he could barely stand upright.

She seemed finally to notice. "You're tired," she said. "What else should I do?"

"Pile everything that's left into my camper," he said as he repacked his tackle box.

He placed the .22 inside, then pulled it out. Seeing Errol's hair still stuck between the grip and butt, he pulled the hairs out one by one, and dropped them on the ground. He should have sunk the gun. But since he hadn't, he'd keep it in his belt. For now.

With Claire helping, they were soon ready to go. Scott cleared a space inside the camper, spread his sleeping bag, and told Claire, "Ride in back."

She looked surprised. Afraid.

"We shouldn't be seen together," he explained. "Sleep if you can. You may have to spell me at the wheel."

"Okay," she said. "Can I use the bathroom first?" She mustered a wan smile. "It's important."

"Go ahead," Scott said, then watched her hurry, toilet paper-roll in hand, toward the woods. Would he end up on Death Row because a woman had to take a crap?

He started to unlock his truck, then opted for a last camp-check.

Nothing left behind, as far as he could tell. The ground, though, was stained red-brown where Errol had been. Damn. One mistake like this could doom them.

A few scrapes with his boot, and the dark stain was gone. The ground looked scarred, but rain would soon take care of that. The dark sky looked ready to release a flood.

Pulling out his pocket knife, Scott cut a leafy whisk-broom from a nearby bush. Finished cutting, he glanced down and saw a giant toad—the one he'd seen before?—staring from under the bush.

He had an urge to soccer-kick the thing into the woods. But why kill a helpless animal?

Turning his back on it, he placed Errol's .22 on the ground, and attacked the earth-scars with his broom. When the ground was as smooth as he could get it, the toad was gone. Scott gave his boots a quick once-over, tossed the broom into the trees, picked up the .22, and opened his cab.

A stench almost knocked him down. Like the dead cow, but worse.

His parka lay on top of something on the floor. He yanked it off, then leapt away. Underneath—fur matted with blood, eyes wriggling with maggots—was the head of the bear cub from Oso Lake.

Scott raised the .22 and spun around. "McGee!" he bellowed. "Where are you?!"

He wanted to rip the man apart. At the same time, he needed cover. McGee could be sighting down on him from anywhere. How had he tracked them here? How had he known?

The best that Scott could do was crouch behind his truck with his back to the lake. "Come out, you fucking freak!" he screamed. "I know it's you!"

The woods were still as death.

He scanned the lake. No boat that he could see.

Had McGee captured Claire? Or killed her? Was he watching? Waiting for Scott to come for her?

There'd be more cover in the woods. He gripped the .22, its cold weight reassuring as he tensed for the short dash to the trees.

Something moved, just to the left of where Claire had gone in.

Using his truck's hood as a rest, he aimed the pistol at the sound.

Twigs crackled. Branches moved. A figure burst out of the woods. Scott's finger tensed to shoot.

No! It was Claire!

She saw his gun. Stopped. Edged backward. "Scott? I heard you yell . . ."

"Get in the camper!" he said. "Bearclaw's here!"

As she scrambled to obey, he jumped into his stinking cab and slid the .22 under his seat. The truck might be rigged to explode. He barely cared, as long as this tension broke.

He thrust the key in the ignition and turned. The engine fired up. No bombs.

He backed up. No unusual jolting. No flat tires.

He cranked the wheel, turned the truck around and, fearing to be shot at any second, roared away.

His truck seemed sluggish, laboring up the long incline. Had McGee sabotaged it in some way? Scott whipped his head around, fearing to see him in the camper window, holding up Claire's head.

Nothing there but the blue curtains Sara'd bought so they could make love in the back.

Still no ambush as he came to the first cliffs.

He stopped the truck, set the brake, threw open the passenger door, and kicked the bear's head outside. He hadn't touched it with his hands. Still, he wiped them on his jeans before he slammed the door and roared away.

For an instant, in his side mirror, the bear cub's head seemed to snail-glide after him. Then it was gone, leaving two maggots on the floor-mat, wriggling.

Scott tried to think as he jolted ahead, a sheer mountain on one side, a sheer drop on the other. If McGee meant to kill them, wouldn't he have tried just now? Or was he savoring the hunt? Prolonging the torture? Maybe the head was a taunt. Or a message: "We've both got things to hide."

4:45. It seemed to Scott that, in the past three hours, he'd endured more strain than in his whole past life. Those Houston cops had been nothing, next to this.

"We're not home yet," he said. His body didn't care. He felt it weakening. His throat and stomach throbbed from Errol's attack. Even his fear of Jim McGee was running down.

Images swarmed: Errol's howling face. The red bullseye on his sweatshirt. The dark green blanket sinking in the pale green lake.

Police with grappling hooks were raising Errol's wrapped body. Hikers searching Errol's truck picked up a credit card, read a serial number, found some clue—maybe Errol's gas can—that he'd missed. He was being wakened by "Open up! Police!" Kidney-kicked. Beaten with nightsticks. Thrown in jail. That judge in Houston—bald, with jowls—scowled down from the branches of a pine.

The truck banged on through chugholes and over split-log bridges, clinging to the road as it skirted cliffs and wound through timber stands that had delighted him two days before. The strip of sky that he could see was almost black. But still no rain.

Passing the place Errol's truck had plunged, Scott looked away. If the truck was visible, what could he do except feel doomed?

What if he met another car? What if the driver recalled the number on his US plates?

Three times he started shivering and had to pull over until the shaking stopped. Each time, he hoped that Claire would offer help. When she stayed in the camper, he drove on, checking his gas gauge, praying that he really did have half a tank—that the rain would hold off half an hour—that he wouldn't have a flat or engine trouble, wouldn't run off the road and have to be towed out by men who would appear in court to nail his coffin shut.

At the turn-off to Dick's Dude Ranch, his will ran out. While his vision pitched and swayed, he spied an indentation in the woods, pulled in, and stumbled from his truck. He thought for certain he'd throw up. In movies, normal people who'd killed someone always threw up. Instead, once he'd stretched out on the ground, his head stopped swimming. He felt famished. His last meal had been Instant Breakfast several lifetimes ago.

He lay still, almost relaxing, then heard a car.

Ducking behind a fallen tree, he watched a red Ford truck rumble up. Oregon plates. A man, a woman, and three kids were stuffed inside.

They stopped at the fork in the road. As Scott's heart readied to leave his throat and make a break for it, the driver, with no sign of having seen him, started up the road to Dick's.

Relief rolled over Scott in waves. The waves turned into sobs, which he choked back at first, then yielded to. He lay on his face in the woods, crying as he hadn't since his dad spanked him for "talking back," and afterward he'd vowed, "Never again!"

A hand touched the back of his head.

He turned, and saw Claire kneeling beside him. She looked better. Almost herself.

"I'm sorry," he said, wiping his face with his sleeve. "For everything."

"I'm sorry, too." She stroked his hair the way his mom used to. *Everything's all right*, she used to say back when, for the most part, everything *had* been.

"We'd better move," he said, but didn't try to rise. "Bearclaw may come. Or rain. Or both"

"His real name's Jim McGee," Claire said.

"I know," Scott said. Pointless to protect Errol now.

Quick as he could, he told her everything they'd found at Secret Lake. Then she told what Ted Brumley had told her.

"McGee must think he *is* Bearclaw," she said. "Or possessed by him."

"He's schizophrenic," Scott said. "Like that *Psycho* guy. Ed Gein."

"The one who made clothes out of women's skin," Claire said, and shuddered visibly. "I don't want McGee wearing *me*."

"He'll stay in Canada," Scott said. "He's got a perfect set-up here." He raised his head and, only half joking, addressed the woods. "Your secret's safe with us, McGee."

"While we're stopped, I'd better pee," Claire said.

"Okay," Scott said. What else *could* he say? "Don't go too far."

"I won't, believe me," she said, then moved around the camper, into the woods and out of sight.

He felt that he should follow to protect her. But even in a life-or-death crisis, there was the privacy thing. He peed where he stood, then, careful to avoid the spot, sat back down and tried to rest till she returned.

A minute later, she was back. "I can drive, if you want," she said, and took his hand as he stood slowly.

"Maybe after Winoma," he said. "Stay out of sight till we're past there."

"Okay," she said. "If you need me . . ." Squeezing his hand, she walked back to the camper and climbed in.

It struck him, as he pulled back onto the dirt road, that he should have grabbed a protein bar from the camper. But stopping now would waste time that they didn't have. Winoma was on the one road south, and had the only gas station for miles. They had to reach it during working hours—reach it, and pray they didn't meet big Ted or the RCMPs.

He rolled his window down and took a breath of cool and wholesome North Woods air. The break had left him feeling better: weak and drained, but better. As if a high fever had cracked.

Light rain began to fall, and had soon turned the dirt road to mud. But there was the highway straight ahead. The way home.

Except a gate now stretched across the road.

Had those Oregonians shut it? Had McGee locked them in? Or set a trap?

Halfway expecting to be shot, Scott left the truck to idle, and jumped out.

There wasn't even a padlock on the gate. It opened easily. There were no cars or pseudo-Indians in sight as Scott jostled between the cracked gray fenceposts and pulled onto the paved highway, slick with new rain.

34

Seated on the floor of Scott's camper, trying to fend off sliding piles of out-doors *stuff*, Claire lifted one curtain's edge just enough to see that it was rainy outside, getting dark. She let the curtain drop, lay back on Scott's air mattress, and pulled his sleeping bag around her like a robe. His smell, a mix of musk and woods and lake, was comforting. But not comforting enough.

Now that she was headed there, she saw how tricky the border would be. Scott was leaving with the truck he'd arrived in. He'd have no problem, alone. But with her? Ted's beating aside, Customs would know she'd entered Canada with Errol. They'd want to know where he was. *And* his truck. Even if she concocted a lie they would accept, crossing with Scott could trip them up later on.

Scott, of course, would see this too. Would he decide she wasn't worth the risk, and leave her? She couldn't be sure.

The Canadian border was five thousand miles long. Her best bet might be to cross it through the woods. But border agents would have thought of that. There must be cameras. Maybe buried sensors, too. She was no woods-woman. What if she got lost? Or caught. *Oh, I was just taking a walk . . .*

And afterward? Relationships were hard enough with *no* baggage. She and Scott were starting with a freight train full. Benjamin Franklin had said, "Two can keep a secret, if one of them is dead." They'd have to spend their lives proving Ben wrong.

She should knock on the window behind Scott's head, and get him to stop. They should make a plan while they had time. But she was *so* tired. The movement of the truck and the warmth of Scott's sleeping bag, combined with the stress of the day made her feel ready to sleep for a year.

Stress of the day. What a way to think about her husband's death. Yet even when she tried, she couldn't force the memory to coalesce. She'd been in shock. And still was, apparently. If she needed to sleep, that's what she should do. She would need all her wits about her when she woke.

A gentle dream-current kept nudging at her thoughts. It seemed to come, though, from outside her mind. She saw herself trudging up a rocky trail through high mountains. On her right, she saw a cave, and walked inside. Errol had found some kind of cave. Was it this one? Was something about it Freudian? All she remembered about Freud was *penis envy.*

She heard a voice, and crawled to the edge of a pit that swirled with mist. Below, Jim Bearclaw stood in front of a stone altar anchored at each of its four corners by a stone toad. Camp Robbers swooped around Bearclaw, or perched on his shoulders and head. A red-haired woman lay on the altar, nude.

Claire wasn't scared. She recognized the scene from one of Errol's "collector's item" *Conan the Barbarian* comic books.

Bearclaw wore a bearskin robe. The bear's head, jaws open, hung over his forehead. She saw his puckered scar and his strange eyes: one brown, one yellow as a cat's.

The toads' eyes glowed like rubies as Bearclaw raised a gourd rattle and started chanting in some Native tongue. His wheezy voice turned resonant and strong. His words shot into the sky and burst like fireworks.

His rattle had become a knife: curved and yellow as a claw. Still chanting, he raised the knife. Claire tried to scream, but no sound came. She was the woman staring up at Bearclaw's face, which became Scott's as the knife plunged toward her chest.

◆ ◆ ◆

The rain had fizzled as darkness swept in on Scott like a black fog. But the road stayed wet. Passing the Oso turn-off, he hoped that McGee had come back, and would stay. Strange to realize they were both killers now.

There were few cars on the highway, but each approaching pair of head-lights seemed to scan his cab before hurrying on. Any lights behind him never stayed for long.

He entered Winoma, trying to embody innocence. Compared to Errol's truck, his was nondescript. That was good. It was good, too, that the gas station was open.

It wasn't good that he was the one customer. Luckily, the gaunt attendant seemed too drugged-up to remember his home planet, much less Scott's face.

"Filler up," Scott said, and praying Claire stayed hidden, made for the restroom. Better to kill time where he wouldn't be seen.

He shut and locked the restroom door, used the urinal, then, glancing around the little room, saw a newspaper on top of the commode. "NO NEW CLUES IN LOCAL DEATH," a headline blared, above a picture of big Ted!

Scott's heart threatened to break out of his rib cage as he stood in the piss-reeking restroom, and read. "Ted Brumley" had been found "leaning against a tree," dead of "head injuries." Police were "following clues that point to Paul Benoit, also suspected in the killing of Jane Ryan at Oso Lake." There was no mention of Errol. And no mention of Scott, though he'd held the man for the fatal blow. No mention of Americans at all.

The attendant was still filling his truck when Scott returned. He didn't dare rush the man, and risk lodging in his memory. All he could do was get his cash ready, keep his head down, and wait.

Scott felt bad about Ted. Objectively, though, his death was a plus. He could have placed Scott, Errol, and Claire together. It was good, too, that the dead girl's boyfriend, Benoit, was distracting the police. As for McGee— the world, it seemed, was full of killers, running free.

This thought sparked another, even more unsettling. The RCMP office was a stone's-throw away. He could walk in, with or without Claire, and confess. He could do what his mom would have seen as "the right thing": tell the truth, and face the consequences "like a man."

Standing in a drizzle already halfway to a rain, he teetered on the edge of a cliff much steeper than the place he'd crashed Errol's truck. It might feel good to ease his conscience and *take responsibility* for his acts. But that phrase meant, in practice, to hand responsibility to others: to place his fate in their hands, and face the "Authorities" not as a man, but a naughty child.

No. He would not jump off that cliff.

The attendant replaced the gas nozzle, and fumbled with Scott's gas cap. "I can get it," Scott said. "Thanks."

He screwed the cap on, paid the man, and pulled away from Sunoco. One RCMP car was parked outside the station. An officer knelt beside it, checking the front tire. Scott's heart thumped hard as he drove by—but thumped less hard, he noted, than it might have done.

The Mountie never looked up. Only Howdy Do's fiendish blue eyes watched Scott leave Winoma behind.

◆ ◆ ◆

Half an hour later, Scott was still making good time. The storm had managed only a few splats of rain. His whole body ached and throbbed. Still, he felt alert and able to drive on.

Was McGee following? Had he hidden some kind of tracking device in Scott's truck, like on TV? Or did his tracking powers come from somewhere else?

Scott thrust that thought away. The North Woods only seemed uncanny when you were there. Once he got home, his thoughts would normalize.

First, though, he had to get safely out of Canada. Approach Customs with Claire, and they'd be linked. And what if someone cross-checked, and asked Mrs. Wolfe, "Where's Errol?"

He didn't relish telling Claire, *You'll have to hike in through the woods.* But at the moment, he could see no other way.

"Just drive," he told himself. "Cross bridges when they come."

A tapping from behind spun him around. As if she'd known what he was thinking, Claire had pulled the curtains back.

"Pull over," her lips said as she pointed right, to the side of the road.

He wanted to protest. But he nodded, and her head disappeared.

Did she need another bathroom break? Otherwise, stopping made no sense. Best to keep moving while momentum was on your side. And yet, he had to keep her calm. With the border coming up, they'd both need to be cool and rational.

A dirt road opened on the right, and he turned in.

Like the road where they'd slept en route to Ursula, this was a tight fit. With no room to turn around, Scott drove in far enough to be seen from the highway, but not too far to back out. Motor idling, headlights showing a muddy road and rain-glistening woods, he left the cab and trudged back to his camper.

Claire looked spectral in the camper's one dim light.

Scott tried to sound upbeat. "What's going on?"

"I'm carsick. And claustrophobic." She came into his arms and held on tight. "Oh, Scott, how can things have gone so wrong?"

"I don't know," he said. Her touch had gone wrong, too. Errol's ghost might as well have stood there, holding them apart.

Her lips sought his in the dark. "Make love to me," she whispered.

"Now?!"

"Please, Scott," she said. "If we live to be a thousand, I'll never need you more."

She seemed to wobble on some personal precipice. Upset her and she might fall.

"I'm not in a real sexy mood," he said.

"Leave that to me," she said. "Bring us a blanket. I'll get the flashlight."

She started toward the cab. He almost stopped her, then stepped into the camper dutifully.

Gear lay jumbled everywhere except the nest she'd made out of his sleeping bag.

"We'd be drier in here," he called.

"It smells bad," she said. "It's too cramped. I need to be outside."

Reluctantly, he grabbed his orange blanket, turned off the camper's light, and shut the door. The thought of sex made him feel sick. How would Claire react if his libido went on strike?

Up front, she killed the truck's headlights. Then the engine died.

"Set the brake and lock the cab," Scott called. "Make sure you have the keys."

"I do," she said.

The truck's front door slammed shut. The cab's light died.

Scott touched his camper, its firmness reassuring in the blackness that pressed in.

His flashlight winked on, then bounced toward him, Claire walking behind.

"I'll take the keys," he said, holding out his hand. "Don't want to lose those out here."

She lifted them to show she had them, then shoved them into her own pocket. "Don't you trust me?"

What could he say but, "Sure. I do."

The woods grew colder as they walked, the dampness adding its bite to the air as they followed another faint deer trail. Enormous black trees hemmed them in on both sides. Above the road, a star or two blinked into view, then ducked behind thick clouds.

"It's really dark." Claire sounded scared. But not enough, it seemed, to counter her sex drive. She jolted forward, the flashlight's yellow beam groping ahead.

Stopping beside a pine tree with a double trunk, she said, "Here's a good marker," and left the path.

Scott followed reluctantly. The underbrush was thick and wet. The ground squished underfoot. The blanket he carried would never keep them dry. Could they even find the truck, once they were done?

"Don't go too far," he warned. "That flashlight's temperamental."

She shone the light around a little clearing overhung by shadow-trees. "This is good," she said.

Spreading his blanket, Scott thought of the other blanket he had spread that day. Whatever love potion he'd swallowed had worn off. Claire's charms, at least for now, had lost their charm.

She yanked her pants down as if she had dysentery. Not bothering with her shirt, she dropped to her knees, opened his jeans, and pulled them off his hips.

"This feels so weird . . ."

Her efforts quelled his protest. And produced results.

"Lie down," she said.

The blanket lay on top of sharp pine cones and rocks. But Claire was not concerned with comfort, his or hers. The sounds she made seemed less pleasure than pain as she straddled him.

Her foot kicked the flashlight, which went out. In cave-darkness, Scott's hand closed on the metal tube, and shook. The light came on as Claire—dry as sandpaper—kept forcing him inside.

Instead of loved, he felt abused. It made him want to punish her as she seemed to want and need. Disgust rose in his throat. He felt a lust akin to rage that swelled and swelled until it burst and he was pounding into her, groaning as much from relief as release.

She dropped down onto him when he was done, and held on tight. "Thank you, Scott," she said at last. "I'm better now."

Rocks bored into his back, but he held her until she said, "We should go."

In the dark, her voice sounded small and sad.

While she rearranged her clothes, he stood, pulling up his jeans. Might as well discuss the border when they got back to the truck. If they could find it.

He bent to touch his toes and stretch the dents out of his back, then noticed, at the far edge of the flashlight's beam, Errol's pistol on the ground.

"Ready?" Claire said, and moved to grasp the flashlight, her body between him and the gun.

"Claire—why'd you bring . . ."

She lunged away. He grabbed for her.

The flashlight died. Darkness crashed down.

He'd caught her shirt. She pulled in silence: a monster fish hooked in the dark. Then her shirt ripped. She lunged away. The flashlight came on as she whirled, pistol in hand.

He dove behind a spectral tree as the gun barked.

The light went out. The pistol barked again. He saw the flash, heard the shot, knew he wasn't hit, and ran. Blind. Terrified. Slamming into trees. Smashing through thickets. Stumbling through the blackness, arms thrust forward, trying to force a passageway.

The yellow flashlight beam sprang on and moved toward him.

He crouched low. No need to ask what she was doing, or why. Both answers had become too clear.

The pistol cracked. A bullet zinged close to his head.

He froze. She was aiming by sound. Aiming well. So she could shoot. What else about her didn't he know?

She'd fired three times. How many shots were left? He'd loaded the clip, but not counted the bullets.

The flashlight swept across the woods. Claire tramped behind, moving in the wrong direction now. He held his breath and prayed she kept moving that way.

Instead, she squared the corner of the line she had been making, walked a few steps, squared the line again and, flashlight sweeping side to side like a flamethrower, moved back his way. She was searching like a pro. Could someone be directing her, or was she simply using common sense?

Scott crouched as low as he could get, and still move fast. His body had forgotten to ache. He felt afraid, but not terrified now. He felt focused. Intent.

The yellow light came near. An instant before it hit, he leapt away. The pistol barked just as he slammed into a tree.

Orange and purple spots flashed in his eyes. Claire thrashed toward him, her flashlight dogging his zigzag among the trees.

Thick brush caught his foot and threw him down. The light closed in, then died. Claire's "God damn!" sounded less woman than man.

Scott floundered up and crashed deeper into the woods. His face and hands felt gouged by trees and raked by brambles when, at last, he stopped and looked back.

Only darkness.

In the distance, the flashlight flickered on. The ghostly shape behind was Claire. The woman he'd thought he loved was hunting him.

Her light cut a broad arc, slicing back toward him. His path must be clear as a bulldozer's.

She stopped, the flashlight hanging by her side. "Scott?" she called. "Can you hear me?"

He crouched, silent. If she ran out of bullets, he could take her one-on-one. But how many did she have left?

"Well . . ." Her voice was as clear as if she stood next to him. "I hope you do."

A long pause. Then, "I'm sorry, Scott."

She moved the light in a slow circle around her. He pressed behind a tree until it passed.

"I really wanted us to work . . ." Her voice caught. Was she crying? "We'd be like each other's jailers," she said. "I can't spend my life hiding. Running away . . ."

No freaking out. No hysteria. Chilling clarity.

"I've got to go to the police," she said. "It's the only way."

When he did not respond, she said, "If you claim self-defense, I'll back you up." Then she started to walk away from him.

He followed, guided by her light. His wallet held an emergency key. But even if he beat her to the truck, he couldn't drive away. She'd tell the cops that he'd killed Errol and raped her. That's why the rough sex. Internal abrasions, plus his sperm. If she escaped these woods alive, he was done for.

She walked as if she knew the way. When the truck did not appear, she stopped, looked around, then set off confidently to the right.

At last she stopped, looked around again, then turned, seeming to gaze straight at him. "I hear you," she said.

He froze behind a screen of leaves as the light came at him. It passed by, finished its arc, started back, and died. Batteries rattled as she shook the flashlight. Which didn't come on.

"I can sit here until daylight," she said. "I wouldn't wait, if I were you."

Try to flee, and he'd look guilty. She'd be off the hook. And he'd be on.

Her voice had stopped. The woods were silent. Nothing moved. Not a leaf fell.

She couldn't shoot him in the dark. She'd hear him, though, if he tried to sneak up. Was she pretending the flashlight had failed? Where was she? Doing what?

He strained his ears. Not a sound. Then—*pit-pit-pit-pit*—rain began.

Squatting, he groped for a weapon, found the ground covered with rocks, and placed a good-sized one between his feet. Then he touched what he wanted: a sapling the size of a spear. As kids, he and his friends had fought battles with homemade spears, rattling them off tree houses while the same kind of spears rained down on them.

They'd pulled their spears up, roots and all, to leave a dirt-cushioned tip. Even so, bruises from the spears could last for weeks.

He slid out Dad's pocketknife and opened it. The little blade wouldn't stab, but it would slice. He started making angled cuts, beaver-style, into the sapling's inch-thick base. He and his friends never used pointed spears, but always made a few, "just in case." They never said in case of what.

The tapping of rain in the trees would make it hard for Claire to hear him. And just as hard for him to hear *her*.

One day when he was six or seven, Becky VanDeventer—four years older, twice his size—had yanked his baseball glove off his hand. When he reacted with fists, his father boiled out of the house and, leaving Becky with the glove, hauled him inside.

"Only a coward hits a girl," had been seared into Scott's brain on that day. Now, a tapered point took shape in his cold hands. A point to spear the woman of his dreams.

When the last wood fibers let go, he eased his sapling to the ground, trimmed off the bottom branches, then whittled the soft wood into the sharpest point that it would take. It would blunt easily. But if it hit soft flesh, it might penetrate. Just once.

Sliding his knife back into his pocket, he squatted, shivering. Straining to hear.

The rain had stopped. The woods were silent as before.

Scott felt around until he touched a chunk of rotten wood, then flung it toward where he had last seen Claire. He heard it crash through foliage, followed by a flash of red-orange light, and the .22's *crack!*

She hadn't moved. And she was jumpy. That was good.

Filling both hands with rocks, he faced the flash, and underhanded the rocks: high, and thirty degrees to her left. As they crashed down, he crashed through the woods toward Claire.

Drawing no fire, he stopped and crouched close to the ground, shivering hard. How long before hypothermia set in?

A minute passed. Two. Three. He squatted like a Stone Age warrior, spear in his right hand, knees against his chest for warmth. He knew what he had to do. No quibbles. No regrets.

Something like slobber hit his face. A snapping stick made him look up. A yellow eye was glaring down. And below that, the glint of the .22!

He leapt up, howling, smashed the gun with his spear, then drove the point straight into the darkness below the yellow eye.

The spear hit something and sank in. The eye vanished. The thing he'd speared gave a heron-like *kwuark.* Thrashing like a giant gigged flounder, it ripped the spear out of his hands.

He fell backward and rolled away. The yellow eye said Jim McGee. The voice was Claire's.

Crouched low, Scott groped for a rock.

A big one slid like a stone ax into his hand. He raised it, ready to attack.

There was no need. Whatever he had speared was thrashing, gurgling like a catfish on a dock.

It seemed to take hours, but finally, it went still. No more rain fell. No moon or stars glowed in the sky. The woods were dark as any cave. Silent, except for his breathing.

He stood, poking with his foot until it struck something big on the ground.

He prodded. And prodded again. When the something didn't move, he knelt and felt it.

Claire.

Close to her left hand, he felt the cold tube of the flashlight. He picked it up, and it snapped on.

She'd pulled the spear out of her neck, but not before it did its work. Her mouth grimaced as if tasting something vile. Her eyes stared, wide.

There wasn't a lot of blood. Asphyxiation must have killed her: windpipe and larynx crushed.

The .22 lay a foot from her right hand. Scott's hands shook as he lifted the gun. Still, he felt less panic than after Errol. Either he'd gotten used to killing, or his fear-tank had run dry.

He turned the flashlight's beam in a circle. Incredibly, his orange blanket lay nearby. Whether Claire had known it or not, they'd circled back almost to where they'd begun.

A sallow moon moved in and out of clouds. The yellow eye had been moonlight, not Jim McGee. All the same, he killed the light, raised the .22, and listened.

Only raindrops—*pit-pit-pit-pit*—in the trees.

Grasping Claire's ankles, he dragged her to the orange blanket, then, leaving her, headed back the way they'd come. Helped by the flashlight, which didn't go out once, he followed their trail of broken brush back to the double pine, then the deer-trail and the dirt road.

Reaching his truck, he dug out his hatchet, matches, and stove fuel, re-locked the truck, and hustled back to Claire. The woods were wet. With any luck, they wouldn't burn.

Every tree, bush, and shadow hid potential horrors as he chopped saplings, then piled damp leaves and pine needles to make a pyre. Heat from the stove fuel would dry them out, he hoped.

No need to sneak Claire across the border now.

Placing a layer of small twigs on the pyre, he crisscrossed three layers of saplings, then spread the blanket over them.

Before moving Claire, he went through her pockets and pulled out a wad of Kleenex and his keys. Her rings came off easily. Faced with a need to cut them off, he wasn't sure what he'd have done.

He couldn't bear to gather her into his arms, so he moved her as he'd moved Errol—legs, then torso—onto the pyre. Unlike Errol, she was easy to lift.

Once her body was in place, he picked up his spear, bloody on the end, and laid it beside her. He half-expected her to rise like a vampire. When she did not, he doused her body, the blanket, and the pyre with fuel, and backed away.

None of this seemed real: what she had tried to do, what he had done, how deeply he had felt for her. He moved through a fog of pain, fatigue, disbelief, and fear. Another nightmare, with no chance of waking up.

Using his flashlight, he found a twig with brown leaves still attached, then struck a match and lit the leaves. The fire sputtered, then took hold. When it did, he tossed the twig onto the pyre where Claire lay like a warrior queen.

It landed on her knee, balanced there for an instant, then fell and flared.

SEVENTH DAY

35

For the thousandth time, Scott's watering eyes urged his odometer forward. The rain had stopped. He rolled both windows down, hoping the night air would rouse him. Any second a spotlight might hit, sirens would blare, and he'd be caught.

Vaulting out of the dark no more than thirty yards ahead, a big buck blurred across the road, its rack branching like a small tree. Scott felt himself thrown forward as he braked, his seatbelt stopping him inches from the steering wheel. His tires screeched as he fishtailed past where the deer had been. No impact. He was clear.

"Pieces of feces!" An instant slower to the brake, he *and* the deer could have been dead. Even now, he wasn't sure he would survive. His face and hands were lacerated from the woods. His forehead felt like a single, throbbing lump. His stomach was a fireball of pain radiating from Errol's punch. Houdini died after a punch ruptured his spleen. Scott feared the same. And would have feared it more, except his fear was split between so many things.

Had his fire burned Claire to ashes, then gone out? Had it fizzled in the rain, leaving her body identifiable? Had it escaped the pyre, and charred the woods for miles?

Her rings, at least, would not be found. He'd thrown them as he drove across the Fraser River: deep and swift and wild.

He wished his license plates did not scream "Foreigner!" On any road in Canada, his truck stood out. If a dead Yankee were found, some RCMP might stop another Yank. Some local might remember one. While night protected him, he had to drive, shaking his head to clear cobwebs, fighting the pain that tightened like a spring in his gut.

Only when he woke in the oncoming lane did he decide, *No more.*

He didn't dare park on the shoulder. Even if it was legal here—he wasn't sure—he might get hit. Someone might note his license plate, or stop to check on him.

Up ahead, his headlights showed what looked like a dirt logging road. He braked too fast, skidded on the wet blacktop, but managed to make the turn without sliding into a half-filled drainage ditch.

This road felt harder-packed than the one he'd used with Claire. It was also twice as wide. He drove in thirty feet, then had enough room to turn around and face out. Moving to the far right in case of trucks, he killed his lights and engine, then sat and stared into the gloom. The woods were thick and threatening, and felt more so when—first a few drops, then a steady drum—rain started again.

Locking both doors, he reached under his seat to make sure Errol's .22 was there. As he did, he touched a water bottle that proved to be half-full of Tang. It wasn't his, so it must have been Claire's.

In a weird way, this was their last kiss, he thought as he gulped the liquid down: stale, but at least it quenched his thirst. Once he got home, he'd never touch Tang again.

The rain's white noise was soporific. Shutting his eyes was like lowering a movie screen. The fight with Errol, which had happened in a blur, played back in bloody detail. After that, his ordeal with Claire began.

◆ ◆ ◆

Scott knew before he cracked his eyes that Jim McGee was there. "What do you want?" he asked, relieved the wait was over.

The rain was over, too. McGee's eyes glowed outside the truck: the yellow and the brown. "You called *me*," he said.

Scott glared at the scarred face. "What would I want with you?" he asked with what he meant to be corrosive scorn.

"Likes attract."

"You sound different," Scott said, then realized why. "You sound like Errol!"

McGee smirked. "I sound like *you* sounding like Errol. You're the one mixing us up."

"I didn't call you here," Scott said.

McGee laughed Errol's big laugh. "Who did, then? It's your dream."

Was it a dream, or was McGee trying to make him *think* it was?

"You're like the Devil in Ivan Karamazov's room," Scott said. "But I don't have brain fever."

"Are you sure?"

Lunging through his open window, Scott grabbed McGee's greasy shirt. "You psycho freak . . ."

With startling ease, McGee pulled free. If he'd had a mustache, he'd have twirled it. "I'm what you make me," he said. "See you soon."

"If I see you again . . ." Scott was standing, now, outside his truck.

"I know," McGee said. "My ass is grass."

Scott slammed a straight right to McGee's chin.

McGee fell backward like a cardboard man.

Scott slammed his foot down on his throat. McGee's head came off his body, and hopped away. A toad!

More toads hopped out of McGee's clothes. Foot-high toads ringed Scott like gargoyles: red eyes glowing.

"Hello, Scott," Claire said, and stepped into the light.

◆ ◆ ◆

He jerked awake: safe in his truck, heart shuddering as, in deep darkness, raindrops pounded down. He rubbed his eyes—less heavy now—and sat upright. No glowing red eyes in the dark. No Jim McGee. No Claire.

The glow-light on his watch showed 3:53 a.m. His stomach hadn't gotten worse. His spleen might not be ruptured after all.

He was hungry, but his food was in the camper. Not the time or place to get it now.

His engine started with no trouble. *Good truck*. His headlights shone on nothing more deadly than woods. He thought so, anyway, until he tried to drive and found the rain had turned the road to glue. Mud gripped his tires like death. And would not let go.

He tried rocking his truck. Forward. Reverse. Forward. Reverse.

If anything, the movement mired him more.

"Come on!" he begged, and shoved the accelerator to the floor.

His truck responded, as Errol's had, with an enraged roar. His tires spun and spun, then miraculously grabbed. Fishtailing and spraying muck, the truck charged up from the mud, out of the woods and onto a highway empty as the dark side of the moon.

◆ ◆ ◆

The sign—KAMLOOPS 10—should have said LYTTON.

Trying to stay calm and keep one eye on the road, Scott checked his map. Somehow he'd missed the turn-off onto Highway 1. Now he'd have to take the 5 down from Kamloops, and spend more time in Canada. More time to get caught.

The rain was lighter, but still coming down. Scott gave the sun little chance against the gray clouds overhead. That was okay. Rain might keep witnesses inside.

By the time he reached Kamloops, though, the rain had slackened to a drip. He picked the busiest gas station, for anonymity. A restaurant meant delay and lots of eyes, so he used his one Canadian ten-dollar bill to buy, from the automated Refreshment Centre, a cardboard-tasting turkey sandwich and a carton of milk. Then he drove on.

The midtown junction of highways was a British-style "roundabout." Scott found himself circling, veering, spun around and, before he knew it, on his way to Banff. When 5 SOUTH—MERRIT flashed by on his right, he cranked the wheel instinctively, running his truck off the highway, over soaked grass, and onto Highway 5.

By great good luck, there were no cops—only a red van driven by a man who honked, flipped him off, and drove away, bouncing in his seat with anti-American rage.

Scott's face, seen in the mirror, showed less damage than he'd feared. The bump on his head had shrunk. His scratches weren't conspicuous. Every muscle in his body moaned. But the pain seemed survivable.

Emotional pain was another thing. Images of Errol and Claire kept smashing into other thoughts. Yes, he'd killed in self-defense. But if he'd been less stupid, there'd have been no need.

"Drop it," he told himself. The Sufis claimed there was no *fault*, only chains of events, every link lucky for some, unlucky for others who, to make life feel less random and irrational, assigned fault to the link preceding the unlucky one. Or maybe it wasn't the Sufis. Maybe it was the post-structuralists. Either way, a trillion factors could have altered everything.

He rolled through Merritt at ten thirty and, blessing his faithful truck, entered the home stretch.

Overhead, the gray had thinned, letting in patches of blue. As if the sky were saying, *The worst is behind you.* He'd driven several miles before a sign told him he'd lost another highway. Instead of heading for Vancouver on the 5, he was on 97C, Osoyoos-bound. Yesterday's shock must still be playing with his brain.

He looked for a dirt road. Not finding one, he pulled onto the shoulder and checked his map.

97C would take him well out of his way. But it was still heading south, toward the border. It was probably less traveled than the 5. Plus, he'd enter Washington near Brewster Lake.

"What the hell?" he said. "Brewster it is."

As he pulled back onto the highway, he felt a jolt and heard a clunk, but thought no more about it until, five minutes later, his truck began to bump and shake as if trying to wrestle him off the road. A hollow thumping screamed, *Flat tire!*

Pulse on overdrive, he wrestled his truck to the shoulder, and jumped out to see what could be done.

His right front tire couldn't have been flatter. A long slit in the side showed why.

"Be cool," he told himself. His jack, as he recalled, was in his camper. Before he looked, though, he pulled the jack-handle / tire tool from behind his seat, and cranked the spare tire down from its storage place under the truck. Good thing he'd filled the tire up before this trip.

He was rolling the spare tire toward the flat one when he heard a siren. In the distance, red light flashing, an RCMP cruiser was bearing down.

He dropped the tire and looked desperately for a place to hide. Open fields stretched out on both sides of the road, a few horses grazing peacefully. Across the road, a sign proclaimed, BAR T RANCH. FINE QUARTERHORSES.

Scott hadn't ridden a horse since Kiddieland. He'd break his neck if he tried. Besides, where would he run? Nothing to do but wait, he told himself as the RCMP car whizzed toward him.

It didn't stop. Siren screaming and light flashing, it whizzed by with a *whoosh* of air.

Scott dropped the new tire next to the old, then, body shaking as if it were on springs, walked to the camper to retrieve his jack.

"You're fine," he said aloud. "False alarm."

His sleeping bag, bright green and blue, lay nested just as Claire had left it. Scott kicked it aside and rummaged through his gear. If he had lost the jack . . .

No, there it was, poking from under his half-spilled sack of extra clothes.

"Good," he said, and reached through the clothes to grip the jack.

Something clammy touched his hand. He jerked back, then leapt forward again, scattering clothes.

A toad, almost as flat as Scott's tire, lay pressed against the camper floor. Eyes fixed on Scott, the animal began to swell.

In one motion, Scott scooped it up and shoveled it through the open camper door. When he climbed out, the thing—injured, apparently—lay on its back beside the road. The yellow of its eyes was like McGee's eye in his dream.

Could McGee use the toad, somehow, to track him? Could the toad *be*

McGee? Scott half-expected it to disappear when he raised his foot to stomp. But it popped like a fat grape, the soft body reflattening as blood splurted onto the road.

In a mix of disgust and rage, he stomped some more, grinding the toad into the gravel and the dust. Not supernatural in any way. Just an ex-toad.

He wished he hadn't killed it, now. There'd been no need. All the same, he gave the remains a kick that sent them skidding off into a muddy ditch. So much for Bearclaw's *eyes*!

Seeing his right boot covered with toad blood, Scott scraped as much as he could onto a bank of tall green weeds, then climbed into the camper and gathered up his jack and the tool bundle that had come with the truck. When he stepped back outside, a Mountie car was pulling up.

As the white car with its red, yellow, and blue stripes slowed to a stop, Scott set down his tools and moved away from his truck, hands at his sides in what he hoped was a non-threatening posture.

The Mountie, when he left his car, looked close to Scott's age. Close to his size, too. He had a pale blonde mustache and, instead of the iconic red coat, wore all-purpose cop-khakis.

"Everything okay?" he asked, sounding a trifle tentative.

Scott gave his best impression of a relaxed nod-and-smile. "Just a flat."

No chance, now, to slip unnoticed out of Canada.

The Mountie moved closer. "Need any help?" His voice cracked slightly on *help*.

Nervous, Scott thought. *Like me.* Except the Mountie had the power of The State to buck him up. At Scott's expense, if need be.

"Thanks," Scott said. "I can handle it."

"I'll stick around," the Mountie said. "Make sure you're okay."

"That's fine." As if The Law required his consent. "Thank you," Scott said, picked up his tools and, hands shaking, walked to the flat tire. *Concentrate.*

Positioning the jack, he inserted the tire-tool / handle and, pumping up and down, began to lift the truck.

"Better set the brake," the Mountie said.

Scott jumped to his feet. "Oh, yeah. You're right."

As he opened his cab, he remembered Errol's gun under the seat. If this guy searched the cab . . .

It would be stupid to act preemptively. Shoot a cop, and all Canada would come after him. Still, Scott was surprised how easily the idea came.

"Thanks," he said, and shut the door. "I'm no mechanic."

Mechanic was slang for hit-man. Was that true in Canada? He kept his breath under control as he crouched by his flat tire and jacked up the truck. If he had another flat before he got home, he'd be screwed.

A screwdriver pried off his hubcap easily. The lug nuts were tight, but came off, too.

When the Mountie walked up behind, Scott braced for a punch.

When it came, it wasn't physical. "Know anyone with a green truck?" the Mountie said. "From the States?"

Scott focused on the tire. "Let me think . . ."

"I mean someone that's here. In Canada."

"Oh. In Canada."

If the guy caught Scott in a lie, it would be bad. Admit to knowing Errol, it could be worse.

Scott lifted off his flat tire. "I don't think so," he said, and tried to seem distracted by the tire's weight.

"Just checking," the cop said. "I hate it when I'm in the States, and people say, 'Hey, I know Joe Blow from Canada. Do you know him?' Like all Canadians know each other."

Scott set the spare tire in place, and started to replace the lug nuts. "Yeah," he said. "People do that."

"Anyway," the Mountie said, "if you *do* see a green Chevrolet truck—oldish, with Montana plates—I'd appreciate a call."

Jim McGee was from Montana.

The Mountie handed Scott a card. Royal Canadian Mounted Police. Dwight Randall.

A non-threatening name. In fact, the guy evoked little or no cop-phobia. Maybe because he seemed a peaceable, non-coppish guy. Maybe because— how could it be otherwise?—something in Scott had changed.

"I'll keep an eye out," Scott said, and tucked Randall's card in his pocket.

Unless this was a trick, the green Ford truck had no connection with Errol. There could be problems, though, if the cops caught McGee.

Officer Randall peered into Scott's open camper. "Been fishing?"

"Yep," he said, calmer than he would have believed. "Canada's the place."

Randall was standing right where Scott had killed the toad. For all Scott knew, the toad was Canada's national amphibian. Thirty years for killing one.

Scott saw the toad blood clearly. Red as human blood. Or was this paranoia, like Poe's "Tell-Tale Heart"?

Officer Randall seemed oblivious. "Catch anything?" he said.

"I did okay." Tightening the last lug nut, Scott was hyper-aware of the tire-tool in his hand. Would the Mountie check his fishing license? Search for over-limit fish?

"Where'd you go?" Randall asked.

As Scott stood up, a name flashed into mind: a sign he'd blown by, coming down here. "Salmon Lake," he said.

Randall nodded. "I hear that's a good spot."

Scott replaced his hubcap, kicked it on tight, and faced Randall, tire-tool dangling by his side. "Beats the hell out of the States," he said.

At that moment, Randall's radio squawked. He walked back to his car while Scott threw his tools and the blown tire into the camper, then shut and locked the door. While the Mountie talked—about Scott?—on his phone, Scott edged closer to his driver door. Closer to Errol's gun. If Randall looked the least bit threatening . . .

A moment later, the Mountie replaced his phone in his car, then dropped into the driver's seat and closed the door. "Gotta go," he called out the window, innocent as a neighbor who'd dropped by for a chat. "Drive carefully."

"Thanks for your help," Scott said. "I will."

The guy hadn't even asked for ID.

Scott waited while the cruiser pulled away, headed north. Then he stuffed the .22 under his shirt, and hustled it into the camper. Pulling out the clip, he rolled both gun and clip into his sleeping bag—which, he noticed, smelled of Claire's perfume. The gun was evidence against him. And his best defense if he met Jim McGee.

◆ ◆ ◆

Coming into Canada a week ago, Scott had been interrogated by a skinny carrottop who, despite a line of cars, badgered him for ten full minutes, then searched his truck before letting him pass. US Customs were famously pickier than Canada's. And this station wasn't busy. They could hassle Scott as much as they liked. And what if Officer Randall had regretted not asking for ID? What if he'd radioed ahead: *Hold the Yank in the old blue Datsun truck?*

There were three stations here, manned by six officers with nothing to do but make trouble. Scott chose far right and, trying to seem calmer than Buddha, more innocent than Jesus, drove up.

His officer, puffy-cheeked with a thin gray mustache, sat as if bolted to his stool. He seemed adrift in some other world as he checked Scott's passport, then droned through a list of questions, all of which Scott answered casually until one—"Are you bringing any firearms into the country?"—hit him like a crowbar to the head. Errol might have filled out some form for the .22. If Scott said *Yes*, and Gray Mustache asked for a form, he would be screwed. If he said *No*, and the gun was found, he'd be doubly screwed. Triply screwed if the gun was traced to Errol. How had he failed to think of that?

Trying to keep his voice calm, eyes unconcerned, he took the only chance he had, and answered, "No."

Gray Mustache didn't even blink.; he just droned on. Finished with his list of questions, he favored Scott with a little nod, said, "Welcome home," and as Scott showered thanks on any Power that would have them, waved him through.

36

Scott spent his first few miles in the US fearing he would be pursued. Then that fear died away. Driving with Washington plates in Washington, he wouldn't rate a second glance.

In four hours, he could be home. On the other hand, he'd told Julie he'd be gone two weeks. He was barely an hour from Brewster Lake.

The thought of fishing seemed, in ways, a blasphemy. A time of penance seemed required. But what good would it do? Survivors of disaster had to cut their losses, cauterize their wounds, and restart their lives. That, or increase the list of casualties.

Fishing might even be therapeutic, like remounting a horse that had thrown him. And if, somehow, McGee was still in the picture—better not to bring that problem home.

The rain had stopped in Merritt. Now Scott drove out from under the remaining clouds into blue-skied Okanogan country. As US 97 unspooled south, he found himself hemmed in by crumbling basalt cliffs cracked into columns like the ruins of titanic fortresses.

He and Errol had spent some great times here.

On his right, a sign said TRUCK STOP, and his truck obeyed. Trying to hide his eagerness, Scott walked in and ordered his first restaurant food since Howdy Do's.

His waitress—a woman of Wagnerian dimensions, frosted hair piled high—had just delivered his salad when a trio of green-uniformed Highway Patrol officers barged through the door. Scott squelched the urge to bolt. Better to wait and see what they were looking for.

As it turned out, they were looking for a meal. Settling at an empty table, they opened their menus wide as wings, and beamed benevolence. One of them, as big as Errol, said something that provoked a roar of mirth.

Scott felt like laughing, too. The cops made him uneasy, but not panicked. Not helpless. Not post-traumatically stressed. When he turned back to his food, he could almost forget that they were there.

He'd never known that lettuce leaves, even soaked with Thousand Island, which he normally despised, could taste so good. He cleaned his salad plate, inhaled his chicken-fried steak, and wiped up the last of his white gravy with the last of his bread. He ordered, next, a chocolate shake and when it came, leaned back in his booth to savor it.

Maybe it was the food, or just the sugar after a week without, but he felt better than he had a right to, filled with an energy on the verge of glee. Was this how warriors felt after a victory?

A fat guy in straining jeans and one of those bent-down-in-front-and-back cowboy hats waddled to the old-fashioned jukebox where, hunched over the glowing, red-green-and-blue machine, he considered his options.

Straightening up, he clunked a few coins into the slot, pushed some buttons, and lumbered away as Merle Haggard's classic "Today I Started Loving You Again" began to play.

Funny how country hits, like the singers who made them, never went out of style. Scott pictured the fat guy doing an old-fashioned slow dance with his waitress. The thought was oddly comforting.

Merle's lament segued into "Truck Driving Man." Talk about apt. Every five minutes, another big rig rolled up. The drivers, all shapes and kinds of men, seemed friendly and at ease, enjoying the food, the music, and each other. They joked with all the waitresses, and didn't let metallic hair colors, lined faces, and elephantine rears stop them from flirting. This was *their* place. Others might eat here and take a respite from the road, but only truckers were full members of The Club.

When a new waitress with a smiling, red-lipped face, platinum hair, and curves straight out of the '50s, asked, "Like some coffee?" Scott was tempted to mention Marilyn Monroe. But he guessed she heard that fifty times a day, and so he said only, "No thanks." Still, the impulse to flirt felt good. As if an evil spell had cracked and set him free.

When his bill came, he thanked his waitress, left a good but not unforgettable tip—in cash—and bought some groceries at the mini-mart next door.

Five minutes later, he was crunching down the dirt-and-gravel road to Brewster Lake, winding through pine forests considerably more sparse and dry than the woods he'd left behind. By midsummer, this road would be mostly dust. Now, it was one long bouquet: white daisies, black-eyed susans, foxgloves, and Indian paintbrush, which made him think of Jim McGee.

Pulling to the side of the road, he opened his camper to retrieve Errol's .22.

Instantly, a bad smell hit. Not bear's-head-bad, but bad enough.

His nose led him to his ice chest where, to his relief and chagrin, he found nothing more sinister than his trout from Ursula. It was many hours past being saved by ice. All the same, he should have bought some at the mini-mart. His brain was still jangled. Still not working right.

He lugged the chest off the road, and dumped the fish among an outburst of daisies. Ripe as it smelled, something would find and eat it soon. Nature let nothing go to waste. All the same, he hated to see the trout rigormortised into a slimy U. No way around it: death was an ugly thing.

Trying not to think of Errol or Claire, he shut the ice chest, shoved it back into his camper, and climbed in behind it.

Unrolling his sleeping bag, he thought he'd find the .22 and clip.

They were gone!

Panic gripped his throat and held on tight. He scattered gear in a frenzy until—there! The gun lay in plain sight, jammed against the water bottle where it must have slid. The clip lay close-by. If the Customs guy had glanced inside . . .

The moral was clear: intelligence and planning were fine, but all it took sometimes to get away with crimes was human error and dumb luck.

Back in his cab, Scott filled the clip, clicked it in place, then restashed the gun under his seat. A lot of people carried guns out here. If McGee showed up, he'd learn that Scott was one of them.

He was four miles or so from Brewster Lake when he started passing signs of a fire. The road had acted as a tourniquet, holding back the flames. On Scott's left were living woods; on his right, acres of black stumps and charred trees, their naked branches like black veins against the sky. The blaze had most likely been caused by lightning, or possibly a campfire or cigarette. Yet he felt as if *his* fire had tracked him here. Errol had been right: the wild was losing out. There'd soon be nothing left.

In a half-mile, though, the desolation had changed back to green, flourishing woods. These woods, as the Cascade Mountains stole more of the moisture flowing from the west, gave way to scrublands, which turned into desert as the road dipped down. Sagebrush now covered the flat earth, its gray-green interrupted by a line of brighter green, sometimes far from the road, sometimes near, and once, spanned by a one-lane bridge, directly underneath. This bright green line marked the area's main water source: the aptly named Rattlesnake Creek.

Rabbit brush was in full bloom, explosions of yellow flowers everywhere. The air was sweet with sage and the liquid calls of meadowlarks. Every so often, a magpie, stroboscopic black and white, flapped across the road, its cry rasping ahead, its plume-tail trailing behind.

In the distance, a cluster of cars and trucks materialized.

"All *right*," Scott said as, dragging a dust cloud worthy of a buffalo stampede, he closed in.

There were the two familiar sanicans, the incongruous phone booth, the white sign pocked by target practice: BREWSTER LAKE. FLY FISHING ONLY. The campground was packed with vehicles, their owners either on the lake fishing, or asleep. Only two men waved as Scott jostled by.

He rejected a parking space beside the sanicans—bad smells, worse memories—and settled on a spot between a jeep and a Ford truck lugging a camper so immense it looked like a bread-loaf swallowing a ladybug.

There were no trailers or big boats. Motors were illegal on Brewster, and the three-quarter-mile hike ruled out all but the lightest skiffs. This eliminated power-boating hot-doggers and, coupled with the lake's one-fish limit, kept angling good.

It was just past four. Scott could be fishing by five.

Two boys strolled by, swinging a pair of fourteen-inchers. When Scott gave them a thumbs-up, they grinned, waved, and gave him back the sign.

◆ ◆ ◆

Scott woke, in cave-blackness, out of exhausted sleep. Something was in his sleeping bag!

Reaching down, he felt a ball of springy cloth between his feet: Claire's stocking cap, he realized as he pulled it up. He couldn't see it in the dark, but felt the pom-pom, and smelled the shampoo-and-lake perfume of her hair. She'd left the cap when she got out to murder him.

He placed the cap beside his sleeping bag and shut his eyes. But the cap's presence, infused with Claire's scent, unnerved him. As if she were hovering nearby.

Trying to stay asleep, he cracked his camper door and laid the cap on his bumper. Tomorrow, he'd sink it in the lake.

At first light, though, when he got up, the cap was gone. If it had ever been there.

BREWSTER LAKE

37

Days passed quickly, the fishing typical of Brewster: steady catches of one-to-two pound trout, with an occasional two-and-a-half-pounder to keep things interesting. The sky stayed clear, the temperature cool, the fishing good. Brewster was maybe a fourth the size of Oso, an eighth the size of Ursula, and much more heavily fished. There were no thirty-pounders here. Scott felt no need to work from dawn to dusk, wringing every ounce of fishing from each day. He got up late, fished or loafed as the urge hit, and felt himself recovering.

He started telling other fishermen about his "two weeks" at Brewster, scribbling his hearers' license numbers in case he needed witnesses.

Faster than he would have believed, Errol and Claire were drifting into memory. Errol was his best friend from college. Claire was a beauty he used to know. More and more, like his whole time in Canada, their deaths seemed part of a bad dream.

He started carrying paper and pencil to the lake, jotting down song lyrics and melodies that jumped into his head. He pictured Julie often, and liked what he saw.

As for McGee—he hadn't come to Brewster, that was clear. The thought of him free to murder again was hard to take. But that was Canada's problem. Even an anonymous note, now, would be too big a risk.

He kept expecting to be slammed by self-loathing. He was not. He understood why Mafiosi had to "make their bones," placing themselves outside the rule-of-law that held most people back. "Thou shalt not kill" was the wall between civilization and the ages when humans and hominids raped, murdered, plundered, betrayed, and by so doing, lived to pass their genes to him. No wonder soldiers struggled, coming home. Trained and encouraged to kill, they were expected, suddenly and absolutely, to re-install the homicide taboo.

Was that possible, once you'd broken down the wall? Or been thrown through?

If there's no God...

Day by day, Scott healed: fresh air, sage, lizards, coyotes, and trout in place of crappy bars, back-stabbing bandmates, bills, insurance, traffic jams— the picky little things which, if there was a hell, it would be full of. Errol had said, "Life drags along like nothing's gonna happen—then, wham, something cracks you on the head." Scott's head had been cracked hard. Time for a long "nothing's gonna happen" phase.

38

He rose before dawn on Sunday, his last day at Brewster Lake. Gulping his last packet of Instant Breakfast—strawberry—he filled his water bottle from the last gallon container in his camper, then dropped Errol's pistol into his backpack. Opening his glove box, he brushed aside the Secret Lake feather, and pulled out Errol's box of .22 shells. He stuffed these in his pocket, locked his truck and, fishing rod in hand, set off for the lake.

Dawn's luminous purple turned bluer and bluer as he strode. The moon was fading, its pale light dissolving into day. To his right, Venus increased its tranquil glow. The air was cold enough for his stocking cap, but not too cold for comfort. Judging from the lack of clouds, it would warm soon.

Meadowlarks were out in force, their clear warbles blending with the scent of creosote and sage as Scott topped a rise and saw the lake: unexpected, in this dry land, "as a Playmate between law briefs," Errol had said. The lake was flat, except where reed beds ruffled it, or trout dimpled its black sheen.

As many times as Scott had seen the place, it never failed to thrill. He stumbled down the sandy path, hoping his rubber boat hadn't blown away in the wind that scoured this country every night.

There it was, tied securely to a troll-shaped creosote bush a few feet from the lake.

Scott gave the boat a few quick pumps of air—it always leaked overnight—then wrestled it to the water and set it down, half out, half in. He stowed his gear, placed both hands beside the oarlocks, shoved off, and jumped in as trout sloshed on every side.

To be first on the water was "like making love to a beautiful virgin," Errol had said. "Not that I've known a lot of *them*." Today, though, Scott ignored the feeding fish and rowed straight to the middle of the lake.

On shore, more fishermen were trudging up. Quickly, while he was alone, Scott dug the pistol from his sack. He rubbed it with his shirt in case fingerprints survived underwater, then slipped the gun like a fish into the still-dark lake. He paused a moment, remembering the last time he'd sunk something in a lake, then let the gun slide from his hand.

Rowing a little ways away, he dropped the shells just as a scream cracked the silence. His eyes flashed left and right, then overhead to where a lone gull soared, crying like a tortured child. The rocky bluffs that overlooked the lake exhaled the coos of doves, the hoots of owls. Blue-green swallows skimmed insects off the lake, twittering as they veered, dipped, and dived like fighter jets.

Scott made a long cast, let his line sink for a count of ten, then started rowing as dawn overflowed the hills.

◆ ◆ ◆

Three hours and many fish later, the bite had died. Scott moved his gear to one side of his rubber boat, chewed a protein bar, drained the last of his water, and lay down with his head under his boat's thin rubber seat. As he'd done many times before, he rolled his stocking cap into a pillow and, his seat a perfect sunshade, sighed and shut his eyes.

The sun was warm as any blanket. A light breeze kept wavelets slapping at his boat, lapping a lullaby. Rocked by the water, he thought of holding Sara in her retro waterbed, and could have cried. If he had been more realistic, she'd still be his. He would never have seen Errol again. Never met Claire. He could be fronting his own band, and maybe making records, too.

"Get a white man's haircut and marry my daughter, I'll start you off managing one of my papers," Sara's father had said. A hundred grand a year to start, with advancement as he earned it, plus co-ownership with Sara of all the Boswell holdings when Mr. B died. And Scott, with the moral arrogance of the young and ignorant, had told the old racist, "Sorry, Sir, I'm not for sale."

"Forget the newspapers," Sara had pleaded. "We'll have money to produce your songs. We'll hire you a manager and publicist. Let me help you, Scottie. Please."

"I won't take your father's money on false pretenses," he'd declared, pious as any Puritan.

A year later, Mr. Boswell was dead of a heart attack, and Sara was married to Jim Torgerson, a tax attorney who played keyboards in a band she'd helped to sign with Capitol.

No failure-of-nerve there.

Scott squeezed shut his eyes. But the harder he tried to squeeze these thoughts out of his mind, the tighter their tentacles wrapped, dragging him down into the gloomy depths of sleep.

♦ ♦ ♦

He woke abruptly. Sara had called his name. Sounding irked.

He sat up, dazed. No one was near. Only the lake and empty shore.

The wind had blown him to within five feet of land, his progress stopped by lily pads. On every side, green placemat-leaves covered the water, interspersed with bowl-shaped flowers yellow as the sun that soared in the noon sky.

Purple and yellow irises opened their beauty to the sun. Red-winged blackbirds bounced on cattails, flashing epaulets for females to admire and males to fear. With an uproar of creaks, whirrs, rasps, and screeches, a hundred males puffed out their chests, proclaiming their magnificence.

Scott had just noticed a leopard frog staring from a lily pad when, out from behind a clump of rabbit brush in bloom stepped Jim McGee.

Scott's hand closed on the fishing knife that lay, unsheathed, at his feet.

McGee limped forward, palms face up in what he must have thought was an Indian pose. A few feet from the lake, he stopped.

"How'd you get here?" Scott said. This was happening in the bright light of midday. Still, it wasn't real. Brewster Lake did not have lily pads. He saw no other fishermen.

It wasn't real, yet it felt deeply serious. He gripped his knife. Maybe he knew how to throw it in this dream.

McGee sat, crossing his legs creakily. His scar crinkled like sun-baked mud. His stink reached Scott across the water.

To keep his voice from carrying on the lake, Scott spoke softly. "What do you want?"

"To help you."

"Right," Scott said. "We're the best of friends."

He was in water only inches deep. Less than ten feet divided them.

Without warning, Scott sprang out of his boat, charged through the shallows, and jumped on McGee. Knocked on his back, McGee grabbed Scott's knife-hand. He stank like death, writhing and twisting: much stronger than he'd been at Oso Lake. Snarling, he rolled to the right and sank his teeth into Scott's arm.

Scott howled and jerked away, his flesh ripping like cloth. His arm, now free, plunged the knife down.

McGee blocked with his own arm. He gave a shriek, and thrashed as Scott's blade opened the arm up like a fish. Scott raised the knife again, and drove it straight into the wrinkled throat—once, twice, three times—as McGee bucked, fish-flipped, and gasped out his life.

Panting, Scott rolled off McGee's body, and sat, too weak to stand. A chunk was gone from his right arm—soaked, now, with his blood and McGee's.

His arm was numb. Pain would come soon. He'd wake up then.

"Scott?"

He jumped, knife poised to strike.

"Scott?" a woman's voice called. Sara's? No, the voice was Claire's!

＊ ＊ ＊

"Scott?"

He woke as the nose of his boat scraped against sand. He'd drifted the length of Brewster Lake. Gulls white as clouds soared overhead, calling his name. The bright sky dizzied him.

The world shuddered and swayed, then settled down. His knife was clean. So were his hands. Both arms were fine.

On shore, where McGee's body would have been, a horned black beetle scrambled over smooth lake sand. A pair of mallards flapped past, quacking, then U-turned and flapped, quacking, past again. And still the gulls called, "Scott?"

A sense of well-being suffused his body, warm as the whisky he and Errol would share on their trips here. He felt himself soaking up the blackbirds' joy as they called *eee-a-reee* along the shore. He'd killed McGee symbolically. And killed his fear.

Something he'd heard from a Vietnam vet suddenly made sense. "Once I started wasting things, I couldn't stop," the man had said. "It was like coming."

As he rowed toward the center of the shimmering blue-green lake, Scott saw clearly how his first fight with Errol had fed his PTSD. He'd felt helpless, just as he had against the Houston cops and the drunk who'd hit his mom. With Errol, though, he'd finally fought back.

Muscles contracting and relaxing with each oar stroke, Scott felt a surge of sadness over Errol and Claire. He also felt strong, confident, and, oddly enough, free. The cliffs surrounding Brewster Lake, the sun-struck water, and the azure sky vibrated with Van Gogh intensity. Scott felt the same excitement as when, after hours of wrestling with some tune, the perfect melody jumped into his head. He trailed his hands in the water: so cold and fresh that he splashed some onto his face before making a perfect sixty-foot cast.

Errol would have been proud.

Scott let his fly sink deep, to where big trout lurked at midday, then started a slow troll, feeling a heavy weight slide off his shoulders and sink into the depths. Law would demand he justify what he had done. Law would try to weigh his culpability, and Errol's, and Claire's, then decide in what proportion each was wrong, and what he, the survivor, would have to pay. But *right* and *wrong* meant nothing in the wild. And the wild was everywhere. He was no more Sir Galahad than he was a Turkey-Drowning-in-the-Rain. Life had dropped a bomb, the smoke had cleared, and due to a blend of courage and luck, he'd been left standing. He'd done what he had to, and survived.

His pensive mood broke as a big trout boiled to his right. Suddenly, fish were all around him, tails and dorsal fins exposed as they swirled like sharks beside his boat. Feeding, but on what? Cast after cast, they shunned Scott's fly.

He tried a second, then a third, and was changing to a fourth when, approaching from behind, he heard a noise. A boat was rowing straight for him!

He grabbed his oars and tried to think. Police would not chase him down in a rowboat. They'd call with bullhorns from the shore. Or surround his truck and wait.

Had he dumped Errol's gun too soon?

Lodging his rod under his rubber seat, he placed his knife in easy reach, and started toward the oncoming craft: a small, green johnboat, its oarsman rowing steadily.

The gap between their boats was closing fast. If Scott slipped overboard and swam underwater, could he reach the johnboat before getting shot? He hadn't seen the man's face yet—only a tan cowboy hat and matching vest. Then the man hooked a fish and turned. His features were obscured by aviator sunglasses and white sunblock, but Scott could see this wasn't a cop or McGee.

Pudgy-faced, with a banner-sized Fly Fishing Unlimited patch sewed to his vest, the man landed and releasing his fish efficiently, then cast again, and hooked up instantly.

Scott waited till the fish was in the net, then called, "Whatcha using? They're avoiding me."

Apparently, the man sided with the fish. He replied, with the soft priss of the Expert, "Flies."

"What color?" Scott persisted, rowing closer.

The man could have been da Vinci, asked what made *The Last Supper* great. "Different colors," he said, and made a textbook cast: stiff and precise.

Let it go, Scott told himself. But as the man's next backcast unrolled, Scott whipped his own line over it, and—fuck being reasonable!—dragged it down.

The startled Expert spun around.

"You caught me," Scott said as he gripped the man's line. "Gimme some slack."

When the man obeyed, Scott pulled both lines into his boat. The mystery fly was tiny—20 or 22—a pale green body with brown hackle.

"What kind of fly is this?" Scott said.

"A cow dung," the man huffed.

"Suits you," Scott said. Lifting the fly, he snipped it off with his clippers, and dropped the man's line into the lake. "Sorry, guy, your fly broke off."

Adrenaline made Scott's hands shake. He'd have to fight now. Draw attention to himself. Fine. Bring it on.

Cow Dung reeled in furiously, sat down, and seized his oars. Instead of coming for Scott, though, he rowed away. To call in the Authorities? No. In thirty yards, he stopped and hunched over to replace the fly that Scott was tying onto his own line.

The guy's johnboat was meant for standing. But when he did, he looked unsteady on his feet. He made a shaky backcast, tried to correct it, and made it worse. Then his hand slipped. Scott heard a muted cry, and saw Cow Dung's rod and reel—top-of-the-line, you could be sure—fly from his hand and splash into the lake.

Scott laughed out loud, watching the man row frantically around the spot, as if the Lady of the Lake might rise with his rod in her soft white hand. When she did not, Cow Dung skulked, head down, back to shore.

Scott made his first cast with the cow dung and—bang!—nailed a two-pounder. He landed that one, hooked and landed another smaller one, then hooked a third which wriggled and splashed strangely, flopped on the surface, and came into his net with someone else's leader wrapped around its head.

The wrapped leader, on which the cow-dung fly was snagged, had damaged one of the trout's yellow-and-black eyes, and destroyed the other one. Without thinking, Scott gripped behind the fish's gills, and pulled back on the head. He felt a crunch, and heard a sound like celery breaking as the fish went limp.

"Sorry, trout," he said, and slid the fish into the water for the gulls.

The feeding frenzy, when he looked around, had stopped. The time seemed right to go.

39

An hour later, Scott stood in the battered phone booth beside the Sani-cans. Cow-Dung, if he were still around, stayed far away.

It felt almost perverse to call Julie after what had happened with Claire. All the more reason to call. To move back toward a normal life.

"Julie?" he said when she picked up. "Great White Fisherperson here."

She knew his voice right away, seemed happy he had called, wanted to hear about his trip—to Brewster Lake, not Canada—and agreed to postpone the pleasure until nine that night, when he promised to be at her door.

He hung up, and had taken two steps toward his truck when the phone rang: loud, harsh, and alien in the sage-scented air.

Thinking Julie had called back, he plucked the receiver up. "Hello?"

"Who is this?" asked a woman's voice—a voice so much like Claire's that Scott stepped back and, receiver still clutched in his hand, nearly yanked the cord out of the phone.

Rather than give his name, he said, "This is a pay phone at Brewster Lake. In Eastern Washington. Do you want somebody here?"

"What's Brewster Lake?" the woman said. With Claire's hint of British accent.

"You must have the wrong number," Scott said.

"I'm sorry," the woman said. But didn't hang up.

"Do I know you?" Scott fought not to freak out. "Is this a trick?"

"No." The woman sounded hurt. "Why would I trick you?"

She hadn't said she didn't know him. Rather than press the point, Scott asked, "Where are you calling from?"

She hesitated. "I shouldn't say . . ."

Not unreasonable for a woman in these freakazoid times.

"Who are you trying to reach?" he asked, then nearly dropped the phone when she said, "My husband."

"Where's he supposed to be?"

"With me."

Scott tried to slow his heart and dial his panic down. This wasn't Claire. It couldn't be. "I hope you find him," he said. "I've got to go."

"You sound nice," she said. "Maybe we'll meet some time."

He saw, now, what he should have guessed. The woman was disturbed. Probably dialing random numbers to find someone to talk to. Guilt had made him think of Claire.

"Goodbye," he said. "Good luck."

"Thank you," she said, then mumbled something that could have been, "See you in Seattle," before the line went dead.

Scott stood in the booth, afraid to move. When the phone rang again, he nearly jumped out of his skin. "Hello?!"

No answer.

"Hello?"

Dead air, with a slight hiss in the background. The phone must be malfunctioning. The woman had most likely dialed the right number, but gotten the wrong place.

Double-timing to his truck, Scott recalled a *Twilight Zone* about a phone that picked up calls from the past. Or was it from the dead? Either way, it was pure fantasy. Still, he felt jangled and on-edge—feelings that morphed into gloom as his truck crunched across the dirt-and-gravel parking lot and turned onto the dirt-and-gravel road. Returning home meant facing his old problems and more. How would he feel around "normal" people, knowing what he'd done, and that the Law might track him down at any time?

At the Rattlesnake Creek bridge, he eased onto the road shoulder and stopped. A parting ritual had sprung to mind.

Opening his glove box, Scott pulled out the eagle feather he'd found at Secret Lake. Errol had said it meant *good luck*. Talk about wrong . . .

Scrambling, then almost falling down the steep, crumbly bank, Scott stopped barely two feet from the creek. It glittered in the lowering sun, eight feet across at most, but swift and noisy as a full-sized river. The ground he stood on was dry, red-brown sand.

He stared into the water's roil, then chose a slick near the far shore, and sailed the feather like a paper airplane.

"Take it away," he said as the feather arrowed down into the rush, bounced up, and sped off, bound for the Columbia.

He gave a slight wave and a grim smile like the hero in an old Western, then turned back to his truck.

A battered green Chevy truck sat next to it. Beside the truck, in a black cowboy hat, sunglasses, and an ankle-length black bearskin coat, stood Jim McGee.

Scott felt as if the freezing muck of Oso Lake had swallowed him. This was no dream.

Without a word, McGee scrambled down the bank toward Scott. No limp at all. He held a small cloth bundle tucked under his arm.

"Hold it, McGee!"

The man skidded to a stop six feet from Scott. When he pulled off his sunglasses, the yellow eye was less yellow than Scott recalled. The face was scarred, but less ugly. A light wind, which seemed to be increasing, was blowing any bad smell away.

"How'd you find me?" Scott said.

"Indians are good at tracking."

Scott wanted to say, "You're no Indian." But the man was crazy. Who knew what would set him off?

"These are yours." McGee tossed his sunglasses at Scott, who plucked them out of the air. The ones he'd left with the dead girl.

He dropped them into his shirt pocket. No way he'd ever put them on.

"I found a gas tank near your camp," McGee said. "Bright red. Name and address on the side."

Scott's attempt at a poker-face must have failed, because McGee said, "Don't shit your skivvies. I scratched out the name, and sunk the bugger in the lake."

McGee reached into his coat pocket. Scott stepped back. But McGee's hand was empty when he pulled it out.

"Where's the woman?" he said. "In the camper?"

Scott shook his head no. "She took off."

"Too bad. That was some Grade A stuff," McGee said. "What was her name?"

"Jill. Lassiter." The name was out before Scott had time to think. *Jill Lassiter* had been his mom's best friend.

"I passed a fire, driving down," McGee said. "I had to help it out some. But it did the job."

He took the bundle from under his arm, laid it on the ground, and unrolled it. Inside were a gold ring, and chunks of what looked like charred wood.

He tossed the ring to Scott. "Read what it says."

Scott caught the ring, trying to steady his hands. "University of Washington. C.G.," he read aloud. "Who's C.G.?"

Claire had been looking for this ring.

"Can't be Jill Whatsits," McGee said. "I wouldn't hold onto it if I were you."

Scott almost dropped the ring, then realized what was meant, and shoved it in his pocket. "Maybe it's worth something."

"Worth more'n these bones." McGee nudged the charred material with his boot. Then he lifted his foot, smashed it down, and crushed whatever-it-was into dust.

He threw a handful of what looked like pebbles into the creek. "Cops can I.D. a body from the teeth."

Picking up the cloth wrapper, McGee shook it out, his yellow eye fixed on Scott. The wind caught some of the dust. The rest rained on Rattlesnake Creek.

McGee wadded up the cloth, and threw it in the creek, too. "That guy you left beside the road—I finished him. So you'd be clear."

It hardly mattered, but Scott was glad that Brumley's death wasn't on him.

"What do you want?" he asked McGee. "Why are you here?"

He expected a demand for money. Instead, McGee said, "That first day you came to Oso, I thought, *That wuss'll never beat those other two.*"

"Beat them at what?"

"Survival, man. You were playing for your life. You fuckin' won."

Scott was tempted to rush the guy and try to finish him. But something made him hesitate. "Are you here to kill me?" he said.

McGee looked wounded. "No, man. I'm here to help."

Keep him talking. Wait your chance, Scott told himself. To McGee, he said, "Help how?"

"When your tire blew? If that Mountie'd made trouble . . ." McGee drew his finger across his throat, and smirked. "Uncle Sam, my ass. *Bearclaw* wants you."

"Wants me for what?"

"He wanted *me*, but I got burned," McGee explained, all seriousness. "They don't like uglies in Los Angeleeze-rhymes-with-sleeze."

"Bearclaw's going to LA? What's he want there?"

"He wants the woods back. All of it."

"That's good," Scott said, as if this made perfect sense. "I love the woods."

"When everybody follows Nature's Law, cities die," McGee said, avid as an evangelist.

"What's Nature's Law?"

"Take what you want. No mercy. No restraints." McGee slapped at the air as if brushing off cobwebs. "Restraints can channel power. Like rivers squeezing between rocks. Whites stole America that way." His injured eye twitched. "But you've dammed up your power with too many laws. You've gone too soft and stupid to defend yourselves."

"What does Bearclaw want with me?" Scott said.

"You'll spread Nature's Law. Like the flu."

The man was psychotic. If Scott played into his delusions, he might get him to drive away. Or find a way to take him out.

"So you want to go to LA?" he asked. "With me?"

McGee shook his head no. "Jes gon' be him'n you," he said, and smirked.

Scott tried not to show dismay. McGee had watched them like some omnipresent ghost.

"You mean I'll be *possessed*?"

McGee's shoulders sagged. His burn-scar puckered as his face went slack.

"You want to be a hot shit rocker?" he wheezed. "That's good. The hotter you get, the more cities'll burn."

In Bearclaw mode, McGee seemed physically weaker. Like the man Scott had tackled at Oso Lake.

"I see what you mean," Scott said and, as subtly as he could, eased into *ready* stance. "People thought Elvis would wreck civilization. Maybe he did," he said, and charged.

McGee reached under his coat. Next thing Scott knew, there was a shotgun in his face.

"Back off, white man," McGee hissed: all Bearclaw now.

Scott pulled back, inches from the gun. He raised his hands as if to stop a load of shot.

"Thought you lost this?" McGee made small, rotating motions with the gun.

Scott nodded. It was Errol's gun. "You win. Again," he said. Flatter the guy. Keep him talking. Maybe someone would drive up.

"I fixed your Tang," McGee said.

"*Fixed* it? How?"

"Ground up 'shrooms. To let you see what's really there."

Scott skin seemed to tingle and shrink. Could this be true?

The shotgun was definitely real. One flash of pain, and he would be as dead as Errol.

McGee's eyes, the yellow and the brown, fixed on Scott's face. The shotgun fixed on his heart. "Too bad about your friends," McGee said. "But you and me, we're *more* than friends."

Fury swelled inside Scott's chest. Go down swinging! Do damage before he died!

Gentle as Jesus, McGee said, "Why do you still fear me, brother?"

Before Scott could start his lunge, McGee shoved the gun under his own chin, stretched his hand to the trigger and, with a yell like a war cry melding with a scream of terror, pulled.

His head exploded in red spray. His body dropped.

Scott stared at where it lay, half-covered by the bearskin coat, a bloody spine-stick where a head had been.

This was no dream.

Scott looked around. The only witnesses were rabbit brush, creosote, and sage.

He bent toward Errol's shotgun, then yanked back his hands. Leave no fingerprints! If the shotgun were traced, let Errol's death be on McGee.

He had to leave quickly, before anyone came. Still, he made himself take time to think. What was he forgetting? What else should he do?

He didn't like leaving McGee's truck in plain view. But there was nothing odd about a truck parked by the creek. It could be a while before anyone drove by, let alone stopped.

"Hell with it," he said, scrambled up the incline to his truck, and saw, just where he'd left it on his bumper days ago, Claire's stocking cap. No question now where it had been.

Whisking it up, he carried it into his truck and dropped it, pom-pom up, on the passenger's seat. He checked to be sure McGee's body hadn't moved, then, hands shaky on his steering wheel, pulled back onto the road. The wind was on the rise. Any footprints in the sand wouldn't last long.

There was no law against seeing a suicide. Or finding a corpse. If he were stopped, he'd say he was going for help. Otherwise, once he reached the highway, he'd be free.

Scott-free.

As he drove, a premonition made him scan the road for deer. But all he saw were rodent skitterers.

The more he thought of McGee's plan, the crazier it got. The part about too many laws did make some sense. If the US fought World War II today, judges would block the actions it would take to win. "Nature's Law," on the other hand, had never gone out of style. Next to some Iraqi warlord or Wall Street impresario, the most revenge-crazed Indian shaman would seem like a nice guy.

As for Scott's harboring the spirit of Bearclaw—not only did he not feel invaded, he felt good. Claire was the one who, in the woods, had seemed possessed. But if some powerful spirit had controlled her, she would not have wound up dead.

Jim McGee had been schizophrenic. The black stuff he'd stomped on was likely charcoal or dirt. If he'd taken time to sift Claire's ashes, he could never have trailed Scott to Brewster Lake. Unless he'd planted a device. Scott would have to search his truck when he got home, and clean it thoroughly. Especially his sleeping bag.

He'd throw Claire's ring in the Columbia when he crossed. And her hat, too.

He pictured Julie standing in her door. If they clicked, she might ask him to move in. He could write songs, put together a new band, and save money for LA. Nordstrom's most likely had stores there. Maybe she'd head south with him.

He checked his mirror. No cars. No dust clouds except his own.

The Law wanted people to think crimes were always solved, and its God-like eyes were everywhere. But Law was the Wizard of Oz: a small bald man behind a screen, controlling munchkins with trickery and fear.

Claire's hat in the passenger seat brought to mind the woman on the phone, and gave him a dose of the creeps. Keeping his eyes on the road and his left hand on the wheel, he used his right hand to open his glove box. He planned to stuff the hat inside. As the box opened, though, a folded sheet of paper slipped out, and down onto the passenger's floor-mat. The paper looked like it had come from Claire's sketchbook.

Scott pulled instantly to the side of the road. Shifting to neutral, he engaged his emergency brake, then snatched up the paper and unfolded it.

Someone had printed, in unisex block letters, "See you in Seattle. XXX."

Claire must have written this. How, though, had he missed seeing it? He'd taken Errol's .22 shells out of the glove box in the morning, then taken out the feather at the bridge. He'd seen no note. Yet it must have been there. It couldn't have magically appeared. Could it?

Don't be an idiot, he told himself. Claire would have left the note as a surprise. It could have gotten stuck at the top of the glove box.

That must be it, he decided as he disengaged his brake and, spraying gravel, pulled back onto the road. Claire was dead. He'd handled her corpse, and felt not the least twitch of life. He'd dumped stove fuel on her, and lit the fire himself.

Up ahead, he saw the burnt forest he'd passed on the way in. To his left, the trees were black and stark. To his right, everything was green.

A grouse exploded from the green side, sailed across the road to the burnt side, and dropped in what, he saw now, was foot-deep vegetation. Pine seedlings sprouted everywhere, mingling with other greenery fresh-sprung out of the char. White daisies freckled the clearing. Beside the road, a wild rose bloomed.

Fire, as all nature shows preached, was *natural*. Trees and animals died; the woods survived. An hour's fire did the work of decades of decay, freeing nutrients to feed the new woods springing up even as the old lay smoldering. Birds and animals returned. Young plants flourished in the unimpeded sun, burying, in time, the last trace of disaster.

Another mile, and the roadside turned to flowers flanked by unburned woods. He'd left his fish somewhere near here.

It would have been eaten that first day. But to his left, a dark animal rose from a profusion of daisies, and shambled back into the trees. A small bear? Maybe. It looked more like a wolf. Or wolverine. Both were said to be returning to the state.

The real Bearclaw would have liked that. Scott did too. Especially the wolverine.

If he returned to the Rattlesnake Creek bridge, would McGee's body be there?

He wasn't going back to see.

Once he got home, the magic of the woods would fade. The bones, the corpse, the Spirit of the Lake, McGee—all would seem strange but natural. Uncanny but not occult. Psychedelics-in-their-Tang could explain what had occurred. Psychology could, too. A distressed Unconscious. Old-fashioned lust. The wilderness effect.

Possession-by-Bearclaw was delusional. But to a schizophrenic, that was natural, too.

Flicking his radio on, Scott heard a roar of static, and punched *Seek*. Seconds later, a Queen song tuned in. Dying of AIDS—barely able to stand, Scott had read—Freddy Mercury sang "The Show Must Go On" with a fire undimmed by disease. When Brian May soloed with that same fire, Scott welcomed the tears that blurred his eyes. This was what music could do. What *his* would do some day.

Up ahead, Highway 97 undulated like a black snake across the dusty earth. To his left, the Cascade Mountains glowed with snow that sparkled brighter as the sun slid down the sky.

Maybe, to freak him out, McGee had written the note and stuck it in Scott's glove box at the same time he placed Claire's hat on his bumper. More likely, Claire had left the note while he was out fishing with Errol. She would have pictured him finding it and smiling. Feeling warm.

"I wonder if brains can leave their energy behind," she'd said. Scott wondered, too.

As he neared the freeway, the gravel road began to circle left. This made the sun seem to wheel around until it blazed into Scott's eyes. Its perfect roundness made him think of a golden drainage pipe. That, or the entrance to a magical cave like Errol had found. The golden glow could come from lava, or some treasure like pirate doubloons. The lava would kill him; the doubloons would make him rich. But only if he had the gonads to go in.

His road began to parallel the freeway. Then, in a quarter-mile, the two roads merged. The sun, straight ahead, drilled into his brain.

He touched his front pocket. His sunglasses were there.

He hesitated. Then, before his retinas could fry, he put the glasses on.

No weird energy, as far as he could tell. He was sniffing for bad smells that might have seeped into the plastic, when an air horn's blast nearly blew him off the road.

In his mirror, a monster truck like in that old movie, *Duel*, was bearing down. The driver no doubt assumed Scott would rabbit out of his way. Instead, he mashed his accelerator down.

The truck roared closer, its horn blasting: frantic now. Scott had the crazy thought that Claire was driving. Or her ghost. Made of undetectable dark energy, she would catch up to him, pass through, and be waiting in Seattle. Maybe at his front door or in his bed. Maybe in nightmares. Maybe even in Julie.

"Don't be an idiot," he said aloud.

The truck's air horn blasted again. Then Scott began to pull away. The

road was climbing. Laboring against the grade, the monster truck fell farther and farther behind.

"Vacation's done," Scott told the sky, its wisps of cloud tinged with violets
and pinks, its powder-blue fading to gray.

The line of smooth highway blacktop had straightened out. The monster
truck had disappeared. Accelerator to the floor, Scott settled his sunglasses
on his nose, and sped straight into the cave's blinding light.

BIOGRAPHICAL NOTE

Called "Southern California's most inventive and accessible poet," Charles Harper Webb is the nation's foremost proponent of stand up poetry. A former professional rock singer/guitarist and licensed psychotherapist, he is professor of English at California State University, Long Beach. His latest of twelve collections of poetry is *Sidebend World* (University of Pittsburgh, 2018). Webb has published a collection of essays, *A Million MFAs Are Not Enough* (Red Hen, 2016), and edited *Stand Up Poetry: An Expanded Anthology* (University of Iowa, 2002), used as a text in many universities. His awards include a Whiting Writer's Award, a Tufts Discovery Award, and a fellowship from the Guggenheim Foundation. An avid fly-fisherman, he lives in Los Angeles, CA.